" 'Tis very dark hen she put them against his chest and tried to push him away.

" 'Tis dangerous. Ye can never say what might happen." He threaded his fingers through hers, then held her hands out to the side and against the wall.

"Aye. I could be accosted by some randy fool." She tried to keep her tone of voice cool and steady, but it quickly wavered and grew husky when he rubbed his body against hers. She could feel his arousal and that fed her own. "What game is this? Do ye mean to take by force what I have refused to give ye?" He kissed her throat and Ailis knew that if he released her hands, her only hesitation would come as she tried to decide whose clothes to rip off first.

"Nay, but I could make ye want it—at least once."

"That ye could and that could also make me angry with ye."

"I will take my chances."

She gasped with a pleasure that she could not hide when he nipped at her bodice. Then he kissed her with a hunger she quickly matched. When he released her hands, she wrapped her arms around him to hold him closer. He slipped his hands down her back, cupped her backside, and pressed her more tightly against him.

"Lift your skirts, Ailis," he asked in a soft, demanding voice.

The shadows and her own hunger made her bold. Slowly, she lifted her skirts . . .

# BOOKS BY HANNAH HOWELL

*Only for You*

*My Valiant Knight*

*Unconquered*

*Wild Roses*

*A Taste of Fire*

*Highland Destiny*

*Highland Honor*

*Highland Promise*

*A Stockingful of Joy*

*Highland Vow*

*Highland Knight*

*Highland Hearts*

*Highland Bride*

*Highland Angel*

*Highland Groom*

*Highland Warrior*

*Reckless*

Published by Zebra Books

# HANNAH HOWELL

# RECKLESS

## Zebra Books
## Kensington Publishing Corp.
http://www.kensingtonbooks.com

ZEBRA BOOKS are published by

Kensington Publishing Corp.
850 Third Avenue
New York, NY 10022

All Kensington titles, imprints and distributed lines are available at special quantity discounts for bulk purchases for sales promotion, premiums, fund-raising, educational or institutional use.

Special book excerpts or customized printings can also be created to fit specific needs. For details, write or phone the office of the Kensington Special Sales Manager: Kensington Publishing Corp., 850 Third Avenue, New York, NY 10022. Attn. Special Sales Department. Phone: 1-800-221-2647.

Zebra and the Z logo Reg. U.S. Pat. & TM Off.

First Printing: September 2004
10 9 8 7 6 5 4 3 2 1

Printed in the United States of America

# 1

"A toast to the bride who will one day unite the Mac-
Farlanes and the MacCordys in her womb."

The bride Ailis MacFarlane's deep brown eyes narrowed
as she surveyed the men at the head table in the great hall of
Leargan. Her lips thinned by a growing fury, she needed to
unclench her even white teeth before she could take a reluctant sip of wine from an ornate goblet. The knuckles of
her long slim fingers were bone white, but she was unable
to ease her grip upon the goblet as she set it back down on
the tapestry-draped table. Beneath the heavy oak table she
agitatedly tapped her small booted foot. Her rage craved
some outlet. None of the men so jovially toasting each other
and making plans were paying any mind to her or her increasing fury.

She wondered if they would pay her any heed if she stood
and screamed out her fury. Probably not, she decided. They
rarely noticed her or her moods. She sent a hard glare at
Donald MacCordy.

The cause for the increasingly rowdy celebration was
her betrothal to Donald MacCordy, the eldest son and heir
of the laird of Craigandubh. The union would strengthen
their alliance of arms. The two families would now stand

shoulder to shoulder against their enemies. Of which there were an ever-growing number.

For years the MacFarlanes had had a tentative connection to the MacCordys, occasionally coming to one another's aid. Now it would be a much stronger tie, one of a common heritage in the children to come. As yet unconceived despite Donald's intensive efforts whenever he chanced to catch her alone, Ailis thought furiously.

For the past few days Ailis had struggled to avoid the man she was soon to marry. She was as determined to delay the fateful day when Donald MacCordy would make her a woman as the lecherous Donald was eager to precipitate it. His clammy hands were much too swift and cloying. His too full lips reminded her too much of the leeches the physicians so prized. As yet another toast was raised to the approaching nuptials, Ailis raised her goblet and briefly wished it held poison. She loved life far too dearly, however, even if it meant suffering bondage to Donald MacCordy.

At twenty she knew she was over ready to be married. Her uncle and guardian had no children of his own, and as she was the only surviving child of his only brother, she could inherit the small but prosperous holding of Leargan. There was only a slight chance that her uncle's new wife, Una, who was young, lovely, and somewhat simple, could yet produce a child, and that slight chance faded more every day the poor woman suffered in Colin MacFarlane's grasp. It was with a covetous eye on Leargan as much as enhancing the alliance that the MacCordys accepted her for a bride for their future laird.

Suddenly Ailis tensed. She realized that in all the talk of marriage, living arrangements, dowers, and the future of their clans, there had been no mention of her nephews and niece. Since her sister Mairi's death two years ago, Ailis had cared for the three children conceived during a six-year liaison with a wild but unnamed man. Rath and Manus, the seven-year-old twins, and Sibeal, their five-year-old sister, were the only source of happiness in Ailis's life. Ailis began to fear that she would not be allowed to keep the children with her. She decided it was time to find out for certain.

"Uncle? What about my sister's bairns?" she demanded.

"The bairns have been considered," Colin MacFarlane said in a cool, calm tone.

Ailis did not trust the smoothness of her uncle's reply, a smoothness echoed in Donald's smile. "I dinna expect any great cost to be expended upon them," Ailis said. "I just want them to remain in my care as my sister wished and as I promised her they would."

"We are all well aware of that promise, lass. Dinna worry on it."

Her uncle then ignored her and returned to his drinking. Ailis silently cursed. A few minutes later she slipped away to go to her chambers. To stay and participate in the betrothal revelry would be like dancing at her own funeral. She was trapped and they all knew it, just as they all knew she would rather wed one of the devil's own horsemen than Donald MacCordy.

"And now that I ponder it, Donald probably *is* one of the devil's horsemen," she grumbled as she paused in front of the door to the tiny, damp room that had been grudgingly allotted to her late sister's children.

The poor quarters had been reluctantly offered by their uncle. Colin MacFarlane called the children the Bastard Trio. There were times when Ailis was hard-pressed not to do violence to the man, for his attitude hurt the children. They had suffered enough pain. Instead of being welcomed and comforted at Leargan, the children were crowded into a small, drafty room by a cold, unfeeling man. Ailis could do nothing. She could not even get the children into her more comfortable quarters. The few times she had tried, her uncle had had them forcibly removed, for, he claimed, her chambers were to be her bridal suite, and her groom would not appreciate it if it was cluttered up with bastards. Ailis had swallowed her fury, for she had finally realized that the bickering and confrontation were hurting the children more than if she simply let the matter be.

As she quietly entered the children's room, Ailis looked at their faces, searching yet again for some clue as to who had fathered them. No one had been able to stop the besotted Mairi from meeting her lover, and after her father had died, no one had really tried. The twins had already been born, and Mairi had been considered unweddable. Ailis had only once stooped to following Mairi, but she had just managed to get lost. All attempts to get Mairi to tell her the man's name had also failed despite their close relationship.

Although Ailis sorely missed her sister, she often thought that it was for the best that Mairi had died before their mother had, and before the onslaught of their uncle's guardianship. The shame Mairi had brought to the family and the fury that stirred within her too-proud uncle would not have been tempered by a parent's love. Colin MacFarlane would have made life a sheer misery for the lovesick, erring Mairi. Ailis doubted that she could have protected the sensitive Mairi from Colin's venom any better than she had the children.

All three children were smiling at her and, although she smiled back, her attention was centered on the twins. She was sure they held the greatest clues to their father's identity. They were handsome boys with rich blue eyes and gleaming black hair. The hair was like hers, like Mairi's but the eyes and the lean faces were definitely from that unknown father. Little Sibeal had strawberry-blond hair.

Yet another clue? The big brown eyes and small oval face were just like hers and Mairi's. What bothered Ailis was that of all the men she could think of who held such features, none were friends to the MacFarlanes, and one clan, the MacDubhs, were the bitterest of enemies, for her uncle had stolen Leargan from them. Ailis hid a grimace as she thought yet again that it was bad enough her sister had carried on a liaison with a married man. She dared not let herself believe that it had been with one of their deadliest enemies as well. She forced the chilling thought aside and bent to kiss each of the three children.

"Are ye to be wed to Donald MacCordy, then?" asked Manus as Ailis tucked him in.

"Aye. There isna a thing I can do to alter that dire fate, laddie."

"Are ye certain?"

"Very certain. I have thought on it long and hard, but there is naught for me to do."

"I dinna like the man, Ailis," Sibeal whispered. "I ken he doesna like us at all."

Ailis tried not to place too much weight on the solemn little girl's words. "No man can be at ease with another man's bairns, sweeting. 'Tis all that is." Ailis could see that the children had as little confidence in her soothing words as she did.

A half hour later, when Ailis finally sought her own bed, she found sleep annoyingly elusive. Sibeal was right—Donald could not tolerate the children. In truth, Ailis was beginning to fear that Donald deeply hated them. He had been betrothed to Mairi when her illicit liaison had become common knowledge, but Ailis did not think that was the whole of it. She began to suspect that Donald knew who Mairi's lover had been, knew and hated the children for it. Unfortunately, Ailis did not believe it would be easy to get that knowledge from him.

She tensed as a noise yanked her from her musings. It took only a second to recognize the sound as that of her door being stealthily opened. Ailis slipped her hand beneath her pillow to grasp her dagger, a weapon she was never without. When the shadowy figure finally reached her bed and bent over her, she struck, driving her dagger deep into the man's flesh and just as swiftly yanking her blade free as she leapt to her feet. The ensuing bellow of pain brought several people bustling into her room with candles held high. As the light filled her chamber, Ailis was not surprised to see that her erstwhile ravisher was Donald. The man was on the floor clutching his badly slashed arm and making an inordinate amount of noise. She watched scornfully as his father, brother, and cousin rushed to help him.

"What the devil are ye about, ye daft lass?" bellowed Colin MacFarlane. "Ye have just skewered the man ye are supposed to wed." He swung at her, but she was used to his quick, brutal hand and neatly avoided the blow, returning his fierce glare as she clung to the bedpost. "Ye could have killed him!"

"I treated him as I would any man who comes a-creeping to my bed in the dark of the night," she snapped. "He has no right to be here."

"He was only a wee bit eager, lass," growled the Laird of Craigandubh. "There was no need to nearly hack his arm off."

"Ye exaggerate. 'Tis but a flesh wound, even though he bellows like a gelded bull. And if he meant no harm, he should have brought a light with him. Aye, and spoken out, instead of creeping about like a thief."

Ailis was disgusted when the men tried to dispute the truth of her words. By the time all the shouting was over and she was again alone in her chambers, she was exhausted. She replaced her knife beneath her pillow, relieved that her infuriated uncle had carelessly forgotten to confiscate it. The dagger could still prove necessary to discourage Donald's unwanted attentions. With a sigh and a curse for Donald MacCordy, she snuggled beneath her covers, refusing to let her troubles and worries rob her of sleep.

"Ye great fool," snapped Duncan MacCordy, the bulky Laird of Craigandubh as, once in his chambers, he began to bandage his heir's wound. "The lass could have killed ye. She was right to attack any man who crept up on her in the dark with nary a word. Do ye mean to spoil all our plans with your lust for the wench?"

"How was I to ken that the bitch slept with a dirk at hand?" Donald glared at his handsome cousin Malcolm, who laughed softly. "She will pay dearly for this come our wedding night. I will ride her hard and long just as I should have ridden her whore of a sister."

"Ye, Mairi was a whore, but she gave us a cursed fine tool for blackmail and revenge," said Duncan. "And soon wee Ailis will give it to us to do with as we please." He rubbed his blunt hands together in anticipation.

William, the laird's young, homely son, frowned and smoothed his hand over his receding chin. "Are ye sure that old Colin MacFarlane doesna ken who fathered the bairns?"

"Aye, I am very sure," answered Duncan, and he shook his head, his lanky gray hair shifting clumsily with the movement. "And the old fool isna even interested. All he can see or think about is the shame of it, the mark upon the Mac-Farlane name. What we must hope for is that Barra MacDubh kens who the wee bastards really are."

"He kens," snarled Donald. "The cur kens well that he twice filled Mairi MacFarlane's belly. His slut of a wife,

Agnes, told me as much ere she died. For two long years I have ached to have my revenge on that whoreson. Soon, very soon, I will have it."

Duncan scowled at his son. "The bairns are to be used to gain us the MacDubh land and naught else. Remember that, Donald. Ye arena to use them to soothe your poor wounded vanity. Ye had best keep in mind that the bairns are also of MacFarlane blood. Your wee bride is their aunt."

"In her heart she is more than that," remarked Malcolm, drawing all attention to himself. " 'Tis a very strong bond she has with those bairns, and ye, Donald, had best begin to see it clearly. If ye want as little woe as possible, ye had best tread warily in all your plans for those bairns."

"The bitch will be my wife, and she will do as I tell her or she will sore regret it," snarled Donald. "She willna fight me for long, I vow."

Malcolm sighed but said no more. Yet again he wished he had the wherewithal to be free of his cousins or to be in the service of some other man. He had so little in common with his kin.

But he was bound to his rough, unperceptive relatives. Unlike the others, Malcolm could see the finely honed steel that straightened Ailis MacFarlane's lovely backbone. He also saw that she had as much feeling for those babes in her care as if she had borne them herself. There was no doubt in his mind that if she thought those children were in any danger, she could be as lethal as any she-wolf guarding her cubs. It was plain, however, that Donald would take no advice in the matter. Malcolm suspected that that blindness would eventually cause them a great deal of trouble.

"Aye," muttered Donald. "Ailis will learn, and I suspect that she will grieve little for those bastards when she discovers who their father is."

"If Barra MacDubh really is their father, why has he made no claim upon them?" asked Malcolm.

"He doesna care to have his kin aware of who his lover was just as Mairi didna want any one to ken it," answered Duncan.

"Let us pray that he remains reticent, for I ken that his brother, Alexander, isna a man to sit back and wait to deal," drawled Malcolm, then sighed as he was virtually ignored.

Alexander fought valiantly to stem his swiftly rising temper. His younger brother, Barra, was oblivious to his efforts, however, and blithely continued to add to his fury. The evening meal was becoming an ordeal, and the quiet in the great hall told Alexander that the other men expected matters to grow worse. The pages and the occasional serving woman crept amongst the men with the tense air of people awaiting an attack.

Yet again Barra was drunk. While Barra's shrewish wife had been alive, Alexander had been somewhat sympathetic, believing Barra had sought peace in the wine. Yet Agnes had been dead now for two years, and Barra had remained almost consistently drunk since the day of the woman's death.

That in itself was a source of extreme annoyance to Alexander. He simply could not believe that grief for the woman prompted Barra's wallow in ale, and all of the man's shame should have faded by now. Even more unsettling was that this night was the anniversary of Agnes's death, and Barra was clearly worse than most nights. He would have to be carried to bed. If Agnes had been a worthy wife, Alexander might have found some sympathy for his brother, but his opinion was that the only drink that should be taken in Agnes's name was a loud toast to her absence. Agnes had been a vicious, unpleasant wench who had delighted in making every man, woman, and child within her reach utterly miserable.

A grimace twisted Alexander's mouth as he silently admitted that even if Agnes had been a sainted angel, he would have been hard-pressed to feel any sympathy concerning her untimely death. Even the women whose bodies he used received little more from him than a few grunts and a coin or two. It was difficult to believe that he had once been so flattering and gallant. He marveled at his own naïveté. The women his family had been cursed with over the last dozen years had certainly cured him of his amiable innocence as thoroughly as they had decimated his clan's fortunes. Barra was simply yet another good man who had been caught between a woman's thighs and drained of all good sense and strength. If Agnes were still alive, Alexander was certain that he would kill her himself.

Unable to restrain himself any longer, Alexander leapt to his feet, wrenched the tankard from his brother's hand, and hurled it toward the far end of Rathmor's great hall. "Ye have had enough." His tall, broad-shouldered frame taut with anger, Alexander glared at Barra.

Barra calmly took the tankard belonging to the man seated next to him, refilled it, and took a drink. "I can *never* have enough."

Alexander raked his fingers through his thick golden hair, agitated by his inability to understand his own brother. "Curse ye," he snarled. *"How* can ye wallow in drink for two long years because of that whoring bitch Agnes?"

"Agnes?" Barra blinked owlishly at his brother. "Ye think this is for Agnes?"

When Barra suddenly burst into laughter, Alexander's blood ran cold. The laughter was not the free, contagious sort customary to Barra in earlier, happier times. There was a sharp note to it that made Alexander fear for Barra's mind. That fear was enhanced by the wild look in Barra's red-stained eyes, eyes of a less intense blue than his own. Drink had been known to destroy a man's mind before, Alexander thought, and uttering a foul curse, he slapped Barra, knocking the slender man off the bench he sat on. As he watched Barra pick himself up off of the rush-strewn floor and resume his seat at the table, Alexander clenched and unclenched his hands, fighting the urge to slap his brother until Barra was both sober and sane. The fact that there was no sign of anger in his brother only added to Alexander's fury.

"I am *not* mad, Alex," Barra murmured. "However, I have often wished that I were. Madness might finally release me from my hell."

"I had thought ye released when your bitch of a wife breathed her last. *She* made your life a living hell."

"Oh, aye, that she did, and she saw to it that her death wouldna put an end to my purgatory. Ere Agnes, died, she took from me the only thing that made my life worth a farthing." He laughed hoarsely. "Although I dinna doubt that ye would thank her for it."

"I wouldna thank Agnes for a thing save, perhaps, for dying."

"Aye, ye would thank her. Do ye have any idea why, when she was so near to death with that fever, she took herself out of Rathmor and thus caught the chill that killed her so quickly?"

"Nay." Alexander began to feel uncomfortably tense.

"Well, no doubt this shall lift your dark spirits. Agnes went to a crofter's hut on the far western side of our lands and murdered all that made me happy, all that could ever make me happy. She cut Mairi MacFarlane's bonny throat."

Alexander grabbed Barra by the shoulders, a dread suspicion growing in his mind and making his grip painful. "And why should ye care that Agnes killed a MacFarlane?"

"Why? Because Mairi MacFarlane and I had been lovers for six years." Barra barely stopped himself from falling when Alexander thrust him away as if he had suddenly contracted the plague. "Mairi was but fifteen and I was nearly twenty, newly wed to dear, vicious Agnes—the lass ye thought would bring heirs to Rathmor. God's blood, six months wed and I was already in purgatory."

"So ye went and lay down with the niece of the man who murdered our father?" Alex hissed.

"Aye, lay with *and loved* her is just what I did."

"Nay!"

"Aye! Mairi was the very breath I needed to live, the food that kept my soul from dying, as yours had. Agnes couldna abide it. I couldna speak to ye, for I kenned your hatred for the MacFarlanes." Barra sighed, his expression and tone of voice becoming maudlin. "Agnes took my Mairi. Aye, and my wee bairns, my sons and my wee bonny lassie."

All the color fled Alexander's face as Barra's final words seared through his mind. "Ye had bairns? Agnes killed your bairns?" He spat out the words through tightly gritted teeth.

"Nay." Barra awkwardly shook his head. "Nay, she didna kill them, although what happened is much the same. I canna see them, canna even hear how they fare in health and spirit."

Alexander gave Barra a rough shake. His temper was stretched thin. "Cease bawling like some lass and tell me about your bairns. Tell me everything!"

"I had twin sons. We named them Rath and Manus. They would be seven now." Barra sniffed as he sought to still his tears and vainly struggled to put some order into his thoughts. "Then there was Sibeal. The lass must be five now. I brought her into this world myself, slapped the breath of life into her with my own hands. My own tiny lass with Mairi's bonny eyes. All four are lost to me now.

So now ye ken why I drink. Agnes not only cut my love dead that black day, but she made certain that I could never see my bairns again." He shook his head and took a long drink. "Aye, 'tis as if they, too, have died." he whispered.

"Ye had bairns—sons, curse ye—and yet ye said naught to me?" The sting of hurt mixed with Alexander's anger.

"Nay, I didna think ye would care to hear it," Barra groused. "They are bastards with foul MacFarlane blood in their veins."

"And MacDubh," Alexander snapped, and several of the men at the head table growled their agreement.

"My Sibeal has hair just like mine," Barra sighed. "The laddies have my eyes. In truth, they have the richer blue that ye were blessed with. God's tears, 'tis as if the very heart has been torn out of me."

Alexander grit his teeth and fought against his anger. Maudlin drunks had always infuriated him, but now he had a new understanding of Barra. His own opinion of love and of Barra's appalling choice of a lover did not matter. The man had lost his children, had spent two long, dark years with no sight or word of them. Alexander was all too aware of how such a loss tore at a man, but he swallowed his own still-raw pain, for he needed to be decisive. He knew that his own loss intensified his fierce need to retrieve Barra's children. Any MacDubh children belonged at Rathmor. He leaned toward his brother.

"Just where do ye think your bairns are now, Barra?" he asked in a soft, smooth voice as he watched Barra from beneath partly lowered eyelids.

That deceptively gentle question roused Barra from his misery. He looked around the table, his eyes widening as he met looks of sympathy and accusation. As he slowly turned his gaze to Alexander, he swallowed nervously. The drunken haze he had been sheltered in cleared a little, and he knew what caused Alexander's eyes to shine with rage.

"At Leargan," he rasped, cringing slightly in anticipation of Alexander's response.

"Aye, at Leargan—being raised by a man who murdered our father and stole Leargan from us. The heirs to what scraps of wealth we still clutch on to are in the hands of the one who has ever sought to take even that." When Barra gave an incoherent cry and fled from the great hall, Alexander sighed, sank down into his heavy oaken chair, and rested his head in his callused hands.

"What do ye mean to do?" asked his burly cousin Angus. "Ye canna intend to leave the bairns in Colin MacFarlane's blood-soaked hands, can ye?"

"Nay," answered Alexander. "Nay, I willna allow that whoreson to have the raising of them. It sore grieves me that MacFarlane blood flows in their veins, but they are Barra's for all that. They are MacDubhs. They will be brought here and raised as MacDubhs. Please to God that the poison which is MacFarlane hasna seeped into their hearts as yet. Say naught to Barra, for he is useless as a warrior now, but we ride for Leargan at first light."

# 2

The soft, fragrant grass felt good beneath Ailis's tired body as she sprawled next to her recumbent friend Jaime and left the children to play on their own for a while.

"Och, Jaime, I must be getting old. The bairns fairly wore me out." She grinned when the big man laughed, a deep rich sound that suited him well.

"It does them good to run. They dinna get to do it much. Wee ones need to have a run now and again, mistress."

Ailis nodded, briefly studying the big, dark man at her side. His muscles strained his dull brown jupon, and his hands were so large and strong that Jaime could easily kill a man with little effort. She felt perfectly safe with him and trusted him with the children's lives. Jaime knew how to control his great strength, when to restrain it and when to unleash it.

She was sure that Jaime was not as slow-witted as people thought. He could learn a great many things if one just had patience with him, but Ailis knew that the most important thing she had taught him was self-worth, something his vicious father and others had stolen from him. She could not help but feel proud of that. It had also made Jaime utterly devoted to her, a devotion so complete it occasionally made her uncomfortable, but she did not dissuade him. It was good to have such an ally, for she had few at Leargan.

A sigh of pleasure escaped her as a cool breeze soothed

the heat of the midsummer sun. " 'Tis true that the children are forced to be quiet at Leargan so as not to anger the laird."

"Aye, he can be a mean one." Jaime sat up to watch the children more closely.

"He can, indeed. And yet 'tis sad, for a child needs to be a child. They grow so fast." She watched the children laugh and chase each other, reveling in the beauty of a cloudless summer's day.

Jaime cast her a nervous glance before blurting out, "I ken that it isna my p-place to speak so or to press ye, but— what will happen to m-me when ye wed Donald MacCordy and go to live at Craigandubh?"

"Why, ye shall come along with us." She patted his large clenched hand. "Dinna fret yourself. I willna leave ye behind." She knew no one at Leargan would protest his leaving, for they all thought that Jaime was a half-wit and one to be feared.

He unclenched his massive hands and spread his palms flat on the ground. "Thank ye. Ye and the children dinna tease me or fear me. Ye are my only friend, and I dinna want ye to leave me."

"Well, I shallna, and the children certainly wouldna wish ye to be separated from us. They love ye dearly." She frowned when he tensed, oblivious to her words, and stared intently at the ground beneath his hands. "What is it?" She placed her palm flat against the earth and was startled to feel a faint tremor. "Jaime?"

"S-someone c-comes," Jaime spat out, then cursed the stutter that had marked him as an idiot, a stutter Ailis had helped him overcome until it only affected him when his emotions ran high. He clenched his jaw and struggled to speak quickly despite the stutter. "They c-come from the n-north."

"MacDubhs," Ailis whispered, terrified for the children

because Jaime was unarmed, their horses were unready, and they were all far away from the protective walls of Leargan.

"Maybe. A goodly number and they ride hard. We must flee from here."

"There is no time!" Ailis cried as she leapt to her feet, able now to hear the swift approach of horsemen from a direction where only her enemies dwelled.

With a speed that Ailis found truly astonishing in such a big man, Jaime collected the children. Ailis nodded when he suggested that they seek shelter in a large tree at the edge of the clearing. It was hardly impregnable, but it could hide them from the riders thundering their way. If not, it would buy them time, time that could bring rescue. Ailis nimbly swung up into a large gnarled tree and got ready to haul up the children as Jaime handed them to her. Jaime was just handing Rath up to her, the last of the three frightened children, when the riders galloped into the clearing. Ignoring her urging to join them, Jaime turned to face their enemy alone.

Alexander reared to a halt mere feet from the huge dark man. His soldiers quickly reined in around him. After studying the giant by the trunk, Alexander looked up into the branches of the tree and felt almost lighthearted. Twin boys and a small strawberry-blond girl child peered down at him. Such luck did not often come his way.

"The fates have truly smiled upon us this day, Angus." He grinned at his cousin, who held his usual place of honor on his right. "The fruit we seek is here for our picking."

"Aye, but there is a muckle great tree to fell ere we can collect the harvest." Angus nodded toward Jaime.

As he signaled to his men to go after the man guarding the tree, Alex advised them, "Dinna kill him if ye can help yourselves. He is unarmed and outnumbered thirty-five to one. 'Twould be naught but murder."

From her perch in the tree Ailis watched nearly half of the men dismount, toss aside their weapons, and approach Jaime. Her blood ran cold when she recognized the Mac-Dubh badges they wore. They apparently did not intend to kill Jaime, but she was not particularly comforted by that. Jaime could not defeat all of the men. Unless some help miraculously arrived, she and the children would fall into the hands of her clan's deadliest enemies. Tales of the horrors the MacDubhs visited upon any MacFarlane luckless enough to fall into their bloodthirsty grasp ran rampant at Leargan, and she had the misfortune to suddenly and clearly recall each and every one. Calm reason told her that not all of the tales could be true, but, she decided, fear was a highly unreasonable emotion. At that moment she could, and did, believe all the very worst that had ever been said about the infamous MacDubhs.

Relaxed in his saddle, Alexander watched the battle as his men rushed the giant standing guard by the tree. It was a fight that could only end in victory for his men, but the dark behemoth was taking a heavy toll. The fact that the huge man would face several MacDubhs with only his bare fists was pure lunacy, but Alexander could only respect such madness. It was evident that the big man intended to fight to the death, with whatever weapons were at hand, in order to protect the four who huddled in the tree. Loyalty such as that could only be honored, although Alex wondered if the man's protectiveness would be as fierce if he knew who had fathered the children he so valiantly fought for. When the large man finally fell, Alexander felt no surge of victory. He dismounted, approached the tree, and gazed up at four small, pale faces.

"Come down, mistress, and bring the bairns with ye," he ordered. A second, closer look at the little girl's strawberry curls and the twins' eyes and features confirmed Alex's belief that he and his men had chanced upon Barra's brood.

"Your gallant protector has fallen at last, so ye must accept defeat and climb down."

"Accept defeat? Never!" replied Ailis, successfully subduing her very real fear for the children, herself, and the unconscious Jaime. "If ye want me and the bairns, ye will have to come up here and collect us."

Alexander ground his teeth as he signaled to a select few of his men to answer the girl's challenge. He knew she was trying to gain herself some time. Whether or not she had any sound reason to think that that would gain her rescue, Alexander was determined to give her as little time as possible.

When the first man who tried to ascend the tree was sent groundward by the simple but effective application of one dainty booted foot in his face, Alexander was as surprised as anyone. As each man went up, he was cleverly routed. The men planned a defense for the move that sent their predecessors tumbling to earth, but the woman, with the agile assistance of the boys, simply adjusted her methods to suit the new attack. Despite a MacDubh advantage of physical size, muscular superiority, and greater number, the girl held the stronger position, for she had a highly advantageous point of defense.

As the eighth man tumbled to the ground, Alexander decided he had had enough. Valuable time was being wasted. He drew his sword and held it to the throat of the now conscious, but still groggy, giant who had proved such a valiant protector despite having been overcome in the end. The threat was a bluff, and Alexander could not guess how she felt concerning the welfare of her guard, but it was a ploy worth trying.

"Mistress," he called, and everyone looked his way. "There has been enough of this play. Come down or I shall cut this man's throat here and now."

Ailis knew she had finally lost the battle, but said, "Ye

didna kill him when ye had to fight him; why should I be-lieve that ye would do so now?"

"Because we both ken that ye are trying to gain time. Well, I have no more time to waste."

That cold statement confirmed Ailis's decision to sur-render. A plan was of little use when it was known by the enemy. Neither could she use Jaime's life to buy time to wait for a rescue that might never come. No one knew she and the children had left Leargan, let alone where they had gone to. She doubted that they would even be missed for several more hours. Jaime's life meant more to her than gaining a little time. Ailis could only pray that she was not just delaying Jaime's fate even as she hurried forward the fate of herself and the children. She glared down at the man who threatened her dearest and truest friend.

"I want your oath that no harm will come to us," she said. "Your solemn oath."

Alexander stiffened with outrage and snapped, "We dinna make war upon helpless women and bairns."

"I didna ask ye for a debate on what ye will or willna do. I asked for your *oath* that the bairns will come to no harm whilst they are in your hands."

A soft growl through tightly gritted teeth was Alexan-der's first reply, but then he said, "Ye have my oath on it. Now, get your backsides out of that cursed tree ere I skewer this giant."

"Someone must catch the children," Ailis said, trying not to let the man's obvious fury frighten her. "'Tis too far for them to come down unaided." Over and over she told herself she had to remain brave before the children, for she did not wish to add to the upset they were already suffer-ing.

It was difficult for Alexander to just stand and watch as the children were lowered down. As he took a close look at them, their relationship to his brother, to the MacDubhs,

was clear to see, and he felt himself swell with emotion—
an even mixture of a still raw grief and a deep joy. In order
to conquer that wealth of feeling he turned his full attention to the slim, shapely, raven-haired woman nimbly
descending from the tree and ignoring the offered assistance. The vision also caused something to stir inside of
him, but he was almost certain most people would not consider lust an emotion.

The woman was small, yet had a sensual air equal to,
even surpassing, that of a voluptuous woman. As she
moved to the fallen giant's side, her walk held an explicit
invitation, although instinct told Alexander that it was not
only unintentional but unknown to her. Nevertheless,
Alexander was immediately determined to accept that invitation.

Jaime sat up, looking a little groggy and his swarthy
face reflecting his upset, an emotional turmoil further il-
lustrated by the heavy stutter he spoke with. "Och,
m-mistress, ye shouldna have come d-down. I am n-nay
worth it. Ye should have s-s-stayed in that t-tree."

The twins were patting Jaime's broad back, and little
Sibeal held one of his large hands in her two tiny ones in
an attempt to calm the distraught man, so Ailis patted
Jaime's dark, curly head. "Nay, I couldna desert ye. Dinna
fret so. If it will make ye feel any better, dinna believe I did
it for ye, but for myself—for the ease of my own heart,
soul, and mind. Nary a one of them would have given me
a moment's peace if I had let ye be slain."

A frown settled on Alexander's face as he ordered his
men to collect all the items that belonged to the MacFarlanes. It was clear that Jaime was a little slow. It was also
clear that even the woman held some affection for the
brute. That puzzled Alexander, for it went against what he
had come to believe about women. So did her surrender
simply because he had threatened the giant. He pushed his

confusion aside and considered the problem now confronting him. He wanted the girl, but lust was not sufficient reason to drag her along with them. So, he mused with an inner smile, he had to find another to salve his conscience.

"What are ye to these bairns?" he demanded of Ailis. "Are ye their nurse?"

The very last thing Ailis wanted the man to know was that she was Colin MacFarlane's niece. Although he had been kind to the children, she could not forget the blood feud between the MacDubhs and the MacFarlanes. She suspected he might not be so charitable to an adult Mac-Farlane. "Aye, I am their nurse."

"Ye look a wee bit young to be a nurse."

"I am twenty. 'Tis old enough."

"Then ye are to come with us. I will have need of a nurse to tend the children, and there is none at Rathmor." He grasped her by the arm and frowned when she did not immediately fall into step at his side.

"What of Jaime?" she asked as she fought the tug he gave on her arm.

"What of him? He can stay here."

"I didna surrender to save his life just so that ye can leave him to Colin MacFarlane's fury. 'Twould be a certain death for Jaime."

Alexander knew he was making a mistake even as he looked into the eyes of the three children. Just as he had expected, the plea he could read upon the children's face was his undoing. It was undoubtedly foolish to take such an admirable fighter into the very heart of his stronghold, but Alexander knew he could never tell the children that he was going to leave the brute behind to an uncertain and, most assuredly, unpleasant fate.

"Very well," he snapped, irritated by his own weakness. "He may come with us if he swears to cause no trouble."

Jaime hesitated only long enough to exchange one long look with Ailis, then managed to utter the promise Alexander had demanded. Alexander's men eyed the huge man warily as he mounted. The MacDubhs did what they could to disguise any signs of their presence. They swept the ground with branches to obscure their tracks, patted down any turned-up earth, and even cleared away any horse droppings. The last thing Alexander needed or wanted was to be caught up in a mad race for the safety of Rathmor.

Alexander sat the young girl Sibeal on his horse in front of him while the twins were mounted together on another horse. The somewhat haughty-appearing nurse rode alone, and astride, much to Alexander's appreciative amusement. He wrenched his gaze from her slim stockinged legs and signaled the start of the ride back to Rathmor. He ordered his men to keep the horses at a steady, ground-covering pace, yet one that would not tire the animals out too quickly.

It had all gone far too well for his liking. Alexander could not believe his luck. It made him uneasy. Except for a multitude of bruises and a possible broken bone or two, he and his men had gained their objective with very little violence. He had been prepared to attack Leargan itself, hoping that the advantage of surprise would compensate for his small force, but he was pleased that he did not have to take that risk now. Nevertheless, he could not shake the feeling that trouble and complications aplenty waited just around the corner. He cursed himself for a superstitious fool and concentrated on getting back to Rathmor before his remarkable good luck ran out.

As Ailis rode along on her sorrel mare, she felt relieved that her ploy of claiming to be the children's nurse had worked. She suspected the man had very little knowledge of such things; otherwise he would have realized that she was too young to hold such an important position in her clan.

She prayed that none of the children would give her away. It was enough for now that her quick, sharp look had silenced them. She did not like to force them to lie, but the truth now would only cause them all a great deal of trouble.

Although there had been sporadic violence between the clans, she had no idea why the MacDubhs should want Mairi's illegitimate children. They could not possibly know what she had only suspected. Yet stealing the children had clearly been the MacDubhs' plan. She could not believe that the fair-haired leader who had spared Jaime's life could be so vile as to harm children. Ailis hoped that she was not letting the man's handsome face blind her to his true nature.

There was only one thing she was sure of, and that was that she faced rape at the hands of the beautiful if grim-faced man who led the MacDubhs. A chilling shudder ripped through her when she had finally realized who he was—Alexander MacDubh, the most famous and feared member of the MacDubh clan. From a very young age she had been taught what the man looked like, a description it had been easy for any young lass to recall. Those tales of a beautiful man, altered by grief from a charming courtier to an embittered, cold-hearted raider, had always fascinated her and won her sympathy. As a young girl, she had suffered from a confusing mix of a need to see such a beautiful man and a dread that she might some day get her wish. Dread was what she felt now, for she had caught a glimpse of a familiar look in his rich blue eyes, a look she regrettably knew all too well. Alexander MacDubh desired her. Now that she was his prisoner, he could simply take her whenever he wished.

The arrogance of it annoyed her even as the inevitability of it chilled her. She would have no allies at Rathmor; Jaime would only be slain if he tried to come to her aid. Her true identity would certainly not help her. It could easily inspire an even harsher treatment.

In the guise of the children's nurse she might be able to talk Sir Alexander out of what he was planning for her. Rumor said that he had once been a very charming seducer. If he discovered that she was Ailis MacFarlane, however, MacDubh would find the use of her a thing to savor, for he would know how it would stab at the heart of the too-proud Colin MacFarlane. The more she considered the matter, the more inevitable rape seemed, so she tried not to think about it, something she failed miserably at. She vainly fought an encroaching sense of resignation.

When the dark walls of Rathmor came into view, her air of calm was even harder to maintain. Rescue would now be difficult and costly, in both time and in men. It would all depend on how badly the blood tie between the Mac-Cordy and the MacFarlane clan was desired. There could well be no rescue attempt at all. As far as the children were concerned, Colin MacFarlane could consider himself well rid of a heavy and embarrassing burden.

Suddenly the time she had struggled to gain back in the clearing was no longer desirable. Time could now lose her her maidenhead. Time could now tear away her disguise as a mere nurse. Time could now buy her nothing but trouble. In fact, she thought as the thick gates of Rathmor thundered shut behind her, time could now become her worse enemy.


"If we continue on like this, we will kill the horses." Malcolm MacCordy dragged his forearm across his face, using his shirtsleeve to wipe the sweat from his brow. He scowled up at the afternoon sun and then looked around the clearing they were in.

As he reined in beside his cousin, Donald snapped, "We havena found them yet." His father, brother, and most of the ten men-at-arms with them muttered agreement. "Do we just quit, then?"

"The moment ye kenned that the children were outside of Leargan, ye tumbled into a panic." Malcolm spoke in a low voice, for he did not want the men-at-arms learning of the MacCordys' deep interest in the children.

"And so we should have. Colin is a fool. Letting the bairns roam free is much akin to dropping a full purse in the town square and hoping it will be left untouched."

"And riding about hour after hour like crazed idiots makes us wiser than Colin?"

"We need those children!"

Malcolm bit his tongue against all the words he wished to say. If the MacCordys had not been so grasping and dishonest, they might well have an ally or two left. Then they would not have such a need for the children. In truth, they were nearly encircled by people who had a grudge against them, and first amongst those were the MacDubhs. Malcolm suspected that the MacDubhs were behind the disappearance of Ailis and the children.

"We arena succeeding this way." Malcolm struggled to be tactful and finally said, "I think we need to rest and rethink our plans."

"Aye," agreed William. "That sounds like a good idea."

"Oh? And what would *ye* ken about a good idea?" Donald yelled at his younger brother. "Ye are naught but a witless fool!"

With a shake of his head, Malcolm dismounted as his cousins began to bicker in earnest. He watered his horse, loosely tethered the animal, then collapsed beneath a large tree. He watched in bored amusement as the graying Duncan joined in the argument between his two burly sons. The rest of the men dismounted, watered their horses, and let the animals graze as the three men continued their quarrel. Malcolm mused that it did not require any great wit to know that riding around the countryside at full gallop and shouting was no way to proceed, but there was no way to tell his cousins that.

Malcolm sighed, idly brushed some grass from the front of his elegant black jupon, and reached for his waterbag. Then he grew tense and still. He narrowed his eyes as he searched the ground for exactly what had so briefly yet fully caught his eye. It took several moments of close scrutiny, but then he understood. Someone had done a good job of trying to conceal it, but he knew some sort of confrontation had occurred on that very spot and not too long ago. He could now discern where the moss and grass had been trampled, even gouged in a few places. When he made a wider search of the ground, he discovered a few splotches of blood still sticky to the touch. Instinct told him the blood must be from a fight between Jaime and whoever had tried to kidnap Ailis and the children.

But in which direction had they ridden? Silently Malcolm searched the area in an ever-widening circle. His efforts brought him rewards just as the others ended their tirade and began to eye him warily. Malcolm paid his bulkier cousins no heed. Not far beyond the clearing there was ample sign of the recent presence of a large force of mounted men. Malcolm followed the trail of the riders a few yards. Now it was clear who had Ailis and the children. It surprised him some that, as all evidence indicated, they had also taken Jaime. Malcolm's thin face tightened into a grim expression as he acknowledged the possible death of all the MacCordys' grand plans and the fury his kinsmen would display when he told them. He strolled back to his cousins.

"They were here, but they are long since gone," he announced.

Donald scowled at him and scratched his softening

stomach. "What do ye mean? We were here but a short
while ago and saw nothing."

"We didna look close enough." With his cousins at his
heels, Malcolm began to point out all he had just discovered. "I think the blood is from that brute your tiny bride
keeps at her side, Donald. Aye, and some from the ones
who brought him down. The ones who did this made a
nearly perfect job of concealing their tracks. It bought
them the time they needed to get back to their lair before
anyone came to look for the bairns and Mistress MacFarlane." Having shown his cousins all the clues he had
uncovered, Malcolm leaned against the gnarled tree he had
sprawled beneath earlier. "From the direction the riders
took when they left here, I think we all ken who has taken
the lass and the children."

"Aye," snarled Duncan after indulging in a hearty and
profane bout of cursing. "The MacDubhs. If Alexander
MacDubh doesna ken who the bairns are now, he will ere
his brother sets eyes on the bastards."

"I think he kens very well who those bairns are," said
Malcolm, running his long fingers through his dark brown
hair. "A man doesna come on a raid at midday without
good reason. Nor does he leave his lands at this time of the
year if he can avoid it. There is just too much work that
needs to be done. Pulling men from their work now could
well bring hunger in the winter months ahead. Nay, Mac-
Dubh came here for a reason, a very good reason, and I
ken that it fell into his very lap. The man probably canna
believe his luck. I think ye have lost this game, Cousin."

"Nay!" bellowed Donald, then quickly lowered his voice.
"There may yet be a chance to retrieve our loss. Aye, the
MacDubh will want to hold fast to the children, but he
willna keep Ailis. A ransom will be asked for her. Why, even
the greatest of fools can see the worth of such a prisoner."

"Aye, and the MacDubh's no fool. However, if the lass

is as wise as I feel she is, she will do her utmost to try and hide the truth of who she is."

"I canna see that," muttered William, revealing to Malcolm that he could easily be as thick-witted as so many accused him of being. "The MacDubhs will ransom her, free her, if she tells them who she is."

Malcolm refrained from telling his young cousin how wrong he was, for he had learned years ago that pointing out his faulty reasoning did no good. "The MacDubhs have sworn vengeance against the MacFarlanes for the treacherous murder of their father. It would greatly please them to have Colin's niece, his only heir unless that half-wit Colin married has a bairn. The MacDubhs *will* ransom Ailis, but they will use her ill first. The chance to taste vengeance by abusing Colin's heir will be a temptation too sweet to refuse."

Donald swore viciously. "That bastard MacDubh will use her anyway."

"As any man would do if he found himself in possession of as sweet a piece as Ailis MacFarlane is," agreed Malcolm. "I was meaning that she wouldna be passed amongst the men if she can hide who she really is. She willna be returned a maiden, but that is a small loss compared to what she could be if she were used roughly by all at Rathmor. Ye might yet get a taste of what ye have so hungered for, Donald."

"Aye, but only after a MacDubh has savored it first. A cursed MacDubh was between the legs of Mairi ere I could have her. Now there will be one between the legs of Ailis. I am sore weary of MacDubhs taking the maidenheads of the lasses I am betrothed to."

"Ye werena betrothed to Mairi," said William, and he ducked to avoid Donald's swinging fist. "Ye werena."

"I was soon to be betrothed to her." Donald ceased trying to strike his young brother and put his gloved fist on his hips. "I had to wait until her idiot of a father decided she was of an age to marry, but Barra MacDubh slid his sword into my sheath ere the betrothal toasts were raised."

"Ailis is Colin's heir, and that is more important than her cursed maidenhead," snapped Duncan, cuffing his eldest son offside the head. "We are after her land, her dowry, and the alliance with the MacFarlanes, not her twice-cursed chastity. I dinna care who has bedded the wretched lass so long as ye are the one she weds."

"I care!" yelled Donald, his pockmarked face turning a choleric hue. "The MacDubhs will pay dearly." He tightly gripped the hilt of his sword.

"Ailis's lost maidenhead is the least of our concerns," Malcolm drawled, a quick glance assuring him that Colin's men-at-arms remained out of hearing range. "The MacDubhs now hold the weapon we had planned to use against them, to break them. Bastards or nay, those children could be the only heirs Rathmor has. Barra MacDubh courts no woman save for Dame Ale, and Alexander has become so embittered that he trusts no woman and will take none to wife. He takes care not to seed any woman he uses. He doesna wish to give them the means to drag him before a priest. The children were a strong weapon whilst ye held it, but I think ye will never get it back now. MacDubh will expect ye to try and will be ready for ye. Rathmor is a nearly impregnable keep. Have ye any plan at all? Did ye never think that such as this could happen?"

"Aye, we did," Duncan grumbled. "However, whatever we decide to do will take time, something we dinna have at this season of the year." Duncan scowled and scratched his beard-stubbled chin. "Come the spring, the bairns will be back in our hands. The question we need to answer is— do we leave Ailis unransomed until we grab the bairns? I canna stomach giving the MacDubhs all they could demand in return for such a valuable captive. Colin willna be too pleased to part with the large ransom the MacDubhs could ask for the heir of Leargan."

"Nay, Colin holds tightly to his purse," William agreed, a brief look of confidence firming his round face.

Duncan nodded after looking at his youngest son in some surprise for his insight. "This must all be given some careful thought if we are to gain as much as we can out of this."

"When the ransom is asked, willna Colin *have* to pay?" asked William. "If he deserts his own blood, he will never be trusted again by anyone who might hear about it."

"Willie"—Duncan spoke with an exaggerated patience—"Colin MacFarlane is little trusted by anyone even now."

"I think the question of ransom must remain unanswered for now," Malcolm said. "I feel certain that Ailis will try and hide her identity. She isna stupid. It may be some time ere MacDubh kens that he holds someone who is worth ransoming."

"I hope ye are right, Malcolm," Duncan said, his voice heavy with doubt. "We need time to work out our plans."

"Aye," agreed Malcolm, "and right now time could prove to be our worst enemy."

**3**

"Curse ye, Alexander!" roared Barra as the victorious MacDubh raiding party entered Rathmor's great hall. "Why did ye leave me behind?"

"Ye would have been more of a danger to us than a help, for ye suffer the ills of too much drink," Alexander explained, then frowned as he realized that Barra was no longer listening. His gaze was fixed on the other side of the great hall.

It was not the three children Barra stared at as if the Devil himself had suddenly reared up out of Hell. The three children were still difficult to espy amongst the crowd of men. Barra's wide gaze was fixed upon Ailis, who was gently urging Jaime to sit down as she attempted to tend the man's facial abrasions and bruised knuckles.

Barra rose from his seat at the head table and took a few unsteady steps toward Ailis with one of his shaking hands outstretched toward her. With each step Barra took, Alexander saw the shock upon his brother's lean face lighten just a little bit.

"Mairi," Barra whispered, but then he shook his head and rubbed at his temples with trembling fingers. "Nay, how foolish of me. Mairi is dead. I but let wishes and dreams cloud my sight for a moment. Ye must be her sister, Ailis."

Ailis gave a small involuntary cry. Her time had

abruptly run out. Her shock increased as, in Barra's handsome face, she saw the blue eyes of the twins as well as their narrow faces. So, too, did she see thick strawberry-blond curls identical to those that crowned Sibeal's small head. There was no denying the devastating revelation that flooded her mind. The way Barra's gaze settled upon the children, his look filled with love and a hunger born of long denial, Ailis was left with no doubts. Her sister's lover had been Barra MacDubh. Now she understood Mairi's reason for such intense secrecy concerning the identity of her lover.

"Sister?" Alexander hissed, and he gave Barra a slight shake to gain his attention. "Did ye say *sister?*"

"Aye," Barra briefly forced his gaze back to Alex. "Ailis." He looked at Ailis. "Ye do look much like my Mairi, but now that the first shock of it all has left me, I can see the differences. I am so very sorry, Ailis," he said, his voice muted and sincere. "I brought your poor sister naught but misery."

There was such melancholy in his voice that Ailis's heart was touched. "Nay. Mairi was happy, very happy, with ye and with the bairns."

"Ye said you were their nurse," Alexander hissed, glaring at Ailis and fighting to ignore the way she spoke to Barra, for it created a dangerous, unwanted softening inside of him. "Ye lied." He decided to center his attention upon this sin. "Ye are Ailis MacFarlane—niece and heir to that murdering bastard Colin MacFarlane."

"I ken well enough who I am." Ailis was determined not to quail before the man even though she only reached his collarbone. "I didna lie. Ye didna ask *who* I was, only *what* I was, and I answered that truthfully. I do act as their nurse. I just didna mention a detail or two." A page brought her a cloth and some water to clean Jaime's wounds, and Ailis took swift advantage of them even as she glanced toward the children. "Didna I care for ye and I alone?" she asked them, and the children nodded. "Didna I help your mama before God took her into His arms; didna I help her and care for ye when she couldna?" Again the children nodded, and Ailis sent Alexander a brief sharp glare. "That sounds much akin to a nurse to me. So how did I lie?" She shook her head as she rinsed out the rag she had used to bathe Jaime's wounds. "I now ken why ye were after the children."

She tried to keep her attention fixed upon Jaime. Alexander MacDubh was far too unsettling. None of the stories of his beauty had been exaggerated, she decided. He was tall, lean, and exquisitely formed. His hair was thick, had an attractive wave to it, and hung a little past his broad shoulders. There was that taint of a cynical twist to his expression, but that face was still breathtakingly lovely. Ailis did not think she had ever seen a man's features cut so perfectly. And his eyes, she mused with a silent curse. Those startlingly blue eyes stole her thoughts even though they glinted with fury and mistrust. And his temper had not been exaggerated, either, she thought. Ignoring the man was her best defense. If his beauty did not leave her witless, then seeing that anger would surely have her trembling. She had no wish to appear either way in front of the man. When Alex spoke, she fiercely resisted the urge to turn toward that deep voice.

"Aye, I was after the children," Alexander said, his voice hard and cold. "I wasna about to leave anyone with a drop of MacDubh blood in the murderous hands of a MacFarlane. The children are still young. We should be able to scrub them clean of the taint."

Despite what Ailis thought of the method her uncle had used to obtain Leargan, she was a MacFarlane. Alexander's insult stung. Since she, and before her, Mairi, had had the sole care of the children, she saw his remarks as a personal affront. The soft voice of common sense told her that Mac-

Dubh could have no knowledge of who raised the children or how, but she paid it no heed. She curtly tossed aside the rag she held, forcefully placed her small fists on her slim hips, and glared at the man.

"Oh, aye, the raising of the bairns is so clearly a concern for ye." She gave a soft, sarcastic laugh. " 'Tis so much better if the bairns learn to be the bloodthirsty, cold-hearted bastard that ye are."

Alexander backhanded Ailis across the face. His action stunned him and—he could tell by their faces—astonished and shocked his men. Despite the depths to which his opinion of women had sunk, he had never before struck one. He had always seen such an action as dishonorable, even cowardly, for a woman could not match a man blow for blow.

A low growl escaped Jaime as Ailis tumbled to the floor. Four men rushed to hold the brute down, but tiny Sibeal reached Alex first, and she demonstrated that she carried an ample load of the now legendary MacDubh temper. Alexander grunted in pain as the little girl delivered a punch to the part of his anatomy most within her reach. He clutched his groin and doubled over slightly, needing a moment to catch his breath. When he looked at his tiny niece, she faced him squarely with her small fists set firmly on her hips in imitation of her aunt. Through his discomfort, Alex briefly noted that he was not the only one staring at the child in openmouthed silence.

"I hope I crippled ye!" Sibeal said, fury adding strength to her childish voice. "Ye hit my aunt Ailis ever again, and I will cut your pintle off and stuff it in your ear, ye rammish whoreson."

Even the pain in her jaw could not extinguish the laughter rising up in Ailis. Neither could swallowing hard, coughing, or any of the other tricks she sometimes used to stifle a laugh. The gaping looks upon everyone's face and

the sheer astonishment on Lord Alexander's overwhelmed
her. She released a peal of laughter. The twins were the
first ones to join her, then Jaime and Barra, as well as
many of the MacDubh men. As she fought to control her
mirth, Ailis noted that Alexander himself was very close
to outright laughter.

"Och, lassie," she finally said, grinning at Sibeal. "Ah,
my sweet Sibeal, ye shouldna have done that. 'Tisna
proper for a lady to act or speak so."

A frown creased the child's angelic face. "But ye did the
same to Sir Donald MacCordy. I was peeking, ye ken. Ye
said just those things and more, too."

Ailis could feel the color rush into her face, and she
groaned softly, then attempted to look stern as Barra
helped her to her feet. "I am sure ye are mistaken, child."
She tried to speak with calm assurance, but it was not easy.
She knew she *had* said such things. She silently vowed
that, if there was a next time, she would be certain to as-
certain that no small but keen ears were close at hand.

"Nay, she isna mistaken," said Rath, a glint of mischief
in his eyes, and his upset over the treatment of his aunt
briefly pushed aside by a highly amusing memory. "Donald was screaming like a stuck pig. I ken it well. He was
saying that he burned for ye, and ye said that ye would
snuff out his flame for all time." Ailis softly yet vehe-
mently urged him to hush, but he was spurred on by the
obvious enjoyment of the MacDubh men. "Donald said
that he would warm ye up until ye begged for him, and ye
said that if he put one filthy hand on ye, ye would knock
his cullions back so far that he would never be able to
swallow again. Then he touched ye and ye did it."

"Nasty little piece," Alexander murmured and grinned
at Ailis's embarrassment. His amusement faded as he studied her, fighting to ignore the bite of guilt he suffered over
the mark of his blow upon her small, oval face. "And just

why does Sir Donald MacCordy feel he can take such liberties with Laird Colin MacFarlane's niece?" When she started to turn away from him, he caught her by the arm.

"Mayhaps he is just a lecherous dog." Ailis knew it would be a mistake to let him know that she was betrothed to a man the MacDubhs hated almost as much as they did her uncle.

"Aye, he is that, well enough, but I think there is more." He grasped the hand she was trying to keep hidden in the folds of her skirt and stared at the ring she wore before looking directly at her. "I think the man merely tries to gain what will soon be his anyway. Ye are betrothed to Sir Donald MacCordy."

Ailis frantically searched her mind for some name to give him, any name that would not add to her usefulness as a tool of revenge.

"Ye dinna like him, either, do ye, sir?" Sibeal said to Alexander in all innocence. "I can tell it. He doesna like me and my brothers, ye ken, but it doesna matter. We shall still have Ailis. We will live with her. She has promised us. I am going to help her care for her bairns."

Although it was faint and quickly disguised, Alexander felt the tremor that ripped through Ailis. He also saw the fleeting look of revulsion that clouded her beautiful dark brown eyes. Alexander wondered if it was only Donald MacCordy who repulsed her or if it was all men, then wondered why he even cared. When he bedded the girl—and he would—it would not be for pleasure, his or hers, so her warmth or lack thereof should be of no concern to him.

"Your value rises by the moment, wench," Alex drawled. "It appears that I not only hold the heir to Leargan and all else that filth Colin possesses, but the bride to the heir of Craigandubh." He tightened his grip on her soft hand when she tried to wriggle it free, then tugged her closer to him. "Now, what do ye think I ought to do with ye, a lass who is so closely tied to two men I sorely ache to run my sword through?"

The very softness of his lovely voice made her blood chill, but she faced him squarely. "Ye already ken how ye will act, so I willna waste my breath to answer ye." She glared when he slid his gaze over her in a slow, insolent inspection, for she saw it as nothing less than an insult.

"Aye, I ken what I shall do with ye. That ye should have been saved for the poor abused Sir Donald MacCordy will only sweeten my cup." He glanced at Jaime, whose huge fists clenched and unclenched. "Ye had best warn your large friend not to try to be gallant, or all your valiant efforts to keep him alive will have been for naught." The way the color seeped from her face told him that she truly cared for the brute, yet Alexander wanted to deny that truth, for it undermined his bitter, unflattering opinion of women.

"Jaime, ye swore that ye wouldna raise your hand against a MacDubh." Ailis kept her voice calm yet firm, for it was the surest way to pierce through Jaime's fury. "Ye must hold to your oath."

"But, mistress," he protested, "I ken what he wants with ye."

Hold to your word, Jaime," Ailis stressed. "I willna have your blood upon my hands. Ye can do naught to change my fate."

"I can snap the rutting bastard in twain," Jaime grumbled, his dark eyes hard with fury and his gaze fixed upon Alex all the while he flexed his big hands.

"Aye, ye can do that." Ailis looked at the man who still gripped her hand and idly wondered why the Lord sent her a persecutor hidden beneath such a lovely shell. "And I shall be right there to enjoy it when the time comes, but that time isna now, Jaime." She looked back at her big friend. "Nay, not now. I may have more need of ye when I face my uncle and my betrothed again."

Before Alexander could reply, servants arrived with food and drink. When the children, Ailis, and Jaime held back from sitting at the table, Alexander none too gently pulled Ailis to a seat by his side. The children and Jaime cautiously followed, but an outright command was needed to get them to sit. Alexander found it a little confusing. The children acted as if they expected to be forcibly expelled from the great hall.

"We canna eat in the great hall," Sibeal blurted. "Grandmère forbade it. So did Uncle Colin. Are ye sure we shouldna go to our room? We do have a room, dinna we? Rath makes naughty noises, ye ken. Aunt Ailis can come with us, too. She often does." She sat stiffly at Barra's side, tensed as if prepared to flee.

"Well, we dinna mind sharing our table with children," said Alexander. "Did your uncle and grandmère often have company, then?"

"Nay," mumbled Sibeal, who suddenly grew intensely interested in the food Barra set before her.

Ailis felt her heart contract as it always did when the children revealed how their elders' scorn had touched them. She was also relieved when Sibeal grew quiet. Ailis did not think it would help her at all if Alexander Mac-Dubh found out how the children had been mistreated by the MacFarlanes. She saw Barra exchange a look of puzzlement with Alexander and knew that her sister, Mairi, had never told Barra how the children had been treated like pariahs. She suspected Mairi had feared that Barra would insist upon taking the children out of the reach of that scorn, and Mairi would never have been able to give up her children. She prayed that Alexander would not press the matter, then glanced at the man and inwardly groaned. Alexander had a look of determination on his almost pretty face, and instinct told her that he would indeed press the matter. He had questions, and she knew that he was a man who would doggedly pursue the answers.

"There appears to be something tying up the wee lass's tongue." Alex looked at Ailis. "She willna reply to any questions."

"Mayhaps that is because what ye are asking isna any of your concern. Ah!" she cried softly when he took hold of a hank of her hair and none too gently pulled her toward him until their faces were but inches apart. "Brutality will gain ye naught, Sir MacDubh."

"I *will* have the answers," he said in a low, quiet voice, ignoring Barra's soft admonitions and noting that, although Jaime was as taut as the finest drawn bowstring, the man held to his promise to stay his powerful hands. "'Tis by your command that they remain silent, mistress. I wish to ken what poison your cursed family has fed to them."

Even if he threatened to snatch her bald, hair by hair, Ailis swore that she would not answer. She set her chin and gave him her most stubborn look.

"Leave her be!" Manus cried, grasping Alexander's wrist. "I will tell ye all ye might wish to ken."

Alexander loosened his grip on Ailis's thick, midnight-black hair and mused that the boy looked far older than his seven meager years. "Fine. Why were ye made to dine in your chambers?"

"Because we are bastards." Manus blushed, cast a brief, nervous look at a tight-lipped Ailis, and continued, "Our mother's kinsmen, except for Aunt Ailis, couldna bear to look upon us. Grandmère MacFarlane said that we were produced from sin and shame and that we reminded her that her eldest daughter was naught but a whore." His clear voice wavered slightly. "Grandpère was much the same, though he was dead ere I was old enough to care much. Colin Mac-Farlane sees us as a mark of shame—'a sordid stain upon the name MacFarlane' is what he calls us. He says we are naught but a whore's misbegottens and that he canna bear the stench of us. That, sir, is why we stay within our chambers." He returned to his seat and, after one last glance at Ailis, began to eat.

As Ailis fruitlessly tried to put some order into her wild unbound hair, she hissed at Alexander, "Are ye satisfied now, Sir MacDubh? Now that ye have opened up all of their wounds? They see and feel the scorn and pain it stirs all too often. They dinna need ye making them face it so fully and hear it discussed."

Her words held a truth that Alexander chose to leave unacknowledged. He could easily read the wounded look in the children's eyes. For a moment he said nothing as he valiantly fought to control his temper. It was not only the heartless way the children had been treated that stirred his fury, but how the knowledge of it brought even more grief to Barra.

"What have ye been told about your father?" Alexander asked abruptly, glancing at each child in turn as he awaited a reply.

"Only what our mother and Aunt Ailis have told us," answered Manus. "We couldna go with Mama to see our father once we began to speak, for the secret could have been revealed. Children dinna always think before they speak. Mama told us that there were people who would kill our father if they kenned who and where he was. Mama said he loved us, but she didna want us to have to bear the weight of such a secret or suffer the guilt if we couldna keep that secret. I can understand all of it now. We often exchanged gifts with our father. Wee tokens."

"Aunt Ailis told us what Mama did," Sibeal added. "Aunt Ailis says our birth canna be a sin in God's eyes because Mama acted from love. God understands love." She patted Barra's tightly clenched hand where he had rested it upon the table and smiled at his taut, wan face. "Ye must not feel sad for us. Aunt Ailis says that when we die, we will be taken in God's arms like Mama was. God has very big arms." She suffered herself to be held tightly for a moment by a smiling but moist-eyed Barra. "I hope Mama willna be cross if I dinna go to God's arms too soon."

"Nay." Barra's voice was unsteady as he released the little girl. "Your mama willna mind if she has to wait four score years or longer."

"Was there more?" Alexander pressed.

"Our mother told us that Manus and I have the look of our father except for the color of our hair," Rath answered. "Sibeal has hair like our father's. Mama once said that it was for the best that we were kept much out of sight, for there was a big danger that somebody would see in us the clue as to who our father is."

Manus nodded. "Then those people who wished him dead could have found him and killed him. Aunt Ailis says that would have killed our mother as quick as that knife did."

"Who wished to see your father dead?" Alexander asked, curious to see how much they had been told.

Alexander found himself admiring the children's skill at conversation. It was evident that an adult had spent time with them, talked to them a lot and as equals, and thus developed their skill with words. Although a great deal of what they said was clearly a lesson well learned and recited back, he sensed a keen intelligence in them. Manus replying to his question drew him from his thoughts.

"Grandpère and Uncle MacFarlane and Donald MacCordy," answered Manus. "Aye, the MacCordys were very angry about our father, and they still are."

"Why should the MacCordy clan care that Mairi MacFarlane had herself a lover?" The tension Alexander felt in Ailis only increased his curiosity.

Sibeal looked at Alexander. "Donald MacCordy was to be betrothed to my mama. Isna that right, Aunt Ailis?" She did not wait for Ailis to reply. "It had all been settled, but then Mama had the twins. Aunt Ailis said 'tis best that the betrothal never happened because my mama could never have borne being wed to a man with leech lips."

"Leech lips?" Alexander looked at Ailis, noticed how she avoided his gaze and blushed brightly, and he nearly laughed.

Rath nodded, smiling faintly. "Aye—leech lips." He dodged his aunt's attempts to pinch him into silence. "Aunt Ailis says that Donald MacCordy's kisses are akin to having a big fat leech stuck over your mouth." He giggled when Alexander and his men laughed.

Some of Alexander's amusement had nothing to do with Ailis's colorful description of Sir Donald MacCordy's kissing skill. To think that Sir Donald MacCordy, a man Alexander hated almost as much as he hated Colin, had lost one of his brides to Barra and was soon to lose the chastity of another to Alexander was truly something to savor. Even if he did not desire Ailis with a strength hitherto unknown to him, Alexander knew he would have bedded the girl anyway. The carnal use of the woman Sir Donald MacCordy considered his might be a petty revenge, but it was still an enjoyable one. Alexander knew that it would send Sir Donald into a towering rage, and if the way Mairi and her children had been treated was any indication, the loss of another of his niece's chastity would certainly raise Sir Colin's choler.

Ailis saw Alexander's amusement and inwardly cursed. She instinctively understood what the man found so funny. Her annoyance was increased by the realization that she found his laugh attractive. It stirred an unknown yet frighteningly pleasant feeling in her blood. Even reminding herself that her impending shame was one of the things that fed his amusement did not stop her from liking to hear that deep, rich laugh. She ruefully admitted to herself that she disliked Donald intensely enough that the thought of how both women intended to be his bride were bedded by his bitterest foes did have the flavor of a fine jest. That did little to soothe her abused feelings, however.

"Methinks ye will make Sir Donald MacCordy a very poor wife," Alexander said, his enticing voice intruding into her dark thoughts.

"That should please ye," she snapped, keeping her voice low so that their conversation remained private. "If ye do as ye plan, however, that marriage might never come about."

"Aye, 'twill please me if ye torment MacCordy. I also ken that MacCordy badly needs to make a firm alliance. There are too many around who wish to see him dead or run off. 'Tis the same with the MacFarlanes. As separate clans, their enemies could prevail against them, but united they could stave off the wolves of vengeance. Aye, Donald MacCordy will still take ye as his wife no matter how ill I use ye, but he might not be too pleased to do so."

"Och, well." She sighed, twisting her full mouth into a wry smile. "I ken that Donald already regrets it. 'Twill make little difference." She decided it was a good thing that the children were so young, for they did not fully understand the danger she faced.

"Ye have been greeting his wooing with a rough hand, mistress," Alexander said, his tone and attitude jovial. "I ken that MacCordy will be here with his sword a-swinging as soon as he kens who has ye. Aye, he will be fair eager to run me through."

The anticipation Alexander felt about such an event was revealed in his rich voice, and Ailis wondered why she was not more afraid of the man. "'Twill be a while ere Donald raises a sword for any reason or cause."

"Oh? Is your eager groom ill or, mayhaps, wounded?" Alexander watched her lick the wine from her full lips, felt his loins immediately tighten, and inwardly groaned.

"Aye, Sir Donald is sorely wounded," replied Manus. "His sword arm was bandaged and in a sling. I heard it said that his injury needed many a stitch."

"Donald MacCordy was ever quick to take to a sword or the fist," Barra said. "Who did this deed, one that could buy us even more time ere our enemies strike back? O-ho," he whispered when he saw the color flooding Ailis's face. "A fight over ye, was it, mistress?"

"Ye could say that," drawled Jaime, his dark eyes alight with laughter, his fear and anger forgotten for the moment. "My mistress took a knife to the rogue when he crept into her chambers."

"Oh, but ye *are* a vicious piece, Mistress MacFarlane!" Alexander gasped the words out as he was again seized with laughter, a laughter that began to fade when he realized that he had indulged in it more since the MacFarlanes' arrival at Rathmor than he had in many a year. "Sir Donald MacCordy may never survive marriage to ye." He grabbed Ailis's wrist and tugged her close to him, noting that even the smell of her, that scent of clean touched with lavender, stirred his body's interest. "Ye had best not be thinking to deal with me in such a fashion," he murmured. He fixed his gaze on her mouth for a moment before looking into her wide, dark, and anger-filled eyes.

A quick glance told Ailis that Barra and the rest were keeping the children diverted, so she hissed at Alexander. "It wouldna be your sword arm I would be slashing, Alexander MacDubh. I can do naught at this moment, but heed this, my fine rutting reiver—for every drop of blood ye draw from me, I will have the same from ye tenfold. Once I am free, be it through rescue or ransom, it willna be the men ye had best keep a wary eye on."

"Such hard words from such a soft mouth." He lightly touched her lips with his finger and held her steady when she tried to pull away. "Tell me, does your uncle or your groom MacCordy ken who fathered the bairns?" He watched her closely in hopes of detecting any evasion in her reply.

"How could they? I didna ken it myself, yet there was no one, save for your brother, who was closer to Mairi's heart than I was."

"Your kinsmen and betrothed have eyes, mistress, and they ken very well what Barra looks like."

Ailis frowned as uncertainty crowded into her heart. She had been so relieved that the children would be allowed to stay with her that she had not really given much thought to how unusual it was for a man like Donald MacCordy to agree to her request. Under the law the children were her uncle's responsibility more than they were hers. In Donald's eyes they were living proof that his first intended bride had desired another man over him. Ailis had always thought that Donald hated the children. Although she now saw that he could easily be plotting something concerning the children, she was not at all sure of what such plots could entail.

"I dinna ken," she said, her voice quiet and unsteady. "Donald never said a word, but the MacCordys may indeed ken just who fathered the children." Her deep concern for her niece and nephews made her repeat her thoughts to Alexander. "Do ye see? I now have some doubts, some questions. The MacCordys might well ken the truth."

"Aye," Alexander mumbled, idly caressing her wrist with his fingers as he thought the matter over. "What about your uncle?"

"Nay," she replied with no doubt at all. "Uncle wouldna be so quick to give them over to the MacCordys if he did."

"True." He hid his surprise and appreciation over her perception. "Those children are too good a weapon to lose. Old Colin would have found as much use for them as the Mac-Cordys think they have. I wouldna have left the bairns within his grasp, but Barra only told me his secret yestereve." Alexander made a quick decision and, turning toward the children, called, "Children, would ye like to ken who your father is?" He ignored Ailis's soft, hissed protests and Barra's abrupt loss of color.

"Aye, sir," replied Manus. "But not if it will put him in danger." His siblings nodded their agreement.

"It willna, for ye all now share a roof." With a slight flourish of his hand, Alexander pointed toward Barra. "Allow me to introduce ye to your father—Barra Mac-Dubh."

# 4

"Is he really our father, Aunt Ailis?" Manus asked as, in the bedchamber he would share with Rath, he donned a clean, linen nightshirt. "I feel he is and I think we look a bit alike, but do *ye* ken it for sure?"

Ailis sat on an ornately carved oak chest near the window and settled Sibeal on her lap. As she began to brush out the little girl's bright hair, she wished with all her heart that Alexander had not made his announcement. Such startlingly important news should have been delivered gently, slowly. The words could not be called back now, however. Now it was best to stay with the truth and to try to ease any doubts or fears the children had.

"Aye, he is your father," she replied. " 'Tis true that we dinna have anyone's word on that save for the word of the MacDubhs. However, enemy or nay, the word of a MacDubh is good." She grimaced. "Even if ye canna abide what they tell you, 'tis the truth. They are known for their honesty. Though I dinna care for the way Sir Alexander told ye, I canna deny what he said."

"And ye feel really sure that 'tis the truth?'

"Aye, Manus. Ye share a look with Sir Barra, especially ye and Rath. There was the way Sir Barra looked at me and called your mama's name. 'Twas the face of a man who had seen a ghost. Then there was the way he looked at ye lads and wee Sibeal, as if he couldna see enough of ye. A man can ply many a trick, but he canna put such raw love in his eyes unless the feeling rests in his heart. Nay, nor can he look so at a child who isna his."

"If he loves us, then why didna he come for us when Mama died?" asked Rath as he crawled into the bed he would share with Manus.

"Ah, sweeting, there are so many reasons." Ailis sighed when she realized that the children expected her to explain. "The MacDubhs and the MacFarlanes have been enemies for years. Leargan was once a MacDubh keep until our uncle took it through treachery and murder. Your father met your mother after that hatred had begun. He couldna speak of ye or of her, just as your mama couldna speak of him. And he already had a wife. The laird of the MacDubhs, Sir Alexander, makes his loathing of the Mac-Farlanes plain. Do you understand what I am trying to say?"

"Aye," Manus nodded as he snuggled down next to Rath. "If it were kenned that we had MacDubh blood, we wouldna have been safe with MacFarlanes, and our father felt that our MacFarlane blood put us in danger with the MacDubhs."

"Exactly." Ailis stood up with Sibeal in her arms and kissed each boy's forehead. "Now ye are all together as ye should have been years ago."

"What will happen to ye?"

"I will be ransomed, Manus." She forced aside her many fears about her fate.

"But then ye will be taken back to Leargan," Rath said, a slight tremor in his voice. "We will stay with ye."

"Nay." Ailis spoke firmly despite her own pain. "Ye belong with your father. He loves you, so much so that he kept away from ye even though 'twas the very last thing he wished to do. I have had ye since the day ye were born. 'Tis his turn now."

Ailis realized that she had never foreseen a time when the children would not be hers to care for. Now she saw that she had been foolishly blind. The chance of Sir Barra claiming his children had always existed. Now it had happened, and despite how deeply it cut her, Ailis knew she had to step aside.

"Canna ye stay here with us?" asked Sibeal as she tightened her arms about Ailis's neck.

"Nay, lass. I have no place here. Mayhaps later, when the troubles have eased between the clans, we will see each other again."

"If our father lets the laird hurt ye, I will hate him," Rath swore fiercely.

"Nay, ye willna, laddie." Ailis spoke as firmly as she could. "Barra MacDubh is your father. He is the man your mama loved and the man whose seed made ye. He also isna the laird here—Sir Alexander is. A man must do as his laird says. He may argue and disapprove, but he canna stop his laird. Ye arena to hold your father to blame for Sir Alexander's actions." She ruffled each boy's hair. "I will be fine."

"He hit ye, Aunt." Sibeal touched the slight bruise marring Ailis's cheek.

"That is something I have experienced before. Uncle Colin and Donald MacCordy have both knocked me about some from time to time. I have a wretched sharp tongue that can sorely try a man's temper. And did ye see Sir Alexander's face when he did it? 'Twas a great surprise to him, so 'tis clear that he doesna do it much, if at all." Ailis sat down on the edge of the bed. "Dinna fash yourselves over me, children. There is naught that Sir Alexander can do that I canna overcome. He isna going to kill me. I am much more valuable alive. Now I must be putting this lassie to bed." She stood up, turned toward the door, and came face to face with Barra. Instinct made her certain that the man had been standing there for a while.

Barra stared at Ailis for a moment. He was confused about her after all he had just heard. It was clear that Ailis had Mairi's capacity for love and understanding, but that softness was clearly tempered with finely honed steel. Mairi had often chosen to ignore reality, whereas Ailis evidently never lost sight of it, faced it bravely, and did her utmost to make the best of things. Ailis was a survivor, whereas Mairi had been a dreamer. Barra suddenly knew, deep in his heart, that his Mairi never would have lasted long. Mairi had simply not possessed the inner strength needed to survive.

"Will ye come to me, Sibeal?" Barra asked in a soft voice as he tentatively extended his arms toward the child.

After a brief hesitation Sibeal allowed Barra to take her into his arms. Ailis watched as the man bid a rather shy good sleep to his sons, then followed him as he walked to Sibeal's room just across the hall. As she watched him tuck Sibeal into bed, Ailis knew she was right to believe that the children should stay with their father. The man truly loved them, and the children were already responding to his kindness. Ailis kissed Sibeal good night and left the room. She briefly wondered if she should warn Barra about Sibeal's special gift, but decided that revelation should wait until they had all come to know each other better. She turned to seek out the bedchamber allotted to her, and Barra caught her by the arm, halting her. As she turned to face him, she fought to hide the sadness she felt over the impending loss of the children.

"I wish to thank ye, Mistress Ailis," Barra said, his voice soft and husky with emotion. "Ye could have turned my bairns from me with but a single word."

"Ye are their father. My sister loved ye." Ailis sighed.

"Without ye I wouldna have had the children at all. There is naught ye have to thank me for."

"Allow me to believe that there is." He grimaced and ran a hand through his thick hair, which so closely matched Sibeal's. "I wish I could repay ye by keeping ye safe, but I fear that I canna. When my brother wants something, there is naught a body can do to stop him."

"It matters little. When 'tis learned who holds me, there is no one who shall expect me to escape here still a maid. Donald MacCordy will add the loss of my chastity to his lengthening list of grievances against me." A slow, wry smile curved her mouth. "Dinna tell your wretched brother that I said this, but the jest he so savors has something of a pleasant taste for me as well."

"Dinna try to soothe me. 'Tis dishonor he means for ye, and we both ken it. I canna understand it, for 'tisna his way, yet 'tis clear that he means to excuse his actions by claiming his need and right for vengeance."

Ailis lightly placed her hand on his arm. "Do ye really think Donald MacCordy would take me gently?" At his expression of sudden understanding, she nodded. "Aye, ere now my fine betrothed has seen the taking of my chastity as a means to avenge all the wrongs and slights I have heaped upon him. I dinna wish to be 'taken,' dinna mistake me. However, thinking on how it will thwart Donald will make it easier to bear. If I am fated to be used as a tool of revenge, let it be *against* Donald and not by him against myself. And, too, I canna help but believe that your brother willna be as cruel as Donald."

"Nay, and yet, Alexander has no love for women and a temper that can burn hot."

"Aye, I ken that. If ye wish to do something for me, have some wine sent to my bedchamber."

"Och, nay, Ailis. If ye are thinking of drinking yourself into senselessness, dinna do it. 'Twill enrage Alexander."

"Ye mistake me," she said in a gentle voice and smiled faintly. "I ken that I might yet try to resist my fate. I shall fight your brother as I have fought many over the years, if only because his arrogance will irritate me. I speak eloquently of resignation and turning matters to suit myself, but I am not the meek submissive sort. I want to chain both fist and tongue with the numbing effects of wine so that I will not bring more pain upon myself by word or deed."

Impulsively Barra gave her a quick hug. It was somewhat fumbling, but his genuine concern touched her. As he left he muttered that her wine would be delivered presently, then strode off, leaving Ailis feeling decidedly confused. She shrugged over the vagaries of men, which she was beginning to think were as plentiful as any woman's, and went to her room.

One quick glance as she entered her bedchamber told her that she had been sent to the laird's chambers, and she cursed softly. It was very clear that the laird of Rathmor was not planning to waste any time in claiming his prize. As she studied her surroundings more carefully, she angrily mused that she should probably consider herself lucky that he had not taken her right there in the great hall.

The room was sparsely furnished, as was common, but it was also warm. What drew her attention the most was the massive bed. She found it difficult to look away from the ornately carved piece of furniture.

Hot water had been provided for her in a large earthenware bowl. Ailis briefly considered the thought that it would serve Sir Alexander MacDubh right if she stank of horses and a hard ride, then she shrugged and began to wash. A little dirt would not stop the laird of Rathmor from collecting his vengeance.

The robe provided for her was much too large, so she

put her chemise and undertunic back on, finishing just as her wine was delivered. Ailis poured herself a full goblet, sat on a chest beneath the narrow window, and stared out at the moonlit bailey of Rathmor. Thoughts tumbled through her mind, a mind too active and aware for her liking. Ailis decided to seriously consider what her next step should be.

As had many another young maid, Ailis had occasionally dreamt about the legendary handsome Sir Alexander MacDubh. It was disappointing to discover that he was not terribly different from other men except in his abundance of good looks. Those fine looks, however, could prove a great help to her. It would be very easy to imagine Sir Alexander as a lover, as a man who was bedding her out of need instead of vengeance. Her own earlier reaction to him, the feelings he had stirred within her as he had held her wrist and had gently caressed her with his long elegant fingers for a moment, told her that the man could easily catch her interest. And very firmly, too, she mused.

She refilled her goblet and thought that over for a minute. Instinct told her that the man was no rapist, not when he had looked so shocked about striking her in a response to her insults. There was no doubt in her mind that he would get what he wanted, however, through coercion, through skillful seduction, or even through patience. She could save them all a lot of trouble and just let him bed her. There was so little she could do to strike out at Donald MacCordy that it truly appealed to her just to give her maidenhead away to his bitterest enemy. What she would guard against was giving away her passion or any other, deeper emotion. She would strike at Donald by the act and defeat Sir Alexander by not allowing him to cause her any pain. That decided, she drank her wine and idly mused that it might not hurt to also pray that Sir Alexander became insensibly drunk while toasting his easy success of the day.

* * *

Alexander thought of Ailis and savored the shiver of anticipation that went through him. So intense was the feeling that he barely noticed the other people in the great hall who were drinking with him. It had been a very long time since he had felt eager to bed a woman. He could almost wish that the taint of vengeance did not hang over them all, but it did, and there was no way of shaking it. Neither could he fully shake a sense of guilt, even of distaste, over his plans. It was right there mingling with the anticipation. He had never forced himself on a woman, not even after his emotions had soured. As he tried to convince himself that he had every right to treat a MacFarlane in any way he chose, Alexander noticed that Barra's glances his way were less than filial.

"Something troubling ye, Barra?" he asked his brother. "Ye dinna look much like a man who has just had his lost bairns returned to him. I begin to suspect that what gnaws at ye has naught to do with the children."

"Ye are right to suspect that, brother. Curse it, Alex, canna ye leave the lass alone?" Barra demanded.

"Nay." Alexander's reply was succinct, but then he sat up straighter and leaned closer to Barra. "Have ye forgotten that the lass is a MacFarlane?"

"Nay, and neither do I forget that she is the beloved sister of my lover Mairi and the aunt of my bairns."

"A fact that I would sorely like to forget. Ye had best keep an eye on that lass, and on your bairns. Or she will soon have the children turned against ye."

"She has already had the chance to do so," Barra said in a solemn, quiet voice. "She turned from it. Ye judge this lass wrong, Alexander."

Barra's words angered Alexander for reasons he knew he could not begin to understand, and that annoyed him even more. "I dinna judge this one at all save to see that she is a fetching wee piece for which every inch of me is afire." He finished his ale and refilled his tankard, staring moodily into his drink.

"If ye are feeling amorous, why canna yet take one of the willing lasses scattered about Rathmor? Ye have made certain that there are more than enough of them." Barra muttered a curse. "The lass is a virgin, for the love of God."

"Love of God had naught to do with it. 'Twas swift unladylike fists and skillfully wielded knives." Alexander could not restrain a faint smile as he thought about how his enemy, Donald MacCordy, had had his wants thwarted by the young girl. "I would wager that he was planning to avenge her slights and insults in their wedding-night chamber. 'Tis the way MacCordy would think, I am certain of it. 'Twill enrage MacCordy to ken that I have had what should have been his, that a MacDubh sword will be the one to pierce her maidenhead. Aye, and he will ken that I enjoyed it."

A few men were near enough to overhear Alexander's words, and they laughed crudely. Barra glared at them before turning toward his brother and snarling, "Dinna speak of her as if she were some whore."

"Ye are concerned about a MacFarlane wench? Do ye forget . . . ?"

"Nay, Alex, I dinna forget, curse ye. But dinna *ye* forget that the lass ye plan to wreak vengeance on was but a child when her uncle treacherously murdered our father. Do ye think a wee lass not much older than my sons is guilty of that crime? Mayhaps she honed the knife her uncle used? Mayhaps ye think she planned the crime?"

Alexander was somewhat taken aback by Barra's sarcasm, then he frowned. There was going to be trouble between himself and Barra over his treatment of the MacFarlane wench. That did not change Alexander's plans, but he recognized the danger of it. Barra had some good arguments and good reasons to take the girl's side, but none of that mattered compared to how strongly Alexander desired the young woman. The strength of Barra's defense, however, was unusual if only because Barra was doing it with clear-eyed sobriety. That was something Barra had lacked for far too long. For that reason alone Alexander decided not to simply brush aside Barra's arguments.

"She carries the name MacFarlane," Alexander said. "'Tis all that matters." A mutter of agreement amongst the men echoed his words. "I dinna care if Mistress MacFarlane was naught but an itch in her father's loins at the time her uncle began to strike against us. She is that murdering bastard Colin's niece, his only heir for now."

When Barra started to speak again, Alexander snapped, "Enough! I will concede that ye are right in all ye say, but it doesna matter. From what little I have seen of the lass, she holds all that used to be good in the MacFarlanes before that adder Colin tainted the strain. That also matters naught." A few of the men sharing the head table nodded thoughtfully. "Through Mistress MacFarlane I may strike at both MacFarlane and MacCordy. 'Tis too sweet a chance to ignore. They would think the same if they held a MacDubh woman. Aye, and ere ye say it, I run hot for the wench. I willna even try to deny that. That alone is reason enough to bed her. Have done with it, Barra."

After a measuring look at Barra's compressed lips, Alexander turned his attention to where a comely maid named Kate was collecting the remnants of Jaime's hearty meal. They had placed the huge man in the far corner of the great hall, but Alexander knew that everyone still keenly felt the man's presence. "I want that brute watched closely even though he has vowed to stay his hand. The bond between him and the lass is a strong one. 'Twas certain death to face us alone and unarmed as he did. I could have cut him down in a winking. Aye, but stand firm he did. That sort of loyalty may prove stronger than his word." Alexander studied Jaime and saw how the man's gaze was fixed upon him and how Jaime's massive hands clenched. "Aye, I ken that it is."

"Jaime loves his mistress," Barra murmured.

"Aye. Beauty and the beast. Watch him, Barra, for I have no wish to kill the man."

Kate paused in refilling Jaime's tankard when she saw how he eyed the Laird of Rathmor. The size of Jaime fascinated her. She was a buxom, healthy girl, yet he made her feel like a dainty lass. She did not think him any less of a man because of his stutter. In truth, for the first time in her life she was really interested in a man. To watch him threaten her laird in his every look and gesture made her afraid of him. Without any thought except to calm him, she placed her hand over his and met his startled dark gaze.

"Nay, sir, the laird will have ye killed, and then ye will be useless to your mistress." She wondered at the astonishment in his fine eyes when he looked at her. "There is naught ye can do to halt what is to happen."

Jaime saw the concern in the woman's pretty hazel eyes and nearly forgot what he was troubled about. His stutter was strong as he said, "Your l-laird means to d-dishonor Mistress Ailis. Aye, and he c-could hurt the wee lass. I c-canna bear it."

"Ye can bear it and ye must," Kate ordered. "Did your mistress not ask it of ye herself?" Jaime gave a reluctant nod. "If 'twill ease your mind, I will tend to her come the morning. She may wish for a woman's help."

"Aye." Jaime smiled at the girl. "Aye, that would ease my mind some. Thank ye, mistress."

"Kate," she murmured, slightly bemused over how his

smile softened his broad, not unhandsome face and caused a softening within her. "Call me Kate."

Alexander watched the byplay between Kate and Jaime then looked at Barra with his brows raised slightly and amusement turning his gaze a gentler blue. "The beast has a way with the lasses. Do ye see how our Kate moons over him, our cold Kate, who usually scorns men?"

Barra's smile was real if small. "The lasses see the lamb beneath the lion, the loyal and mayhaps too soft a heart beneath the brawn."

"Aye, ye have the way of it," agreed Angus. " 'Tis wrong to think him a poor idiot as well. Aye, he may be a wee bit slow-witted, but he isna an idiot."

His eyes narrowed slightly, Alexander studied Jaime as the big man shyly conversed with Kate. "Nay, not an idiot, but often thought to be one. He carries the mark of a man scorned or ridiculed at every turn. Ofttimes great size can stir such feelings. The MacFarlane wench chose well. A kind word and the brute is her slave." He shook his head when he saw Barra stiffen, clearly preparing to argue that cynical observation. "I ken that Mistress Ailis means her kind words, so dinna rage at me again. Even I canna feel that she just feigns caring for the man."

"Aye, the children care for him as well." Barra frowned slightly. "Ye are right in thinking that his loyalty and need to protect the lass could prove stronger than his word. The promise could well be pushed from his mind as his concern for his mistress grows stronger. Is there no way to secure him for the night?"

Alexander slowly nodded. "Aye, we could place him in the dungeons. I hadna wanted to. It seemed an insult, a sign that we didna trust him to honor his word."

"It could save the brute's life in the end," Angus said.

"Far better to endure an uncomfortable night, mayhaps a sense of insult, than a taste of cold steel."

With a sigh Alexander ordered some of his men to take Jaime to the dungeons. He was not worried that his men might think fear prompted his command, for his bravery was unquestioned and well proven. It was simply an expedient move to keep a man alive. Alexander truly did not want to have to kill Jaime.

Jaime sensed what was about to occur as soon as he was approached by four burly men. Fear kept him from acknowledging Kate's soft promise to see him on the morrow. Ever since he had been a small child, he had feared dark places. He knew the MacDubhs meant no intentional harm, but they were about to inflict the worst kind of torture on him. He dragged his feet, but they treated it as a mild protest. He knew they saw his blank expression as stubbornness or stupidity and not the blind terror that it was. Fear stilled Jaime's tongue so that he could not explain himself. Only his promise to Ailis to stay his fists kept him from using his great strength to break free.

A small whimper escaped Jaime as the door to the cell was shut, but no one heeded it. He sank down onto the cold stone floor as the light from the men's torches faded. He curled up into a ball and tried to stave off the horrors his mind invoked. It would work for a while, but in the dark close space of the dungeon, Jaime knew that his fears could not be conquered, would only grow stronger. He called out for Ailis. But that did little to halt his growing panic, for he knew she could not help him, that she would soon be far too busy fighting the Laird of Rathmor.

* * *

As he finished off his ale, Alexander decided that he had savored his anticipation long enough. He rose from his seat prepared to savor reality. Alexander paused by his brother and noted the white-knuckled grip Barra had on his goblet. It was but one of many signs that heralded an uncommon tension in Barra. Although Alexander did not wish such dissension to exist between him and Barra, he was not ready to turn away from Ailis.

"Ye thought she was Mairi when ye first saw her," he murmured. "Is there a great likeness?" As Alexander had hoped, the mention of Mairi caused an immediate softening in Barra.

"Aye, though Ailis is smaller. Mairi wasna only taller but rounder, fulsomer. Ailis is also a fighter. I fear my Mairi was not."

"The woman risked a lot when she took ye as her lover. MacFarlanes are bred to hate MacDubhs."

"True, but Mairi was ever afraid. At times she shook with fear, shook as if she had the ague. My Mairi was soft of spirit, but wee Ailis isna. Methinks Ailis would spit in their eyes."

"Aye." Angus chuckled. "The lass may be a MacFarlane, but ye canna help admiring her spirit." A quick glance at Barra caused Angus to abruptly fall silent.

Barra guessed that Angus had wanted to make some remark about how that spirit could affect what Alexander planned to do. He looked at Alexander, intending to make one last plea. "Alex, canna ye—"

"Leave it, Barra." Alexander leaned close to his sibling so as to ensure the privacy of his next words. "Though I have come to scorn the more tender emotions, I still savor the baser ones betwixt men and women. Ye say that Ailis looks akin to Mairi, so ye ought to ken why your pleas fail with me."

Barra sighed, for he did understand. "Just dinna hurt the lass. I ken ye can get what ye seek without much force or fear. Use those skills of seduction ye had so finely honed years ago. Ailis has done naught to deserve pain added to the shame ye mean to visit upon her."

Alexander briefly clasped Barra's shoulder in a silent promise, then started out the hall. He understood Barra's torn loyalties, and the lack of ribald comments as he left told him that others understood, too. Alexander was grateful since he sensed that Barra's capitulation was far from complete. By the time he reached his chambers, however, Alexander's only thoughts were upon what awaited him inside. The enticing sense of anticipation was heady as he entered his chambers.

Ailis eyed Alexander warily, and a bit unclearly, as he entered. On one or two occasions she had been drunker than she was at the moment, but she felt her state of inebriation would suffice. In fact, she was feeling decidedly free of tension and even a little cheerful. All moral questions aside, if it was not Alexander MacDubh who bedded her, it would be Donald MacCordy. She had no wish for either man's services, but if given a choice, she would most certainly take Alexander. He simply wanted to humiliate Colin and the MacCordys. Donald wished to subjugate her. She also knew that Alexander MacDubh would accomplish the act with less brutality and more finesse than Donald. The fact that Alexander was the most attractive man she had ever seen did not hurt, either. In truth, she was a little worried that that could severely undermine her resolve to remain cold and distant.

When Alexander correctly judged Ailis's state, he experienced a brief flash of anger. That eased when he realized that she was only slightly inebriated. It would probably make matters easier for him. He really had no wish to fight with her.

"Still dressed?" he murmured as he moved toward her.

"Did ye expect me to be naked and laid out on the bed for ye?" she snapped.

His lips twitched as he suppressed a grin. "Nay, Mistress Ailis. 'Twould be more your way to meet me fully armed and hot for my blood."

She frowned when he sat down near her and calmly removed his boots. It was a very poor time to so clearly notice his good looks and virility. Coldness was what she needed to maintain, coldness or at least disinterest. When he stripped down to his hose, she abruptly stood up. She definitely needed to fortify that disinterest with another drink. One look at his smoothly muscular chest had stolen every bit of coldness she had mustered.

Alexander guessed her intent and, moving quickly, clasped the decanter at the same time she did, preventing her from getting another drink. "Ye have had enough, wench. I dinna care to lie with an insensible female." He pried her hand from the bottle and grasped her by the shoulders, surveying her gentle curves with undisguised hunger. "Undress," he ordered.

That curt demand made Ailis ache to hit the man, but with great effort she refrained and replied with an equal curtness. "Nay." She gave a startled yelp when Alexander deftly tore both her undertunic and her chemise down the front.

As Ailis made an instinctive move to flee, Alexander grasped her by the shoulders again and pressed her against the wall. It was an effort for him to tear his gaze from the soft golden beauty he had uncovered. Finally he looked at her face, meeting her wide, angry, but fearless brown eyes.

"If ye intend to screech so, then I am glad we put your burly guard in the dungeons for the night."

"Jaime is in a cell?" she whispered, and her concern for her friend ended her embarrassment over being naked before a man as well as her anger over his rough manner. She was all too aware of Jaime's terror of such places.

"Aye," Alexander murmured as he discarded her torn clothing. " 'Tis more for his good than for mine."

A desperate need to free her friend from the mental horror she knew he was suffering prompted Ailis's next move. She reached out to the table to their side and grasped the wine decanter. She knew Alexander saw her move even as she swung, but it was too late for him to stop her. He fell beneath her blow, the shards of the broken bottle and its contents surrounding him.

# 5

Ailis stared at the man sprawled at her feet. When he groaned and began to move, she felt a mix of relief and fear. It was evident that she had not even put Sir Alexander into a satisfactory state of unconsciousness. Nevertheless, she discovered that she was heartily glad that she had not injured him, either.

She stepped gingerly over him, grabbed his fine linen shirt off the bed, and put it on. It was far from decent, did not even fully reach her knees, but there was little else right at hand. She could not fret over modesty now. Knowing that her time to act was swiftly passing, she dashed out of the room. She had to reach Jaime and help him before Alexander could stop her.

Barra and several other MacDubh men were just stepping out of the great hall as Ailis raced down the narrow, winding stone steps. They gaped at her, and a quick glance in a mirror on the wall as she careened to halt in front of them told her why. Ailis doubted that the men had seen many half-naked lasses, with waist-length raven hair in wild disarray, racing through the hallways of Rathmor. Ailis easily shrugged aside the pinch of modesty she suffered. She was far too concerned about Jaime and about Alexander's impending pursuit. Kate then stepped out of the great hall to join the men in their astonishment. Even

Alexander's bellow from the upper chambers did not move the men to act.

"Where is Jaime? Tell me how to find him," Ailis begged of Barra as she kept a nervous watch for Alexander. "Tell me, ye gape-mouthed idiot!" she cried when Barra just continued to stare at her.

"I can tell ye, mistress," Kate said and stepped forward.

"Ye wouldna try to trick me?" Ailis did not really trust such a quick offer of help.

"Nay. I ken that whatever troubles ye concerns Jaime and that this isna some game ye play to try and escape."

"Well, please, let us hurry, then," Ailis urged even as Alexander could be heard running along the upper hall toward the stairs.

Kate rushed toward the dungeons, and Ailis followed her. She had just grabbed a torch from its place upon the wall and handed it to Kate, who started down the steps to the dungeons, when Alexander reached his men. Ailis knew that from hearing the curses yelled out in Alexander's distinctive voice. She clutched at Kate's hand as, with as much haste as they dared to use, they made their way down the steep, narrow steps into the bowels of Rathmor. They had barely gone half a dozen steps when the sounds of Jaime's terror reached their ears, his deep manly voice only adding to the pathos of his cries. Ailis did not need to prompt Kate to try and move faster.

"Why arena ye going after her, ye great fools?" snapped Alexander, and his men quickly reacted, rushing after the two women without any further hesitation.

One glare from Alexander's hard blue eyes told Barra that it would not be wise to reveal how much humor he found in the situation. He faltered on the steps with the others when the eerie, unsettling sound of a grown man's torment echoed up from the dungeons. A harsh oath from Alexander got them all moving again. Ailis's clear, even voice was soon added to the din rolling up from the cells beneath Rathmor as she sought to calm Jaime.

Both Kate and Ailis cried out in sympathy and alarm as they reached Jaime's cell. The huge man was moving incomprehensively as he made a continuous circuit of his cell. His big hands were bloodied from his blind, frantic attempts to find a way out. While Kate grabbed the ring of keys from a hook embedded in the dank gray wall and sought the one needed to free Jaime, Ailis talked to him. She tried to break the hold terror had upon her friend, but it was hard, for there was nothing but a small barred window to speak through and that was above her head. Jaime needed far more than her voice in the dark. When Kate finally opened the cell door, she handed Ailis the torch, but Alexander was already there. He grasped Ailis by the arm when she started to step inside the cell.

"He isna in his right mind," Alexander warned, eyeing Jaime warily. "Ye had best not go in there."

Ailis ignored him and, pulling against his hold, walked deeper into the cell with her torch held aloft. " 'Tis Ailis, Jaime," she called to her friend. "Look—'tis no longer dark in here."

With his wide back pressed to the wall, Jaime stared toward Ailis, his gaze fixed upon the torch light. "L-light."

"Aye, my poor friend, light. I have come to take ye out of this place."

"I am in the hole. 'Tis the hole. He has buried me again."

"Nay, Jaime. Ye arena in the hole. Ye arena in that box. See the light? 'Tis Ailis and I have come to take ye out of this place." She stepped closer to Jaime when Alexander reluctantly eased his grip on her. "Can ye see me, Jaime? 'Tis Ailis." She set the torch into a holder on the wall before stepping up to the shaking man and placing a hand on his wide chest. "I will take ye out of here now. Ah, my poor bedeviled Jaime, what have ye done to your fine hands?"

Jaime was soothed by her voice and the light and began the slow crawl up toward sanity from the depths of his fears. He frowned at his much-abused hands, and his stutter was very thick as he said, "I was t-trying to d-dig out. I had to d-dig out of the hole." He wept silently as he met her gaze, fat tears rolling down his beard-shadowed cheeks. "I canna b-bear it, mistress. I tried, truly tried, but I c-canna b-bear it." Kate tore strips from her petticoat and began to bind up Jaime's hands.

After giving Kate a look of gratitude, Ailis told a still-agitated Jaime, "'Tis all right now, Jaime. Can you see? Now there is a light to chase away the dark. Ye arena in the ground, ye arena buried in that box, ye are in a cell and now the door is open. 'Tis unlocked and open. Ye arena shut in here any longer."

He looked toward the open cell door, was recovered enough to see the men crowded around it, and hung his head. "I have shamed ye."

"Nay," Ailis protested in a soft voice as she reached up to pat his sweat-dampened curls. She did not wish him to lose the confidence she had been able to instill in him after rescuing him from his cruel family. "There is nary a person here who doesna have a fear of something. Aye, and if they had the cruel bastard ye had for a father, they would act as ye do. I dinna think any the less of ye for this."

"Nor do I," murmured Kate. "Ye need some salve on these hands, but this bandage will do for now."

Jaime cast a shy glance toward Kate, then asked Ailis, "Am I to be let free now, mistress?"

Alexander had to suppress a smile when Ailis looked his way. Her glance dared him to say no. He nodded.

"Aye." Ailis smiled at Jaime. "Ye are to be freed. Come along, my friend."

"I will see to the laddie," Angus offered in a subdued voice as Kate and Ailis began to lead Jaime out of his cell.

"Laddie?" Alexander choked out the words as he gave Jaime a sardonic look.

"He canna be more than twenty no matter how big he is," Angus muttered. "He willna be doing much with those hands of his for a wee while, either."

"True." Alexander caught hold of Ailis's arm as she came abreast of him. "Ye heard us. Angus will tend to Jaime. *Ye* will come with me."

Jaime turned to look at them, his eyes widening as he suddenly realized how little Ailis was wearing. "Mistress," he gasped, "where are your clothes?"

She could not really tell her overprotective friend that her clothes lay in shreds upon the laird's chamber floor, for she feared how he would react. So Ailis grew evasive. "I spilled some wine on them."

Looking at Alexander with narrowed eyes and wrinkling up his nose, Jaime muttered, "I ken that ye were sloshing it about a fair bit."

The sound of badly stifled laughter assaulted Alexander's ears, and he snapped at Ailis, "Come along, wench." He ignored the angry looks he got from Jaime, Ailis, and, to his well-hidden astonishment, Kate, as he dragged Ailis out of the dungeons.

As soon as Alexander and Ailis were gone, Barra started to laugh. "God's teeth, 'tis a poor time to be laughing, I ken it—but I canna help myself. Did ye see our fine laird?" He laughed even harder as others began to join in.

Alexander heard the sound of laughter following his retreat. He did not appreciate being the source of such amusement to his men, especially not because of some tiny, dark-eyed female. As he towed a wisely silent Ailis back to his bedchamber, he muttered curses under his breath. His act of rightful vengeance should not draw laughter. Once in his bedchamber Alexander slammed the heavy door shut and pushed Ailis toward the bed before he moved to wash up.

Ailis continued to stay quiet, a course of action she knew to be the wisest and safest. She silently edged toward the table, where the remaining jug of wine and her goblet stood, then helped herself to a hearty drink. As Alexander rinsed out his wine-stained golden hair, she managed to down two more goblets full and tip herself out a third. Then he saw what she was up to. He spat out an oath, strode over to her, yanked the wine jug from her, and had a long draft. With a calm she knew was heavily supported by wine, Ailis decided the fine-looking Laird of Rathmor could use a few lessons in simple manners.

Her blasé attitude well restored, Ailis sprawled on her back on the big bed. "Go easy on that wine, sir. I dinna care to lie down with an insensible man."

Alexander nearly choked on his last swallow of wine and glared at a softly chuckling Ailis. "Ye have dirty feet."

She frowned at him in confusion, for, even though a glance at her feet confirmed their filthy state, she thought his remark odd and unrelated to what she had been saying. "I didna think ye made use of my feet in what is to come."

He blinked at her, then burst out laughing. Even though a small voice in his mind told him that her ability to make him laugh was dangerous, he ignored it as his anger melted away. He kept chuckling as he busily washed her feet, tossed the damp cloth in the general direction of the washbowl, then laid down on the bed next to Ailis. Alexander turned on his side and, propped up on one elbow, cupped his chin in his hand. He studied her closely for a moment, savoring the way his body tightened with desire for her.

"Ye are very calm for a lass who is soon to be ravished," he murmured. "Or—is it the wine?"

It was undoubtedly the wine, but Ailis had no intention of admitting that to him. "If I weep and wail and cower at your feet, will that stop ye from carrying out your plans?" She tensed slightly when he began to unlace the shirt she wore.

"Nay, none of that would matter save that I would need to be rough with ye." Alexander discovered that he had absolutely no wish to be rough with her even if she denied him, but he prayed that she would not guess at that weakness in him. "Tell me, why is your big friend so afraid of that cell? He spoke of a hole? Was he trapped in one at some time?"

"Aye. His father and other kin often shut poor Jaime up in a box, and sometimes they buried him. Oh, not so it would kill him, as they needed his strength to do the work they should have done. But they did it often enough and from a young age. Now poor Jaime has such terror of being in the dark or being confined."

"Aye. 'Tis understandable. I put him there to save his life. I felt he might not be able to hold to his word and we would be forced to kill him. I now ken that he would rather we did that than put him back in the dungeon."

"That he would. I think Jamie would commit the sin of dying by his own hand rather than go into some closed, dark place."

"And he will keep his word to stay his hand."

"He will."

Alexander slowly trailed his fingers down the opening of the shirt she wore, watching the color creep into her face and her eyes darken nearly to black. That indication that he could stir a passionate response in her had Alexander suddenly short of breath. It disturbed him a little, for it was a strength of reaction he had never tasted before, but he relished it. Although he had lately scoffed at the tales of women who made the bedding of others a mundane chore, if not actually distasteful, due to the fullness of the act when shared with them, he had always envied the men who had claimed to have had such an experience. He could not stop himself from wondering if he was finally going to taste something akin to that. For the first time in far too long it became important to him that the woman in his arms reacted, strongly and honestly, and did not just act as a tool to relieve his needs in some superficial way.

Ailis fought desperately to attribute her reactions to his touch to nerves and fear, but she failed. Nerves and fear would have made her push him away, but she held herself still, tried to drink her wine, and awaited his next move with an aching anticipation. His eyes, which had warmed to a deep, captivating blue, held her spellbound. The way he trailed his long, softly callused fingers between her breasts caused a sweet warmth to curl around her loins. That tempting warmth spread like a fire in dry grass when he moved his elegant hand over her slim legs from toe to thigh and back again. She was certain that she could not blame the wine for that.

"Take the shirt off, little one," he ordered her in a thickened voice. He ached for a fuller view of what he would soon possess.

For one brief moment Ailis contemplated denying him, but realized he would simply tear the shirt off, and she did not want even the mildest form of violence to intrude. She tossed off the rest of her wine, set her heavy goblet down, and, taking a deep breath, removed the shirt. The heat of a deep blush flooded her face as Alexander stared at her. No man had ever seen her so exposed. She tried to hide her breasts from his gaze with her arms, but he easily thwarted that attempt at modesty. To her shame she discovered that his blatant appreciation excited her.

"God's beard, lass, ye are lovely," he murmured and

slowly ran his hand down her side to rest upon her hip. "Ye feel like silken gold. Dinna be afraid."

The only reply she could make was a soft noise deep in her throat as he brushed his lips over hers. He tantalized her mouth by tracing its full shape with his tongue until she was tempted into begging for a fuller, deeper kiss. Alexander granted her silent demand with a leisurely thoroughness that pulled a low moan from deep within her. He lightly pinned her to the bed with his tall, lean frame, but she knew such gentle restraint was unnecessary. The sweet seduction of his kiss was chain enough. His kiss left her wanting more when he finally moved away. It was then that she realized fighting him was the very last thing on her mind, and her heart sank.

"Touch me, lass," he whispered in a hoarse voice as he traced the dainty lines of her small ear with his tongue. "I want to feel your hands against my skin."

A voice in Ailis's head commanded her not to give in, but its warning was easily ignored, quickly drowned out by the loud cry of her own wants. Her intention had been to acquiesce to his demand, to make herself less of a tool of vengeance. Instead she found herself not only surrendering to his touch, but participating in her own dishonoring. As that thought flickered through her mind, she found that it was also easy to discard. It left the moment she moved her hands over the smooth hard skin of his torso. All that really concerned her now was that the delicious feelings he created would continue.

She began to eagerly move her hands over his broad back, tracing his taut muscles and the hard ridge of his spine with her fingers, before slipping her hands around to his strong chest. There was very little hair on his chest, but she enjoyed the texture of the small blond triangle. She lightly rubbed her palms over his nipples, feeling them harden beneath her skin. When she slowly trailed the fingers of one hand down the thin line of fair hair leading beneath the waistband of his hose, she felt him tremble. A soft groan escaped him as he brushed kisses over her long neck, and she knew that he was caught up in the same sensual whirlwind that she was.

Alexander began to fear that he would not be able to go slowly, as he knew he should. Her shy but deft touch was swiftly breaking his nearly legendary control. The way she was turning to fire beneath him was intoxicating, stroking his own passion to a height he had never tasted before. It both pulled at him and alarmed him.

"Sweet, so very sweet," he mumbled as he cupped her full breasts in his hands and lathed the tips with his tongue. "Say my name, lass. I want to hear ye say my name."

"Alexander." She groaned with a mixture of plea and pleasure as he continued to torment the hardened crests of her breasts. "Ah, it aches."

"Aye, and I ken what for, Ailis." He covered the hard nub he had been idly torturing and began to suckle gently.

A soft, purely sensual sound escaped her as sensation flooded through her. She arched her body, seeking to touch her hips to his. When Alexander shifted his body and the hard proof of his own arousal was pressed against her, Ailis trembled. She wrapped her legs around him as she fretfully fought to pull him closer. Her cry was more of relief than shock when he edged his hand between their bodies to caress the heated center of her need, easing her wanting even as he deepened it.

When Alexander stood up to shed the last of his clothes, Ailis made no attempt to flee. The prison his touch and kisses had placed her in was made all the stronger by the sight of his lean, hard body. Despite that, she shivered a little at the sight of his fully erect manhood. A touch of fear seeped through her passion. She greedily accepted him back into her arms, for the return of his warmth swiftly began to soothe her fears and press her back into unthinking desire. It was certainly far more pleasurable than fighting with him or worrying about some future sense of shame.

"Ah, now that feels lovely," he murmured as he savored the way their forms and textures blended.

He moved his hands over her slim body as he devoured her mouth with his. The way she moved her hips, searching out his in a clear sign of her honest hunger, intoxicated him. Finally his body told him that the time had come to fully possess her. He kept his gaze fixed upon her desire-flushed face, watching for signs of tension or fear as he prepared to end her girlhood. Either feeling could dim the blaze, something he was eager to avoid. So, too, did he recall his promise to Barra not to hurt the lass. If he could pleasure Ailis, he would certainly be honoring that promise.

Slowly, gritting his teeth with the effort needed to restrain himself, Alexander eased himself into her body. She clenched her fingers, her nails digging into his hips, and she pressed her lips together tightly to muffle a cry as he breached her innocence. For a moment he was still, hoping to allow the pain she tried to hide to fade, but also to savor the feel of her and the strange exultation he felt over the knowledge that no other man had found that haven. He realized it was a first for him, although a few women had attempted to trick him into believing he had taken their virginity. Even as he hesitated, however, he stroked her with his hands, unable to resist touching her and wanting to rekindle the fire her pain had briefly doused. He needed that fire he had briefly tasted in her to return in full.

"The pain will ease soon, lass," he said in a soft, gentle voice as he stroked her thigh.

"It didna hurt," Ailis lied even as she felt the sensation of being torn asunder begin to fade.

Alexander smiled faintly. "Aye? Then why did ye turn ghostly white and nearly bite your tongue clean through?"

"'Twas from revulsion." She gasped as he cupped her breast in his hand and teased the crest until she shook with need.

A low husky chuckle was all the response she got from him. She decided that his rich seductive voice had to be a sin. It could not be right for a man's voice to be so much like an intimate caress. She also thought that he was far too arrogant, but she was too caught up in her returning passion to really care.

She cried out with a desire she could not hide when he drew the hard tip of her breast deep into his mouth and began to suckle, drawing on it with a slow greed that devastated any vestiges of resistance she had tried to cling to. At the same time he began to move. Ailis needed little urging to wrap her legs around his taut hips and to parry his every thrust. She clutched at him, all thought save for what was happening to her body fleeing her mind. Some lingering sense warned her that she was being watched, and she quickly opened her eyes to catch him staring at her. She wondered how such blue eyes could look so hot.

"Ah, Alexander, it aches so." Ailis clenched her body around his, trying to draw him deeper inside of her. "Canna ye cease? I will go mad." She gasped as that ache suddenly changed and a wild, blinding feeling swept through her body.

Alexander cupped her face in his hands, watching in fascination as her desire peaked and hurled her past all thought and reason. The tremors that shook her, inside and out, grabbed hold of him as well and dragged his release from him. He collapsed on top of her, shaking from the strength of that release, her name a hoarse cry upon his lips. The echo of his name, called out in her passion-thick voice, still delighted him. It had been all he could have hoped for and more.

Ailis stared up at the ceiling. She felt torn between horror and wretched self-disgust. It was one thing to be ravished by one's enemy, but quite another to squirm with vocal delight while it was happening. She cared little about her lost innocence, for there was no man she truly loved and for whom it should have been saved. In truth, she was glad that Donald MacCordy would not have the pleasure of tearing it from her. However, the warmth with which she had responded to Alexander MacDubh troubled her deeply.

She could not honestly say that Alexander had forced that passion from her with his widely reputed seductive skills, for it had come far too easily. In fact, she did not want to believe that she was so foolish as to succumb to some artful seduction. Nor could she convince herself that it was the wine's fault. Confused and distraught by what had just happened, Ailis began to think that her uncle Colin MacFarlane was right in his oft-repeated belief that her mother's Spanish blood made her a whore by nature. At the moment that seemed the only possible explanation for how she had welcomed the touch of a stranger, of an enemy, of a man she had been taught to hate.

As he rose from her arms, Alexander watched Ailis with a keen wariness. Her silent staring up at nothing began to worry him. He looked down at the bed and winced. He had never possessed a virgin before, but he did know that they were apt to bleed. Blood upon himself or upon the linen had always been the ploy used by women who had tried to deceive him. However, he knew this to be real and, to his uknowledgeable eyes, he thought there was more blood than there ought to be, especially for a lass of such a delicate build.

Suddenly Ailis became acutely aware of the fact that she was being looked at and that she no longer had any cover-

ing on her body. She sat up with a gasp, intending to grab
the covers and hide her nakedness. Even as she got ahold
of them, she looked where Alexander was staring. She
gave a soft cry of shock, certain that she had lost too much
blood. Even reminding herself that she could easily be
overreacting to the sight of her own blood could not ease
her agitation.

"Ye have killed me," she accused Alexander, then she
groaned and fell back onto the bed with the covers still
clutched tightly to her chest. "I kenned it, but then ye made
me think that I was wrong. Now I ken that ye *have* split me
in twain just as I had suspected." Her voice raised slowly
to a dramatic wail as she added, "Ye might as well have run
me through with your sword. I am finished. I will bleed my
life away in my enemy's bed."

Her dramatics eased Alexander's concern, although he
knew he would be hard-pressed to explain why. If naught
else, he mused with a smile, if she were truly bleeding to
death, she would not have the strength to carry on so. He
did not even try to hide his grin as he rose from the bed,
moved to wash himself off, then returned to the bed with
a damp cloth in his hand.

Ailis screeched in shocked surprise when he yanked the
covers off her. She tried to grab them back only to find
herself firmly pinned to the bed with one strong hand
planted firmly on her chest. A groan of embarrassment escaped her as he washed away the last traces of her
shattered innocence. The man had no respect whatsoever
for a woman's modesty, she decided. She refused to admit
that she felt much better when he was done. She glared at
him as she repossessed the covers, sprawled on her stomach, and hid her face in the pillow. Despite all her efforts
not to do it, she burst into tears.

Alexander sighed, snuffed all the candles except for the
one near the bed, and slipped beneath the covers. He

watched her for a moment as she wept and told himself that it should not matter to him if some MacFarlane wench drowned in her own tears. When his bitter anger toward her clan and toward women failed to encompass her completely and he still felt disturbed by her crying, he scowled and gave her a brief rough shake.

"Cease your wailing, lass," he snapped. "Tears willna bring back what ye have lost this night."

She slapped his hand away from her shoulder and replied in a shaky voice, "I weep not for that, ye great fool, but for myself. My uncle was right."

The latter was said with such a wealth of despair that Alexander felt compelled to ask, "Right about what?"

"My Spanish blood." Her tone of voice implied that she had just contracted the plague, but she was unable to soften that.

"Ah," he murmured and now understood the source of her somewhat unusual coloring. "What about it?"

Little by little the tone of his voice penetrated Ailis's misery. His voice held an air of mild condescending interest that stirred her anger, pushing aside her self-pity. It was entirely his fault after all, she thought furiously. No one else amongst the overardent men she had fought off in her life had so exposed this wantonness in her. If Alexander MacDubh had not turned his pretty and lustful eyes her way, she could have continued on in blissful ignorance of her own failing. Still clutching the linen sheet to her breasts, she sat up to glare at him, seeing him as the true cause of all her misery and trouble. She ignored the small voice of rationality in her head which whispered that she was being unreasonable. At the moment she simply did not care.

"My uncle says that the Spanish are a hot-blooded, licentious people and that blood will tell." She wondered how Alexander, so clearly a man of some worldly knowledge, could be ignorant of this truth.

"Oh, aye? I never believed your swine of an uncle would ever say a word I agreed with. 'Tis glad I am to be proven right."

She saw the reply as hard proof of the man's total lack of understanding, as well as exhibiting a callous attitude toward her shame, and Ailis grew even angrier. In the tongue of her grandmother, the source of the Spanish blood her uncle so bemoaned, she railed at Alexander. She derided his fine looks, slandered his ancestors, scorned his abilities as a lover, and shredded his manhood in terms that would have made the coarsest stablehand blush. When it all worked only to increase his impudent grin, she heartily cursed men in general and lay back down.

Alexander leaned over her, placing a hand on either side of her head. He was fully aware now of what bothered her. Due to some time at court spent in the company of two Spanish noblemen looking to hire mercenaries, he also had a clear idea of how colorfully she could turn a phrase, but he felt he would keep that knowledge to himself. It could serve him well at some later time. If she thought him ignorant of the language, she would probably use it when she felt a need to say things she had no real wish for him to hear.

"There isna any people who are more or less hot-blooded than another, only those who dinna try and hide their nature," he said. "Ye bear no shame for this."

"How can ye say so?"

"Ye could do naught to stop it. What harm, then, if ye can find pleasure in that which ye canna change?" He watched as she thought over his words and he subtly eased the covers from her loosened grip so that he could have a freer access to her soft skin.

Ailis knew she believed his words mostly because it suited her to do so. She finally nodded her agreement, but then frowned at him. Despite how his touch was stirring her blood, she grasped his hand as he slid it over her stomach.

"Now that ye have what ye wished of me, where am I to sleep?" she demanded. "I am weary and I wish to seek my bed."

"Your bed is here," Alexander lied, for a bed in the chamber next to his had been prepared for her, as his habit had been to send a woman away once he had his fill of her.

"But ye have had your vengeance." She felt a trickle of alarm, for she sensed a real danger to her emotions in such enforced proximity to him.

"Aye, I have taken what should have been MacCordy's, but I find that vengeance has a very sweet flavor, and I mean to taste of it again." He covered her mouth with his, using a deep kiss to silence any possible protests.

# 6

Kate frowned as she stood in the doorway. She knew Ailis was to have slept there, yet the room looked as if it had not been used at all. But that was impossible. She knew the girl was not with the children, for Barra had tended to their dressing and brought them into the great hall. Neither was she with Jaime, who was still closely attended by Angus. Nevertheless, she had checked the children's rooms and turned up nothing. Her heart pounding with growing concern as she tried to understand how the girl could possibly go missing, Kate hurried back toward the great hall only to meet Barra walking to Alexander's room.

"How fares the lass?" Barra asked in honest concern, for he saw that Kate was clearly upset. "She hasna been hurt, has she? Or become too despondent?"

Although unable to believe Ailis had escaped, especially without the children or Jaime, Kate mumbled, "I dinna ken."

"What do ye mean, you dinna ken?" Barra demanded, giving the agitated girl a slight shake. "Come, Kate, explain yourself."

"I dinna ken how she fares because I canna find her." Kate wrung her hands as she became more and more agitated.

"Ye canna find her?"

"Nay. The bed that was readied for her looks unused, and she isna in the bairns' rooms."

"God's teeth, do ye think she has managed to escape?"

"Without even Jaime?" Kate asked, her doubt clear to hear in her voice.

"Nay." Barra frowned, but then his eyes widened. "Alexander." He wondered if they had been foolish not to suspect just how far the spirit they had admired in Ailis might take her in a fight for her honor, a fight against Alexander.

Kate hurried after Barra as he strode to Alexander's chamber. She, too, suddenly realized that if the girl had fled, she might well have done something to the laird. Barra's gasp and broad back prevented her from entering the laird's chamber. She saw that Barra seemed rooted to the spot he had stopped on inside the doorway, so she peered around him only to echo his astonishment.

Barra had to fight a brief, sharp twinge of jealousy as he studied his brother. Alexander's golden crowned head was easy to see against the black and gold which pillowed it. His face was tucked up against Ailis's long slender neck while one of his hands gently cupped the breast not covered by his body. One of Ailis's slim arms was curled around his broad shoulders and, though covered, it was easy to see that their legs were entwined beneath the sheet. The look upon Alexander's face was one Barra had not seen for years, the tension completely washed away. That was as surprising as the clear proof that he had kept Ailis in his bed the whole night through. Barra started to smile as he saw his brother begin to wake up.

Even as he first opened his eyes, Alexander knew who was tucked up in his arms. He eased himself partly off of Ailis, keeping his gaze fixed upon her full breasts, which had provided him with such a delectable resting place. Despite having enjoyed the passion they shared several times during the night, Alexander felt his loins tighten. He could not deny that what he had experienced with Ailis was the richest, fullest he had ever enjoyed, and he wanted more. Neither could he deny that it simply felt good to wake up next to her.

He traced the dusky tip of her full breast with one long finger. He watched as her nipple hardened in response and Ailis's slim body begin to stir. Alexander did the same to her other breast, and it brought the same reaction as well as a swat from one slim arm. Ailis then turned onto her side and cuddled up to her pillow.

As Ailis turned away from Alexander, she muttered, "Leave me be, ye rapacious rogue. By all the Saints, do ye never give it a rest?"

The sound of smothered laughter from the doorway caused Alexander to turn. He changed his grin to a frown but could not hide the laughter in his eyes. One jerk of his thumb was enough to send Barra and Kate silently retreating. Alexander wanted no audience for what he was planning.

Barra's amusement fled as he walked toward the great hall, Kate shadowing his steps. "It isna good."

"Nay," spoke up Kate with a familiarity born of having grown up within the keep, her parents old and trusted retainers. " 'Tis very good that the MacFarlane lass wasna hurt nor afrighted, but 'tisna good that his lairdship finds such pleasure with her. Nay, not when she is the first to bring it to him. She is a MacFarlane. She must be ransomed and sent away."

As he watched her sleep, Alexander briefly wondered how long Ailis's stay at Rathmor would be. He reached out and gently but firmly turned her onto her back. He met her heavy-lidded glare with a smile. His smile widened when she muttered something about being left alone to sleep, and she closed her eyes again. The hard tips of her breasts told her she was not as disinterested as she was acting.

"Ye sleep, then," he said as he moved to lie between her shapely legs and propped himself up on his elbows. "I will just carry on."

Ailis was still drowsy, but that did not stop her from being stirred by the feel of his body against hers. She had no intention of admitting that, however. All through the night she had kept her resistance only vocal, and that very little, for she had realized that after Alexander came Donald MacCordy. The very thought of Donald doing to her as Alexander had turned her stomach. She decided she would be a fool not to enjoy what she could while she could. And, she mused, not enjoying it would only have made her suffer anyways, for it might not have stopped Alexander and it certainly would not help her elude Donald's fury later.

"Carry on whilst I sleep?" she murmured in a voice still husky with sleep and enhanced by her growing desire as Alexander stroked her breast. "That is disgusting."

"If ye go to sleep, ye willna care," he said in a cheerful tone before he drew the tip of her breast deep into his mouth.

There was no way for Ailis to hide how that stirred her desire. A soft cry escaped her as she buried her hands in his long thick hair. Her mind slipped from the hazy realms of partial sleep into the ones of passion. He was her enemy, the thief of her virtue and her honor, yet his touch enflamed her. It did not matter that she had been taught since she was a small child to loathe MacDubhs—she craved his touch. When Alexander slowly entered her, she sighed with a delight she could not disguise despite how her body ached as a consequence of such a new experience.

"Ye seem to have come awake quite nicely, lass," he said as he brushed soft kisses over her face.

" 'Tis hard to sleep when some rogue is mauling me about." She clutched at his lean hips to pull him much closer even as she wrapped her legs around him to urge him on.

A husky laugh escaped Alexander as he met her gaze, and he slid his hand over her body in a sweeping caress. He found it intensely exciting to watch her as she gained her release. It was satisfying to know that he was the one who had brought that look of blind ecstasy to her face, that he was the first man to do so. He barely got a glimpse of that look this time for he found himself swept along with her as they simultaneously reached the pinnacle the bodies strove for. They clung together as their bodies trembled from the force of release and from the echoes of it. It was a long time before Alexander had the strength and inclination to free himself of the intimate tangle of their bodies.

He gently extracted himself from Ailis's languid embrace, rolled over onto his back, and pulled the cover over them. Now that the pleasure was past, Alexander found that he was deeply troubled. This time there had been no chance for him to ignore or deny the rich sense of unity he felt with her. So full was the sex act with her that he was hard-pressed to conjure up the barest memory of any one that had gone before. He realized that it was going to be very hard to give that up, but she was a MacFarlane and there was no place for her at Rathmor. There was Mac-Dubh blood on her family's hands and deep treachery, which needed to be avenged.

Those were facts he knew he would have to constantly remind himself of. He would try to console himself with the theory that if there was one woman who could thrill and sate him so completely, then somewhere there had to be another. When Ailis was gone, he would start his search for that other one.

Ailis watched Alexander as he rose to dress. His sudden

silence troubled her as did the remote look upon his face.
There was little hint of warmth or any expression in his
blue eyes. She could grasp no hint of his thoughts or feelings. Since he had not acted like that before they had made
love, she could only assume that there was something
about that which had changed him. It hurt to think that
something she had thought was so beautiful could be a
source of trouble and worry to Alexander, and she did not
question that hurt.

Her eyes widened as a possible explanation firmed in
her mind, one it was impossible to scorn even if scorn was
what it deserved. She was the niece and heir of the man
who had killed Alexander's father and stolen his land. She
was also the betrothed of a man he detested. Their lovemaking should not be beautiful, should not leave him
shaking and clinging to her. It should be no more than an
act of vengeance with a touch of lusting. Ailis knew it was
not vanity which made her certain that Alexander had enjoyed her, hungered for her. That a MacDubh should feel
so for a MacFarlane was what troubled her captor. She
prayed that it would not drive him to treat her harshly.

The thought that Alexander could yet hand her over to
his men crept insidiously into her mind, and she shivered
as an icy fear seeped through her. She did not want to believe that he could be so cruel, but she had to admit that
despite their intimacy, he was a stranger to her. Alexander's
goal was, after all, to strike at her uncle and Donald, and
to make her the whore of his men-at-arms would certainly
do that. It would also rid him of something he now found
troubling. He could do it to prove to himself, and her, that
there was nothing extraordinary about what they had
shared. So, too, could such an abuse of her work to end
whatever desire he held for her.

When Alexander moved to leave, she put aside her fears
and spoke up. "Am I to be kept within these chambers?"

She pushed aside the hurt caused by the evidence that he had forgotten her presence.

Alexander turned, blinking, as he pulled his mind back from its wanderings. "Ye wouldna get a foot away from these walls if ye did try to flee. There is no need to keep ye locked up. 'Tis time and gone to break our fast. Get dressed."

She reached down by the bedside and collected up her torn clothes, holding them up for him to see. "Dressed in what, m'laird?"

He muttered a curse that caused her eyes to widen, then he snapped, "That wouldna have happened if ye had undressed as I asked ye to."

"Of course," she murmured.

It was not hard for Alexander to read her low opinion of his reasoning in her look as she dropped her clothes back onto the floor. The problem was that he no longer knew what fashion was being worn by ladies and even unfashionable female clothing was rare at Rathmor. She did need something, there was no denying that, but what?

He agitatedly paced the chamber as he spoke his thoughts aloud. "I canna think of any wench about Rathmor who is of a size with ye. Ye are such a wee lass. By the saints, even if there was a lass your size, she wouldna have a spare gown. Can your clothes not be repaired, stitched back together?"

One glance was enough for Ailis to be certain of her answer, and she shook her head. "I dinna have a great deal of skill with a needle, but even if your best seamstress took on the chore, 'twouldna help. The clothes were closely fitted ere they were torn. What of Barra's wife's things?"

"They are gone. When that slattern died, we cleared away all sign of her. So it was with my traitorous stepmother and my own late wife. They were all larger than ye anyway." As he talked he studied her, then slowly smiled.

"Aye. Aye, it just may do, although 'twill certainly widen a few eyes."

Ailis watched him in growing confusion as he moved to a heavy chest that had clearly been kept shut a long time. Her confusion grew when she saw that the chest held clothes that, if they were Alexander's, he had not worn for many years. It struck her as odd that all of those women's clothes would have been cleared away, yet he cared for clothes that could only have been worn when he was a small boy or youth. She pushed the thought aside when he laid out a set of those clothes, his gaze bright with enjoyment. She realized he meant her to put them on.

"Is not making me your whore vengeance enough?" she asked, stung by what appeared to be another attempt to cause her shame and humiliation.

Alexander was immediately sobered. "Nay, I dinna do this to humiliate ye. 'Tis all I have unless ye wish to stay naked within these chambers until something can be made for ye."

For a long moment she stared into his eyes, but there was no sign there that he was lying. It could be quite a while before a new set of clothing could be made up for her. When the only alternative was to be chained to the bedchamber by her own nakedness, donning boy's clothing suddenly did not seem so abhorrent. Ailis was also sure that everyone would know why she had been brought to such a pass. That would be embarrassing, but she felt she could endure that if only because it would undoubtedly be short-lived.

"Will ye leave or turn your back while I dress?" she asked as, with a sigh, she reached for the clothes.

A mix of a grin and a leer curved Alexander's mouth as he replied, "I am well acquainted with your charms, m'lady."

Several tart replies sprang to her lips even as color

flooded her cheeks, but she knew better than to utter them. "Please."

After a brief hesitation he shrugged and turned his back. If nothing else he owed her some small measure of courtesy for the pleasure she had given him. The only reason he lingered at all was so that he could escort her to the great hall, for he knew she would need some support at first. He told himself he was being kind just to placate Barra's sensitive conscience, that a few small kindnesses would be necessary to ensure that there was no further quarrel between himself and Barra.

Ailis took a deep breath to steady herself, then stood up and began to dress. As she tugged on each piece, she found that they felt strange, yet not unpleasantly so. There was no musty smell to the clothes, either. She wondered if such good care had been taken in the hope that an heir would make use of them. Alexander had certainly not worn them for a long time because they fit her rather well. She found it a little difficult to picture him as a lad of her small stature.

She gave a fretful tug on the gray jupon as she strode toward the table where he had left his brush, for she needed to fix her hair. The clothes made her feel very aware, too aware, of her form, and she strove to forget that. A soft noise similar to a swiftly indrawn breath caused her to quickly turn, the brush clutched tightly in her hands, and look at Alexander.

Impatient, Alexander had turned to tell her to hurry only to nearly choke on his abrupt inhale at his first look at her. If Ailis was any example, there was a very good reason why women were not allowed to dress in men's clothes. Every man at Rathmor would be set aflame by the sight of her. He certainly was, and he should have fed his lusts enough during the long passion-filled night. A man who allowed his woman to dress so would undoubtedly be driven to the grave by the never-ending need to protect her from lust-crazed men, he mused with a dark scowl.

"Is something amiss?" she asked.

"Nay," he managed to grunt.

"What am I to do about my hair?" she muttered mostly to herself as she brushed it.

Alexander pulled himself free of his stupor and replied, "Braid it. That will do fine enough. Canna ye hurry it along a wee bit?"

She swallowed her annoyance and tried to hurry. She tried to figure out his strange mood. He seemed so edgy, yet she could not understand why he should be. The full, lusty night they had just indulged in should have put him into a far more amiable state. She began to wonder if he possessed anything similar to a good humor. When he grumbled a curse and proceeded to braid her hair himself, she stood quietly, deciding it best not to press his temper. If she did she feared he might yet decide that robbing her of her chastity was not punishment enough for being Colin MacFarlane's kinswoman.

Her good intention faded when he grabbed her by the arm and hastily started out for the great hall. "Will ye slow down a pace? I find more freedom in these clothes, 'tis true, but I have no love of a race. Nor do I wish to enter the hall at a dead run. I shall be too winded to eat."

His steps slowed a little, but he grumbled, "Ye have made us both late. We may find naught but scraps left for our meal."

"If a meal in your belly will make ye less of a surly dog, mayhaps we should run."

He ignored her even as he mused that she was very pert, especially for a woman in her precarious position. They stepped into the great hall, and his eyes narrowed in a dangerous expression as he watched the men seated there. Their reaction to Ailis was all he had anticipated and more.

The scowl on his face sent their lusty glances into hiding, but he knew that lust remained. He dragged Ailis to the head table, seating her at his side with a distinct lack of manners, then threw himself into his own chair. Alexander sternly told himself that he should not care how his men looked at one of the hated MacFarlanes, then glared another of his men-at-arms into submission.

"Ye look fine," Rath said from his seat on Ailis's left. "Now ye can climb trees without cursing your skirts."

"I never curse," Ailis lied out of habit as she idly mused that her odd attire was being accepted very calmly.

Rath giggled along with his sibling. "Nay, I must have been mistaken. What shall we do today, Aunt?"

"That must be decided by our, er, host." She flicked a glance at a still-frowning Alexander. "What may we do and not do, sir?"

Glad to have some diversion from his thoughts, which threatened to have him dragging her back to bed, Alexander replied. Unspoken but clearly understood throughout his brief litany of directions was the fact that she and Jaime would be well watched. The freedom of movement he appeared to be allowing her was all a delusion. He would make very sure that she was allowed little chance to escape. Ailis was a little dismayed to realize that she had not really given escape much thought for a while.

Once done with her meal, she left the great hall to go and walk the grounds of Rathmor. Jaime and the children followed but not too closely. She was well aware of her constant guard despite how subtle the men were about it. Ailis was determined to ignore them. There was no real chance of escaping the fortress of Rathmor, so she felt it would be foolish to brood. If a chance presented itself, she would grab it with both hands, but she would not allow herself to fret over her captivity. She knew all too well that it could be a great deal worse than it was.

"Are ye feeling all right, mistress?" Jaime asked as he finally stepped up to her side.

"Aye. He didna hurt me save in spirit mayhaps." She paused, then realized that, if there was one person she could be fully honest with, it was Jaime. "There was no chance of my stopping what has happened. None at all. Kenning that, I put up *no* fight, my friend. Fighting would have gained me naught but pain. In truth, I enjoyed myself, for he is such a beautiful man, and all I could think of was that, after this, came Donald MacCordy."

Jaime nodded slowly. "Aye, that was best, I think."

"Well, that makes me feel a great deal better." She clasped his hand as they walked.

"Mayhaps MacCordy willna wed ye now."

"Nay, he will certainly be furious that I have lost the chastity he so prized. Aye, and more so because of who stole it. However, he will still wed me. MacCordy craves my dowry and the firm alliance such a marriage will gain him." She shrugged. "I have resigned myself to these facts. 'Tis a fate I canna avoid." She heartily wished that was not so, but she had yet to see how her fate could be changed.

"Then ye enjoy yourself, mistress," Jaime said, "and dinna think poorly of yourself as ye do. Ye deserve some frolic ere your wedding day. I dinna think there will be the cause or the heart for frolicking after ye have been given over to Donald MacCordy."

" 'Tis how I think on it, m'friend." She watched as the children hurried to greet Barra, who was just coming out of the keep and walking their way. "At least I have seen the MacCordys denied the children." Despite the pain of losing them herself, she was glad of that.

"Do ye think they meant to use them?"

"Aye, Jaime, I am fair certain of it. I thought Donald was granting me some favor when he said I could keep Mairi's bairns at my side. But Donald MacCordy does no one a

favor. I should have kenned that from the first. Donald
kenned who Mairi's lover was and whose children they
were and sought to gain them through marriage. He meant
to use them to hurt the MacDubhs and to gain either
wealth or land. He canna do that now." She sighed. "It sore
grieves me to lose them, but they are better off here with
their true father, a man who clearly adores them. Here the
bairns will ken naught but kindness, love, and guidance.
With me, where I must go, they willna have any of that."
That thought helped ease some of her pain.

"Aye, the bairns will be happiest here. Ah, their father
means to play a little ball with them."

"I had best join in so that poor Sibeal doesna feel too
alone."

Jaime grinned as she skipped off to join Barra and the
children in a game of ball. Ailis could be as rough-and-
tumble as the boys. When Barra gently scolded his sons for
tumbling their aunt in the dust, Jaime laughed, for Barra had
barely finished the lecture when Ailis tumbled him and
raced off with the ball. Little Sibeal did her best to try and
run interference for Ailis as the twins and Barra tried to re-
claim the ball. It did not take long before Barra realized that
treating Ailis like a lady would only give her an advantage
she made swift use of. Jaime roared with laughter every time
Barra succumbed to his gentlemanly instincts and upbring-
ing, for it never failed to cost the man.

The game grew in size as other children, youths, and
even a few men drifted over to join the game. Jaime soon
found himself one of a large crowd who were not shy
about yelling out encouragement or derision. Although it
looked like a melee, Jaime knew there were rules, and he
could see teams taking shape. He did begin to wonder if it
was growing too rowdy for Ailis and Sibeal, however. He
saw Alexander enter the bailey and decided to let the Laird
of Rathmor decide.

Alexander was starting toward the stables, intending to go for a ride through his fields, when he stopped and gaped. It was not the game nor the lack of work being accomplished that caused his amazement. He was stunned by the sight of a small, lithe figure with a long raven braid disappearing beneath a pile of boys. Even as he strode toward the crowd encircling the player, Angus at his heels, Ailis was back on her feet. Yet again she was in possession of the ball and running with it. He fleetingly wondered if putting her into a lad's attire had helped lead to this activity.

"What in God's sweet name is the lass doing?" he demanded when he reached Jaime's side.

"Playing ball," Jaime answered, then bellowed, "Run with it, Ailis. There's a lass!"

"She is very good," Angus murmured. He earned a glare from Alexander. "Well, she is. Bad temper doesna change fact."

"Angus, just because she is dressed as a lad doesna mean she must act like one," Alexander scolded his cousin.

"She likes to play ball," Jaime protested. "She likes playing with the children. They need someone to play with, and Ailis was the only one."

The urge to immediately yank Ailis out of the rough game was strong, and Alexander gritted his teeth as he fought it. He stood for a while as part of the audience and soon had to concede, albeit reluctantly, that she was good. Her small stature combined with an admirable speed made her a worthy player. This was clearly not a new game for her. It was all the bruising her delicate figure was enduring that made him wince. He could not believe that such a tiny female could endure such a physical game. She would easily be seriously injured.

A moment later he watched his fears realized. The game came to an abrupt halt when Ailis was brought down but

did not rise as she had each time before. Alexander raced
to Ailis's side, telling himself that the panic he felt was
over the possibility of losing her services in his bed. He
did not wish to give up that particular delight until he was
forced to.

He knelt at her side and quickly checked for any broken
bones. When he found none, he partly raised her up in his
arms. Although he could feel no wound upon her head, it
eased his concern only a little.

"She should rouse in a wee bit, sir," Jaime said as he
leaned over Ailis, but there was a hint of fear on his face.

Sibeal nudged in beside Jaime and patted his arm.
"Dinna worry, Aunt will be fine," she said in a voice strong
with conviction.

Jaime sighed and smiled. "Good."

Alexander almost told Jaime not to be a fool, that a child
could not guess at Ailis's health, but bit back his words.
There was probably no sense in trying to explain it to the
man. He had a more immediate problem anyway.

"Get me some water to splash on her face," he ordered,
hoping that might rouse her.

Manus and Rath did not hesitate. They raced off and returned an instant later with a bucket brimming with water,
their clothes damp from carrying it. Before Alexander
fully realized what the twins intended to do and could stop
them, they poured the bucket full of water over Ailis
splashing him, too. For a moment Alexander sat there in
the mud, speechless and dripping, as everyone around him
struggled valiantly against laughter.

"I wanted to splash a bit of water on her face, not drown
her," he finally snapped at his nephews.

"Oh. But it worked, sir," Manus said and pointed at
Ailis. "See, she wakes."

Ailis sputtered awake. She looked around her groggily.
Her first clear thought was to wonder why she was all wet

and lying in an equally wet Alexander's arms. She could feel dampness seeping through her hose to her backside and wondered why they were sitting in a puddle. Then, suddenly, she recalled the game and sat up a little straighter.

"Did we win?" she demanded.

After gaping at the muddy woman in his arms, Alexander replied in a choked voice, "I would say it is a draw." He burst out laughing, and the others quickly joined in.

# 7

"Is this how ye mean to play your game?"

Alexander muttered a curse, then turned to face Barra, heavily wishing that his young brother had not followed him up to the battlements. It was annoying, but it was also embarrassing. He had come up on the high walls to try and covertly watch Ailis work in the kitchen garden with the children. Alex suspected it was rather obvious, especially since Barra had caught him doing such spying several times in the two weeks since Ailis had been brought to Rathmor.

"And what is that supposed to mean?" he asked, meeting Barra's sardonic look with a calm he did not feel.

"Ye may not have noticed, brother, but I am no longer the dim-witted drunk."

"I noticed. 'Tis one of the few good things that have happened to us in the last few years."

Barra shook his head, rested his arms on the parapets, and stared down at Ailis and the children. "Ye sounded like a petulant child just then. We are alive, Alexander. There must be some good to find in that."

"Ye found little good in these last two years."

"True enough. 'Tis why I can so clearly see how wrong ye are and fear it. I have seen the wretched depths grief and hopelessness can take a man to. I have seen how easily it can steal a man's strength and reason. In ye, I see how it has stolen all that made ye such a good man. Ye have lost your gift of understanding, of forgiveness."

"Forgiveness?" Alexander spat out the word as he glared at Barra. "Do ye ask me to forgive Colin MacFarlane for dishonoring us by cuckolding our father but months after his marriage? Or for his cowardly murder of our father and his theft of our lands? Do ye expect me to forgive our adder of a stepmother for leading our hapless father into that Mac-Farlane trap? She may as well have cut his throat herself. Should I forgive her for helping her lover Colin gain all he coveted? She even used her wiles and the power of her many lovers to help MacFarlane gain the king's acknowledgment of his false claims, thus stealing our right of vengeance. If she wasna already dead I would kill her with my bare hands. And, despite the crimes done us, we risk the taint of outlawry each time we act against Colin or what few allies he has clung to. Am I to forgive all that?"

"Nay, and ye ken that I dinna ask ye to."

"Then who am I to forgive?" Alexander continued before Barra could say any more. "My wives? The first one mayhaps. She was just a whore—an embarrassment but little else. That leaves my second wife—the mad Frances? Am I to forgive her? She who killed my Elizbet, my only child?" he asked in a tight whisper.

"Nay. Cease trying to silence me with a litany of the crimes done to us. Ye ken that I would never ask ye to forgive such things, that I would think ye a saint if ye were able to do so. What I ask is that ye forgive womankind, that we cease faulting the innocent for crimes done by a few of their ilk."

Alexander gave an unpleasant laugh. "A few? The course of my life has been littered with whores, liars, and adulteresses. I forgave too often. 'Tis why we lost so much. They sensed my weakness. No more. I have finally seen the rot that lurks beneath the soft skin and pretty face. I shallna be fooled again."

"Ye canna believe all ye have just said. What of the brides of your closest friends? What of the MacLagan women?"

"They are proof of what I say. They, too, brought trouble with them."

"And good, but I can see that ye have blinded yourself. It also explains why ye have turned cold toward your old friends, even refusing their help in this fight."

" 'Tis our fight, not theirs. I willna risk their lives for our gain."

"Nay, nor will ye risk meeting with women ye ken will prove your accusations and beliefs are all wrong, all born of your pain. Ailis—"

"Ailis is a MacFarlane."

"A trick of birth, 'tis all, and well ye ken it." Barra shook his fist at Alexander. "She doesna deserve what ye are doing to her. Ye bed her every night, and I dinna need to witness it to ken that ye do so with gentleness and lustiness. That can be seen on your faces—briefly—each morn. Ah, but then ye recall that she is a woman, a MacFarlane, and ye turn cold. Ye lurk about watching her, hungering for her, but rarely speak to her or treat her very kindly at all."

"She is a MacFarlane!"

"Aye, and ye are a fool!"

Before Alexander could strike Barra, as he ached to, he heard young Sibeal's voice saying, "Papa, Uncle, I need ye to help me." He fought to control himself as Barra immediately turned to Sibeal.

Barra picked the child up and gave her a kiss on the cheek before gently scolding her. "Ye ken that ye shouldna be up here, dearling. 'Tis dangerous. Why didna ye stay with Ailis? Ye looked to be having fun in the garden."

"I was." Sibeal lightly chewed on her bottom lip and

twirled a fat reddish curl around her dirty finger. "I needed ye."

"Well, I am pleased to help, but what can I do that ye canna do? Or that your aunt canna help with?"

"Ye must save the wee puppies."

"What wee puppies?"

"The wee puppies that will fall in the water." She tugged on the front of Barra's jupon. "Come, Papa, ye must save the puppies." She began to cry, and her words became jumbled.

"Do ye ken of any puppies, Alexander?" Barra patted Sibeal's head in a gesture of awkward helplessness.

"Nay." Alexander shook aside the unwanted pang of jealousy he suffered while watching Barra with Sibeal. "A few of our bitches are due to whelp soon, but I dinna think they have. The earlier broods are too big to be called wee puppies."

"But they are puppies!" Sibeal yelled. "They are! Ye have to get them out of the water. Ye have to!"

"I think we had better speak to Ailis," said Barra when nothing he did soothed Sibeal.

Alexander grumbled a curse as he followed Barra down from the walls. He really did not want to see Ailis. Barra had been painfully close to the truth before little Sibeal had interrupted them. Alexander could not resist the draw of the sweet passion he shared with Ailis in the night, but he refused the woman all else. It was the only way he knew to keep some distance between them, although he felt the worst of hypocrites, for he had once lectured a friend on the wrong done by such a game. Despite that, at night he fed the hungers of his body, but by avoiding her for most of the day, he also hoped to evade becoming emotionally drawn to her.

It was a plan that was not working very well at all. He was finding that he ached to see her, wanted to talk to her, to hear her laugh. It was why he had taken to spying on her. That weakness in his plan would not make him discard it, however. It was the only plan he had. It was the only defense he had against Ailis—a woman he was certain was a great threat to the shield of bitterness he had encased himself in. He knew instinctively that Ailis MacFarlane could touch him, so he would stay out of her reach.

As he and Barra, who still carried Sibeal, approached Ailis, Alexander hardened himself. Ailis looked endearingly dirty. She still wore one of his boyhood shirts, but skirts and petticoats had replaced the hose. The women of Rathmor had been quick to sew her up some women's clothing after seeing her dressed as a lad. Her rich black hair hung in a thick braid down her back. The sleeves of the linen shirt were rolled up and she had dirt on her up to the elbow as well as several broad smudges upon her face. She was no cleaner than the twins, who had been helping her. Alexander found it very hard not to smile, and that irritated him.

One look at Sibeal's tear-stained face, and Ailis forgot her interest in Alexander. She wiped her hands on her apron and quickly took her niece into her arms. "Hush, my loving." She kissed Sibeal's forehead, then looked accusingly at the two men. "What have ye done to her?"

"Naught," snapped Alexander. "She keeps weeping about puppies."

Barra hastened to explain how Sibeal had come to him and what she had said. "Once she started crying, 'twas impossible to understand. She just keeps wanting us to help with the puppies." He frowned when he saw an odd expression settle on Ailis's face, one echoed on the begrimed faces of the twins. "What is it? What is wrong?"

"The child is upset is all," Ailis muttered. "Ye need not linger here. We can tend her."

"Nay," Sibeal wailed and lunged back toward Barra,

who quickly caught her in his arms. "We have to go out-side, outside the walls. Ye canna go, Aunt, but Papa can. Papa can."

"All right, Sibeal." Ailis rubbed the little girl's back. "Calm yourself, sweeting. Ye ken well that ye must be calm, that ye must think hard and speak carefully."

"Aye, and that ye were supposed to be quiet," grumbled Manus, earning a slight punitive nudge from his aunt.

"Quiet about what?" demanded Alexander. "Have ye been keeping some secret, Ailis?"

"Oh, aye, just a wee one." Ailis gave a sour laugh. "However, now is not the time to discuss it."

"Now is the perfect time." He reached for her.

Ailis slapped Alexander's hand away. "Nay, it isna." She easily ignored his look of astonishment over her blatant impudence. "Now we must calm Sibeal, find out what she needs, and get it. After that we may pay court to your petty suspicions and animosities." She immediately turned her full attention to Sibeal. "Now, take a few deep breaths, lassie, and still those tears. If we are to save these puppies ye speak of, then we need to ken a few things—such as where."

"They are in the water," Sibeal answered, calmer, but with her high clear voice still unsteady.

"Are they standing in the water?"

"Nay, they are in a sack. A man tosses them off of a cliff."

"Now, wait a minute," Alexander interrupted, ignoring Ailis's cross look. "There are no cliffs in Rathmor nor streams running through the bailey. The child but had a bad dream. Some old memory haunts her."

"I saw it! I saw it!" Sibeal began to cry again as she protested.

"Now ye have fixed it." Ailis saw that Barra was doing as good a job of calming his daughter as she could, so she turned her attention to Alexander. "I hadna wished to reveal this so soon. I had wanted ye to come to ken Sibeal better. She has the sight." Ailis was not surprised by the look of shock on Alexander's face, a look that quickly changed to disbelief tinged with fear and anger. Barra looked much the same, but he said nothing, simply continued to calm Sibeal and try to get some answers from the child.

"Now ye try to make game of me," Alexander snapped, grasping Ailis by the arm and giving her a little shake.

"Nay, but I dinna think anything I can say will change your mind on that." Ailis did nothing to hide her annoyance with his suspicion, for, after two weeks of suffering his distrust, she was heartily sick of it. "The only solution is for ye to play along and see the truth for yourself. Unless ye have something else ye must do."

"Not at the moment. So, go ahead, make a fool of yourself."

Ailis ached to tell him exactly who the fool was between them, but bit back her words. "Is there a place near at hand where a man could toss something off a cliff into a stream?"

"Aye," answered Barra when Alexander just muttered something crude. "About a mile from here. Pagan's Point."

"Pagan's Point?" Ailis asked.

"When the people in this area first accepted the Christian faith, they remained tolerant of those who resisted it. Then we got our own priest, and he convinced them that those who didna accept God must be accepting the devil. So, the people gathered up all those who clung to the old ways and hurled them off Pagan's Point."

"A good plummet to your death making it easier to find God, I suppose." Ailis shook her head. "Well, let us go to this Pagan's Point, then. If 'tis the right place, Sibeal will ken it as we get nearer."

"Ye will ride with me," Alexander said as he grasped Ailis's hand.

They headed toward the stable, and Ailis used the time to calm herself. Sibeal revealing her strange talent so abruptly was unsettling, but Alexander was more so. He held her close all night, made wild sweet love to her, and spoke the prettiest words she had ever heard. Come the dawn and he became the man he was now—cold and distant, with occasional flashes of anger when he deigned to speak to her at all.

She felt the tension in Alexander as, once their horses were ready, he yanked her up to ride behind him. Sibeal rode with her father, the twins shared a pony, and two men-at-arms rode with them. Alexander grunted what few commands he gave out, and Ailis decided he was an extraordinarily ill-tempered man. She barely had time to tell the stableboy to let Jaime know they had gone so that he would not worry before Alexander urged them all on their way. Her only consolation was that he planned to reveal her as a conniving wench who would trick a child into lying for her, but he was about to suffer a shocking dose of cold, hard fact. Ailis just prayed that Sibeal would not suffer.

Ailis's heart ached and she was weary of the pain. She knew she felt far more than passion for the man, but he ground those more tender feelings beneath his bootheel each and every morning. Each night there was beauty, and each morning there was ugliness. She felt used, yet could not resist the heated sweetness of another night in his arms. Even now, with her arms about his trim waist and her cheek against his broad back, she wanted him, yet he was as stiff as an offended spinster. Ailis knew she was going to have to make some decision soon. If she continued to share his bed, she risked being marked a whore and losing all dignity. To ease that shame she needed more from him than hunger in the night and callous indifference all day, and he was not giving it to her. Soon she would have to accept that one did not always get what one hoped for.

When Alexander reined to a halt, Ailis was abruptly yanked from her dark thoughts about leaving Alexander's bed. She saw Barra dismount and help Sibeal down. They had come to a halt not far from the edge of a dangerous precipice. Across a shallow gorge from them was a piece of land that jutted out farther than the rest. That was undoubtedly Pagan's Point, she decided. Without waiting for Alexander's help, she dismounted and hurried over to help Barra with Sibeal. The poor man was beginning to look very unsure of himself. Even the twins' rushing to his side did not make him look any more confident.

"She says this is the place," Barra murmured, then looked straight at Ailis. "I wouldst like it if ye would now tell me that ye play a game with me."

"I canna, Barra. Believe me, I understand how ye feel. I didna want to hear this myself," Ailis said.

"What ye ken is a lot of nonsense," Alexander said, his tone hard and angry as he joined them, his two men-at-arms watching them all warily as they secured the horses. "I think this game has gone on long enough. 'Tis but some trick to try and escape."

"Without bringing Jaime along?" Ailis gave him a disgusted look and turned her attention to Sibeal. "Is this the place where ye saw the puppies?"

"How could she see them here? She has never been to this place." Alexander's eyes widened at the way Ailis whirled and glared at him. "I grow weary of this foolishness."

"Then leave. We can do well enough without ye. I think the most important thing right now is to soothe Sibeal. Doing as she says is the only way. When she is proved right or wrong, 'tis done, and we can all go home." She turned back to Sibeal. "Are they here now, sweet?"

"Aye," Sibeal answered. "Down there." She went to the

edge and pointed at a spot a few yards downriver from Pagan's Point. "There is where the puppies will be. We have to go down there and catch them."

"There is a steep path over here, Aunt," called Manus a moment after he and Rath began a hasty search for a way down.

"Are ye sure we must go down there, child?" Ailis asked Sibeal even as the little girl grabbed her by the hand and tugged her toward the rocky path the twins were already scrambling down.

"Aye. We canna catch them up here. I am sorry I told Papa, Aunt Ailis, but I had to save the puppies."

"Of course ye did." Ailis heard Alexander order his men-at-arms to watch the horses, and she looked back briefly to see the Laird of Rathmor gracefully climb down after them. "I think ye have upset your uncle the most."

Sibeal nodded. "He is a very sad man."

"That he is, loving." And I grow weary of being battered by it, she thought to herself as she paid closer attention to the uneven path.

Alexander muttered a curse as he quickly followed Barra, the children, and Ailis. He could see nothing on the ground on either side of the stream, yet they were all risking their necks to hurry down a treacherous path because a tiny child said puppies were there. It was tempting to order an end to it all, yet Alexander knew Ailis was right. The little girl needed to have her dreams proved or disproved. It was the only way to put an end to the matter.

Ailis brushed off her skirts when they finally reached the beach, which was nearly as rocky as the path. "Where are the puppies, Sibeal?" she asked her niece.

"They will come soon, Aunt." Sibeal stood and stared up at Pagan's Point as Barra brushed off the child's clothes.

It suddenly occurred to Ailis that she had not adequately gotten the time of the incident from Sibeal. The arrival of

the puppies could be now or several months from now.
Poor Sibeal was still new even to speaking of her dreams.
Just as Ailis was about to ask Sibeal, Alexander gave her a
rough nudge from behind. She frowned, saw him pointing
toward Pagan's Point, and looked to see a man ride up.

At first Ailis did not know which to watch—the point
where Sibeal's dream was being acted out, or Alexander's
reaction. After a second hard look at Alexander, she decided he was the one who bore watching. His face had
gone parchment white. She knew he was not going to accept Sibeal's gift very well at all.

"There are the puppies!" Sibeal yelled, and when the
man tossed them into the gorge, she started to cry.

While Alexander and Barra scrambled to get the sack
out of the shallow, swift stream, Ailis struggled to hold
on to her niece and nephews. The moment the MacDubhs
set the sack on shore and Alexander neatly sliced it open,
Ailis released the children. She hurried after them, reluctantly curious.

"Hurry, Aunt," called Sibeal. "They are so afraid and
hurt."

"What does she mean?" Alexander demanded as Ailis
reached his side.

"She feels things," Ailis answered as she saw Barra and
the twins release six shaken, wet, but living puppies.

"Feels things?"

"Aye, m'laird—feels things. Anyone can guess how
those poor pups must have felt to be stuffed into a sack and
tossed off a cliff, but Sibeal can actually feel it."

"And ye expect me to actually believe all of this?"

"Do as ye please, m'laird, but I would advise ye to learn
to pay heed when Sibeal tells ye something about a person.
It could make the difference between life and death." She
sighed when Alexander just cursed, then hurried back up
the path. It did not surprise her when a moment later she

heard a horse ride away, and she turned her attention back to a badly shaken Barra.

"I ask ye again to tell me that this was some game, Ailis," Barra demanded as he sat down on a rock and stared at the children, who were busily examining the puppies.

Ailis sat down next to him and patted his arm. "I truly wish I could. 'Tis a hard thing to accept. I keep hoping it will yet go away." She gave him a weak smile when he briefly laughed. "People dinna like it. It makes them afraid. I find that fear dangerous."

Barra grimaced and nodded. "We shall have to teach her to be secretive."

"Aye, and I think she can learn that. 'Tis that she has only just begun to talk about what she sees and feels. Talk about it in a way that made me truly understand that she has a gift. I have been so busy trying to teach her to speak more clearly about it and accept that she has such a skill that I havena stressed caution as much as I should. I have told her that people might think bad things about her, but that is such a difficult thing for a child to understand." She glanced up at the top of the rise where the horses were and thought on Alexander's abrupt departure. "The sight is something many people dinna like and dinna want."

After one long look up the path, Barra nodded. "Alexander has always hated such things. He willna hate Sibeal for it, though. He may have changed a lot in the past few years, grown harder and more bitter, but he loves the bairns. 'Tis a shame he lost his own bairn, for he would have been a good father. He was for the short time she was alive."

"Alexander had a child?" Ailis was shocked and, she realized, a little hurt.

"Aye. She was a sweet little girl, much like Sibeal. Her name was Elizbet. She was his child by his first wife, whose morals were very weak. That wife died, and it was a while before Alex married again. His first wife may have been a whore but his second wife was evil, vicious, demented. There was a sickness in her mind. When she finally died, she didna go alone. She took poor Elizbet with her. The child is buried in the kirkyard just beyond Rathmor. I dinna believe Alexander has ever recovered."

"Nay. 'Tis not something ye can recover from, not fully," she murmured, suddenly aware of a better understanding of Alexander, even a sympathy. "He holds a lot of anger in his heart."

"He does, but 'tis past time he ceased to spit it out at everyone. Even his friends lose patience."

"Alexander has friends?" She smiled when he laughed, pleased that the shock of discovering the truth about Sibeal had begun to fade. "We had better return. There is the hint of rain in the air."

Barra nodded, stood up, and helped Ailis to her feet. "I have six new pups, dinna I?"

"I fear so," she agreed, smiling at the children, who were gathering up the wriggling puppies. "Sibeal has a big heart for such a little girl. Ye could find yourself knee-deep in abandoned or hurt animals or people."

"Then we shall have to teach her to be selective as well as secretive," he said as he and Ailis moved to shepherd the children back to Rathmor.


Alexander remained sprawled in his chair as Ailis entered his bedchamber. He had managed to avoid her, Barra, and the children since they had returned from Pagan's Point. He had even managed to avoid dining with them in the great hall. Now, however, it was time to go to bed. Alexander had been tempted to stay away longer, to lurk in his small solar and drink until he was certain Ailis was asleep, but the urge to be with her was ever stronger.

A niece with the sight, he thought and almost laughed. If there was one thing he could have considered worse than a niece with MacFarlane blood, a niece with the sight would have been it. One reason he had avoided everyone's company since discovering Sibeal's skill was so that he could better convince himself that it had all been some trick, even just some piece of inexplicable luck. He had almost done so; only a small uneasiness remained. He hoped Ailis would not talk about Sibeal's unusual skills, but the way Ailis was eyeing him as she moved to wash up told him that he would probably not get that wished-for reprieve. In one last attempt to avoid any conversation, he stood up, shed his clothes, and climbed into bed. It was cowardly, he mused, but it just might work.

Ailis gave a start of surprise when Alexander suddenly got undressed and got into bed. She then spared a moment of annoyance over the way he had thrown his clothes all over the floor. The great laird, she grumbled to herself, is having himself a fine sulk. She shook her head and began to wash up. While she still felt a great deal of sympathy for him, she did not intend to pander to this foolishness.

Stripped down to a short, plain chemise, she walked over to his side of the bed. He lay sprawled on his stomach looking almost endearing except that his manly beauty tended to distract her. Ailis knew her position at Rathmor was precarious, but she was also Sibeal's aunt. She had to know how Alexander would treat the child now.

"What will ye do about Sibeal?" she demanded.

"I havena given it much thought." He opened one eye and heartily wished that Ailis did not look so adorable.

"Hay! Ye have done naught *else* but think about it since ye fled Pagan's Point."

He abruptly sat up to glare at her. "I didna *flee* Pagan's Point."

"Oh, aye, ye did. Ye hied away as if all of the hounds of hell bayed at your heels."

"I think ye forget who ye are, what your place is here, and whom ye are speaking to!"

She had not expected him to grow quite so furious, but she held firm for Sibeal's sake. "I havena forgotten any of that. I am a MacFarlane, I am your prisoner, and ye are the constantly irritated Laird of Rathmor. I am also Sibeal's aunt, the woman who has had the raising of her. 'Tis about Sibeal I mean to speak, and I expect to be heeded."

"Ye do, do ye?" He could not fully suppress some admiration for her as she stood there prepared to defend or protect her niece.

"Aye, I do. Did ye think she wouldna see how ye ran away and have stayed away?"

Alexander felt the heat of guilty color sting his cheeks. He had not thought on the child's feelings, but had been completely caught up in his own tangled emotions. There was no doubt in his mind that the child would have seen his retreat for what it was. And it was now too late to make amends, for the children had long been abed. Alexander looked at Ailis and decided he would not admit that to her, however.

"I needed to think about what I had seen," he finally replied.

"And what great decision have ye come to?"

"I believe ye all give too much weight to mere luck and coincidence."

"I was once blind to the truth, too."

"That is the truth." He saw her shiver and held up the covers on her side of the bed. "Get in ere ye catch a chill."

"The truth is that Sibeal has the sight." Ailis scrambled beneath the covers but kept her gaze fixed upon him. "I fear that comes from her mother's kinsmen. Our grandmother, our mother's mother, had the sight. She claimed she had always had it."

"Did ye see any proof?" He turned on his side to face her.

"She was dead ere I was of an age to judge the truth of her claim."

'So, ye have no one—and nothing—to compare Sibeal to. Ye can only work on superstitions and myths."

Ailis laughed and shook her head, amazed at his stubbornness. "Do ye call what happened today naught but superstition and myth? How can ye deny what ye saw and what ye heard?"

"What I saw was us drag some stray dog's whelps out of the water. The lass could have heard someone talk of drowning the pups. All the rest was just the upset of a tenderhearted child."

It was difficult to resist the urge to pound her heels against the bed in frustration. "Fine, we willna argue the truth of her sight. 'Tis up to ye to believe it or not. However, how do you mean to treat poor Sibeal as ye debate this matter?" When he just stared at her, she pressed, "Well, I want an answer."

"Ye act very arrogant for a wench who is naught but a tool of revenge," he drawled.

That was cruel. Ailis fought desperately to hide the truth of that from Alexander. As she learned more about him, she was beginning to understand him, even to recognize the occasional hints of meanness as his hurt and bitterness lashing out. It was her own fault that she had let her emotions become so entangled that his anger could hurt her. She just had to keep remembering that she was not the cause of that fury, did not deserve to be stung by his bitter words, and therefore would ignore them. She would also not allow herself to be intimidated by this cold, angry Alexander.

"I am as much a blood kin to Sibeal as ye are," she said in a cold voice and noticed a fleeting look of discomfort on Alexander's face. "I willna let ye hurt the child."

Alexander was outraged and cursed. "I would never hurt a child!"

"Not intentionally, but 'tis just what ye did when ye turned from her after she revealed her skills. Ye have to let her see that ye still care for her. Ye are cold, Alexander MacDubh, but—"

"Cold?" He abruptly turned so that he was lightly sprawled on top of her. "I dinna feel very cold now."

Ailis found it impossible to ignore how the feel of him heated her blood, but she refused to let him divert her. "I have asked ye what ye mean to do about Sibeal. I must have an answer." Her last words were muffled as Alexander tugged off her chemise.

"I will speak to Sibeal in the morning." Alexander began to brush soft kisses over her face as he gently stroked her body with his hands and enjoyed the way her desires flared to life with a swiftness to equal his.

"And say what?" She found the speed with which he could make her want to forget everyone but his touch a little frightening.

"That she is my niece even if she grows a beard and a second head, and assure her that she isna what I draw back from. I will make it clear that, although I may dislike or disbelieve her gift, I dinna extend such feelings to her herself. Does that make ye happy?"

"It at least makes me confident that ye will try to spare the child's feelings."

Alexander studied her face, the way her golden-hued skin was blushed by desire's heat and her eyes had darkened almost to black. In the depths of her alluring eyes he saw a sadness and realized that he wanted to banish that sorrow, yet doubted he would be able to do so.

"Ye have never really been happy, have ye?" he asked softly.

"Happy enough. As happy as most people." Ailis did not appreciate the man's sudden insight.

He slowly eased their bodies together, enjoying the expression of pleasure she could not hide. "Does this make ye happy?"

"Aye, for a while. For the time it lasts."

"Then we had best try to make it last as long as possible," he murmured and kissed her.

As Ailis let his lovemaking take her into that welcome realm of blind need, she wished she could make him say such things about far more than their passions.

# 8

"It took them six weeks to say 'nay'?" Ailis muttered. "I kenned that they were slow-witted, but this defies understanding."

Ailis reread the wrinkled parchment missive from her uncle, which bore her betrothed's faint signature. She had been called into Alexander's solar, barely been allowed time to appreciate the large windows and abundant light in the room, before she had been read the letter from her kinsmen. Her tart statement that she could read had drawn a mild response of polite surprise from Alexander, and he had given her the note to read for herself. That had not changed anything. It had simply let her see the somewhat painful truth for herself. Even her own blood wished to use her as a pawn. It did not really surprise her, but it still hurt. She sighed as she sat on a padded bench before one of the windows.

"There is little to understand," Alexander said. "They plainly say they have no wish to pay for ye or the bairns."

She ached to slap Alexander's beautiful face, but crumpled up the message she held instead. "Aye, but they took a long time to do it, and they have taken no action against ye in the meanwhile. Oh, they might cast me aside so callously, but not the bairns. The bairns are far too useful. And now they have lost the good weather. Well, nearly. 'Tis late August. Soon the fall rains will come, then the winter snows."

"And then the spring rain, thaw, and mud." Alexander shook his head. "We could be saddled with your keep for a year."

That was one callous remark too many, and Ailis leapt to her feet. "Ye need not be saddled with my keep for another moment. I can be out of your way in no time at all."

Alexander swore. Moving swiftly he was able to stop her from leaving the room. He put himself between her and the door just as she reached for the latch. Simply getting word from the MacFarlanes and the MacCordys had been enough to put him into a bad humor. When he had seen the hurt in her eyes, a pain caused by the cold rejection of her own kinsmen, he had softened. He had wanted to soothe her hurt. That reaction had stirred his fear, the dread he carried constantly that she could and would stir his emotions, and he had responded as he always did—by slapping her away with cruel words. However, he knew he did not want her to leave Rathmor altogether.

"Sit down, Ailis," he ordered.

"Why? What is the use? My kinsmen and betrothed have cast me out, and ye clearly dinna want me."

"Oh, I want ye." He reached for her, but she slapped his hands away.

"Not that way." Ailis was determined not to allow him to kiss her into unthinking acquiescence.

"Just sit down again." He bolted the door and almost smiled at the way she glared at him before she returned to her seat. The bolt was far above her head, and he knew that disadvantage annoyed her. "We shall try to talk this out like adults, without rancor or anger," he said as he returned to the writing table he had been sitting at.

" 'Tisna me who has trouble with that," she muttered, her annoyance growing when Alexander simply ignored her. "What purpose is served by my staying here any longer?"

"If naught else, ye help with the children. It pleases them well enough to have ye around."

And what about ye? she thought and was briefly afraid that she had spoken aloud. As she had learned of Alexander's troubled past, she had tried to be patient with him, to understand how much history stood between them. Nevertheless, she found it painfully difficult at times. One minute he was cold to her, the next he was gentle and passionate. He could whisper sweet words all night, then insult her with the sunrise. The man would drive her mad. She suspected that she loved him, that that was why she cared how he felt and could be so hurt by his words, but she did not want to confront the emotion, for then she would no longer be able to deny it.

"What we need to decide is—what does Colin MacFarlane mean by this?" Alexander mused aloud.

"That he doesna want us back. What else could he mean?"

"A great deal, lass, and I think ye ken it. Ye ken the man your uncle is. What game do ye think he plays?"

"The game of 'toss my burdens into another's lap'?" She sighed and shrugged when he gave her a mildly disgusted look. "He wants ye to think he has done just that so that ye will ease your guard on us, mayhaps even throw me out so the man can snatch me back at no cost to himself."

" 'Tis what I think," he agreed. "I have it on good authority that your uncle petitioned the king to have me proclaimed an outlaw." Alexander found himself divided in how he felt about her horrified reaction to that news. One part of him was pleased, and the other doubtful of the honesty of her reaction.

"Outlawed?" she whispered and shuddered. "That would have allowed anyone to kill ye."

"Exactly. The king refused. After all, the children are of my blood. I had already sent a man there to make that claim, and it was enough to give me the right to do what I did. Also, a few old friends used their influence on my behalf."

"And will they help ye if there is a battle?"

"Nay, I couldna ask them to. This is my battle; 'tis a private battle. I willna have them risk themselves for the sake of my purse and my pride. 'Tis my vengeance, and I must exact it."

"Oh, aye, and get murdered what family ye have left." She knew that beneath the hurt and bitterness Alexander was a good man, and it irritated her to think that even a good man could get blindly caught up in a matter of vengeance.

"Do you believe that your uncle or your betrothed will just step back and ignore the insult I have dealt them? Aye, or the chance to gain more of what is mine?"

"Nay, but I had hoped ye wouldna be so keen to plunge into battle." She stood up and paced the room. "My uncle wants ye to believe that he is defeated. That could mean one of two things—he has a plan to strike, or he hopes to trick ye into some carelessness. Both things require that ye now let down your guard, that ye believe that he has quit the game." She turned to look at Alexander, her hands on her hips, and frowned when she saw how he stared at her skirts. "If ye wouldst pull your lecherous mind out from beneath my petticoats, we may yet come to some decision over my uncle's latest move."

Alexander felt no embarrassment about being caught indulging in a pleasantly salacious thought. He had been nicely aroused by watching Ailis's slim hips move as she had paced. Despite sharing a bed with her for six weeks, he still found her every move interesting, almost her every gesture inviting. He met her disgusted look with a smile.

"Aye, your uncle does mean to try and trick me into letting down my guard. But he will find that I am not so easily fooled."

"It seems odd that he has left it so late to try this ploy. If it fails, then he has no other choice but to wait until spring. 'Tisna often that one can make a successful attack in the winter."

"He will have to act now and be quickly successful if he is to end this by winter."

"And ye dinna think he will act now or quickly."

"Nay. He hopes to make me take the first step—a misstep, of course. By the time he decides I willna do as he wants, then 'twill be too late to do anything until the late spring, early summer. Soon we will reach the time of the year when, if ye arena hindered by the snow and the cold, ye are caught in the rain and the mud."

"Then I had best be on my way, or I shall soon be trapped here." She saw by the quick, sharp way he looked at her that he would fight her leaving Rathmor, and that both relieved and irritated her.

"And just where do ye think ye would go?" Alexander knew it would be wise to just let her go, but he also knew he would not do it. "Ye are still my prisoner."

"Why? What reason can ye have? My kinsmen willna pay, so ye gain no profit from keeping me. Since there isna a man in all of Scotland who would believe me a maid after I have stayed six weeks with ye, then ye already have your vengeance. There is no more use for me here."

"As I have said—ye care for the children," he said roughly. "They like ye to be near."

"So I shall stay near. I just willna remain in Rathmor."

"Ye will stay here!" he yelled as he stood up and slammed his fist down on the table.

"Why?"

"Because ye can still be useful here. Aye, and ye could prove useful to your kinsmen. There is a lot ye could tell them about Rathmor—about its strengths and weaknesses. Nay, ye will stay here until I give you leave to go."

"So be it, but I willna stay in your bed."

"I hadna noticed that ye found it such a distasteful place to be."

"Ye have some skill, and we both have a passionate nature." She shrugged. "I grow weary of being the pawn in this game between ye and my uncle. Ye took my maidenhead, let that be enough. If I must stay here, then 'twill not be to continue as your whore. Ye shame me before the children, and I willna abide it any longer."

"Fine, have it your way." He strode to the door, unbolted it, and yanked it open. "Get out." As she started by him, he grabbed her by the arm and forced her to look at him. "Ye will soon change your mind."

"I dinna think so."

"Nay? Ye hunger for what we share as much as I do."

"Aye, but 'tis a greed for something offered only at night. Ye slip into the bed, and we grab at the heat we share like bairns after a sweet. Then comes the dawn and ye turn cold, pushing me aside. I dinna think even using me to strike at Donald made me feel quite so much the whore as that does. I have had enough of it. Since ye only spare me such warmth at night, in that bed, then I shall take myself away from ye at that time and in that place."

"Ye willna be able to hold to this plan."

"I will, for ye are a cold, even cruel, man during the day. Ye offer a lass nothing. Ye blame me for things I had naught to do with. I grow weary of being the brunt of your troubles and angers. Keep them. I shall miss your skill and the hint of feeling ye gave me in the night, but it no longer outweighs the shame of how ye treat me all day." She yanked free of his hold and marched away.

Alexander watched her until she was out of sight, then slammed the heavy door after her. He knew what game she played. She wanted him to offer her more than his passion. He would not. Never again would he open himself to some woman, trust her, and make himself vulnerable. He had already given Ailis far more than he had given any other woman in several years. If Ailis was too blind to see that, then it was simply too bad. He would not invite her back into his bed.

A chill wind slipped through the torch- and moonlit bailey, and Ailis held her cloak more securely around her. It was only mid-September, but it was already colder than she liked. She feared it would prove to be a very long, hard winter. That was the last thing she needed, she thought as she glared up at the tall familiar figure on the west wall. He was not looking at her, but instinct told her that he had been. Alexander had become like some persistent shadow, watching her all the time. It was growing almost impossible to ignore.

She released a soft, bitter laugh, then quickly checked to be sure no one had heard her. There were a few people who already questioned her sanity. After all, only a madwoman would leave Alexander MacDubh's bed. At first Ailis had found that attitude faintly amusing. Now she wondered if there might be some truth to it. There were times in the night, when she lay awake twisted with hunger for Alexander, that she questioned her own sanity. All she seemed to get in return for her attempt to regain some dignity was sharing a bed with Sibeal and dreaming about sharing one with Alexander. She also spent a lot of time in the evening walking around the inner bailey, trying desperately to soothe some of the growing emptiness, the tense restlessness, that was stealing so much of her sleep. Ailis hoped people would think her walking was due to her growing tired of captivity, but she feared they all knew exactly why she walked almost every night.

As she started a third circumvention of the keep, she finally caught Alexander looking at her. He stood up on his wall flanked by three men-at-arms and stared down at her. She stuck her tongue out at him. It was childish and she knew it, but there was a mild sense of pleasure in it.

Alexander heard the snickers of the men near him but decided to ignore it. He started to walk along the wall, following Ailis. It had been nearly a month since she had left his bed. Once or twice he had contemplated using one of the other willing wenches at Rathmor to ease the hunger that gnawed at him, but he knew they would be no help. Once or twice he had even contemplated going and getting Ailis and dragging her back to his bed. What could she do to stop him? Each time he had asked himself that question, Alexander had decided that he did not really want an answer. So he slept alone. Or, at least, he tried to sleep. More times than not he lay awake wanting Ailis. He had begun to avoid her as much as possible, afraid that his need would overwhelm his sense of right and wrong, and that he might actually try to forcefully take what she refused him. The thought of that appalled him.

"So why do ye stalk her now?" he muttered to himself as he reached a narrow flight of steps that led to the bailey and started down them. "Ye would be wise to stay away. Ye are in a condition where begging wouldna be beyond all possibility, and she would sore love to hear that from ye."

"Sir?" asked a man-at-arms who waited patiently at the foot of the steps.

"Where did that lass go?" Alexander demanded.

"Around the corner, sir. 'Ware, 'tis dark in that part of the bailey," the soldier called after Alexander before starting up the stairs to take his turn upon the walls.

"Perfect," Alexander mumbled as he caught sight of Ailis and hurried after her.

Ailis heard someone following her and started to turn around only to be grabbed by the arms and tugged over to a sheltered niche in the keep's high walls. "Alexander, leave me be," she demanded as he gently but firmly pinned her against the walls.

" 'Tis very dark here." He grasped her hands when she put them against his chest and tried to push him away. " 'Tis dangerous. Ye can never say what might happen." He threaded his fingers through hers, then held her hands out to the side and against the wall.

"Aye. I could be accosted by some randy fool." She tried to keep her tone of voice cool and steady, but it quickly wavered and grew husky when he rubbed his body against hers. She could feel his arousal, and that fed her own. "What game is this? Do ye mean to take by force what I have refused to give ye?" He kissed her throat, and Ailis knew that if he released her hands, her only hesitation would come as she tried to decide whose clothes to rip off first.

"Nay, but I could make ye want it—at least once."

"That ye could and that could also make me angry with ye."

"I will take my chances."

She gasped with a pleasure she could not hide when he nipped at her breasts through her bodice. He kissed her with a hunger she quickly matched. When he released her hands, she wrapped her arms around him to hold him closer. He slipped his hands down her back, cupped her backside, and pressed her more tightly against him.

They were both panting for breath when Alexander finally ended the kiss. Ailis kept her fingers entwined in his thick hair as he slowly knelt before her. He slid his hands beneath her skirts. She gasped when his lightly callused fingers touched the bare skin at the top of her stockings.

"No braies," Alexander said, his voice soft and thick as he gently stroked her with his fingers. "What have ye done with the braies Jaime convinced ye to wear?"

"I was abed when I thought to take a stroll. I didna bother to put them on." She wondered where she found the wit and strength to talk with her body trembling so from his slow, intimate caress.

"Have I made ye want it at least once more?"

"Mayhaps," she whispered, knowing that she would probably run him through with his own sword if he walked away from her now.

"Ah, but we must be sure about such matters. Lift your skirts, Ailis," he asked in a soft, demanding voice.

The shadows and her own hunger made her bold. Slowly she lifted her skirts until all he had so gently caressed was revealed to him. She gasped with a mixture of shock and rich pleasure when he touched a kiss to the raven curls there. Then he stroked her with his tongue. Ailis started to cry out but quickly stuffed her skirts into her mouth. What protest she had planned to make had already faded. She clutched her skirts tightly, using them to muffle her exclamations of pleasure, even her demand for him to stop as her release drew near. He continued to love her with his mouth, bringing her to her crest and beyond. Weak-kneed and heavy with satisfaction she began to sink toward the ground, but he kept a firm grip on her hips. He continued to kiss and stroke her with an intimacy that swiftly restored her need.

Alexander felt her tense, and he stood up. He released himself from his hose even as he kissed Ailis. She was blind with need for him, and he savored it. He also shared it, stirred beyond bearing by her passion.

"Wrap your legs around my waist, dearling," he ordered, his voice echoing the trembling in his body.

Ailis did as he told her to and groaned her delight as he joined their bodies. She clung to him, savoring the intense pleasure his every thrust sent through her. Even as he tensed and shuddered, holding her tightly as he spilled his seed inside of her, Ailis lost herself in the blind fulfillment of her own passion. She was only vaguely aware of her cloak being removed and of Alexander drawing them down onto the ground.

As Ailis came slowly out of her daze of repletion, she realized she was curled up in Alexander's arms on top of her cloak. She shyly and nervously looked around to make sure that no one could see them, relaxing when she saw that it would at least be very difficult. Then she came to a full realization of what had just occurred, and she cursed.

"Ah, are ye preparing to deny the 'aye' ye just gave me?" Alexander asked, watching her closely and wishing he could see her shaded features better. Her face was always a clear window to her emotions, and he felt better when he could see her expressions as they talked. It eased some of his doubts.

"I never said aye." She wondered if that was the full truth, for, after she had said mayhaps, her memory of what she had and had not said was not particularly clear.

"Not with words but with every sweet inch of your wee body ye said it loud and clear."

" 'Twas but a moment's weakness." She tried to sit up, but he easily pinned her beneath him, and she did not fight it.

"A moment's weakness? 'Twas quick blind hunger. Admit it. Ye miss being in my bed."

There was an arrogance to his tone that made her ache to strike him. Unfortunately, he spoke only the truth. It was also true that he had sorely missed her being there, but she knew he would never admit it. The frenzied lovemaking he had just indulged in was the only admission he would make. She would have to accept that.

Ailis inwardly sighed. Abstinence would pull no words from him. She had been foolish to believe that it would. It had been her pride that she had soothed by leaving his bed—no more. If Alexander ever wanted to speak of his deepest feelings to her, it would not be because she told him no, and it would not be because she had made him so hungry for her that he lurked around Rathmor and seduced her in the shadowed niches of its high walls.

It had also occurred to her not long after she had left his bed that it might not have been the wisest of moves. She had placed herself at a distance, and that was not the way to win a man's affections. That was especially true of a man like Alexander, who carried a lot of hurt and bitterness. What she had to ask herself was—was a man like Alexander worth a few lacerations to her heart and pride? The answer was an unequivocal "aye."

"Did ye miss me in your bed?" she asked him and was not surprised to feel him tense ever so slightly.

"Ye are an exciting lover."

"Such sweet words," she muttered. It was not going to be easy to stay with a man who had locked himself away.

"I am not a man for sweet words. If 'tis a swain of flatteries and constant declarations that ye seek, then ye are looking in the wrong direction."

"Nay, I expect nothing. I begin to fear that ye have no more to give save for your lusts. I have already asked ye for words, spoke my thoughts clearly, and got only a cold stare as I left. Well, ye have shown me that I still crave the one thing ye do offer freely. So I shall take it."

Alexander wondered briefly why he did not feel far more victorious. "Then ye shall return to my bed."

"Aye, but I will make one demand."

"But I have just told ye—"

"No need to run, my timid lover. I dinna ask for any more than common courtesy. Ye will cease to spit your anger at me. I have done ye no wrong, and I deeply resent being punished for sins I havena committed."

He grimaced and dragged his fingers through his hair. "I ken it. 'Tis just that I find it hard to forget that ye are a MacFarlane." He eased himself off her and sat at her side.

"I dinna ask ye to forget that. 'Tis what I am." She sat up and tried to put some order back into her tangled clothing. "However, I dinna have to account for the sins of my kinsmen at every turn. That cold disdain causes me shame. The sneer and the insult ye would heap upon me that made me feel like a whore. 'Tis the cold disrespect ye showed me whenever we were out of bed that made me leave what we could share in bed. I willna be treated that way. I dinna deserve to be treated that way."

"Nay, ye dinna."

"So, 'tis agreed? I will return to your bed, but only for as long as ye treat me with courtesy in and out of the bedchamber?"

When she held out her hand, he shook it. "Agreed. Ye will have that courtesy for as long as ye remain at Rathmor."

"Ye couldna resist adding that, could ye?" she mumbled as she stood up and brushed off her clothes.

"'Tis but the truth." Alexander stood up, picked up her cloak, and draped it around her shoulders.

"Aye, and one should never shirk from the truth."

As she started toward the path that would lead her back into the keep itself, Ailis nearly laughed. There was a strange twisted humor in the way Alexander acted. He could not seem to pull her back to his bed fast enough, but that was enough to scare him, so he reminded her that she would have to be leaving some day. She could not help but wonder if the man needed to remind himself.

He quickly fell into step at her side, and she covertly watched him. His every movement was graceful. The man could set a thousand lasses' hearts aflutter with just a smile. He could seduce any woman with just a few soft words spoken in his deep, sensuous voice or a warm glance from his beautiful eyes. Ailis was certain that even the most saintly of women would have at least a passing thought about how it would be to share his bed. And yet, he guarded himself. The man feared his own emotions, feared more hurt and grief. It was endearing, even hopeful, for such fears proved he had a heart, but it was also frustrating. Yet again she could be paying dearly for something that was not her fault.

"Are ye already changing your mind?" Alexander asked as they entered the keep.

Ailis suddenly realized that her steps had slowed as she had sunk into her thoughts. She could sense a tension in Alexander, could see a look of stubbornness upon his face. He thought she was about to refuse to go back to his bed, and he was trying to think of a way to get her there without making any demands or promises. She was almost tempted to let him try.

"Nay. I am not changing my mind." She was stopped from saying any more when Jaime and Kate stepped out of the great hall. "Ah, Jaime, how do ye fare? I havena seen much of ye lately."

"I have been helping Mistress Kate prepare for the winter. Ye seem well, Mistress Ailis," Jaime murmured.

"Aye, well enough, considering that I must endure Mac-Dubhs day in and day out." She ignored Alexander's frown, and it was as she did so that she realized Jaime and Kate were holding hands and blushing faintly. "Off ye go, then. Dinna become a stranger," she added, then immediately felt ashamed of her twinge of jealousy.

"Nay, I never could."

After Jaime and Kate murmured good sleep and disappeared toward the kitchen, Ailis sighed and started up the stairs toward the upper chambers. Jaime was in love with Kate. The man could not hide it even if he knew how to be discreet. Ailis tried not to worry about him, to discard the matter as being Jaime's business and none of hers, but she found that impossible. Jaime was, in many ways, like a child. She could no more stop worrying about him than she could about the twins or Sibeal. Even knowing in her heart that Kate was a decent, kind woman did not help. She needed some reassurance, and as they reached the door to Alexander's bedchamber, she turned to him.

Alexander saw the frown on her face and reacted immediately. He picked her up in his arms, carried her into his chamber, and bolted the door behind him. In a few quick strides he reached his bed, gently dropping her down onto it, and then pinned her there with his body.

"I suppose ye think this is romantic," Ailis said, her voice muffled by her cloak as Alexander struggled to take it off without completely releasing her. When he reached for the lacing on her bodice, she caught hold of his hands. "I should like to ask ye a question before ye continue to try and smother me with my own clothes."

He easily extracted his hands from hers and began to unlace her bodice again, but slowly. "What is the question?"

"Let me say this first—I believe that Kate is a fine lass, but ye have kenned her for far longer than I, so ye would be a better judge than I. Also 'tisna as simple a matter as it ought to be. What I need to ken is—is Kate quite serious in how she acts toward Jaime? I mean, is she the sort to be intrigued because he is different, then discard him when that becomes a burden?" She grimaced. "No matter how I ask this, it isna kind to her, is it?"

"Nay, it isna."

"Well, I canna help it. Jaime is like a wounded child. He was cruelly treated by the closest of his kinsmen—his own father and brothers. I dinna think anything can cut a person deeper than that. He is such a big, strong man, yet inside he is soft and so easily hurt. He has never been any woman's choice of courtier, although a few have tugged him into bed or the nearest hayloft to see if he is big all over. He would be so badly hurt—"

Alexander lightly kissed her, relieved that she was not about to change her mind and want to leave. "Jaime is the first man our Kate has ever shown an interest in. I shouldna worry about him." He shook his head. "I should have guessed that ye were frowning over your mighty protector."

"What did ye think I was frowning about?" Ailis then recalled their unusual entrance into the room and especially the bolting of the door. "Ye thought I was about to say nay again." When he looked fleetingly guilty, she cursed and shook her head. "If I do naught else whilst I am here, I would much like to prove to ye that not every woman is so fickle of mind—or heart."

He stared at her for a long moment before replying, "I think I would like that," and he kissed her before she could say any more.

# 9

Ailis cursed viciously as Kate wiped her face with a cool, damp cloth. It had only been ten weeks since she had been back sharing Alexander's bed. She did not think it fair at all that she should be paying for that weakness so soon or so heavily. Nevertheless, Ailis knew what was wrong with her, and the look on Kate's face told her that that woman knew, too. Ailis was with child, and, even worse in her mind, she was pretty sure the child had been conceived up against the walls of Rathmor. It was embarrassing.

"Here, m'lady." Kate sat on the edge of the bed and offered Ailis a chunk of bread spread with only a touch of sweet butter. "Eat this slowly, a wee bit at a time. Some women claim it eases the turmoil in the belly."

Ailis did as she was told and did feel a little better when she was done. A slow, sip by sip drinking of some cider further cheered her. Then again, she mused with a wry smile, if I remain ill I need not face all the trouble ahead. She sighed and flopped back down on the bed after handing the empty goblet back to Kate. There was no way to avoid the trouble or confrontation, for there was no place for her to run to. Since it was the fifth morning in a row in which she had been ill, she was little surprised that she had eluded it thus far.

"I begin to think I am cursed," she muttered.

"Nay, m'lady, ye shouldna say such things." Kate quickly crossed herself.

"Oh? And what do ye call it when I have to live with Colin MacFarlane—aye, and call him kinsman—and am betrothed to Donald MacCordy? 'Tis certainly a curse to have to call such a man husband. Aye, and then to be snatched away by a man who hates all things named Mac-Farlane and who isna too fond of females, either. And now this—now another MacFarlane lass carries another Mac-Dubh bastard. It all sounds much akin to a curse to me."

"'Tis difficult, but 'tisna quite as bleak as ye believe."

"Ye havena met my uncle or my betrothed." She smiled faintly when Kate giggled. "They will kill me for this," she added in a far more serious tone. "'Tisna an insult they will be able to abide."

"The laird willna send ye back to them now."

"Well, we shall soon find out what the great Alexander MacDubh will do. I shall go and tell him of his impending fatherhood."

With a hint of caution, still uncertain about the steadiness of her stomach, Ailis got out of bed. She felt a little faint, but that began to fade as she dressed. Her courage, however, consistently faltered. She did not want to face Alexander with the news that she carried his child. There was no way for her to know how he would react. He had never even told her of his first child. Would he think she was attempting to cling to him by trying to replace that lost child? She shuddered at the thought. He would hate her, and she would find such a thing nearly impossible to endure. She would also find such a suspicion nearly impossible to disprove.

"Ye look so afeart," murmured Kate as she finished lacing the back of Ailis's plain brown overtunic.

"Wouldna ye be?"

"I canna say. I have spent my entire life here. 'Tis difficult for me to understand why any lass would fear Laird MacDubh."

"Aye, but a MacFarlane has many a reason to fear a MacDubh."

Kate grimaced and nodded. "A MacFarlane man—aye. A lass—nay, not much. Ye have been with the laird for months. Ye must ken the man he is."

"I have spent many a night with him, but he isna easy to learn about. He keeps his distance now, and he is very good at it. However, I gain naught by sitting in these chambers fretting over what he may or may not do. I shall go and find out. Is he still in the great hall?"

"Aye, he will be there for most of the morning as he hears the complaints of people in our clan and makes judgments."

Ailis paused as she opened the door. "Oh, so he willna be alone. That could greatly complicate matters."

"Sometimes he isna busy every hour. Mayhaps there arena many complaints. Or ye could just wait and be there the moment he puts an end to the hearings."

"Or I could forget it until we both seek our bed tonight."

"Nay." Kate shook her head. "Everyone is weary at the day's end. 'Tisna a good time to deliver such weighty news."

There was no arguing with that common sense, so Ailis just smiled and headed down to the great hall. She glanced back and saw Kate hurrying off in another direction. Kate was undoubtedly going to find Jaime. That made Ailis feel a little better. Jamie was still bound by his promise not to raise a hand against a MacDubh, but his presence was often protection enough.

She slipped into the great hall just as two squabbling women stood before Alexander. As Alexander tried to quiet them so that he could hear their stories more precisely, Ailis sat in a chair near the wall. She watched

Alexander as he listened closely to each woman lay claim
to a pig. He seemed honestly concerned for the woman
who claimed the pig had been stolen from her and that it
had been her only food for the winter. Here was the emotion Ailis hungered for, the softness and concern he so
consistently denied her. Even the anger, she mused, as she
watched his face while he listened to the other woman
speak of her claim to the pig she had so swiftly slaughtered
and was already feasting on. It was an anger free of the bitterness and hurt brought on by crimes she had had no part
in.

As she listened to Alexander question why the woman had
had to kill the pig so quickly, Ailis placed both hands on her
stomach. She had thought of trying to keep her condition
hidden, but common sense had prevailed. It was not something one could hide for very long. Then she had begun to
worry about how Alexander would react—to her and to the
child. She hated the uncertainty, the inability to be able to
guess his reaction despite weeks of intimacy with the man.
Here was the proof that, at least on his part, the intimacy
they shared did not go to the heart of him. That hurt, and despite her intention to accept him as he was, it was getting
harder to ignore.

Alexander's judgment on the ownership of the pig drew
her attention, and she was pleased that she could agree with
it. The woman who had so hurriedly slaughtered the pig was
clearly guilty of stealing it. Since the woman who owned the
pig had planned on it for her winter's food supply, Ailis did
think the thief's punishment should have been harsher. After
all, the woman had stolen the food from a fatherless family
of six. However, Alexander ordered the thief to replace the
pig with one of an equal size, give back whatever was left of
the slaughtered pig, and contribute one sack of ground oats
to the victim's food supply. By the look upon the thief's face
as the two women left, Ailis suspected there would be many

more squabbles between the two. When no one else stepped forward to speak to Alexander for a good ten minutes, Ailis finally met his steady gaze.

"Do ye have a complaint, Mistress Ailis?" Alexander asked with a faint smile curving his lips.

"More than ye could deal with here, m'laird."

He chuckled and looked at Angus, who stood just to the right of his chair. "I shall pause for a midday meal. If anyone wishes to see me, tell him to return in an hour or wait if he wishes. Have a page bring in some fresh wine, bread, cheese, and a bit of fruit." He looked at Ailis. "Will that be enough for ye? Ye did miss the morning meal again."

Ailis nodded and watched Angus leave before she looked at Alexander again. "I am sorry I overslept again."

"Mayhaps ye are working too much, growing too weary." He waved her to join him at the head table as others drifted into the great hall to have a light noon meal.

"Mayhaps."

She said nothing as she joined him at the table and their meal was set before them. The hall was half full of people. No one was bothering them. No one was even close enough to hear whatever she chose to say to Alexander. Yet Ailis did not feel as if she could be private with him. As she started to eat, she realized that there would be little if any chance of being private with him until they went to bed, and Kate was right when she said that would be a poor time to tell Alexander her news.

"Ye are looking a wee bit peaked." Alexander studied her closely as he poured them each some wine. "Do ye think ye have caught some chill?"

"Nay, not a chill." A chill could be cured, she mused, then hastily and silently apologized to her child for any possible insult.

Alexander lightly felt her face for any sign of fever, and Ailis stared at him in surprise. There in his eyes was some of that softness, that concern, she had so wanted to see. It rankled that she could only pull it out of him by looking sickly. She could not, and would not, play the invalid for the rest of her life.

"Ye dinna feel warm. There is no sign of a fever," he murmured and frowned at her. "And yet ye dinna look well."

"Thank ye. Ye are looking particularly bonny yourself this morning." She realized how sharp she sounded and took a deep breath to calm herself. Now was not the time to quarrel. "I will look better as soon as I have eaten."

"If 'tis a lack of meals that troubles ye, then ye shouldna sleep so late."

Ailis decided she had better broach the subject quickly before he made any more irritating remarks, or there would be a further delay that she could not really afford. She certainly did not want him to guess that she was pregnant before she was able to tell him herself. The only thing that would be worse than that was if someone else guessed her condition and told him. She took a deep breath, leaned very close to him, and idly wondered how he could look so attractive eating a chunk of bread.

"I look peaked and I sleep late because I am with child." She sat back and waited for his reaction.

The first expression she glimpsed upon his face gave her some hope. It was fleeting, but she knew it was elation. Then she began to grow very nervous, for the subsequent expressions rippling over his face held some very dark emotions.

"Whose child is it?" he demanded in a cold, hard voice.

There was nothing he could have said that would have insulted her more, Ailis decided. She wondered if he knew that, if that was why he had said such a cruel thing. Then she stood up and, putting all of her fury and frustration behind her swing, punched Alexander square on the jaw, knocking him sideways in his seat and causing all conversation in the great hall to cease. As he cursed and struggled to right himself, she strode out of the great hall, barely nodding a greeting to Barra and the children as they passed her on their way in. She quickly found her cloak, went outside, and began to walk the inner bailey, hoping the chill bite of the air would cool her temper.

Alexander glared at everyone in the great hall as he pressed a linen napkin to his bleeding lip. They quickly stopped gaping at him, but he knew he had not completely quelled their curiosity. He was still muttering curses against Ailis and had almost stemmed the bleeding when he glanced across the table to find Barra, the twins, and Sibeal all staring at him with a mixture of disgust and amazement.

"And what are ye staring at?" he snapped at them.

"A fool, I think," replied Barra, who then quietly directed the children to go to Jaime and Kate in the far corner of the hall before moving to sit next to his brother. "What have ye done now? These last few weeks have been, if not perfect, at least peaceful. Your hatefulness had eased some."

" 'Twas what she demanded as her price for returning to my bed. No more callous, insulting remarks during the day."

"Ah, and ye just broke that agreement," Barra unsheathed his eating dagger and cut himself a large chunk of bread.

"She told me she was with child." He was somewhat relieved to see Barra tense and pale slightly, for it showed that he was not the only one to be taken completely by surprise.

"She tells ye she is to bear your child, then punches ye. A strange sort of behavior which prompts me to repeat my question—what have ye done now?"

"Mayhaps that was just her way of thanking me," Alexander drawled.

"Very witty. Nay, ye said something, and the only thing I can think of that would prompt such fury is an insult that makes me shudder. I pray it isna what ye said to her."

"I asked her—whose child is it?" He tried not to cringe beneath Barra's look of furious contempt.

"God's long beard, Alex! Ye used to have such a sweet tongue with the lasses. Are there no remnants of that skill left within ye? Are there no remnants of even simple courtesy? What has that lass done to ye that ye feel so pressed to cut her so deeply? She has her pride, and ye have sorely bruised it. Aye, time and time again."

"'Twas a reasonable question."

"Nay, it wasna, and ye ken that."

"She was out of my bed for weeks—free and within the reach of other men."

Barra spat a foul curse. "She was out of your bed, but she was never free, and well ye ken it. There isna a single man within the walls of Rathmor who would touch her. Nay, not since ye first lay with her and held her in your bed until morning. The child she carries is yours, brother, and we both ken it. The question ye must answer now is—what will ye do about this? Will ye tend to your duty, to your responsibility, or will ye continue to play the callous rogue?"

Alexander decided he was growing very weary of his now constantly sober brother's skilled, sharp tongue. "Ye seem to be determined to forget what Ailis is."

"Nay, brother, ye do."

"She is a MacFarlane," Alexander hissed, then pounded his fist on the table. "That is all that matters."

"She is a young lass who, I now ken, has struggled to maturity despite indifference at best and cold cruelty at worst. More the latter than the former. She had naught to do with the crimes of her uncle. Therefore, the only honorable thing for ye to do is to wed the lass." Barra met Alexander's stunned expression with perfect calm.

"Ye may have ceased to drink too much, but I think your brain is still well soaked. Are ye completely mad? Me to wed a MacFarlane? Colin's niece and heir?"

"The innocent lass who now bears the weight of your growing seed."

"Sobriety has made ye irritatingly pious."

Before Barra could make any reply to that, Alexander was out of his chair and striding out of the great hall. He did not need his younger brother telling him where his duty lay and what honor demanded of him. After fetching his cloak, he went in search of Ailis. He had been cruel, and she had not deserved that. Shock had twisted his thoughts. It had roused all his suspicions and anger, and he had blindly lashed out at her. There was only one man who could have set a child growing inside of Ailis MacFarlane's womb, and that was he.

When he saw her striding along at the foot of the western wall, he hurried toward her. The girl had a strong stride, he mused, then came to an abrupt stop when, while he was barely a yard away, she whirled around to glare at him. She grabbed up a handful of gravel and proceeded to pelt him with it. He used his heavy cloak as a shield as he slowly advanced on her.

"Get away from me!" Ailis ordered as she backed up a little, grabbed another handful of gravel, and continued to throw the small rocks at him. "I told ye I would have naught to do with ye if ye couldna even be courteous. Well, ye were just as far from that as ye could be, so now be gone with ye. Away with ye, ye bonny-faced, foul-mouthed, unfeeling, lustful sack of meanness."

"Will ye cease?" He cursed and paused to wipe a smear of blood from his cheek after one of her pebbles scratched his face. "I have come to talk to ye. Ye can at least hear me out."

"Why? So ye can spit more poison at me? I think not."
As she bent to grab some more pebbles, he lunged at her,
easily catching her up in his arms. "Brute!" she cried. "I
grow weary of ye grabbing at me!"

While careful not to do her any harm, Alexander got her
pinned on the ground beneath him. "And I grow weary of
being pelted with rocks. Now ye must heed what I have to
say."

"Nay, I dinna. If I wasna afraid it would fall back on me,
I would spit in your face, ye heartless rutting pig." Even
though she knew it would not get her very far, she tried to
squirm out from beneath him.

"Be still!" he yelled and cursed with exasperation when
she did as he ordered, but glared at him, her lips pressed
tightly together. "I shouldna have said what I did. 'Twas a
baseless accusation."

"If that is meant to be an apology, 'tis a very poor one."

"Ye canna tell a man such news as abruptly as ye did and
expect him to act sanely."

"This apology isna getting any better. Get off me. Ye
grow heavy."

Recalled to her condition, he quickly got off her but sat
right next to her, ready to grab her if she tried to run.
" 'Twas wrong of me to speak so, but ye might have done
better to restrain your own temper."

Ailis almost laughed as she sat up, brushed off the
bodice of her gown, and idly smoothed her hair. The man
clearly found the words *I am sorry* more of a mouthful
than he could tolerate. She doubted that she really wanted
to hear his explanation for why he felt he was wrong to
have so grossly insulted her. It would probably only make
her angrier. What she wanted to do was to tell him to go
away and stay away, but both her heart and her mind gave
her a dozen reasons to strongly resist that urge. He richly
deserved such treatment, but if nothing else, she had to

consider the child she carried. She would have to compromise her own honor—again. It was growing tiresome being the one who always compromised, who always gave and tried to be understanding.

"Ye deserved far more than I gave ye," she snapped. "If I were a man, we would be fighting to the death over such a bitter insult. In truth, sticking ye with a dagger holds a great appeal for me just now."

He grabbed her by the shoulders and gave her a light shaking. "Will ye set aside your anger for a moment so that we might talk? Aye, I misspoke and 'twas an ill thing I said. However, I was set aback by your news. I had thought I had taken care not to seed ye."

"Aye—except for that night against the walls of Rathmor, when lust overtook my good sense and your fine care." When he began to smile, she swatted him on the arm. "Only a man would find such a thing something to take pride in."

Alexander fought his amusement, knowing it was a poor time to reveal it. "Are ye sure that is when it happened?"

"One can never be *sure,* and yet, in my heart I do feel certain that conception took place that night."

"Then we must be wed."

"Wed? But a moment ago ye accused me of lifting my petticoats for all and sundry, thus putting the parentage of my child into serious question. Now ye wish to wed with me? Your wits are sadly addled, my fine laird."

She stood up and began to brush off her clothes. Alexander stood up as well and studied her closely. He had admitted his wrong, and considering she was a prisoner at Rathmor, he felt that was more than enough. In his heart he knew that she deserved so much more, that there was so much more he wished to give her, but he could not. That there was now a child only reminded him of how deeply he could be hurt if he did not hold himself at a distance. He would not allow himself to weaken, to soften, for it could too easily break him.

"My wits are quite fine, Ailis," he said. "We will be wed as soon as I can find a priest. Ye ken better than most what pain can be dealt to a bastard child. The one we have created will be legitimate. My child may have to carry MacFarlane blood, but by all that is holy he willna carry that accursed name."

He turned and walked away, leaving Ailis to gape after him. She threw one last pebble at him but missed. Not only had she not gotten any real apology, but his parting words had been another insult. Ailis closed her eyes and took several deep breaths to calm herself. It was time for some cold, hard truths, and getting angry at a swine of a man would not help. She needed cold, unemotional, common logic.

The first fact she had to face was that she was carrying Alexander MacDubh's child. That made her choices very limited. Alexander was still not softening to her for all his passion remained hot and sweet. There was always the chance that he might never do so, that he was too badly scarred by past hurts to feel again. His pain could be too complete, and no amount of caring, love and sympathy from her would ever heal him. Nevertheless, he had said that he would marry her, and her only real alternatives to that were to run off and be the poor mother of a bastard child—a life she knew could be a hell beyond bearing—or to return to Leargan to marry Donald, which would be no better and quite possibly a great deal worse. That left her with Alexander, a man who could turn her insides hot with a glance, or freeze her heart with one cutting word.

"There is no choice," she muttered as she started back to the keep and her bedchamber. "It must be Alexander. I really dinna want another man despite the sad fact that I dinna have this one anyhow. And he willna beat me or our child. 'Tis very sad when a lass's life holds such choices. Donald would be the worst choice of all, so I shall take Alexander and pray for the best."

It was her plan to formally inform Alexander that she would accept his proposal. She knew it had been a command, but she decided to ignore that if only to recall him to his own arrogance. There was no sign of him, however, either inside of the keep or in the bailey and its clutter of sheds and huts. When she finally espied Angus coming out of the stables, she set her shoulders and hurried over to him, determined not to let him be evasive with her.

"Where is Alexander?" she demanded as she caught hold of the sleeve of Angus's jupon and forced the stocky man to stop and face her.

"Ah, isna he with ye?" Angus grimaced and flushed beneath her look of disgust.

"Do ye see him? Mayhaps I have tucked him into a pocket inside my cloak and I but forgot."

"Enough. He has left Rathmor."

"Left Rathmor?" Suddenly her own anger seemed a small thing as she recalled all the dangers awaiting Alexander outside the walls of his keep. "Is it safe for him to leave Rathmor? What of my kinsmen or even some other enemy?"

Angus rubbed a grubby hand over his stubbled chin, leaving a smear of dirt. "He wasna of a mind to heed any warnings. He has gone to the kirkyard. Ye ken the one. 'Tis just inside the trees to the west of Rathmor."

"Aye, I ken the one. He has gone to visit with Elizbet." She sighed and wondered how she could fight the hold of that tiny ghost.

"So, he told ye about his daughter?"

"Nay, he never has. Barra mentioned her, that she died with his second wife. I have gathered a bit more of the tale, but only a wee bit. Somehow the second lady of Rathmor caused Elizbet's death."

"Oh, aye, that demon's wife did that. She murdered her."

"Murdered the child?" Ailis realized that was what had been constantly hinted at, but she found it hard to believe.

"Mind ye, she didna put her dagger in the child's heart or the like, but what she did do was murder nonetheless. Aye, the second lady MacDubh had Satan's spirit in her, and it broke free that day. There was no stopping the woman. She set that child on the back of a half-wild stallion and herself on a beast that wasna much tamer. Then off she raced, over the fields and moors and along the cliffs where we found those puppies some weeks back."

"Oh, sweet Mary, dinna tell me that they came to harm at Pagan's Point."

"Nay, but 'twas not too far from there. We took chase, but there was no catching her. Whenever poor Elizbet's steed eased its pace, Lady MacDubh whipped it back into a frenzied speed. Ye could hear the poor child weeping with fright whilst Lady MacDubh laughed. Alexander could see how the mad chase could end, but we all tried to cheat fate. 'Twas no use. Even as Alexander drew near, Lady MacDubh laughed and lashed out at the stallion Elizbet clung to, driving the beast over the edge of a gorge, and that devil's woman leapt out after them. She laughed all the way to her death. Even if the fall hadna killed them, the high waters they fell into would have. We never did find that stallion."

" 'Tis almost more than I can believe. Ye wouldna tell me such a tale to win over my sympathy and ease my anger against Alexander, would ye?"

"Nay, m'lady." Angus looked at her with an expression of outrage clear to read upon his plain face. " 'Tis a tale born of madness."

"Aye, of course it is. I meant no insult. I just dinna wish

to believe that Alexander had endured such a tragedy." She felt the weight of hopelessness but struggled to push it aside. "When did this happen?"

"Two years past come today. Aye, 'twas a clear but bitter day, just like this one."

"And I pick this day to tell him my news," she muttered and shook her head.

"The when of such news makes no difference, m'lady," Angus said, revealing that Ailis's pregnancy was no longer a secret. "He wanted no more children, for he fears to lose another. However, 'tis past time the lad learned that he canna keep tussling about without some seed taking root." He smiled faintly when Ailis blushed.

"Quite so. Show me where this kirkyard is."

"'Tis outside the walls of Rathmor, m'lady. Ye arena supposed to leave this bailey. Ye could try to flee."

"Angus, I am a MacFarlane lass seeded with a Mac-Dubh child. Do ye really believe I would wish to go back to my kinsmen?"

After meeting and holding her gaze for a full minute, Angus came to a decision. "Nay, of course ye wouldna. Your fate is locked to ours."

"Irretrievably so."

"Just go out of this gate, lass, and follow the path that leads west into the wood. 'Tis but a wee stone, chapel, and the poor lass's grave is just behind it."

"And ye think it is safe for Alexander to linger there?"

"As I said, there was no stopping the man." Angus shrugged. "We ken that your kinsmen watch us, and there is talk of coin offered for ye—or for the laird. We watch, but there isna much else one can do. I sent a few men out after him and told them to stay out of his sight, yet watch out for him."

"Do ye think that those men will try and turn me back?

They willna ken that ye said I could walk outside of Rathmor."

"As long as ye walk straight to the laird and stay with him, they willna try and stop ye."

With every step she took toward the kirkyard, Ailis debated the wisdom of going after Alexander. He could become furious with her for intruding upon a very private moment. The thought worried her, yet she did not falter. Instinct told her to go to him. She inwardly cursed and wished that her instinct would tell her what to do when she got there.

Her first sight of Alexander tore at her heart, and she knew she would endure more coldness, even more insults, in her attempts to reach him. The man knelt before a tiny grave marker, sprigs of dried lavender sprinkled over the brown grass. His hands were tightly clenched and rested on his knees. His head was bowed, the cold but gentle wind lightly tousling his thick gold hair. As she neared him, he tensed and turned to face her even as he nimbly got to his feet. The first expression she saw was not a welcoming one, but then he smoothed his features.

"Did no one accompany ye? They just let ye walk out of Rathmor?" he demanded.

"Aye. Where would I go? To Donald so that he can take his fury out on me? Or mayhaps to my uncle so that he can tell me how deeply I have shamed him?"

"Are ye saying ye willna try to leave now?"

"There is no gain in it for me." She looked at the stone, which held a simple carving of a few sprigs of lavender and the name Elizbet, under which was written "The beloved daughter of Alexander—a wee angel whose memory will ever linger in her father's heart."

"Your daughter."

"Aye. So ye have learned about her."

"That took no skill or cunning. 'Tis no secret."

"Nay." He idly nudged a sprig of the dried lavender with his feet. "She loved the scent of lavender."

" 'Tis a good one—neither too sweet nor too strong." Ailis paused, trying to form her next words. "I dinna try to replace her," she said in a quiet voice and did not cower beneath Alexander's intent stare.

"Ye never could."

"I ken it."

"Do ye? Can anyone understand how it feels to bury one's own child unless she had buried one of her own?"

"Nay, probably not, and if it pleases God, I hope I never have to learn how it feels." She placed her hands over her stomach.

Alexander's gaze fell to her hands. He placed one of his over hers, and he met her gaze. For one brief, stirring moment Ailis knew they were in complete accord. She felt as if they had touched in a deep, personal way and felt her first honest taste of hope. She prayed it was not a false one.

# 10

"Why canna we go? Jaime's going," Manus grumbled, and Rath nodded.

"We shall be very, very good," Sibeal promised.

"I am sure ye will be, but ye must stay here," Alexander said, his voice firm as he helped Ailis mount.

Ailis looked at her nephews and niece. They ached to get away from the confines of Rathmor, and she dearly wanted to grant them their wish, but she also knew that Alexander was right to make them stay behind. She questioned the sense of their own journey, but Alexander was determined. He said they would be married by a priest, and the day she had told him of her pregnancy, he had sent out riders to find one. After nearly a week of inquiries, they had finally located a priest, but the man had suffered a broken foot in a strange accident, and so they would have to travel to him. Ailis had a bad feeling about their journey, but Alexander was in no mood to heed her.

"I truly, truly, truly want to go, Aunt," Sibeal said.

"Well, I fear I must say nay, loving. Dinna forget that there are people who would like to take ye away from your father." She gave Barra a brief smile as he stepped up behind his children. "When the danger is finally past, I am sure he will let ye run quite wild."

Sibeal took her father's hand in hers and stared at her aunt. " 'Ware the chickens."

"Pardon, dearling?" Ailis was slowly becoming used to the odd things Sibeal often said, but thought that this was particularly strange.

"Just be careful of the chickens."

"Aye, I will." Ailis looked at Alexander. "Shall we be on our way?"

The men gathered around the inner bailey were eyeing little Sibeal warily, and Ailis decided it was best to at least agree to whatever the child said. She did not like the attention brought to bear upon Sibeal's unusual skill. Although she still had no idea what Sibeal had been talking about, Ailis did not want to keep discussing it out in the bailey with so many people listening. It troubled Ailis, however, when she waved farewell to the children as Alexander's small party rode out of Rathmor. Sibeal had that intently solemn look on her sweet face that always made Ailis nervous. The child had been trying to warn her, had clearly had some premonition. Ailis swore to herself that she would be extra vigilant.

In the group that would ride the ten miles to the tiny village where the priest lay recovering from his injury were only six others beside herself. Ailis wondered if Alexander, Jaime, and Angus plus three men-at-arms was really enough protection. Sibeal's warnings could be for simple things, but they could also be warnings of larger events with dire consequences. The group had been kept small to avoid drawing too much attention to themselves and to allow for a great mobility if they had to race back to the safety of Rathmor. It was a lot easier for seven people to flee and hide then for twenty or more to do so. Rathmor and the children also needed to be protected. Ailis understood and agreed with all of that, but she began to wish that she could convince Alexander to wait at Rathmor until the priest was healed and could come to them. The warning of a five-year-old child was not enough to accomplish that.

Alexander rode up beside her and watched her for a moment before saying, "Ye look worried."

"We both have enemies."

"I have enemies. Ye have your kinsmen and your betrothed."

"Who will act very much like my enemies if they catch me. Aye, and especially if they guess that I am with child by ye. I shudder to think of how Donald will take such news, and I would rather not be with the man when he does learn of all this."

"Is that why ye chose to wed me?"

"Oh, aye, and such a fine choice I was given," she muttered, then nodded. "'Twas certainly part of the reason I accepted your proposal." She met his wry glance with a sweet smile, almost daring him to deny her talk of a proposal. "At least ye willna take your fury out on a wee bairn despite how quick ye are to blame the blameless."

"Blameless, are ye?"

"Well? What have I done to ye save to be born a MacFarlane? And I challenge ye to show me how I can be faulted for that." She knew he would ignore the challenge just as he had every time she had made it, but it was interesting to see a glint of humor in his eyes, for that was new. Unfortunately, it was also fleeting.

"What was Sibeal talking about when she said that ye must beware the chickens?" He could tell by the look on Ailis's face that she understood why he had made that abrupt change of subject, but her insight was beginning to irritate him less and less. "Is the child afraid of chickens?"

"Nay, she wasna referring to some fear she has. She was warning me."

"About chickens?"

Ailis heartily wished he had directed their conversation to something other than Sibeal's parting words. She was not comfortable with the child's premonitions. Alexander certainly was not comfortable with them and would question any implication that the child would have such things. It was not a discussion she wanted to get into. Her growing knowledge of Sibeal's abilities would make her defend them, and that was certain to irritate Alexander.

"Aye, about chickens," she grumbled.

"What could she possibly believe chickens could do to ye?"

"Chickens willna do anything to me." She took a deep breath and readied herself to say things she knew would annoy him. "There will be something about chickens to warn me that a threat is at hand, 'tis all. I will see them or hear them or it could be that someone will mention them. Why, it could be that the danger will strike whilst I am dining on chicken."

"So, ye must be alert each time ye hear, see, smell, or even *taste* a chicken? Do I have that right?"

She ignored his sarcasm. "Aye, 'tis something about a chicken I must pay heed to."

"Since nearly every poor crofter betwixt here and London has a chicken or two, that seems a poor warning to me."

"The lass is but five years old. She hasna learned to be exact yet. Also, I didna have time to carefully question her. I certainly didna want to talk about it much within the hearing of so many of your people."

"Such caution is wasted. All of Rathmor is whispering about it." Alexander shook his head, irritated at how quickly the tale had spread and how nothing he had tried to do had stilled it.

That was exactly what Ailis did not want, and she cursed. "Well, if we continue to be careful and to hide her moments of vision, the talk should soon ease. Soon people will, more or less, forget."

"Do ye really believe that?"

"I hope that is what will happen. 'Twould be best, safer, for little Sibeal, and that is what is important."

"Then mayhaps ye should cease feeding the child's fancies, cease treating these things as real."

Ailis sighed and shook her head. She was able to muster some patience for Alexander's attitude, for she understood it. She had also tried to argue away the truth. Her understanding was being stretched to its fullest limits, however. He could just be quiet and watch Sibeal, listen to the child, and then decide without the constant arguing. It was as if Alexander wanted to make her agree that it was all nonsense, too, and he should know that she was not about to do that.

"Ye keep pulling me into this argument," she said. "I have no wish to participate in it. Sibeal is what she is. I canna explain it, and I willna deny it. If ye have trouble with it, then ye must sort that out by yourself."

"Ye canna expect a man to react reasonably or with awe to a warning about chickens."

"Nay, but she will get better. She will learn to explain about what she has seen, to give more precise warnings."

"She will learn, eh? She will get herself killed is what she will do."

There was just enough intensity in his voice to cause her to look at him in some surprise. Ailis could see that look of discomfort and even that hint of fear that had been there from the moment he had been told of Sibeal's gift, but there was more. He was deeply concerned about Sibeal. Alexander might fight the truth for a long time yet, but he understood that many others did and would believe, and he understood what could happen.

"Nay, we must see that she learns what is needed to prevent that," Ailis said. "And I think one shouldna be so quick to discard all that she says. Mayhaps she doesna have the sight; mayhaps she just sees and hears clues that we dinna. Mayhaps she just reads signs, all signs, far bet-

158 *Hannah Howell*

ter than most people. Whatever she has, she hasna been wrong yet—not in sensing danger or in guessing the true nature of people."

Alexander slowly nodded. That the child might have a true gift at reading signs and interpreting the odd over-heard piece of information was something he could believe in. It was far more palatable then his niece having the sight, visions, dreams, or premonitions. It was also far less dangerous for them all. Alexander just wished he could believe it wholeheartedly, but he realized that he had already begun to grant credence to the talk of Sibeal's gift.

"Do ye believe that we should be proceeding with some added caution, then?" he asked.

"We are proceeding with as much caution as we can. The only way we could be more cautious is to return to Rathmor and stay there."

"Nay, we will go on to the priest."

Ailis nodded but inwardly cursed Alexander's stubborn nature. If he was being driven by love, she might have been less condemning, but he was prompted by duty and honor. There were times when she was sorely tempted to suggest that he put his honor and duty in a very dark and uncomfortable place, but she bit back the words. Both were good for a man to possess. She just wished that this time they were not all tangled up with her marriage.

She kept battling the temptation to refuse to marry him. It would be interesting to see what he would do. Her main fear was that she would never reach the man's well-armored heart. She did not demand much, just some softness, some caring, yet there was only the occasional glimpse of such emotion in Alexander. Her own emotions were so tangled that she was not sure she could trust her own judgment about those occasional glimpses. Simple common sense kept her from retreating, though. She needed a husband, and for all his faults, the Laird of Rathmor would not beat her, would be a good father, and would provide well. After having faced the prospect of wedding Donald MacCordy, Ailis could see the worth of such small blessings.

"Alexander?" When he looked at her, Ailis took a deep breath and asked, "Once we have spoken vows before this priest, I shall be a MacDubh. Will that be enough to make ye cease blaming me for being a MacFarlane?"

"Ye will always have MacFarlane blood in your veins."

He rode off to the head of his small band, and Ailis cursed. The man apparently took some perverse pleasure in hurting her, although she prayed that he did realize how successful he had been. She worked very hard at concealing her pain.

Then she frowned at his broad back as she silently repeated his response in her mind. He had not really answered her, she thought with a start. His reply had been a simple recitation of a fact. Alexander had never actually said whether or not he would blame her for crimes committed by people of that blood, just that she had such kinsmen. Ailis thought it over and over, but it still came out the same—he had not answered her. It infuriated her. She had to fight the temptation to ride up to him and keep asking the question until she got a real answer. What she would do, she decided, was to listen far more carefully and be less quick to hear some insult behind his words. Ailis suspected that she might discover yet another ploy to hold her at some distance.

"Well? Where is this priest?" Ailis asked as Alexander and Angus rode up to where she and the others waited on the outskirts of a little village.

"At the inn," Alexander replied as he reined in beside her.

"The inn? 'Tis a strange place for a priest to await a wedding party. Especially when there is a fine wee church close at hand." She pointed to the little stone church on their right.

"The inn is where he hurt his foot. He fell as he left the place late one evening."

"Oh, nay, nay. Are ye about to tell me that the man tipples?"

Alexander grimaced. "Tipples? He fairly bathes in the ale. However, he is sober enough to help us repeat our vows."

Ailis sighed, then frowned as she realized the man-at-arms who had ridden off with Alexander had not returned. "And where is Red Ian? Was there some trouble in the village?"

"Nay. Red Ian stayed at the inn to try and increase Father MacNab's sobriety. Come, dinna be so nervous."

"I just have a bad feeling about all of this, Alexander. A very bad feeling," she murmured as she looked around and fixed her gaze upon a small clutch of hens in the churchyard.

When Alexander saw where she was looking, he muttered a mild curse. "I would have thought ye too clever to be unsettled by a child's warnings and bad dreams. Ye have let them turn ye into a coward," he added, hoping to goad her out of her hesitation. He did not like being outside of Rathmor, either, and he wanted to get their business with the priest done as quickly as possible so that they could return to the safety of his keep.

"Caution is not cowardice," she snapped and nudged her horse toward the village. "I just practice it differently. So, since there was no sign of the enemy, let us go and see this wine-soaked man of God."


Malcolm MacCordy grunted as he dragged the unconscious MacDubh man into a back room of the inn. He dropped the burly redhead down next to the unconscious

priest. It was an insult that he was made to perform such
menial chores, but it had one advantage he could not ignore. There was less killing. Donald or any of the others
would have cut the men's throats. Malcolm was satisfied
just to tie them up and ensure that they would stay quiet.

"Hurry on with it, Malcolm," Donald grumbled as he
strode into the room and scowled at the two men Malcolm
was tying together. "Ye make extra work for yourself with
these acts of mercy."

"I have no wish to get the blood of a priest on my
hands." Malcolm donned the priestly garb he had stripped
from the drunken Father MacNab.

"I hadna realized ye were such a religious man."

"I am not, but I see no wisdom in courting excommuni-
cation or worse. Are the men all placed as we had
planned?"

"Aye. The trap is set. It but awaits ye to take up your
place and for the prey to step inside."

As Malcolm pulled the cowl over his head to conceal his
features, he inwardly sighed. Everything was going as
planned. The spy they had insinuated into Rathmor had
proved well worth the coin paid to him. They had all worked
so hard since the MacDubhs had taken Ailis and the children, and now their hard work was to be rewarded. Malcolm
knew he should be echoing the gloating of his kinsmen. He
suspected that his character was weak enough that he would
be if he was to share in some way in the rewards for this act
of treachery. But there would be no benefit to him, so he
could afford the hint of morality, even a small, silent act or
two of rebellion. Malcolm would do as his kinsmen demanded, but he would pray that the trap they set would fail.
He would pray that their traps failed and that there was very
little blood spilled.

He would also pray for little Ailis, he decided. At best
the day would end with her escape; at worst she would end

up back in Donald MacCordy's hands. If Donald meant even half of the threats he had made, Malcolm would not wish the fate of marriage to the man on any woman. From all he had heard, the Laird of Rathmor had become a cold, cynical man, but Ailis would not be brutalized. Malcolm could not say the same for the lass's treatment at Donald's hands. Donald was furious, and he would undoubtedly take that anger out on his bride—a bride who now carried the taint of an enemy's touch.

Malcolm sat in a shadowy corner and bandaged up his foot to match the priest's. He was just resting his foot on a stool when the arrival of MacDubh and Ailis was announced. The way his kinsmen scurried out of sight reminded Malcolm a little too much of vermin rushing to the shadows after being abruptly exposed to the light. Since he was about to help them gain a victory, it was an uncomfortable insight to have. He tugged the cowl over his face a little more and swore to himself that he would work harder to break free of his kinsmen before his hands became too stained with their crimes. In an attempt to steady his nerves, he took a long drink of ale as he waited for the confrontation with MacDubh and Ailis.


Ailis frowned at the low, thatched-roof inn when they reined in before it. She found the name of the place a matter of concern and almost said something to Alexander as he helped her dismount. One look into Alexander's alluring blue eyes told her that she would be wise not to comment on the inn's being called the Red Hen. Nor the unusual number of chickens clucking about the deeply rutted road, she mused as they walked into the inn and had to shoo away a fat squawking hen right in front of the door. Complete silence on the matter was far more than she could manage, however.

"There are an awful lot of chicken signs," she murmured as he ducked through the low door and tugged her in after him. "Are ye certain this place is safe?"

"Ailis, ye must not allow yourself to be ruled by superstition." Alexander scolded himself as much as he did her, for he was feeling uneasy. "There sits our priest. Angus, ye should watch the door."

"Aye, but ye watch your back. I have an ill feeling about this." Angus scowled toward the priest. "Where is Red Ian?"

"Probably just off relieving himself. We will move quickly, Angus. I dinna mean to linger here."

With Jaime and the second man-at-arms right behind them, Alexander took Ailis over to the priest. She found the way the man was shrouded from view by his cowl and the shadows almost as troubling as the fact that a half-devoured roasted chicken cluttered the table he sat at. One sign she could have talked herself into ignoring, but the signs had accumulated to the point of making her want to turn around and run back to Rathmor. She wondered if Alexander had guessed that, for his grip upon her hand had tightened slightly.

"I hope ye have sobered some, Father MacNab," Alexander said. "We want no delay in the service."

"'Twill soon be done." Malcolm held out his hand toward Ailis. "Come closer, m'child. Let me see you."

"There isna time for all these niceties," Alexander protested, yet released Ailis's hand so that she could step closer to the priest.

"Patience, my son."

Even as Ailis put her hand into the cowled man's, she knew it was a big mistake. She gave a soft cry of alarm and tried to yank her hand back, but it was too late. The man pulled her toward him so abruptly that she fell into his lap. He wrapped his arm around her chest, entrapping her arms at her side. The thought that he was very strong for a drunken priest was just passing through her mind when she felt the touch of cold steel across her throat. As the man urged her to lean against him more firmly, she looked at him out of the corner of her eye, and her heart skipped to a brief stop.

"Malcolm," she whispered. "Nay!"

"Aye, my bonny lassie." He watched MacDubh, Jaime, and the man-at-arms with them. "Dinna move, laddies. She has a very wee neck and soft skin. 'Twill be very easy to cut her throat."

Before any of her companions could move, the room filled up with MacCordy men. Ailis groaned as she saw Donald, Duncan, and William approach. She cried out when the MacDubh man-at-arms tried to prevent his laird from being attacked or taken prisoner, and Donald callously cut him down. Jaime and Alexander were unable to act, for they were quickly surrounded by MacCordy men. Even if Jaime had been armed and could have fought beside Alexander, there were simply too many swords pointed their way. It would be a hopeless fight. Ailis could see Angus's body slumped in the doorway. Along with a touch of grief for the man, she felt the chill of hopelessness. There would be no one to warn Barra, thus there could be little or no chance for rescue, at least not in time to help them before they were trapped at Leargan.

"So, my betrothed, ye are returned to me." Donald stepped forward and, grasping her by the wrist, yanked her out of Malcolm's hold. "'Tis a shame ye havena come back as ye left," he said in an almost friendly tone before he backhanded her across the face.

"Nay!" bellowed Jaime as Ailis nearly fell back into Malcolm's lap again only to have Donald pull her back his way. "Leave her be—ye will hurt the bairn!" A half-dozen men clung to Jaime to hold him in place despite his efforts to reach Ailis.

Ailis stood and rubbed her cheek as she watched Donald's men subdue Jaime and Alexander. Although Alexander said nothing, he had gone a deadly shade of white and his eyes were like blue flames as he stared at Donald with a fury that made Ailis shiver. Only briefly did she wonder if it was her fate or that of his child which stirred such emotion. She then looked at Donald and saw that same expression of anger. Several times she had complained of being used as a pawn. Looking from Donald to Alexander and back again, she truly felt like one, and it frightened her. She cried out in fear when Donald, who still held on to her, stepped up to Jaime and pressed his dagger to her friend's throat.

"What say ye, ye great witless oaf?" Donald demanded.

"That Ailis MacFarlane carries my bairn," Alexander answered before Jaime could.

Donald turned on Alexander with a snarl and would have buried his dagger deep into Alexander's chest if Duncan had not grabbed him by the wrist. Ailis felt weak-kneed with relief. She had really thought that she was about to watch Alexander murdered.

Her concern for Alexander faded quickly when Duncan glared at her, his dagger still clutched tightly in his hand. She tried to step back, but there was no fleeing from his hold. It did not help to tell herself that Donald would not hurt her too badly, that he would gain nothing from her mutilation or her death. The look in Donald's eyes told her that he was not thinking of his gains or his losses at the moment. To her utter astonishment, Malcolm yanked her free of Donald's grasp and put himself between her and her enraged fiancé.

"Dinna touch the lass again," Malcolm said, drawing his own dagger as he prepared to fight his cousin.

"Ye would stand between me and this whore?" Donald was stunned by this unexpected rebellion.

"Aye, I would stand between ye and harming a lass who is with child. There is a crime I will have no part of."

Duncan grabbed his son Donald by the arm and pulled him away from Malcolm. "We only lose if ye hurt the lass. Aye, and if ye hurt the lass while she is in the condition she is now, ye could do her serious harm. Ye canna mean to kill the lass."

"I mean to cut the filthy MacDubh seed from her womb," Donald said in a soft, cold voice.

"Oh, sweet Mary," Ailis whispered as she covered her stomach with her hands and watched Duncan have a hasty and muttered argument with his son. "Alexander," she said, but his attention was on the quarreling MacCordys.

"He has no way to help ye." Malcolm spared her a brief glance while maintaining a close watch upon his kinsmen, including a confused William. "He will soon be dead, lass, and we both ken it. However, as long as I am able, I will stand between ye and them."

"Why?" She tried not to think of Alexander's impending fate, but to put all of her attention upon the fate of her child, whom she had some chance of saving. Malcolm was a strange choice of savior, she mused.

"Lass, I may stoop to many things to serve my kinsmen. Aye, and I have. They are my only means of support. Not even the fear of losing that, however, will make me raise my hand against a lass who is with child. God's teeth, I couldna raise my hand against a lass, bairn in her belly or nay. I have never been forced to this choice before, so I canna promise ye much. I shall try to keep your hulking brute alive so that he can defend ye when I canna."

"Can I trust ye?" Ailis wished she could look the man right in the eye, but he watched his kinsmen as he talked to her.

"What choice do ye have?" He shrugged. "Your acceptance doesna matter. I can do as I must even without your trust."

Ailis nodded and decided that silence was a good idea. She did not want to draw any added attention to herself. That would not help her to protect herself and thus her child, and it could make it impossible to gain any chance of escape. She looked at Alexander and wished she could guess what he was thinking or feeling. He was pale, but his beautiful face held little expression.

Alexander felt as if every muscle in his body was pulled too tightly, so hard and consistently did he pull against the two men holding him. He wanted to get his hands on Donald. The urge to put his hands around the man's thick throat was so strong that it hurt, and for the first time since his feud with the MacCordy clan had begun, it was for reasons other than his father's death or the theft of Leargan. Alexander knew that he wanted to kill Donald because the man had insulted, threatened, and struck Ailis. That he was helpless to defend her gnawed at his soul.

Malcolm MacCordy troubled him as well, but for different reasons. Alexander was grateful that the man would not allow Ailis to be hurt, but he had to wonder why Malcolm suddenly risked the meager benefits his kinsmen doled out to him. All the possible answers to that question did not make Alexander feel any more at ease. Ailis could use all the help she could get, and he was glad that she had the wit to welcome it no matter who offered it. It did, however, trouble him that the help was coming from Malcolm. He knew it was a bad time to suffer the pangs of jealousy, but that was what he felt when he saw the darkly handsome Malcolm standing where he should be—between Ailis and harm.

"So, ye couldna leave my woman be, could ye?" accused Donald as he stood before Alexander. "Just as your rutting swine of a brother did to Mairi, so ye did to Ailis."

"I like to think that I did it a wee bit more skillfully," Alexander drawled, and he grunted as Donald punched him in the side of the head.

A soft gasp of pain escaped Ailis when Donald first struck Alexander. She cried out when he struck Alexander again, then again. Only Malcolm imprisoning her in his arms stopped her from rushing over to try and help Alexander, thus putting herself in easy reach of Donald's fury. She covered her eyes so that she did not have to watch as Donald beat his prisoner into unconsciousness. When she finally did peek it was to see Alexander sprawled on the ground and Donald giving him one last kick before turning his attention on a glaring, but firmly restrained Jaime.

"Dinna touch him," she protested, knowing it was wrong to bring attention back to herself, but unable to bear holding quiet during yet another senseless beating. "He will do naught so long as ye hold me. He will even swear to it."

"Aye," agreed Malcolm. "Make him swear to it. After all, we dinna want to be seen as less brave than the Mac-Dubhs."

"What do ye mean by that, cousin?" Donald demanded.

"Well, 'tis clear that the MacDubhs were willing to let this brute wander about unrestrained, if weaponless. If we canna do as much . . ." He shrugged, leaving the charge of cowardice unspoken, but clearly heard by all.

"I can brave anything some stinking MacDubh can," snarled Donald. "Aye, and more."

When Donald made Jaime swear to be peaceful, Ailis gave a huge sign of relief and slumped a little in Malcolm's hold. She felt guilty over sparing Jaime a beating while Alexander lay bruised and bleeding on the floor, but quickly shook that feeling away. There was nothing she could do to help Alexander. He was an enemy of long standing. Jaime was considered as no more than her bondsman, and she could speak for him.

They made Jaime pick up Alexander, and then they started out of the inn. One of the MacCordy men roughly kicked Angus's body out of the way. As Ailis was pulled through the doorway by Malcolm, she looked back at Angus, who was sprawled on his back beside the threshold. She nearly gasped aloud when he winked at her, and she found it hard to believe that she had actually seen it. But it gave her enough hope to be brave as she was dragged back to Leargan.

# 11

A soft, long groan escaped Ailis as she sat up. Her first concern was for how sore she was and how she had gotten that way. Then her memory flooded in through sleep's lingering haze, and she cursed. She was back at Leargan. Tossed up in the saddle in front of Malcolm, she had been able to do no more than cling to the saddle as they raced to the safety of the MacFarlane keep. Her fear for the condition of her child had increased with every mile, and so she had made little complaint when Malcolm took her to her old bedchamber. A good rest was not only welcome but needed. Ailis refused to let fear, brutality, or intimidation put her child at risk. If she had to harden her heart to everything, she would.

There was a heavy rap at the door, and she was not surprised when Jaime entered with a tray of food and drink. Once Donald had decided that the man was no threat, then Jaime had become a useful servant again. She studied her friend closely as he set the tray on her lap, then carefully sat on the edge of the bed. It was only bread, cheese, and cider, but she welcomed it.

"We are in grave trouble, arena we, Jaime?" she asked as she slowly ate.

"Aye." He sighed and stared at his lightly interwoven fingers. "They mean to kill His Lairdship, MacDubh."

"When?" Her appetite faltered, but she doggedly continued to eat, for her child needed the sustenance.

"Today. I am to bring ye to the hanging tree as soon as ye are done with your meal."

"They intend to hang him—immediately? No bargains? No ransoming?"

"Nay, but they willna let him die so easily."

"Hanging isna an easy way to die."

"True, but 'tis made all the harder if they plan to whip ye near to death first. As Sir Donald says, MacDubh willna be so bonny soon."

That was more than Ailis could bear. She nudged the tray aside and slumped back against her pillows. They were going to make her witness their hate as they inflicted it upon Alexander. They were going to make her see his pain. That was clearly to be a part of her punishment, a punishment she was sure to feel for the rest of her life.

"Jaime, I canna bear that! 'Twill be a torture for me. I will feel every stroke of the lash."

"Aye, because ye love the man."

Ailis shrugged and sighed. "Aye, I suppose I do."

"Suppose?"

"Well, 'tisna something I wished to think about very much. Alexander meant to use me against Donald, and now Donald means to use Alexander against me. I had hoped to avoid the pain such things would, and will, bring me, I have badly failed in that. Now I fear I might fail in protecting the bairn I am carrying."

Jaime shook his head as he took the tray and set it on a small table by the bed. "Ye are a strong lassie. Any bairn ye carry will be a strong one. Aye, and MacDubh is strong. Ye will survive and so will your bairn."

" 'Twould be better if we could all survive this."

"One canna hope for too much. The bairn is the one to pray for."

"Sometimes ye are wise, my friend. I must go now, aye?"

"Aye." He walked to the window and turned his back to her, staring down into the bailey of Leargan. "They will come to get ye if ye take too long."

"I ken it. 'Twould be best if I could go on my own, show a wee bit of dignity."

Ailis got out of bed and found one of her old gowns folded neatly at the end of her bed. She quickly donned the soft brown undertunic over the linen chemise she had donned before going to sleep. A widow's weeds was what she needed, but Donald would never allow that. So she would have to dress in the blue and brown gown and try not to show any emotion. She would not allow Donald to savor her pain. As she finished dressing, she also decided that she must find some way to let Alexander know that she had no willing part in his pain. He might not believe it, but she would feel better if she gave him that message.

"We can go now," she murmured and gave Jaime a sad smile when he turned to look at her. "Let us hurry so that they have no right to drag us where they please."

He linked his arm with hers, and they started on their way out to the bailey. Ailis knew she was clutching Jaime's muscular arm so tightly it probably pinched him, but he made no complaint, and she desperately needed his strength. A great ordeal faced her, and she desperately wished to pass it successfully. If she did, Donald's victory would be dimmed.

A young maid handed her her cloak, and Jaime helped her put it on before they stepped outside of the keep. The cold still hit her squarely as she walked across the bailey. Donald had waited almost too long to spring a trap. Winter would have a firm grip upon the land very soon. She saw the small knot of people on the small hillock beyond the walls of Leargan and could see by the way they stood that they felt the cold, too. She briefly wished that the biting winds would sweep them all away.

The way everyone watched her as she walked toward the hillock made her painfully aware of how she must look, how she walked, and what her expression must be. It was going to be difficult to hide her fear or pain if so many people were going to study her so closely. She needed a little less scrutiny.

When she saw Alexander, she faltered slightly, but Jaime's firm grip on her helped her disguise it. Alexander was spread-eagled between two posts. Despite the cold, he had been stripped down to his braies. It was obvious that Donald wanted Alexander to be humiliated before he was murdered.

Her uncle Colin stood beside the MacCordys as if he were the leader. Ailis suddenly realized that he was not, that he had lost his power the moment he had betrothed her to Donald MacCordy. The MacCordy clan ruled at Leargan. Her uncle was simply too blind to see it. Ailis was sure that the MacCordys would never allow another heir to survive. For a sly, treacherous man, Colin MacFarlane had picked his allies with a fatal blindness.

"I dinna suppose there is much chance of rescue," she said to Jaime.

"Nay, I wouldna think so. 'Tis why they feel so confident about doing this here, outside the walls of Leargan." Jaime shook his head. "Sir Barra wouldna have become worried until we were hours late in returning. Then he would send someone to the village to try and discover what had happened."

"And by then it would be dark, too dark to act. However, someone may have gone to report to Barra soon after we left. Angus was still alive."

"Nay! I saw him cut down. He was on the ground and bleeding."

"He was, but he also winked at me. He was alive and mayhaps could get to Rathmor. Also, Malcolm told me that he left Red Ian alive, only just knocked him down and tied him up."

Jaime frowned and lowered his voice as they neared the MacCordys. "They could get back to Rathmor if Angus survived his wounds and Red Ian wasna killed after Malcolm left. Ah, but then they must try to plan something."

"Still, it *could* be possible."

"It could be, but I wouldna place much of my hopes in it, lass. Look to yourself and to the bairn ye carry."

Ailis nodded even as Donald silently ordered her to stand beside Malcolm glaring at her as he pointed his stubby finger in the direction he wanted her to go. She wondered why she was being shepherded to Malcolm as much as she was. It appeared to be Donald's solution to controlling his own anger—he kept her out of his reach and designated Malcolm as her guard. Malcolm would have the freedom to act against Donald himself, to restrain his cousin. That such a precaution was being taken pleased her, but the fact that it was needed aggravated her fear of Donald.

"Is this necessary?" she muttered as she stood beside Malcolm and stared at Alexander, whose face was no longer so bonny, but bruised and swollen from a heavy beating.

Malcolm looked down at her, studied her pale, taut features, and wondered how much she could endure of what was to come. "It has always been Donald's way to try and make smaller each and every thing he fears. This includes people."

"Ye openly confess that Donald fears Alexander?" She glanced at him, unable to hide her surprise.

"Aye, he always has. And he truly hates MacDubh for the man's fair face and skill with the lasses."

"Jealousy."

"Aye, jealousy. Your pretty lover undoubtedly stirs it in many a man. Donald intends to steal that beauty ere he kills the man."

"And ye can stand here and condone this?" She could not stop her condemnation despite the voice of common sense, which warned her not to insult the man who was protecting her.

"Spoken like one who has land and coin of her own. I have only what my kinsmen choose to give me. And I could stoop to remind ye that I have already even risked that meager income by protecting ye."

"What ye did to aid me is only what anyone would do. However, I thank ye. Surely, though, honor demands that ye put a stop to this. This is a cruelty—naught else. There is no honor or victory in this."

"True, but I willna stop it. I canna. I havena the power. And 'twould be wise if ye kept a stiller tongue in your head. Ye dinna truly want Donald to pay ye more heed than he does, do ye?"

Ailis answered that by becoming very quiet. She wrapped her cloak more tightly around herself. It was late in November, and it was almost a miracle that there had been no seriously bad weather. If she found herself heavily confined to Leargan for too long, then the weight of her pregnancy would begin to hinder her. If spring was too late as a result of a late winter, she could easily be forced to bear her child at Leargan, and she knew that would greatly endanger her child.

She looked at Alexander and caught him staring at her. Even though his eyes were swollen and bruised, she caught the glint of mistrust in them. That stung. No matter which side she chose to stand on, Alexander should know her well enough by now to know that she would never condone such brutality. As she held his look, she made no effort to hide the fear and sorrow she felt, nor the hurt he caused with his misjudgment of her. His battered eyes widened a little, and she knew he had read her expression correctly. She quickly smoothed away that glimpse into her emotional state as Donald walked up to Alexander and gave her one hard look before turning toward his prisoner.

"Yet again you have stained the honor of the MacCordy clan," Donald accused Alexander.

"What honor? A man canna damage what isna there. A MacCordy stains the word *honor* simply by saying it." The pain of the blow to the face Donald gave him was enough to penetrate the numbness inflicted by the cold.

"Such insults dinna change the crime ye will now pay for. Ye stole my bride and ye stole her maidenhead."

"Nay." Alexander turned to look at Ailis and wished he could see her better. "I bedded my wife. Ailis MacFarlane is my wife in the eyes of God."

"Oh, sweet Jesu, that clever devil," muttered Malcolm.

It took only one look for Ailis to understand what Alexander was doing—he was declaring a handfast marriage. Since Donald intended to kill him, it would not protect him or gain her much. It would, however, keep her child from being marked as a bastard. She neatly eluded Malcolm's attempt to grab her and cover her mouth. She used Jaime's bulk to slow down Donald's advance on her.

"And Alexander MacDubh, the Laird of Rathmor, is my husband in the eyes of God."

She did not completely evade Donald's slap, his fingers scraping her cheek as he swung at her, but Jaime and Malcolm silently shielded her from the worst of it. It was probably not a perfect declaration, but it would serve. There were a couple dozen people who had heard it. That would serve as some protection for her child, at least for as long as Donald allowed her child to survive. If nothing else, it was a small strike back at Donald, mayhaps a little petty, but nonetheless enjoyable.

"Well, ye shall soon be a widow!" Donald screamed at her. "Ye have just signed his death warrant."

"Oh, nay, Donald," she replied. "Ye willna try and set that guilt upon my shoulders. Ye have wanted Alexander dead for years. Ye began to plan it as soon as ye netted him in your trap."

"Aye, I did and I planned to enjoy it. Now I shall enjoy it even more, for ye will be helping me."

"Oh, nay. Nay. I willna dirty my hands." She tried to avoid him, but he grabbed her by the wrist. "I said nay!"

Malcolm and Jaime made a cautious attempt to stop Donald, but it was not enough. Ailis could see that they did not dare to do too much. Donald was not going to physically harm her, just ask her to do something that she would find unspeakably hurtful. She wondered how she could resist without tempting a brutal reprimand from Donald.

"Ye will, my wee whore. Ye will wield the lash as I say, or it will be tested upon your skin."

"Do it, Ailis," Alexander ordered.

She stared at Alexander in horror and amazement. "Ye would have me become a part of his disgusting game?"

"Ye have always been a part of the game. Now ye must remember that ye carry my child. 'Tis time to be meek and obedient, to do all ye can *not* to invite retaliation or punishment."

A muffled cry of revulsion escaped her when Donald pressed the whip into her hand. "I canna."

"Ye will, Ailis," Donald said as he stood behind her, forcefully positioning her behind Alexander's broad smooth back. "Think of Jaime."

"What of Jaime?" She stared at the whip in her hand, then at Alexander.

"He lives as a favor to ye. No more. 'Tis a favor that could be easily lost."

"So, if I dinna take a part in your sins, then ye shall

harm an innocent man." She gasped with pain when he grabbed her by the upper arm in a cruelly tight hold.

"Ye always were a clever lass. Now, strike." He stepped back. "Why do ye wait?"

"I dinna ken how to use this," she said.

Donald told one of the burly guards flanking Alexander's bound body to show her what to do. She had to bite back a scream when the man struck Alexander. Twice more he did it until she claimed she knew what to do despite not having seen a thing. Her hands shook as she took the whip.

Her first strike was weak, and the lash barely touched Alexander. Donald cursed her, drew his sword, and walked over to Jaime. He held the sword against Jaime's throat and just stared at her. No words were needed. The threat was wrenchingly easy to read. Her second attempt with the whip was not so weak, and she gagged as a red welt appeared across Alexander's skin.

Five more times she struck. Alexander's body flinched, but he made no sound. She shook until she hurt, and her emotions churned so much that she became nauseated. As she prepared to strike him a sixth time, the whip was yanked from her hand, tossed aside, and she was cradled against a hard, male body. It took her a moment to realize that it was Malcolm. She chanced a quick peek at Alexander and caught him watching her and Malcolm with a cold expression on his face. Then she looked at Donald, whose square face was nearly purple with fury.

"Ye grow too bold, cousin," Donald hissed.

"I but watch over our interests when ye are too twisted with hate and anger to do so," Malcolm replied, his voice soft and calm, and he made no attempt to draw his sword or dagger.

"This was to be part of her punishment. What right do ye have to interfere in my discipline of my woman?"

"Whatever right I can incur in order to keep her alive."

"This willna kill her."

"Nay? This was causing her to shake like a lump of pork jelly. She has also grown quite gray. I feared she could be driven to miscarry the child."

"Good." Donald glared at Ailis's middle with cold-eyed hatred.

"Good, is it? Aye, I hadna realized that ye wished her to be unable to bear ye any children or even to die. 'Tis risky to play that game ere ye actually wed the girl, and ye canna wed her until her husband is dead."

"That girlish-faced cur isna her husband!" Donald screamed.

"As ye wish."

"And what is this nonsense of her becoming barren or dying?"

"Malcolm is right," said Duncan as he stepped forward and put a restraining hand on his son's arm. "A miscarriage can even be more dangerous than a birth. Ye could easily drive her to it if ye continue to torment her so. I am not too sure she should even stay here to watch this. The man has clearly swayed her heart, and she finds his punishment painful to watch."

Donald took several deep breaths in an effort to calm himself. "All right. Get her out of here."

"Nay." Ailis protested. "I mean to stay."

"Ye *will* cease to argue with me!" Donald grabbed her by the chin so tightly that she feared her bones would break. "I can find ways to hurt ye that willna hurt the bairn ye carry whilst ye carry it. I can also make your bairn pay the price for your sins when he is finally spawned. 'Tis your choice."

"Get out of here, Ailis," Alexander ordered her. "I dinna want ye here."

"I should stay here," she murmured as Malcolm led her away and she gave him little resistance.

"Why?" asked Malcolm, his arm about her shoulders as he urged her back toward Leargan. "Do ye want to see his pain and death, simply lack the stomach to do it yourself? I hadna thought ye capable of such things."

Ailis decided she was very weary of cynical men who mistrusted her simply because she was a woman. "Oh, aye, I think ye must have thought of me in such a way, at least once or twice, or such an insulting idea would never occur to ye now."

"My pardons. 'Tis just that I canna see any reason for ye to want to witness his death, especially when we both ken that my cousin shall make it as slow and agonizing as he can."

"I dinna *want* to see it. 'Twill tear my heart out piece by piece. However, Alexander should have at least one friend with him when he meets his fate." She looked at Jaime, who had fallen into step beside her. "Do ye think ye could be there for him?"

"Aye, Mistress Ailis." Jaime turned back to go and stand as near to Alexander as he was allowed, but still some several feet away.

The sound of the whip made her jump, and she fought back her tears. "And so it begins."

Barra cursed and tightly clenched his hands. He crouched in the knotted thickets to the west of Leargan and had a clear view of the place where his brother was meant to die. A quick glance at Angus told him the man was as furious as he, for the mild wound Angus had suffered was not enough to make the man go white.

"There is some good to be found in this," Angus said at last, his voice rough with emotion.

"Aye, and what might that be?"

"They are outside of Leargan. We need not try and storm that formidable keep."

For the first time since Angus and Red Ian had arrived to report Ailis's and Alexander's abductions, Barra felt a stirring of real hope. His only plan had been to get to Leargan as soon as possible, so soon that the MacCordys and MacFarlanes would not be expecting him and the dozen men-at-arms he had with him. After that he had developed some vague idea of surveying Leargan, the MacCordys, and the MacFarlanes and seeing if some opportunity to save Alexander would eventually appear. He was sure it had. The number of people around Alexander was greater than the small force he had, but they were not all fighters or even armed. The only problem he could see was that Ailis was being taken back inside of the keep.

"I willna be able to grab them both," he said and pointed toward Ailis. "Although after what she just did, perhaps that is for the best."

"Come, lad, the lass was forced to do that. Probably threatened into taking part by that filth MacCordy."

"Ye sound sure of that." Barra dearly wanted to believe that, and for that reason alone he was afraid to do so.

"I am. The lass is fair sick of love for the fool. She was given no chance to say nay. Now, we had best get to the business of rescuing our laird ere we lose the chance so sweetly handed us."

As he followed Angus back to the rest of their men, Barra required some assurances. "Do ye really believe we can succeed in freeing Alexander?"

"Aye. If we gallop out of this dark wood, screaming like banshees, we will set most of that lot of carrion racing for the safety of the keep. That will make it hard for the true fighting men of Leargan to do their best. We need but hold them at bay for a wee bit whilst we cut our laird down, and then we hie back to Rathmor."

"Do ye think our mounts are worthy of the challenge?"

"We were but a few hours behind the MacCordys, so they have had as much rest as the mounts they shall need to chase us. Shall I tell the men what to do, or do ye wish that honor?"

"Best if ye do it, Angus," Barra said as he swung up into the saddle. "I understand what we are to do, but I havena much experience in giving orders. Ye do and I want to be very sure that we make no mistakes."

Barra stared in the direction of Leargan as Angus instructed their men. He heartily wished he could rescue Ailis as well, but he knew that would be impossible. That would be hard to explain to the children when he returned without their aunt. He suspected he was going to have a difficult time explaining it to Alexander, too.

Alexander clenched his teeth to halt another scream as the lash seared across his back. He needed something to bite on if he was going to continue to remain silent, but he had no intention of asking MacCordy for anything. Each time he looked up, he met Jaime's steady gaze. He knew exactly why Jaime was there and not with Ailis, and the gesture touched him. Ailis did not want him to be alone amongst his enemies. He knew that with as much certainly as if she had told him herself.

Another sting of the whip and Alexander fought to regain his wits, to prepare for the next. He met and held Jaime's look again. Just as he was about to thank the man for his presence, something Alexander was able to draw strength from, a sound tore through the quiet that left him stunned. The slow grin that spread over Jaime's face told him he *had* heard the MacDubh warcry, but he still found it hard to believe. He was about to be rescued.

"Ailis," he said, finding his thin, hoarse voice difficult to recognize as his own.

"I will watch her," Jaime said as he neatly felled the two MacCordy men guarding Alexander, allowing Barra to get in close enough to cut the bonds around Alexander's wrists.

"Nay, we must get her."

Alexander clung to one post while Jaime undid the bonds at his ankles. All around him was chaos. Donald and his father could be heard bellowing curses and orders, which were going unheard or ignored. Alexander could see people running for the safety of Leargan, and one or two of his men indulged in a short chase now and again to ensure that those people kept right on running. The MacCordy men-at-arms found it nearly impossible to maintain a defense because of the people trying to flee and the need to evade the rearing horses of yelling, sword-swinging MacDubhs.

"She will live. Ye willna." Jaime easily lifted the weak Alexander and set him on the saddle behind Barra. "Go and regain your strength so that ye can rescue your bairn when it comes."

"But that stinking coward Donald will hold her, will wed her, and force her into his bed."

"Nay, he canna wed her." Jaime hastily and lightly secured Alexander to the saddle. "Ye claimed her before witnesses. And methinks he will want none of her until she is rid of your bairn. Now, hie away from here. Donald runs to Leargan to get more men and horses."

Before Alexander could say any more, Jaime sharply slapped the rump of Barra's horse to start it galloping back toward Rathmor. That forced Alexander to concentrate on the simple matter of holding on. An instant later another horse reared to a restless halt before Jaime, and he found himself facing Angus.

"So, ye werena murdered," Jaime said and grinned at the older man.

Angus held out his hand. "Climb up, laddie. There is naught here for ye but cruel words."

"There is Ailis. I must stay with Ailis. She will have need of me."

"Our Kate will wonder why ye have stayed behind."

"Nay, she will ken why." Jaime saw one of MacCordy's men run by, an armed crossbow in his hands. "Nay!"

Jaime tried to chase down the man, but was briefly blocked by Angus's horse. By the time he was able to start after the man, the crossbow was aimed at the backs of the retreating MacDubh brothers. Jaime was just reaching for the archer when the man fired off the crossbow. A bellow of fury escaped Jaime as he watched the bolt bury itself in Alexander's back. Alexander convulsed from the blow and then slumped against Barra's back. Angus shouted a curse on all MacCordys and raced after Barra and Alexander. Jaime looked at the terrified archer he held by the front of his jupon, then tossed him aside. His last sight of Alexander was to see the unconscious and wounded man disappear over the horizon with his men. The MacCordys were racing out of Leargan to follow their enemies even as Jaime started back to Leargan.

Ailis finally kicked Malcolm in the shins. He stopped pushing her toward the keep, but he kept a firm grip on one of her arms. She had heard the MacDubh warcry and tried to run back to Alexander. Malcolm had picked her up in his arms and run for Leargan. He had finally set her down once they were well inside the protective walls enclosing the bailey, but he had tried to drag her inside of the keep itself. What little she could see and hear told her that she had lost her chance to escape with Alexander, and she did not know whether to weep or punch Malcolm until her arms hurt.

"I could kill ye!" she cried, her hands clenched into fists. "I have lost a chance to escape."

"Ye have lost a chance to get yourself killed," Malcolm snapped as he rubbed his shin.

"They have as much chance of getting back to Rathmor as the MacCordys do of stopping them. Now, let me go."

"Aye, I will. Do as ye please. I dinna think ye will get very far. Here comes that brute of yours."

"Jaime?" She felt her heart sink as she turned to see Jaime walking toward her.

"Are ye hurt, Mistress Ailis?" Jaime asked as he stepped up to her and spared a brief, curious look at Malcolm.

"Nay, I am fine. Did they escape, Jaime? Was it really the MacDubhs—and did they free Alexander?" She grasped him by both arms and tried to read the expression on his face.

"Aye, Barra and Angus sent the MacCordys scurrying just long enough. They cut Alexander free, I put him up behind his brother, and they were away toward Rathmor. Alexander wanted to come after ye."

"He did?" Ailis almost felt better knowing that Alexander had wanted to take her back with him.

Jaime nodded, then gently tried to free himself of her grip. "He did, but me and Angus convinced him it couldna be done, that he must save himself now. We all ken that Sir Donald willna kill ye, so that gives Alexander time to save ye."

"And Alexander had no time left." Ailis frowned when Jaime would not meet her eyes and tried to get away from her. "Jaime, what are ye not telling me? What happened?"

She placed herself squarely in front of him and put both hands on his chest. "What are ye trying to hide?"

"I d-dinna want to tell ye."

The slight stutter in Jaime's voice alarmed Ailis. "Ye have to. I will command ye if I must."

"Alexander was alive when he r-rode away," Jaime muttered.

"But? Come, there is a *but* in your tone of voice. Was Alexander hurt?"

"Aye." Jaime sighed, his posture slumping slightly. "One of MacCordy's men fired an arrow ere I could stop him. It hit Sir Alexander high up on his back, near his right shoulder. He wasna dead, though. He wasna."

She clutched his arm and took a few deep breaths to calm herself. "So, he could heal."

"Oh, aye," Jaime hurried to assure her. "He could heal."

"So I must believe. My strength for what lies ahead depends upon it."

# 12

"How long?"

Barra grimaced as he helped Alexander sit up and sip at some honey-sweetened gruel. He did not want to answer that question, for once he did there would be others that would be harder to answer. Unfortunately, Alexander had done nothing else but ask it since he had woken up. Barra sighed as he realized he could no longer evade the confrontation that was so long overdue.

"A month—give or take a few days." He shrugged when Alexander stared at him, in openmouthed surprise.

"A month? Nay, ye jest. 'Tis not the sort of wit I wish to hear just now." Alexander sagged against his pillows after Barra took away his light support and wondered why he felt so weak and light-headed. "Now—how long have I been ill?" He lifted his hand to wipe the light sheen of sweat from his face only to hold his hand before his eyes in horrified surprise. It was bone thin and shook like some old man's. "A month?"

After gently pressing Alexander's hand back down, Barra wiped his brother's face. "Aye—a month. Ye were ill by the time we returned from Leargan. The cold, the beating, and the loss of blood from your wound nearly killed ye."

" 'Tis why I look so emaciated and feel nearly too weak to keep my eyes open."

"Aye. There may even be a chance that the arrow was poisoned. Or carried some filth to sicken ye. There was little we could do but to try to keep ye alive. It wasna easy."

"I remember nothing. Was I out of my head?"

"Nay." Barra tugged a stool over to the edge of the bed and sat down facing Alexander. "There is no way to soften such news. Sometimes ye were out of your wits. We even had to tie ye down a time or two. Other times ye were so deep asleep we feared ye would slip that last step unto death."

"And Ailis?" Alexander found no cause to hope in the expression of Barra's face. "Still trapped at Leargan?"

"Aye. I fear so. Jaime stayed with her. Angus offered to share his horse with the brute, but Jaime wouldna leave his mistress. He said he would protect her."

"Oh, aye, him and that cursed Malcolm," Alexander muttered, an image of Malcolm holding Ailis distinct in his mind.

Barra shook his head. "There are a few things ye clearly remember all too well."

"I also remember that we had to leave her with Mac-Cordy. So, a month. Then winter has truly arrived."

"With a vengeance. Even if we dinna get any more snow, 'twill take till spring for what is already on the ground to melt away." Barra gave his brother a faint smile. "I think it might take ye that long to regain your strength."

Alexander struggled to sit up, dismayed when it proved to be too difficult. "Donald MacCordy willna let my child live for very long after he is born. I must rescue Ailis and our child as soon as I can."

"We are all ready to save Ailis and your child." Barra clasped his brother's hand in his. "Ye ken how impossible it is to launch a successful attack—small or large—in the heart of the winter. And, as I keep saying, ye need to get strong again. This is the first time we have talked since ye left to see the priest. Aye, and 'tis evident to the greatest of fools that this is tiring ye."

"The priest! Did he betray us?"

"Nay, 'twas a man who worked at such chores as mucking out the cowshed. 'Tis strange, but that man was the only one who died. Angus found the man in the inn's kitchen stuffed into an empty wine cask. His throat had been cut."

"The poor misguided fool probably thought that MacCordy would act with honor." He looked toward the narrow window, and although he could not see outside, he could easily imagine what it looked like. "I must wait until spring to retake what is mine—whether I heal quickly or nay."

"I fear so. It willna be easy to retrieve her. We dinna want to fight mud and weather as well as the MacCordys and the MacFarlanes. Ailis is only good to them if she is alive, and the child isna due until May, mayhaps even early June. There is time. Dinna waste your strength in worrying over what canna be changed. Save it for healing. Ailis had Jaime with her. He will watch over her. She will still be alive when we are finally able to go after her."

"That is all true, but after six months under Donald MacCordy's brutal fist, will she still want to live—and will our child survive it?"

Alexander was not surprised when Barra was silent.


Ailis sat on her bed and glared at the heavy door that stood between her and even the smallest of freedoms. For a moment anger overcame the fear that continuously gnawed at her and had done so in the three months she had been a prisoner at Craigandubh. They had fled to the MacCordy keep within days of Alexander's rescue. Even her uncle and stepaunt had come along, although she saw nothing of them, and they gave her no help. She was tempted to throw her meal tray at the door, but she wanted the food too badly to waste it.

She smoothed her hand over her rounding stomach as she munched on a thick slab of honey-coated bread. The quickening she could feel now was her only source of happiness at the moment. Her child was still well. She knew that would continue as long as she and the baby were so intimately connected, so interwoven, that harm to one caused harm to the other. Spring would steal that protection, and she had to keep her strength to fight or flee the dangers she would face then.

Loneliness was her worst enemy. She saw only Jaime, her step-aunt, whose mental confusion seemed worse every day, and Donald, who delighted in threatening her unborn child. Malcolm visited a few times, then decided she was safe enough and traveled on to his own keep, a small peel tower he held for his cousins. She almost missed him. Without Malcolm, Jaime was her only pleasant company. Her stepaunt Una did not always make sense. And Donald, she thought with a renewed flare of anger, came only to frighten her and speak gloatingly of killing her child. Since any sort of physical abuse could seriously risk her life, he had stooped to verbal assault. A lot of times he succeeded in stirring her terror, for her child was her only real weakness.

A soft rap at her door drew her attention, and she waited to see if her visitor was a welcome one or not. A dull, cowed maid entered to take her meal tray, but right behind her was Jaime. Ailis breathed a sigh of relief as the maid left and locked them in together. For a minute she had feared that Donald would arrive, and she was not prepared for the man's almost daily dose of invective.

"I dinna suppose ye have heard any word of Rathmor," she said as Jaime sat down on a heavy wooden bench near the narrow window.

"Ye ask me that every day."

"I am sorry. 'Tis just that I worry so—about Alexander, about the children, and about getting back there."

"Are ye sure that getting back to Rathmor is really what ye wish to do?"

"Where else am I to go? My child would be at risk of his life in the hands of the MacCordys and at risk of being treated like a painful, must-be-hidden shame by his own maternal kinsmen. That leaves the father's clan, the Mac-Dubhs of Rathmor. For all of his faults, Alexander has said that he will wed me, and I am certain that he will do his utmost to keep this bairn safe. That has become of the greatest importance to me. In truth, plots and plans to keep his child alive could well be all that has kept me sane. Months of staring at these damp walls or Donald's ugly face is certainly enough to steal a person's wits."

Jaime shook his head. "The man lets his mind prey on the matter, on ye and the bairn and MacDubh. I fear 'tis turning his wits. His talk grows darker, mistress. I wouldna ignore what Donald MacCordy says no matter how strange it sounds. That fury Sir Malcolm protected ye from hasna died."

"Nay, I ken it. Donald but swallows it, and it begins to rot his innards."

"Aye, true."

Ailis studied Jaime for a moment, realizing what changes had occurred in the man. In the months since the MacDubhs had swept them up and carried them away, Jaime had grown, had matured. The stutter could still appear under extreme duress but not as strongly as it had been. Jaime's confidence had strengthened.

"And how goes it for ye?" she asked. "Ye appear to be doing well enough."

"Well enough. I miss Kate and the children."

"Ah, aye—Kate. I should think ye would wish to return

to Rathmor, to return to Kate." Ailis knew that Kate was the reason Jaime had become so much stronger. Kate's love had finished the work Ailis had started.

"I do want to get back to Kate." A light flush tainted his dark features. " 'Tis my duty to care for ye."

"Jaime, I ken that most people think ye are my bondservant, but ye arena. Ye never were. Dinna start believing it yourself. If ye wish to be with Kate, then that is where ye should be. Ye must not risk your own happiness."

"Kate will wait for me. I ken ye dinna own me, but I *owe* ye. And we are friends—aye?"

"Aye. If God favors us, Kate willna have to wait too long for ye to return."

"I hope not. But how can we return to Rathmor? Either of us? We are kept prisoner here."

"A chance to slip away could come, and we must be prepared. That is what I do. I dinna think on whether or not my opportunity will arise, but that it will and how I must act to take the fullest advantage of it."

"Is there anything I can do? I am allowed more and more freedom as each day passes. They dinna consider me such a great threat since I have sworn that I shall behave. At night I am secured, but not very much during the day. Could that help us?"

"Oh, aye, Jaime, it could help. After all, we shall need to ken where to go once we do get out of here. A route of escape needs to be surveyed."

"And ye truly believe that we will get out of here?"

"I have to believe that, Jaime." She lightly smoothed her hands over her stomach. "I *have* to."

"And ye have to get away from Donald ere that bairn comes out."

"Oh, sweet Mary, aye—as far as I can."

* * *

Ailis tried not to grunt as she hefted herself up onto the
bed and failed. She was not sure which darkened her mood
more—the dull, rainy spring weather or the size of her own
body. Escape had continued to elude her and Jaime throughout the long, cold winter. Now she was not sure that she
could escape even if Donald himself held every door open
for her.

Her fears were getting harder to subdue. Spring was upon
them, and she was sure her child would soon be born. Donald's threats grew more vicious until she was left nauseated
and shaking after each one of his visits. The child she carried had become the symbol of all the insults Donald
believed the MacDubhs had flung at him over the years. He
would use her child to vent his fury and to demonstrate the
increasing hate he felt toward Alexander and her.

"I must escape," she whispered and struggled against
the urge to weep.

Donald's repeated threats to cut her baby's throat before
her very eyes and send the pieces back to Alexander was
the one that lingered the most in her mind. It left her with
tormented dreams, nightmares that caused her to wake up
shaking and sweating. She was sure that that was not good
for her.

A soft scratching at her door and the murmur of voices
drew her attention. Her hopes rose, then fell when her
stepaunt Una entered followed by Jaime, who brought in a
tray holding a jug of wine and three tankards. It was always
welcome to have company who did not threaten or terrify
her, but she needed help now; she needed it desperately. As
dear as the befuddled woman was, Una was no aid and
Jaime was nearly as helpless as her.

"Jaime," Ailis began, her growing desperation clear to
hear in her voice.

"Have some wine, mistress." Jaime urged Una to sit next
to Ailis, then served the two women some wine. "Lady

Una has something she needs to say to ye. Ye had best heed her, I am thinking."

It was hard not to give in to a sense of irritation. Ailis sipped her wine and looked at her plump stepaunt. The woman was barely five years her senior, yet there was an abundance of gray in the woman's hair. Ailis did sympathize with Una's dreadful life, but she needed answers now, not one of Una's jumbled tales.

"Spring is here, Jaime," she said and was surprised when Jaime shushed her.

"I ken. Let Lady Una speak." He patted the timid woman's trembling hand. "Now, tell my mistress what ye told me."

When Una suddenly looked at her, Ailis felt her irritation fade. There was a different look in the woman's gray eyes, a different expression on her round face. Una looked as if all her wits were fully intact. The vague, dreamy air was gone, replaced by torment, fear, and a tremulous determination. Ailis wondered how long the change would last.

"What do you want to tell me, Aunt Una?" She also patted the woman on one plump arm.

"Ye must go away," Una said, her voice soft and tremulous. "It isna safe here for ye."

It was very hard not to make some sharp reply. The woman was suddenly aware of what was around her. Caustic words would not accomplish anything. Ailis did not really want to be responsible for scaring the woman's wits away again. Poor Una had suffered enough abuse and fright from the MacFarlanes.

"I ken it, Aunt Una. Jaime and I have thought on little else since we were caged here."

"Ye must go away now. Now!" Una grabbed hold of Ailis's hands. "Just as I have paid little or no heed to all said and done about me, I have tried to ignore the talk this time. Sir Donald speaks such filth." She placed a hand on

Ailis's abdomen. "They say that I am mad. They havena listened to Sir Donald speak of what he plans for your bairn. I kenned that I couldna ignore it when it began to torment me in my dreams."

"It torments my dreams as well. Sir Donald makes no secret of his plans."

"Your uncle doesna seem to ken what happens about him. But, nay, Donald isna too cautious. He means to kill your bairn before your eyes and then send the child to his father in wee pieces."

She had heard the threat before, many times, but, oddly, she found it even more terrifying when spoken in the fear-shaken voice of her timid stepaunt. "He has told me just that time and time again over these last few months."

"Well, what suddenly made me listen was that he means it. He will do it. He will. I heard it in his voice. I did. 'Twas as if someone slapped me awake. A bairn, a wee innocent bairn. The men sit there listening to Sir Donald talk of this horrible murder and say naught. They are all stinking cowards. Well, I willna sleep through this; I willna dither or dream. Ye are getting away from here tonight."

"Tonight?" Ailis tried not to put all her hopes into Una's prediction, but it was impossible. For far too long she had not even the glimmer of an opportunity to escape. "Dinna tease me with this."

"I would never be so cruel, child. Aye, useless at most times, but never cruel, I hope."

"Nay, of course not. I am just so desperate to get away that I am almost afraid to believe that a chance has come."

Una smiled, sadness twisting her expression. "Especially when 'tis offered by one who canna even recall where she is on most days." She held up her hand when Ailis started to politely protest. "Nay, 'tis true. It began as a ploy to protect myself from my husband, your uncle. I discovered quite by accident that, if he thought me witless, he left me alone. I have been doing it for so long that it isna always an act now. So, we had best make our plans ere my clarity disappears."

"Are ye sure ye can help us get out of the keep?" Jaime asked. "We must be released from our chambers, from the keep itself, and then from the bailey. It does us no good if all ye can do is unlock our chambers door."

"I can get ye outside. Truly, I can. My maid makes it her business to learn the ways of escape in every place we go. She judged my husband well, saw that he would never tend to our safety, and so she did it herself. I will take Jaime and show him the way in case anything happens to me."

Ailis nodded. They all knew what Una feared—the return of the vagueness she could no longer control. It did not need to be talked about. Ailis was glad the woman understood her own weaknesses enough to prepare for any trouble they might cause.

"When should we do this?" she asked, glancing from Jaime to Una.

"Midnight," Una answered. "The witching hour. Jaime says that is the quietest time at Craigandubh. Those who arena on watch are asleep, and those who are on watch arena very alert."

"And they will be looking outward."

"Aye," agreed Jaime. "They watch for an attack. Not an escape."

"We must go on foot?" Ailis patted her heavy belly as she considered that possibility.

"To try and take a mount would be dangerous. Ye canna slip away into the shadows whilst tugging along a horse." Jaime frowned at her. "We shall have to walk—at least at the beginning. Can ye manage that?"

"Aye, I can. I must. There is no other choice. We shall need some food."

"I can gather some without stirring any suspicion."

Jaime stood up and helped Una stand. "Ye just be ready to leave, mistress."

Ailis also stood up and then hugged Una. "Come with us. Ye have no life with my uncle."

"Ye are a sweet lass. Nay, I canna go. I havena the courage. And 'twill be best for ye if I linger here. I would only slow ye down, and my disappearance might raise an alarm earlier than ye would want."

"What if they discover that ye have helped me?"

"I dinna think there is a danger of that. Even if I was directly accused, none of those men would believe it. Take care, wee Ailis. Take care of that baby. Dinna let the one brave thing I have done in my life go to waste."

Jaime led Una away. For the first time since she had been dragged to Craigandubh, Ailis did not mind the sound of the bolt sliding across and locking her in. There was hope now. In a few hours there could also be freedom.

There was not much room to pace in her bedchamber, but Ailis was unable to be still. She had not thought that a half day of waiting would be so difficult, but the moment Jaime and Una had left, time had slowed to a painful crawl. She feared every sound she heard, for it could be Donald coming to torment her with the discovery and thwarting of her escape attempt. Another thing she dreaded was word from Jaime that poor Una had returned to her vague, deluded self and, worse, that she had done so before she could reveal the way out. Occasionally she had the wild thought that the visit from Una and Jaime, the talk of the escape, had all been a dream brought on by her own desperate desire.

She rubbed her damp palms dry on her brown woolen undertunic. There had not been much for her to do in preparation, and she knew that did not help. Some work would have helped to fill the time and make her feel as if she was accomplishing something. Instead, she paced and worried, worried and paced.

Her child kicked inside of her, and she moved to sit on the bed, gently smoothing her hands over her stomach. It was not going to be easy to walk back to Rathmor. She prayed that her escape would not be as dangerous for her child as Donald MacCordy so clearly was. She also prayed that she would not just find more grief at Rathmor. There had not been any definite word on Alexander. It was possible that she could return to Rathmor to find him resting in the kirkyard next to his little Elizbet. She forced that thought from her mind.

"Ailis."

That soft call startled her so that she nearly cried aloud, but quickly clapped her hands over her mouth. She glared at Jaime as he quietly shut the door behind him and walked over to the bed. She had been so caught up in her own worries that she had not heard him arrive.

"Ye frightened me out of a year or two, at least," she scolded Jaime, then realized what his presence meant. "'Tis midnight? 'Tis time for us to escape this place?" She grasped his hands in hers and hopped off of the bed.

"Aye, if ye are hale enough for the ordeal."

"It canna possibly be any more of an ordeal than being entombed at Craigandubh with Donald MacCordy."

"I just dinna want ye to think that all will be well now. It might not be." Jaime frowned as she quickly donned her cloak.

"Oh, I ken the risks well enough, dinna fear, my friend. I ken the risks of lingering here, too. The ones I face by leaving are chanced in an attempt to keep my child alive. 'Tisna too high a price to pay."

"Nay, mistress, it isna. Stay close behind me and, if ye find it grows too dim in a place or two, get a good strong grip on the bag secured to me back." He glanced at her belly. "I think ye will fit through everywhere."

"Ye just push me and pull me until I get unstuck." She took him by the hand. "Come along ere someone comes to check on us. 'Twould kill me to be caught when escape is so close to hand. What is in the bag?"

"Some food, a few other important supplies, and some extra clothing for the both of us."

"I dinna ken what I would do without ye, Jaime."

"Ye would escape on your own."

She exchanged a smile with him as they stepped out of her chambers and Jaime locked the door behind them. He had not been able to hide a slight puff of pride over her words. They both knew that she would have tried to get free with or without him, but that his presence was extremely helpful. Ailis also knew that this late in her pregnancy his presence could all to easily prove to be vital to her.

Without a word they crept along the narrow hall, keeping to the shadows. Ailis was a little surprised at how lax the guard was within the keep itself. She and Jaime were able to get all the way down into the food storage chambers beneath the great hall without once being challenged. All that changed was that what dim light there had been from the occasional torch completely vanished as they crept down the steep stairway into the food cellars of Craigandubh. Ailis had to clutch at the bag on Jaime's back.

Jaime finally paused to light a candle, and Ailis breathed a sigh of relief. They had slowed down to the point where they inched along at a painfully slow pace. The candle gave them enough light for Jaime to move faster, and she allowed herself to be tugged along. It was awkward, but she preferred that to moving so dangerously slowly that they seriously risked being discovered.

When Jaime stopped in front of a wall, she stepped aside to watch. It was obvious that the escape route from the Mac-Cordy keep had not been used in a long while, and in a display of common MacCordy stupidity, it had not been cared for, either. Jaime was hard-pressed to open the small door hidden behind a stack of wine casks. The surge of stale, musty air that escaped when he finally opened it made her cough. It also made her very reluctant to follow him into the tunnel beyond. She knew what kind of creatures called such dark, damp places their home. Then she looked at Jaime and wondered how, with his tormenting fears, he could even contemplate going into such a place.

"Jaime?" She put her hand on his arm and drew his attention away from the dark tunnel. "Can ye do it? Mayhaps there is another way?"

"Nay, there is *no* other way. We must go through here."

She edged closer and peered inside. "It looks and smells like all the places ye so deeply dread."

"Aye, but I shall have a wee light and I shallna be alone."

"Do ye want me to make a noise, a steady sound as we go along, so that ye ken that I am right with ye?"

He nodded. "That would be a help. And keep a firm hold on my hand."

She immediately put her hand in his. "Done. Just keep telling yourself that we move forward, toward freedom, that we are escaping, not being captured, and that at the end of this lies the open air."

"The open, cold, and damp air." He frowned at her. "The weather isna good. It could be dangerous for ye."

"Staying here is dangerous for me, Jaime. Even if the snow were still knee-deep and more were falling, I would leave here. Enough of this talking about it." She stepped into the low, narrow tunnel and tugged him after her.

It was a moment before Jaime shut the tunnel door behind them. Ailis held the candle and struggled to subdue her own rising fear. She eagerly took Jaime's hand when he reached out for her. There was a faint tremor in his grip, and she gave his hand a gentle squeeze. As they started to go through the tunnel, Jaime had to walk slightly crouched over and tug Ailis along behind him. In an attempt to keep his mind from preying upon his own fears, Ailis began to softly hum an old song. She found the sound comforting for herself as well.

Once at the end of the tunnel Jaime hurried to open the small hatch. Yet again neglect had made it more work than it should have been. Ailis stepped back as he put all of his strength and weight behind forcing the door open. When the hatch finally gave, Jaime quickly pushed it open, side-stepping the debris that fell into the tunnel. Ailis took a deep breath of the cool night air as it rushed into the tunnel and heard Jaime do the same.

Jaime climbed out first, then gently helped her get out. As Jaime shut the hatch and covered it with dead leaves and other debris, she looked around. They had come up inside of a tiny, ruined stone cottage. As long as they were careful, they were far enough from the walls of Craigan-dubh to escape unseen. If only the weather were more hospitable, she thought with a grimace and better secured the hood of her cloak in hopes of keeping dry despite the continuous and very cold drizzle. Soft as it was, that rain could easily prove to be their biggest foe.

"Where are we going?" she asked Jaime when, as they left the poor ruin, Jaime turned north instead of west, which was the direction of Rathmor and safety.

"We canna head straight for Rathmor, lass."

"Nay? 'Tis where we want to go. All things considered, I am not sure that adding to the miles we must travel is the wisest thing to do." She tucked her skirts up, securing them under the loose girdle she wore, so that they would not be dragging in the wet and the mud and slowing her down. "I am in no condition to endure a long march."

"If we travel for Rathmor in a fine straight line, we willna reach there. We will just make ourselves very tired ere the MacCordys and your uncle ride out and fetch us back to Craigandubh."

"Do ye think it would be that simple?"

"Mayhaps not that simple, but very nearly so. We are an odd pair, lass. 'Twill be very hard for us to hide. The best we can do is to try and hide our trail."

"Ah, I see, and going in a roundabout way will do that?"

"It could help." He lifted her over a fallen log, then paused. "Do ye think it a foolish plan? I tried to think slow and careful, and to see all my choices as ye once told me to do. I thought this would trick Donald, at least for a wee while."

Ailis nodded and patted his arm. "Ye have planned well, far better than I. My only real plan was to flee, to get back to Rathmor. Ye gave the how of it a great deal more thought. Aye, Donald would never think that we would show any cleverness. He will hie straight for Rathmor. It will take him a while to realize he has seen *no* sign of his prey and pause to consider the why of it."

"So I thought. It could buy us at least a day, mayhaps more. We shall make a gentle turn toward Rathmor. Then, once it lies straight ahead of us, we shall try to move as swiftly as we can, yet stay hidden."

"Do ye think we can stay hidden with all the MacCordys and MacFarlanes beating the bushes for us?"

"Aye, I do. We are but two people on foot. Most times we can see our hunters ere they can see us. Aye, or hear them. If we keep close to shelter, never get caught out in the open, it could prove easier than ye think."

"Oh, it would have to. I think we face a very great challenge."

"We are up to the challenge," he said. "Ye have to believe that."

"I will try," she murmured and prayed that she could maintain the strength she would need not to become a burden.

# 13

"Jaime?" Ailis whispered, certain that she could hear someone approaching her hiding place in the rocks.

She briefly thought of straightening up to peer over the rocks, but firmly resisted the urge. Whispering her companion's name was risky enough. She did not want to chance revealing herself to her enemies. Ailis just wished it were drier and warmer. For three long days the weather had varied from damp to deluge and back again. Another of far too many shivers rippled through her, and she huddled deeper into her damp cloak, finding little added warmth there. Her back was beginning to ache with a worrisome regularity.

"Jaime?" she whispered again, hating her cowardice, yet terrified of being alone and too pregnant to protect herself.

"Here, mistress." Jaime crept behind the rocks and sat down beside her. "I didna mean to leave ye here alone for so long."

"Nay, I beg your forgiveness for being such a weakling that I tremble when left alone."

"There is no shame in that. Ye ken your own weaknesses. Ye arena in any condition to protect yourself. I shouldna like to be so vulnerable, so unable to fight." He patted her hands where they lay tightly clenched together in her lap.

"Did ye find anything? Any sign of MacCordys or Mac-

Farlanes?" She had an urge to get moving again, stillness only adding to the discomfort of being damp and cold. "Can we continue on now?"

"Well, there are signs that there is someone behind us, although I canna be certain they are following us. They could be coming this way for other reasons." He frowned when she sat up straighter and rubbed at her lower back. "Are ye all right?"

"Aye, fair enough. What other reasons?" Ailis began to have a bad feeling about the root cause of all her discomfort.

"They could be MacCordy men riding to warn Malcolm MacCordy," he murmured.

Ailis tensed, then stared at Jaime. "Sir Malcolm? Sir Malcolm resides near here?"

"He does. If ye sit up more and look to the north, ye can see his peel tower through the mists."

"Jaime!" She awkwardly turned and raised herself up onto her knees to look out only to discover that he spoke the truth. "Why have we come here, so near to the enemy we are fleeing?"

He grimaced and rubbed a hand over his rain-chafed face. "I had meant to be farther west of here by now, but I changed my mind last evening. I decided that ye needed a place to rest, some place safe to seek shelter."

"Safe? A MacCordy keep? Are ye mad? And why do ye think I need a place to shelter? I am fine."

"Nay, ye arena fine. I can see it in your face, in the way you move."

"Well, mayhaps I am not perfect, but I can make it to Rathmor."

"Not as ye are now. Ye are weary, cold, wet to the skin, and shudder until your teeth chatter. A good fire would help ye a great deal, but we canna build one out here. It could lead our enemies to us, and 'tis too wet anyway. Ye need to get in out of this cursed weather for a wee rest."

"But at Sir Malcolm's? He is a MacCordy. We canna trust him to help."

"We can trust him to want to keep ye and the bairn safe. We ken that already."

"Well, aye, 'tis why he put himself between me and Donald. However, I wasna trying to flee. In fact, he gave me no aid the one time I might have had a chance to run, to flee with the MacDubhs when they rescued Alexander."

She watched Jaime frown, and then he stared at her steadily. He was trying to think of an argument that would get her to turn to Malcolm for more help. The thought of even one night indoors—dry and warm and on a soft bed—was intensely alluring, but she had to resist it. One act of kindness and chivalry did not make Malcolm a man that she could wholeheartedly trust. She had a chance to reach Rathmor, and she was not about to put that at risk.

"I am certain there are MacCordy men about looking for us," said Jaime. "That will mean another night out here—with the damp and the cold. Is this where ye want to bear your child?"

"What do ye mean? I am not ready to give birth," she insisted, but as she rubbed her lower back, she suddenly knew that she was or would be very soon.

"I think ye are. Even if ye arena there is still the fact that your color isna good, ye clearly have many an ache and pain, and ye are dangerously chilled. Put your fears aside and think on your bairn. This isna good for it."

She sat down, huddled in her cloak. Jaime was right. The shivers she cursed were more virulent, but she had suffered them for most of the day. One of the biggest reasons to risk herself and her child in an escape was because it had offered her child the best chance of survival. Now she had to make the same choice again.

For a moment she forced herself to concentrate on how she felt—besides cold and wet. Her backache was vaguely dissimilar to the ones she usually got at the end of the day, and she had suffered this all day long. That was a sign she knew she should not ignore. Her child had also ceased to move, something he had done with consistent vigor since the day she had felt the first kick. There were no easily recognizable contractions, but she knew that did not mean that she was not in labor already. One glance around her told her the utter unsuitability of the place for childbearing. There was no real shelter from the cold or the constant damp or from their enemies. She could easily be caught out in the open in the most vulnerable of positions. She needed a dry place to hide, and Jaime was right—if Malcolm would agree to help, it was much better to be inside.

"We could lose all we have gained," she finally said.

"Aye, we could." Jaime grimaced as he looked toward Malcolm's peel tower. "He is a MacCordy after all."

"Well, we shall just have to risk it and hope that his distaste of abusing a woman with child carries over to the bairn itself." She started to stand up and readily accepted Jaime's helping hand. "We may have discovered the limits of Malcolm's loyalty to his kinsmen. 'Twould be foolish of us not to take advantage of that."

"He has never been the brutish sinner his cousins have been. However, one ought to be wary of trusting him too easily."

"Very true. I also think that there is a part of Malcolm that takes some pleasure in working against his cousins and, in such a way that they could look poorly or foolish if they chided or punished him for it." She hesitated a little when Jaime started to lead her toward Malcolm's peel tower. "I could be wrong."

"So, we stay?" Jaime frowned at her, his expression reflecting the confusion he felt.

"Ah, poor Jaime, trapped out in the rain with a woman who canna decide whether to go or to stay." She started to walk toward Malcolm's tower. "I have made the decision. I was just a wee bit slow to act upon it. Let us pray that Malcolm will help us and willna demand too high a price for his aid."

"Malcolm, I think ye had best come into the kitchen."

Malcolm looked up from the fire he idly poked at to frown at the young Giorsal, the woman who took care of his meager household. He idly wished that the few guards his uncle had granted him were even half as efficient. After stuffing themselves on another of Giorsal's excellent meals, the men sent to help him protect his tower house were undoubtedly curled up in their beds or crouched over a pair of dice. They were certainly not where they should be—out in the cold rain watching for an army. Malcolm took a deep breath and tried not to allow his annoyance with the rest of his shoddy staff to be wrongly directed at Giorsal.

"The kitchens?" He smiled faintly. "Ye dinna truly expect me to go down to the kitchens."

" 'Twould offend your manhood, would it? Do ye think I wish ye to help me churn some butter or the like?"

"I think ye grow most impertinent. What possible reason could I have for going into the kitchens?" He frowned when she looked around, then edged closer to him. "Such tiptoeing isna needed, Giorsal. We are alone."

"But alone enough not to be overheard?" she whispered.

He looked into her dark gray eyes and was puzzled by the secrecy and the hint of fear he could see there. The girl was acting very oddly. Nonetheless, he felt the pinch of alarm.

"And what might they 'overhear'?" he asked, keeping his own voice low.

"That ye had best come to the kitchens to meet the guests who have just slipped inside."

"Guests?" He tensed. "What guests? There was no alarm called, none of my men announced *any* people."

"Those men your uncle gave ye are not worth the pallets they sleep on. No one is watching. These people slipped into the keep without once being challenged. If they were enemies, I should have been sprawled over my stewpot with my throat cut." She hurried after Malcolm as he strode toward the kitchen. "However, these people are no threat to us."

"How can ye be certain of that?" he demanded as he drew his sword.

"As easily as ye will as soon as ye face them."

Giorsal cursed softly when Malcolm stepped into the kitchen, then stopped so abruptly that she walked into him. She slipped around him to look at the people seated at her work-worn table. The woman looked a little warmer than she should be, but Giorsal quickly refilled her guests' tankards with mulled cider. The pair needed warming inside and out.

"By the look upon your face, I guess 'tis a good thing they found me alone," Giorsal said as she watched Malcolm.

It took Malcolm a moment to shake free of his shock. He could not believe that Ailis MacFarlane and her hulking guardian were sitting in his kitchen. How had they escaped Craigandubh? How had they eluded the MacCordys? Why did they come to him? He did not need such trouble. He certainly did not want to face or make the choices that would be demanded of him.

"What are ye doing here?" he asked as he quickly sat down. "How did ye get away?"

"It wasna so difficult." Ailis sipped her cider and vowed not to let him know too much about her escape. She did not want to cause her poor befuddled aunt any more difficulty. "The weather has proved to be the most persistent obstacle."

"So, ye wish me to aid ye in returning to Craigandubh and soften your husband's fury?" He nodded a silent thank you to Giorsal, who served him some more mulled cider and sat down beside him.

"Nay, I dinna mean to go back to him—ever." Ailis shook her head. "I would cut my own throat first."

"Dinna talk such foolishness. Ye carry a child."

"Aye, I do, which is why I fled your cousin. And why I will never return."

"Then why are ye here? Ye must ken that I will return ye to Donald."

"I had hoped that ye wouldna."

"Hold up now. I am sorry that my one small act of gallantry has made ye think that I am the greatest of fools, a man ready to toss his livelihood, mayhaps even his life, away on a whim."

"Nay, one thing I have never thought ye were was a fool." Ailis smiled faintly, for Malcolm looked mildly irritated and not really much of a threat. "Neither are ye completely your cousin's lackey."

"Ye make some sweeping judgments of a man ye have spent little time with." Malcolm frowned when he saw her wince and noticed that she was clutching the edge of the table very tightly. "Does something ail ye?"

"Is it the bairn?" asked Giorsal. "Do ye need to lie down?"

"Not as yet," Ailis replied and looked directly at Malcolm. "Jaime and I have reason to believe that your cousins' men will soon be here. Mayhaps, because of your aid to me before, they feel this is a reasonable place to search or set extra guards. There is nary another place twixt here and Rathmor that isna guarded. I was very surprised to find ye so unprotected and unwatched."

"I have guards," Malcolm grumbled.

"We saw no one, sir," said Jaime. "That wasna intended?"

"Nay, that wasna intended." Malcolm took a deep drink of his spiced cider. "I am cursed with lazy fools for my men-at-arms. My dear cousin Donald gives me the dregs of the pathetic guard he gathers around himself. Long ago I ceased trying to get any work out of the jesters Donald calls soldiers. If my cousin wishes to waste his money on mercenaries who canna even subdue some sheep in the field, 'tis his concern, not mine."

"I think ye will soon have more guard here then ye might wish for," Ailis said, feeling almost sorry for the man.

"Aye, but it will be here to watch for ye or to watch me. Ye have already cost me dearly, wench. My kinsmen were never the most trusting sort, but before I set myself between ye and my cousins, they had never openly mistrusted me before. Now they do. 'Tis a fine gift ye gave me. Now, here ye sit, eager to cause me even more trouble. Well, no, thank ye."

"Malcolm!" Giorsal lightly punched him on the arm. "Ye canna speak so to a woman with child."

"A woman carrying a MacDubh child," he reminded her.

"The parentage of the child doesna matter to me, and it shouldna matter to ye. All we need to ken is that she carries a bairn. 'Tis enough to move any Christian soul to want to help her. Aye, especially since I believe she willna be carrying that bairn for very much longer." Giorsal's tone carried the faint lilt of a question as she looked at Ailis.

Malcolm stared at Ailis's swollen stomach in horror. "Are ye about to give birth?"

It was difficult for Ailis to completely suppress a smile over Malcolm's reaction. "There is that chance. I do feel odd, but that could be because I am weary and wet. Time will tell. 'Tis just that with MacCordy and MacFarlane men riding ever closer, searching for me, and the weather so very poor, I couldna wait outside any longer. I needed shelter."

"Then why didna ye stay at Craigandubh?" Malcolm finished off his cider and refilled his tankard, all the while wishing that he had some stronger drink. "Ye could have been safe and dry there."

"I would have been, but not my bairn."

"Nay, I ken that my cousin has been angry and speaks cruelly, but ye canna take all he says to heart."

"Oh, but I do." She held Malcolm's gaze with her own. "Donald MacCordy truly means to kill my child."

"Nay, I canna believe that," Malcolm argued, but his voice did not carry the strength of conviction.

"'Tis true. Oh, mayhaps he did not mean his threats while ye still lingered at Craigandubh. That was still just fury, an unrefined cruelty born of hate and anger that was painful, but not truly dangerous. It began to turn as my belly swelled. Donald rarely ever lifted his hand against me, but ye could read the growing truth of his hostile threats in his face, in his voice, even in his eyes. Donald doesna intend to allow my child to live much after its first breath. If there can ever be anything more heinous than the murder of an innocent bairn, then your cousin has thought of it. He means to send the body of my child back to Rathmor, back to the MacDubhs, in pieces."

"'Tis so hard to believe that my own kinsmen would act so low."

"Donald will. He is nearly mad with hate for the child I carry. So I couldna stay there, couldna wait until I had borne my child. I am not the only one who felt so. Ye ken well that someone had to have helped me and Jaime get out of Craigandubh. I willna tell ye who, but mention it only to show ye that someone else shares my opinion."

"Sir Malcolm! Ho, my liege!"

All four people at the table froze as the deep voice echoed through the tower house. Ailis started to get to her feet, Jaime quickly standing up to assist her. Her first thought was to flee, but Malcolm grabbed her by the wrist and put her hand into Giorsal's.

"Hide her, lass," he ordered Giorsal. "Take her to your chamber. I will go and find out what trouble there may be and then tell ye what to do."

As soon as Giorsal had ushered his unwanted guests up the narrow rear stairs to the upper floors, Malcolm strode off to his great hall. It was evident even before he entered the hall that the man-at-arms was just standing in the great hall bellowing for him and could not exert himself to look around. Malcolm cuffed the man offside the head the moment he reached him. The thickheadedness of his men-at-arms infuriated Malcolm. The men Donald had given him to command were little good for anything more than arrow fodder.

"Cease your bellowing," he ordered the man, then slouched in his chair near the fire. "What do ye wish to say?"

"A young page has arrived. He says his master is but a half hour's journey behind him," the guard answered.

"And this is of some importance to me, is it?"

"Aye, 'tis your cousin, sir. Sir Donald is the lad's master."

"Ah, clarification. So, my cousin comes for a visit. Well, assume your post and see if ye can get those other slug-witted dolts to do as they should. I ken that ye think I have no power over ye, but that my cousin Donald is your true master. Well, your true master now approaches our gates. I suggest ye dinna let him see how thoroughly useless ye are." He met the burly man's glare with a faint smile. "Best hurry. Time passes."

As soon as the man was gone, Malcolm hurried off to Giorsal's chambers. He did not have much time to decide what to do about his guests. As he stepped into Giorsal's room, Malcolm grimaced, for the image Ailis presented was one guaranteed to tug at any man's heart, any man except Donald MacCordy. Even lying on Giorsal's bed, her stomach bulging with a MacDubh baby, she looked lovely. He was still drawn to her, to the warmth he knew she could provide. He stepped over to the bed even as Jaime helped Ailis sit up.

"Does trouble ride this way?" Ailis asked Malcolm.

"Oh, aye, my bonny little mother-to-be. Your betrothed rides our way." He watched her become ashen, and when she tried to stand up, he held her in place. "Tell your faithful behemoth to cease bristling," he ordered when Jaime softly growled and took a step toward him. "I will do ye no good dead. In truth, I believe it may annoy Giorsal somewhat if ye kill me, and I believe ye need all the allies ye can get. Aye, even questionable ones like me."

Ailis held up her hand to stop Jaime's advance on Malcolm. "I fear he is right, m'friend."

"I need not kill him." Jaime held up one large fist. "I could just beat some sense and honor into him."

"He could benefit from that," muttered Giorsal, scowling at Malcolm. "No mistake."

"Ye wound me, sweetling." Malcolm spared a mournful glance at Giorsal before fixing his gaze on Ailis. "I fear ye dinna have much time to decide amongst the choices I am about to offer."

"Then I suggest that ye hurry and offer them," Ailis said. "I should like at least one moment to think."

"'Twould gain me a great deal to hand ye back to my cousin." Malcolm held up one hand to silence Giorsal when she started to protest. "So I should gain something for *not* handing ye back to my cousin."

"Ye waste time. Just name your price."

"Ye are my price. When this trouble ends, as it must, and ye are returned to health from the birth of the babe, I want one night with ye." He stepped back a little when Jaime snarled a curse. "That is my price."

"Malcolm, how could ye?" whispered Giorsal, staring at him with hurt and dismay.

"When ye are older, ye will better understand, lassie." Malcolm kept his gaze fixed upon Ailis's face. "Well?"

"I still have a moment. Hush!" She held up both hands when Giorsal and Jaime started to talk. "I thank ye for your concern, but I must decide this for myself."

"I dinna want ye to buy my life in such a way," Jaime said.

"I mean no insult, my dearest of friends, but 'tisna your life I must consider. Or mine."

Jaime nodded and Ailis sighed. She wanted to tell Malcolm to curl up and die, but resisted the urge. It was not a time to be too emotional. She had to coolly consider her options. Malcolm had only named two, but she knew there was a third one. He would never stop her if she tried to get away. Ailis knew that instinctively. Unfortunately, all the reasons she had sought shelter with Malcolm were still there. In truth, she decided as she felt an easily recognizable contraction cut through her, there was now one very compelling one. It was still cold and wet outside and still dangerous. And she still had to avoid falling back into Donald's murderous hands at all costs.

But, she thought, the cost could be very high indeed if she agreed to Malcolm's price. It would destroy whatever chance she had of happiness with Alexander. She was sure that she had softened some of the hard bitterness of the Laird of Rathmor. No matter what her reasons, if she spent one night with Malcolm, what few grains of Alexander's trust and affection she had managed to gather would be blown away. To save her baby she would have to surrender all hope of happiness with the child's father. Ailis knew she could also be giving up any chance of being a true mother to her own child, for Alexander could well lock her out of Rathmor completely, and yet he would never give up his child.

None of that mattered, she told herself firmly as another contraction squeezed her body. It was all of a very small consequence next to the life of her baby. She fought the sense of defeat that threatened to choke her.

"I agree," she said and was glad Malcolm had the wit not to smile or look too pleased with himself.

"Mistress—" protested Jaime.

"Argue with me later," she ordered him. "Where am I to hide?" she asked Malcolm.

"In my chambers. Follow me." He led them out of Giorsal's chambers to his own. "I have a secret room in here. 'Tis a space within the walls. Your big friend may find it a tight fit. Aye and ye, too, since ye have swelled so much."

Glad for Jaime's arm around her shoulders as they followed Malcolm, Ailis asked, "Is there no other place we can hide from Donald? My pains grows stronger and more distinct."

"Giorsal, get her a few things to make her stay within our walls a wee bit more comfortable. Aye and give her what she might need to birth her babe."

Ailis kept a close watch on Jaime as Malcolm stopped before a large clothespress. Malcolm stepped inside of the huge wardrobe and pressed hard against the far side of the back. Slowly the back pivoted. Ailis watched as Jaime paled slightly. It would be a dark, snug hiding place. For a while they would be enclosed within the heavy walls of the tower house. She felt nervous about stepping into the dark narrow passage. Jaime had to be terrified. Ailis did not believe she could ask such a thing of her friend, nor would he be much use to her, for he would be too caught up in his own fears.

"This isna going to work, Malcolm," she said. "Jaime canna abide such places, and I need him to be in his full right senses."

"I will be fine," Jaime said before Malcolm could reply. "I willna be alone. Ye will be with me, mistress. I will also have a light."

"A light could be dangerous." Malcolm frowned. "It could show through some crack and be seen."

"If our enemy is close enough to see that, to espy some small flicker of light, then I suspect he will be near enough to hear us breathe." Ailis grimaced as a contraction gripped her. "Even if Jaime didna need the light to stem his terror of the dark, he would need it to help me. Ah, thank ye, Giorsal," she said as the girl returned and started to brush out the hiding place. "That is kind of ye."

"Ye may be stuck within these walls for some time." Giorsal lined the area with some blankets.

"My plan is to be rid of my cousin as soon as possible," Malcolm said.

" 'Tis already late, sir." Giorsal set a basket of fruit, cheese, and wine inside as well as a supply of clothes, rags, and water. "I fear we will have Sir Donald's unpleasant company until the morning." She handed Jaime some candles and a flint. "And I fear he will be bellowing for ye any moment now," she told Malcolm, then looked at Ailis. " 'Twould be best if ye and your man get into your wee hiding place. I dearly wish we had better."

"To keep my bairn safe, I can abide a wee bit of discomfort."

Ailis stepped inside and sat down. An instant later Jaime handed her some pillows. She lit a candle as he stepped inside and hurried to light another as Malcolm shut them in. As the door closed, sealing them within the walls, she kept a very close watch on Jaime. He closed his eyes and took several deep breaths. She prayed that he would be all right, for the time between her contractions was becoming distressingly small. Soon she would need his help. When he finally looked at her, he was clear-eyed if pale-faced. There was no sign of the mindless fear that could grip him in such places.

"Are ye sure ye are all right, Jaime?" she whispered. "There may still be time to hide in some other place."

"There is no other place." He sat down facing her. "I will be fine. 'Tisna dark and I am not alone."

"And soon I fear we may both be busy." She bit back a groan as a strong contraction tore through her.

"The bairn isna going to wait."

"Nay, I fear not."

"Have ye seen a bairn born or helped in the birthing?"

"Never. Have ye?"

"Nay, but I have helped with the sheep and a calving or two."

"'Tis more than I have done." She panted as she fought to stay clear-headed while a fierce contraction gripped her. "I didna have much time to study the matter before I was made a prisoner at Craigandubh, and no one told me about birthing there. They only spoke of death whenever my child was mentioned."

"Dinna think on them. They willna get hold of this child. All ye should think about is the birthing, the living child who is demanding to be born."

"But, Jaime, bairns make noise when they are born. They scream and squawl."

"Well, aye and nay." He frowned and scratched his head. "I canna think of how to stop it if he wants to do it."

"Neither can I, yet it could lead Donald right to us."

"Dinna fret on it. There is naught ye can do."

"True. Except pray that Alexander's child has the wit to

ken that there is danger all about and keep his wee mouth shut." She smiled weakly when Jaime nodded.

Malcolm cursed when Donald stumbled after him. He had tried to get his cousin so drunk that he spent the night under the oak table in the great hall. Instead, it appeared he would have the lout for company all night. He could only pray that Donald was so drunk that he could hear nothing nor had the wit left to understand anything he might hear. Malcolm dearly wished there was enough time to warn Ailis and Jaime.

"I willna be made to sleep upon the floor in my own keep," Malcolm said as loud as he dared as he and Donald entered his bedchamber.

"*Your* keep, is it?" Donald laughed nastily as he sprawled on the bed. "Ye forget who ye owe everything to, Cousin." He clumsily sat up to tug off his boots, then flopped back down on the bed. "I really thought that little slut would have come here."

"Here?"

"Aye, to beguile her way into your protection again."

"Ye insult me with your lack of trust." Malcolm moved to wash up for bed and prayed that Donald would hurry up and go to sleep.

The sound of men's voices caused Ailis to stop panting. That enhanced her pain and she almost screamed. When she recognized the voices that scream was even harder to suppress. Ailis could not believe Malcolm had brought Donald right into the room, mere feet from where she was. Then she realized that Malcolm probably had no choice. Now, however, she was faced with what could be an impossible task—to bear her first child without a sound.

Ailis stuffed a wet rag between her teeth to cushion

them as she suffered another contraction. Through the blur of her own tears she saw Jaime crouched between her legs silently urging her to push down. Her child was coming into the world with his deadliest enemy but feet away. She cursed as she strained for she could not repress every tiny sound; even breathing made some noise. Keep talking, Malcolm, she silently ordered. Talk long and loud.

Malcolm heard a soft, low noise from within his walls and broke out in a cold sweat. He grabbed the decanter of strong wine Giorsal had left by his bed and poured large goblets full for Donald and himself. As he handed the drink to his cousin he began a long, detailed account of a night he had spent with the king's court. For the first time in his life he set out to purposely bore someone to sleep. He was pleased to see Donald growing glassy-eyed by the second round of wine.

She fought the urge to scream as blinding pain swept over her. The agony of her child leaving her body was equaled by the terror of knowing what the baby's first cry could bring. Ailis was so tense with fearful anticipation that she was only vaguely aware of Jaime yanking open her bodice and settling something warm and wet there. It was a while before she had enough clarity of wit to look down at what she held. Her child lay on her chest determinedly suckling as Jaime cleaned him off. Since there had been no sudden outcry, she relaxed a little.

"A son," she whispered.

"Aye, and a quiet one."

"Thank God." She grabbed hold of Jaime's hand. "And thank ye."

"I just wish I could have stopped ye from promising Malcolm what ye did. It could cost ye a great deal, mistress."

"Aye, I ken it." She looked down at her child and smiled. "But look what was saved, Jaime."

# 14

As he had for far too many nights since his wounds had healed, Alexander stood upon the battlements of Rathmor, his gaze aimed toward Leargan. He ached to besiege the keep and wrest Ailis from her uncle's hold. Unfortunately, the late spring weather refused to accommodate his wants. The recent rains and the imminent threat of more made a direct, heavy attack impossible for the moment. A full attack on a well-defended keep was a dangerous, difficult task. In the adverse conditions they faced now it would be nearly suicide.

For himself, Alexander cared little and would have chanced it. But he could not order his men, some still barely recovered from his rescue, on such a foolhardy venture. It would simply be a waste of lives, and no matter what she was suffering, Ailis would not expect that. She would probably be appalled if he spent even one life in an attempt to save her. Necessity and the need to consider others had forced him to wait, made him bow to common sense, but he did not like it.

The thought of all that could be happening to Ailis, and all that had happened, made Alexander clench his fists in helpless rage. Was the child she carried still safe? Had she been forced into MacCordy's bed despite the fact that she was with child? Had the handfast marriage they had proclaimed in their moment of desperation been honored or had it been ignored despite the fact that several dozen MacCordys had witnessed it? Was Ailis now wed to Mac-Cordy by a priest? Was she even alive?

Alexander shunned that last question almost as it was forming in his mind. Although he usually scorned such things, he could not help but feel that he would know, would somehow sense that Ailis's life had ended. Despite his efforts to hold her at a distance, they had become intertwined in so many ways that he was certain something would occur inside of him if she died, whether he was there to witness such a tragedy with his own eyes or not. He had fought it tooth and nail, but he had to accept that it was true, that she had somehow become that great a part of him. A light touch on his arm took him out of his dark thoughts, and he looked down into the sweet, solemn face of a nightgowned Sibeal.

"Ye should be abed, lass," he scolded in a gentle voice, pushing aside his own grief and fear for the child's sake. He certainly did not want to add to what the little girl already suffered.

"She will come back, Uncle," Sibeal said as Alexander lifted her up into his arms. "Aunt Ailis will come back to us."

"I hope ye are right, sweeting." He headed back inside of the keep, afraid that the damp, cool night air could harm the child.

Sibeal slipped her arms about his neck and said with complete confidence, "I am right. I had one of my dreams, ye ken. It told me she was coming."

It was not unusual for a child to make up tales or to set too much trust in a dream. Considering what everyone believed about little Sibeal, Alexander knew she was probably more susceptible than most children. He paused in mounting the stairs to her bedchamber. After a moment's thought, he sat down on the steps with Sibeal in his lap. He felt he ought to talk to the child, for such delusions, if left unchecked, could bring her great harm. He told himself, sternly, not to allow her words to lift his hopes. To prevent the child from nurturing false hope was another reason to talk to her.

"Ye think I am a silly bairn," Sibeal murmured, staring up at Alexander.

"Mayhaps misled."

"Aunt said that folk would think me silly or might think bad things about me like I am a witch. So I dinna talk about it much. But I had a bad dream about her yestereve, and this night I had a good one. Do ye want to hear?"

"Aye, all right, Sibeal. I will listen. Yet that doesna mean that I believe in all of this or will think your dream means anything." He hoped that by listening to her dream he would lessen the importance she had given it and ease his own superstitious fears about her reputed skills.

"The bad dream made me cry even though I kenned that it didna mean Aunt Ailis was dead."

"What did ye see, child?"

" 'Twas all dark. I could see naught but shadows and a wee bit of her face. There was a big shadow bending over her, but it wasna a bad shadow. Aunt Ailis was hurting, but I dinna think anyone was hurting her. 'Twas a hurt from inside her. She was afraid, but it wasna because of the hurting."

"What was she afraid of, sweeting?" he pressed when she frowned and grew silent for a moment.

"Something outside." She frowned even more. "Aye, the bad thing was near, but it wasna there, and the hurt was inside of her." She shrugged and looked at Alexander. "Aunt Ailis says I will be better at telling as I get bigger and ken more words."

" 'Tis the bairn. Ailis was having the bairn."

Alexander was startled by Barra's words, for he had not realized that his brother had approached him. He had been so intent upon what Sibeal was telling him that he suspected an entire army could have come up behind him. It was taking all of his willpower and concentration to fight the allure of belief. The lack of any skepticism in Barra's expression of interest as he sat next to them forced Alexander to seek some means of protest. He had accepted a great deal since Ailis and Barra's children had come to Rathmor, but there were some things he could not, and would not, abide. Sibeal's skill had to be simply a little girl's fancy.

"Now, Barra," he said with a frown for his brother, "ye shouldna encourage the child in all of this. And I thought ye had sought your bed hours ago."

Barra nodded. "Aye, I had, but I woke. I felt the need to go and check on Sibeal. She had sought my bed yestereve, and I had feared that she might suffer another frightening dream. Is that what happened tonight?"

"Nay, Papa." Sibeal moved to sit on Barra's lap. "I had a good one tonight. Last night was a bad one. I dinna have bad ones often, but they can scare me when they come."

Barra touched a kiss to her scarlet curls and murmured, "Ailis had warned me."

His agitation clear to hear in his voice, Alexander demanded, "Are, ye truly believing that these dreams mean something?"

"Ye saw the proof of that with the puppies."

"I saw luck."

"Come, ye canna tell me that ye think the dream Sibeal just spoke of is a common one for a wee child."

There was no answer he could make, so Alexander fell silent. The sight was a skill much believed in. When he was a beardless boy, there had been a few old women who had professed to having it, and one had proved her claim often enough. He had not liked it then, and he liked it even less now. If he did not understand something, he grew very unsettled, and he had little liking for the feeling. It was appalling to have a cause of that detested feeling within the walls of his keep. Despite all of that, he could not discard her words as nonsense. Barra was completely right in saying that it was an unusual dream for a child, and that gave the claim of Sibeal having the sight a credence he did not really wish it to have.

"What was the good dream?" he asked the little girl, unable to keep his reluctance and inner confusion out of his voice.

"The good dream is why I sought ye out," Sibeal replied. "Ye seemed so sad, Uncle Alex, that I thought ye would like to hear about some good things."

"Aye, lassie, I would." He felt honestly touched by her concern for him.

"Well, Aunt Ailis wasna in the dark anymore, and her hurting had gone away. I couldna see anything clear, but I ken that she was outside now. She was just walking and walking and walking. Jaime was with her. I could see him. They were both looking right at me as they walked and walked. That means that she is coming back to Rathmor."

"If I could believe in such things as dreams and visions—aye—I would say that it meant exactly that. However, I dare not let myself believe, not with all my heart."

Sibeal nodded. The expression on her little face became very solemn. "Aunt Ailis believes, but she says she doesna like to."

"Well, even if I did believe in it all, I canna send my men out riding over the countryside in this weather. Not with the MacFarlanes and the MacCordys hot for our blood and not upon the account of the dreams of a wee lass," Alexander explained as kindly as he could. "My men would most likely think me the greatest of fools, even a madman."

Again Sibeal nodded. "Aunt Ailis wouldna like ye

telling folk about my dreams. She says they will make folk treat me as other than just a little lass."

"Aunt Ailis is right, sweeting." Barra set his daughter on her feet. " 'Tis best to keep such a thing secret. Many people just canna stop themselves from fearing it. Thank ye, lass, for sharing your dream with us. Now—to bed with ye. Do ye wish me to take ye up and tuck ye in?"

"Nay, Papa." She kissed his cheek. "Good sleep."

"Good sleep, lassie."

"I need a drink," Alexander grumbled as soon as Sibeal had gone, and he rose to stride into the great hall.

Barra followed Alexander and watched closely as his brother downed one tankard full of ale and refilled it before he sat down at the head table. In silence Barra filled his own tankard with hearty cider and joined his brother. Although he fervently wished that Sibeal did not possess her special gift, he was able to accept that a few chosen people were born with the sight. He also completely understood Alexander's reluctance to accept it. Alexander was a man who strongly preferred facts and reasoning.

"Mairi's grandmother truly had the sight? That Spanish lady—aye?"

"Aye, Alex. Ailis said that the woman often bemoaned it. According to Ailis, the old woman once said that the only good she could find in it was that it scared the blood right out of Colin."

Alexander gave a weak laugh. "Ailis once told me that her grandmother detested Colin from the moment she met him. It seems she was a woman with some degree of discernment."

"Alex, Sibeal isna a child to tell lies or wild tales wrought from imagination." Barra spoke quietly and kept his gaze fixed upon Alexander's drawn features. "In truth, 'tis often too easy to forget just how young Sibeal is."

"Ah, Barra, ye do ask a lot of me. Since Ailis and the

bairns arrived at Rathmor, I have accepted the children, have I not? I have overcome my dislike of their MacFarlane blood. By Mary's sweet tears, have I not seeded my own bairn in a MacFarlane womb, even handfasted myself to the wench? Must I now accept a niece who can see what will be, who dreams of what is to come? And if I do accept it, what can I do but sit here and wait for this"—he paused as he struggled for the right word—"prophecy to come about? There is naught I can do but wait, naught I can do to prove that the child's dream is any more than a vision inspired by her own hopes. And, let us be reasonable. Am I to believe that Ailis has eluded the grip of her uncle and her betrothed and all of their men?"

"If any lass could do such a thing, our Ailis could. And if not Ailis, dinna forget Jaime."

"Nay, I never forget that brute, but is Jaime still alive? Then, too, he is a touch on the simple side."

"True, although I dinna think he is quite as slow as most believe. And he uses every wee bit of what wit he has when it means aiding Ailis. He may need her brains or the aid of another to get a plan of escape formed or to get them out of Leargan or Craigandubh, but once shown the how of it, there will be no stopping that young giant, even if he dies in the doing of it."

"Ailis is far gone with our child. She could even be newly arisen from her childbed," Alexander snapped. " 'Tis an impossibility."

It was no secret to Barra that his brother was weighted down with the situation. Alexander's fears and pain were clear to hear in his voice. Barra sympathized. He was beset with worry for Ailis. He just wished he had some idea of how deep Alexander's feelings ran. Barra feared that Alexander himself had no clue as to the depth of his feelings. If Ailis was not carrying Alexander's child, there was every chance that he might not be so concerned. It made it difficult to know what to say or do.

Barra took a deep breath to prepare himself, then said, "Aye, it may well look impossible, and if your bairn still lives—whether within or without of her belly—'twould indeed be a very foolhardy thing for her to try and flee. However, neither of those things would stop that lass from trying if she got a chance, any chance at all."

Alexander briefly closed his eyes as he struggled to push from his mind all thoughts of the hazards of such a venture. "Aye, the fool."

"I willna argue that with ye, but 'tis the fate of that bairn she carries that will prompt how the lass acts. Whatever she may think of ye, that bairn is hers. Ye ken as well as I how Ailis will protect her own. Whatever trouble there is between ye and her, she still kens that her child will be safer in your hands. If there is even the scent of a threat to her bairn, that lass would walk barefoot through hell and beyond to save it."

"Sweet Jesu, she would, too." Alexander groaned, his fear for Ailis and their child a bitter taste in his mouth. "I can only pray that there is someone at hand to talk some sense into the foolish lass."

Malcolm glared at Ailis as he talked and paced the great hall. She calmly sat and waited for him to finish his scold so that she could get to bed. She knew she needed a lot of rest for the journey he was so arduously trying to talk her out of.

That his sane and unarguable remarks were being so totally if sweetly ignored put Malcolm into a sour temper. It was an emotional state not helped much by his very real fears for her. In her weakened condition, so newly arisen from her childbed, a hard journey such as she planned could easily kill her. She seemed to be stubbornly oblivious to the dangers she would be facing. Malcolm could not believe that she could be so blind or so stupid.

"Will ye heed me, woman?" he snapped. "This is sheer madness. If ye even reach Rathmor at all, 'twill be only to fall stone dead at the gate."

"Then Alexander can care for our son," Ailis replied. "Malcolm, give it up. Ye canna change my mind."

"I begin to question if ye even have a mind," he grumbled as he sat down at the head of the table. "Just abide here for a few days longer."

"Nay. That would be to sorely tempt fate. The bairn cries very little, but he *does* cry." She smiled faintly. "I would be sorely worried if he didna. Yet his crying may have already reached ears better left deaf to the sound. Donald or Duncan may come back at any moment. Can ye promise me that no one here will betray me?" She could see by the expression on his face that he could not. "Ye ken how close our escape was. Then, too, one must consider the season of the year. If I stay here much longer, I shall be caught in yet another tempest. Or, worse, I could be caught out when many a man is abroad. That is certainly a danger I wish to avoid."

The truth of her reasoning could not be argued with, either, but Malcolm sorely wished it could be. He saw her venture as nothing short of suicide, yet the danger in staying or in continuing to wait was also real. Even if he could find the words to deny that, Ailis had the sense to know that he was lying. In truth the girl was completely encircled, feeling a threat whichever way she turned. He inwardly grimaced, for he knew he was one of those threats, even if a more obtuse one. An innate sense of honor told him to void the promise he had extracted from her, but his body would not allow it.

Ailis watched Malcolm scowl in thought and contemplated the promise she had given him. It was a vow extracted under duress, so she could ignore it without any real loss of honor. She inwardly sighed, for she knew she would not take that route. A price had been asked in exchange for the lives of her and, most important, her child. Malcolm had fulfilled his part of the bargain. She and her son were alive and at no small risk to himself. Ailis knew she would honor the promise she had made. It was just very sad that the promise made to save her life was one that made it only a brief reprieve. Alexander was her life, and her promise to Malcolm was certain to drive Alexander away.

"Go to bed, then, Ailis," Malcolm said, his voice heavy with resignation. "Ye will need your rest for the ordeal ye face come the dawning."

"I thank ye, Malcolm, for all ye have done."

"Aye, ye will, will ye not?"

"Aye." There was an odd note to Malcolm's voice, but Ailis found it impossible to read. "Good sleep."

Malcolm watched her leave, then closed his eyes. "Ye are a bastard, Malcolm MacCordy, a right bastard." He gave a short harsh laugh weighted with self-disgust when even that admission did not spur him to call her back into the great hall and tell her that the promise was forgotten.


Giorsal was waiting in her bedchamber when Ailis finally reached it. The girl stopped rocking the baby's cradle and stood up. With the promise to Malcolm weighing so heavily on her mind, Ailis was loath to meet the girl's eyes. From the start it had been easy to see that Giorsal thought Malcolm was the beginning and end of her world. Ailis knew all too well how that felt. She also knew that the promise and its fulfillment would deeply hurt Giorsal. She sorely regretted that, for the girl had been kind.

" 'Twas a vow made under duress, under threat," Giorsal suddenly said. "Ye need not honor it. None would expect it of ye."

It did not really surprise Ailis that the infamous promise weighed so heavily on Giorsal's mind, too. "Nay, mayhaps not, although I am not so certain one can say 'none.'" She sighed as she lay down on her bed after a brief peek at her sleeping son. "I had hoped that ye had forgotten what was said that night."

"'Twas but two days ago. How could I forget such a thing no matter when it was said?"

"Aye—indeed—how could ye?" She looked at the girl with an unrestrained curiosity. "And why does this trouble ye so? 'Tis certain that Malcolm hasna played the monk since ye came here!"

"Nay—far from it. 'Tis different with ye, though. The others were naught but whores, no more important to him than his chamber pot."

"And I am? I canna see that." Ailis felt that the girl put too much importance on a matter of simple, fierce lust.

"Oh, aye, I ken that ye dinna notice. Ye dinna see what a man does. S'truth, even another woman can see it, for if her heart is involved, as mine is, she can see the dangers and temptations that confound the man she wants. The smallest threat to her heart's desire can usually be seen clearly by a woman in love. Trust me in this, Ailis, ye are no small threat."

"Ye exaggerate."

"Nay. This isna simply a lusting Malcolm suffers from. If it was, I wouldna care. Well, not much!" She sat down on the edge of the bed. "I just dinna ken exactly what he is feeling or thinking, for Malcolm keeps to himself a lot."

"Aye, I ken that sort very well," Ailis drawled, and her thoughts winged straight to Alexander. "However, I still think ye judge this matter wrongly."

"Nay, Ailis, I dinna. Malcolm has never before cared what

his cousins did. He ignored them, for to try and stop them could be to threaten his own holdings, meager as they are. Malcolm has never had very much in life, so he clings tightly to what little he does have now. He would never risk it all for a simple lusting. But by asking ye to share his bed for the night he has done just that for he kens well that his cousin will see it as a gross betrayal if it is discovered. Ye offer a man a fire, and my Malcolm craves a taste of it. He has hungered for it ever since he first set eyes upon ye. Ah, me, ye offer a man so much more than that, but I canna find the words to explain it all. I only ken that Malcolm seeks it. He only sought the easement of a man's aching with all the others. Malcolm dearly wants what ye give Alexander Mac-Dubh."

"He can never have that," Ailis said. "Nay, not even if Alexander throws it aside. Which he will do—quickly—when he learns that I have bedded down with Malcolm."

"Ye and I ken that a man canna grab what can only be freely given, but a man doesna always see it. If Malcolm senses it, he ignores it, calls it foolishness. 'Tisna what he wants to be the truth. Now, although I have never bedded down with him, I ken that Malcolm is a good lover. 'Tis the only reason ladies of a high rank would ever seek out a poor, landless knight, and they do seek him out." Giorsal grimaced. "'Tisna vanity that makes him think the skill that draws so many who would otherwise scorn him could also draw ye to him and away from Alexander MacDubh."

"The skill Malcolm possesses may rouse lust, but 'twill never touch more than that. Canna ye convince Malcolm of this? He has asked a price for my life that, when paid, will certainly kill me. I will lose Alexander and, no doubt, my child as well, for Alexander will surely hold on to his son even as he sets the adulterous mother aside. Because of this thrice-cursed promise, I havena really been spared, only given a wee reprieve."

"I will try, Ailis, but I canna promise anything. Such things are very hard for a man to understand, especially if he has never been in love. Malcolm scoffs at what the poets and ballad singers say as loudly as many another man. He may well scorn what I try to tell him about your feelings."

"Then 'tis as good as done. I am sorry, Giorsal. Very sorry."

"Nay, there is no need for ye to be asking my pardon. Ye were asked a price for your bairn's life, and ye must pay it. Ye dinna seek this, not as so many others did, nor do ye seek what Malcolm does. 'Tis up to Malcolm to put a stop to this, but I truly fear he willna. Nay, not even though a part of him sincerely wants to. He kens well that he asks ye to play the whore and that isna his way." Giorsal rose and moved to the door. "Still, I will try my utmost best to sway Malcolm—for both our sakes. Good sleep, Ailis, and good journey on the morrow."

"Good-bye, Giorsal," Ailis murmured, feeling a strong urge to weep for the girl. "Malcolm," she muttered when Giorsal was gone, "ye are the greatest of fools. If ye truly seek what Giorsal thinks ye do, then ye only need to look around. 'Tis right before your eyes."

Sleep was what Ailis needed, but she soon realized it was going to be elusive. Her mind was cluttered with thoughts of what the morrow could bring. Although she had stubbornly resisted all of Malcolm's urgings to stay, to wait, a large part of her had been strongly tempted to give in. She had to fight her own fears each time she thought of the journey ahead. To leave was to face several dangers, but to stay also held dangers. Ailis wondered when and how her life had managed to get so very complicated.

She slid her hand down to her stomach, which still ached. The womb which had produced her small son still cleaned itself out, still sought to recover from its ordeal of barely two days ago. A woman usually rested for nearly a fortnight, took it easy for a month after birth, yet she busily planned a walk of several days while her body still bled so heavily. She told herself of how a peasant woman, a poor crofter's wife, managed to rise easily from a childbed and work. It did a poor job of easing her fears. She had not been hardened by a life of constant toil such as a peasant woman endures.

There was also her newborn child to consider. He was a strong healthy baby, but she would be asking a great deal of someone only a few days out of the warm safety of his mother's womb. Babies died with an alarming regularity no matter how well favored the conditions. By taking her child on a journey of several days' length, subjecting him to the whims of nature in all its cruelty, she could well be signing his death warrant. She could well be striving to deliver Alexander his son only for the burying on MacDubh land, not for training on how to rule it.

It was hard, for her fears for her child ran deep, but Ailis forced that thought aside. To stay with Malcolm was to risk certain capture by Donald, who would do exactly as he had so often threatened—murder her child and send it to Alexander in pieces. The journey to Rathmor was indeed a risky one, but it was also her only real choice. It also had to be attempted now while the MacCordys searched elsewhere, sent on a false trail by Malcolm. If her son was fated to die, then die he would, but at least he would meet his fate fighting in his own tiny way, and not as some meek sacrifice to Donald MacCordy's mindless hatred.

A shiver tore through her as she suddenly wondered if Alexander was even at Rathmor to receive his son. Her last word of him had been Jaime saying that he had seen an arrow slam into Alexander's back. That wound, combined with the ones inflicted before his men had rescued him, could well have proved fatal. What the beating and arrow wound had begun, the hard ride could easily have finished. Fever and infection could have set in. The more Ailis considered the matter, the more certain Alexander's death appeared.

She violently shook her head. Alexander was too great a part of her. Somehow she would have known if he had died. A person could not remain ignorant when the light suddenly left their world. Ailis was confident that she would know if her love had ceased to be. All she felt was a deep need to return to Rathmor, to be back with Alexander and to present him with his son and heir. Even though she knew there was the chance that she was living on false hope, she preferred to believe that her urge to get back to Rathmor meant Alexander was still alive.

How Alexander would accept her child did not concern her at all. She knew he had grown to love Barra's children despite their MacFarlane blood. She had also sensed his eagerness for the child he had planted in her womb despite how he had reacted at first. He had proved how much he wanted their child when he had tried to rush her to a priest for a church-sanctioned union and then proclaimed a handfast marriage to her before her whole clan. Alexander still did not want a wife, as far as she could tell, yet he had taken one and one who was the niece of his father's killer, the thief of his lands. Nothing could have told her more clearly that he wanted the child.

When sleep finally claimed her, she suffered from nightmares born of her fears. It made her so restless that she greeted the dawn with something akin to relief. Now she could hold her fears at bay with the strength of her own will. She knew that fear had its advantages by making a person wisely cautious, but it could not be allowed to stop her from what she had to do.

She soon discovered that all her strength was needed simply to step out the door, for both Jaime and Malcolm renewed their arguments against their journey. Her own fear urged her to give in to their pleadings and arguments, but she held firm. Her son was held close to her body by a blanket sling and further protected by her cloak. The three of them were then efficiently smuggled out of Malcolm's tower house and beyond sight of his lax guards.

Left alone with Jaime and her baby, Ailis was briefly terrified. It was so far to Rathmor, and it would take so long on foot. Malcolm had been unable to lend them mounts, for they would have been missed. She took the first few steps with a great deal of hesitancy, but then her strength returned. As her pace became more firm and steady, she realized that whatever dangers were ahead, at the end of her journey lay safety for her child. It was enough to give her heart.

Alexander greeted the dawn with a heavy heart. He rose and answered the pull to go to the walls. Word had come at last concerning Ailis. She was not at Leargan but at Craigandubh, but where within that formidable keep was still a mystery. Although the man who had discovered that news felt certain Ailis was still alive, he had no firm word on her health or if she had borne his child yet.

He did not want to heed the message hidden in Sibeal's dream, yet found himself searching the horizon. The foul weather was showing signs of improvement. Soon an attack would be possible. Unfortunately, he was no longer sure of where to attack. Frustration made him clench his fists. Every plan of action that came to mind was merely an exercise in futility. He had to wait, and that had never been an easy thing for him to do. Patience had never been one of his strengths. When Ailis and their child were concerned, it was nearly impossible to find any such quality within himself. He literally ached to take some action and wanted to weep with the knowledge that there was none he could take.

His body was taut with the evidence of his feelings as he searched the surrounding countryside with his eyes and hissed, " 'Tis enough to drive a man to madness. I ken not where to look or who to go after. For the sake of God and my peace of mind, Ailis, will ye send me some word of ye?"

# 15

Ailis heartily wished there was some way to send word to Alexander. She sat down beneath a tree and struggled against falling asleep as her child nursed. Exhaustion had become a constant companion. Each time she stopped walking, she fell asleep. She knew that every step toward complete exhaustion brought her a step closer to what could prove to be a deadly illness, but she was too weary to even worry about that any longer. All she wanted was to reach a place where she could have a safe, dry bed.

Jaime gently removed the child from Ailis's arms and redid her gown, ignoring her sleepy protests. He set the baby at his shoulder and walked, murmuring soothing nonsense to the child as he made certain there was no air in the small belly to give the baby a pain and cause him to cry. Unlike his mother, the child appeared to thrive on the journey to his father's keep. The heir to Rathmor was already displaying his sire's strength. With each new sign of the child's continued good health, and strength, Jaime's concern eased.

It was Ailis who began to truly worry Jaime. They had come so far, but it had cost her dearly. She said nothing, but he was certain she had contracted a severe chill from either the mists that so often assailed them or the rainstorm they had gotten caught in last evening. Exhaustion had sapped all the color from her face, yet there was a flag of scarlet decorating each cheek. Every bit of strength she could muster went to the simple act of placing one foot before another and caring for her child. She had none left to fight a fever. Jaime feared that, in her badly weakened condition, an illness could easily mean her death.

Reluctantly he woke her. She desperately needed rest, but at the moment it was a luxury they could not afford. They had but a half day's walk ahead of them before they reached their long-sought destination. At Rathmor there would be warmth, a bed, food, and people ready and able to care for Ailis. Jaime was sure that moving on was the wisest thing to do. Ailis had also given him strict orders when they had begun their journey—he was not to hesitate for her sake, for reaching Rathmor had to be all that mattered.

"Oh, the bairn is done," Ailis mumbled as she struggled to stand.

"Aye, mistress. We must be walking on. 'Tisna too much farther. We should be at the gate of Rathmor by nightfall. Nay," he said when she reached for her child. "I will carry the bairn."

She gave him no argument. Even her child's slight weight had become too much for her to bear. It was all she could do to stay erect. Her greatest fear was that fever now lurked in her blood. Her limbs felt heavy, and it was increasingly difficult for her to think clearly. Ailis tried not to let Jaime see how poorly she was faring, but she knew she was failing miserably by the way he kept frowning at her. All she could do was pray that he did not stop, that he would obey her orders to get her child to Rathmor no matter what.

As they had slipped across MacCrady lands, they had had to hide from Donald's men several times. They were at least safe from that danger now. She was not sure they could completely trust any MacDubh they met, however. Someone had betrayed Rathmor. Someone had told Don-

ald where to find her and Alexander that day. She could
not be certain that traitor had been captured. Jaime clearly
shared her fear, for he kept them away from any signs of
habitation, traveling close to the trees and keeping near to
all possible hiding places. In fact, he was revealing a real
skill at stealth, one surprising in such a big man.

Although Alexander was constantly on her mind, he was
even more so as they drew nearer to Rathmor. She would
finally see his beautiful face again, see that he had recovered from his wound, and finally put her fears for him to
rest. So, too, would he protect their child. Donald's chilling threat had lain heavily on her mind for what felt like a
lifetime. That burden would soon be eased, for it would be
shared. She would be able to rest for the first time in far
too long. She clung to that thought as she struggled along.


As Alexander walked to the parapets of Rathmor, he
heartily wished for a chance to rest easy with no fears or
the nightmares inspired by them. Reports of the Mac-
Cordys and the MacFarlanes riding over the countryside
searching for Ailis told him that she had somehow escaped
her enemies, yet there was no word on her. That she was
no longer in the hands of enemies should have been good
news except that he had no idea whose hands, if anyone's,
she was in. Again and again he tried to think of where she
could be, and again and again he came up with a thousand
different possibilities.

On thing he knew for certain was that he sorely missed
her. He sighed as he leaned against the wall and stared out
toward MacCordy lands. His bed had never seemed so
empty, yet he felt no urge to fill the space she had left. The
hunger he felt had but one source and but one remedy. He
even missed the way she would argue with him. It contin-
ually surprised him to discover just how fully she had

become a part of his life. He was not at all sure that he liked it. It was exactly what he had tried to prevent, to shield himself from.

He had sent out some patrols, claiming that it was to scout for MacFarlanes or MacCordys. That the men probably suspected his true motives did not bother him. A few scouting forays was a small thing, but at least it was some sort of action taken. If by some miracle Ailis was making her way toward Rathmor, his men would find her. He just prayed that she would not try to avoid them because she feared a traitor. That was a possibility, for she could have no way of knowing that the man had been caught.

"'Tis hard not kenning."

Alexander grimaced as Barra stepped up next to him. "I think even word that she had died would be some relief at this point."

Barra nodded and briefly clasped Alexander's shoulder in a gesture of silent sympathy. "I just canna make myself believe that she is dead."

"Nay, nor can I, although how she could disappear for a week, or more, whilst three clans search for her . . . 'Tis as if she has become the mist—out there, yet not out there." He shook his head. "Heed that. I grow fanciful."

"She is but one person, mayhaps two, if Jaime is still alive. Then, too, 'tis nothing less than their lives that is at stake."

"Aye, true enough. That can serve to make the dullest become crafty, and Ailis isna dull of mind." For one moment he wished that that was not true, for if she were not so clever, she would have stayed where she was, and then he might have had a chance to rescue her.

"And when 'tis his mistress he must protect, Jaime can be very sharp as well. Such a thing brings out the best in that soft-hearted giant. And I hope he does still live, if only for our poor Kate's sake." Barra shook his head. "I hadna noticed how much her cheerful nature mattered about here until she grew so dowie, so solemn and forlorn."

"Well, I hope the man is with Ailis, for she is either near her birthing time or just risen from a childbed. She will be in sore need of his brawn."

Ailis realized that she could no longer fight her weakness or hide it from Jaime. Twice she had stumbled, but, blaming some obstacle, she had regained her feet and plodded on. The third time she could not even do that. She sat where she had fallen and fought the urge to burst into tears. It seemed to her to be the cruelest blow to lose the last of her strength when her final goal was so near at hand.

"Ah, Jaime, I am so close, but I canna take another step." She shook her head. "Ye had best go on without me, Jaime. Take the bairn on to Rathmor and safety."

"Dinna talk such foolishness! I willna be leaving ye." He picked her up from where she sat in the road and carried her to the shelter of some trees.

"I could order ye to do as I say," she said as he sat her down and crouched in front of her.

"Aye, that ye could, but I wouldna heed ye, so dinna waste what little breath ye have left. A bairn needs its mother."

"There will be women enough to hold him. He will be needing a wet nurse anyhow; she could take my place."

"A man needs his wife," Jaime continued in a dogged tone as he tried to rouse her flagging spirits.

"Alexander MacDubh needs no one. He but smiles and a dozen lasses flock to his side. He will miss me little," she said, her despondency causing her voice to tremble. "Och, Jaime, 'tis no use. I can barely lift a finger, let alone walk. My body has said ''tis done.' 'Twas only the thought of how close I was to Rathmor that had kept me going all day."

"I kenned that, lassie. Ye were too soon off your childbed. Ye have a fever, if I judge it aright." He felt her forehead and cheeks, frowning deeply over the heat he discovered there.

"Aye, and that fever is what weighs me down. I canna think clearly. Go on ahead, Jaime. Ye could come back for me."

"I willna leave ye. Nay, and not when we are so very close. And there is rain scenting the air. I will carry ye."

"Nay, that will slow ye down."

Jaime was prepared for argument or, if that failed, to make use of his greater strength, but his attention was suddenly diverted from Ailis. He heard the sound of horses being ridden leisurely down the road toward them. He quickly pushed Ailis down onto the ground and tucked the baby into her arms. With a quiet he had perfected over the last few days, he crept toward the roadside. Even though they were very close to Rathmor, he did not dare to assume that the people approaching would be friends. He crouched behind a small knot of bushes and strained to get a good look at the small band of men despite the diminishing light of an early evening. When Jaime recognized the leader, he was swept with relief.

"I am nay too fond of going back to the laird without any word—again," grumbled one man.

"Aye." Angus sighed and shook his head. "The laird doesna much like not kenning. He needs to act, yet he canna do naught. God's beard, where can that lassie have gotten to?"

"Over here, Angus," called Jaime as he slowly stepped forward, out of his hiding place.

"Jaime?" croaked Angus as the group reined in and stared at him. " 'Tis truly ye?"

"None other. Have your eyes gone bad?"

"My eyes are fine," Angus snapped as he dismounted hastily along with the others in the scouting party. "We have been searching high and low for ye and the lass for over a week. I didna expect ye to stroll up and hail me as if naught is amiss."

"I am a bit surprised to see ye, too, as I would have thought that ye would stay closer to Rathmor with so many MacCordys and MacFarlanes wandering the lands hereabouts."

"Those fools stumble over each other so much they dinna see anyone else. Now, where is the lass?"

"She is over here, Angus."

With his eldest son in tow, Angus followed Jaime to where he had left Ailis, and he cursed when he first set eyes upon her. "Och, lassie, have ye gone mad?"

"Such a fine greeting," Ailis murmured and smiled weakly at the men who knelt by her side. "Look here, Angus—a son." She tugged the blanket open enough for Angus to see the child.

"Sweet Lord, save us! When did he arrive?" Angus stared at the baby in openmouthed surprise.

"About a week past. Nay, a fortnight, I think." She struggled to sit up, but Angus had to give her a helping hand. "He decided he couldna wait any longer, not even for me to get him home to Rathmor."

"Ye are completely mad, lassie! Ye should be abed, not traipsing about the countryside. Do ye think ye are some strapping peasant slut? Sweet Mary, ye look poorly and sorely worn down."

"Always quick with a ready compliment. Ah, but I am sorely tired, Angus. Is Alexander all right?" she asked in a soft, hesitant voice and tensed for the answer.

"Aye, he has healed well. I think his wounds must have appeared worse to ye than they were, although 'twas no light cut he suffered from, true enough. He is sore hot to take a sword to someone, but with ye disappearing as ye did, it left us with none to take up a sword against."

"That must dearly try his patience," she drawled and, despite how bad she felt, she was able to smile faintly.

"Oh, that it does, m'lady. That it does. Here, Jaime, ye take the bairn, and I will take this fool lass," Angus said and then ordered his son, "Ye will ride with Lachlan, Rory."

"I almost made it, Angus," Ailis said as the burly man lifted her up into his arms. "I came so close, but I just couldna take another step."

"Aye, ye did almost make it, and ye almost killed yourself, too. I think ye may have caught a touch of the fever, by the looks of ye."

"'Twill pass," she murmured as they mounted, and she snuggled against his chest, suddenly feeling chilled to the bone and craving his warmth.

Angus wished he felt as confident as she sounded. He did not like her looks, which told him that the fever settling on a woman after a birth had accounted for far too many women's lives. He pushed his and his men's horses as hard as he dared, considering that they had already been ridden all day. It grieved him to think that Ailis may have struggled so hard to reach Rathmor only to die. He dared not even think of how such a tragedy would affect Alexander.


Chaos erupted when Angus's scouting party returned. Alexander hurried into the bailey to see what had caused the uproar. As he stepped out of the keep with Barra at his heels, everyone grew silent, and Alexander felt himself tense. Alexander's eyes widened at the sight of Jaime dismounting to be heartily embraced by Kate. Then his gaze flew to Angus. It was easy to recognize the midnight-black hair that tumbled free of the blanket which shrouded the form in Angus's arms. Alexander raced to Angus's side, then hesitated. He felt his heart skip to a stop when he saw how still Ailis was. It took him a moment to find the ability to speak, for fear choked off his voice.

"Ailis?" His voice was little more than a croak as Angus gently placed her in his arms.

Ailis stirred at the sound of her name spoken in Alexander's enticing voice, and she looked up at him. "I have brought ye your son, Alexander MacDubh."

"Sweet heavens," whispered Barra.

Jaime stepped over to him and Alexander, the baby in his arms, and the small face was revealed to anyone close enough to look.

Ailis slipped her arms about Alexander's neck and tucked her face up against his throat. "Ye must name him, Alexander, and ye must have him christened," she said, her voice hoarsened by her illness, and she felt him tense. "I am sorry. I didna have a chance to do it. I had to stay in hiding."

The heat of her small face as she pressed it against his skin caused Alexander to tense with a deep fear for her. He did not need an extensive knowledge of illness to guess that she had contracted a fever. Alexander looked at Jaime. The expression upon that man's face gave Alexander little hope that what he felt could be disputed, that perhaps Ailis was simply very tired and not ill at all.

"She is afire. How has she come to this state?" he demanded of Jaime as he lightly tightened his hold on Ailis.

"The lass spent barely two days in her childbed before she began her journey to here. We have walked the whole way, save for the last few miles."

"All the way from where? No one has been able to find either of ye for nearly a fortnight."

"First we fled Craigandubh. Then we had to hide at Sir

Malcolm MacCordy's tower house whilst Mistress Ailis had
the bairn. What with hiding from the ones who hunted us, a
rainstorm, a constant mist, and choosing a long, twisted
route so as to stay hidden, we have been trying to get to
Rathmor for well over a week. She wasna ready for such an
ordeal. She wasna strong enough." Jaime shook his head, his
expression mournful.

Her mind increasingly clouded with fever, Ailis was
sure she heard some criticism in what Jaime and Alexander were saying. "They were going to kill him, Alexander.
They were going to cut him up and send him to ye in
pieces."

Again Alexander looked to Jaime for an explanation.
"Donald MacCordy"—Jaime snarled the name—"that
swine was ever telling her what he planned for the bairn
after he was born. He told her that he would send ye your
child in pieces, very wee pieces. 'Tis that which has driven
her so."

"Ye can talk about all of this later," Kate commanded in
a brisk voice. "This lass must be put to bed and tended to."

"The bairn will be needing a wet nurse," Ailis said as
Alexander began to move more quickly, hurrying toward
their bedchamber.

"We will find him one," Alexander assured her. "Dinna
fash yourself, sweeting. He will be well cared for."

"And a name, a name and a christening?" she pressed.
"He must be christened. This journey could have been death
for him, and he would have gone to his grave unshriven. I
canna bear the thought of it."

"Aye, he will be christened. A priest is due here on the
morrow. He will christen the laddie as soon as he arrives.
I will see it done ere the man can remove his cloak. Aye,
and then I will hold the man here until ye are well, and
we will have that church-sanctioned marriage we sought
months ago."

He stayed with Ailis as she was changed, washed, and dressed in a warm nightrail. It eased his worries a little to hear the women tending to her report that she was bleeding no more than would be expected, that they could find no signs that she had done herself any harm in that way. A heavy loss of blood added to the fever she suffered from would have surely meant her death. Ailis was then given a gentle draft, and he sat by her side, holding her hand as he waited for her to fall asleep.

"Ye must keep Jaime here," Ailis pleaded. "Donald wants him dead, and he willna kill him cleanly. He warned us over and over and over again that one more attempt by Jaime to aid me would end in Jaime's death."

"Jaime has a home here for as long as he wants one." He lightly kissed her forehead. "Now, hush, sweeting, and go to sleep. Ye need your rest."

"Just one more thing," she whispered, her voice soft and slowed by encroaching sleep. "If I am still ailing when the bairn is to be christened, I want Jaime named as a godfather. He deserves the honor, for he brought our bairn into the world. Will ye do that for me? I ken he is poor, but his character is a rich one."

"Aye, love, I will do it. I canna think of anyone more deserving. Ye dinna need to tell me that he had a great deal to do with ye and our bairn reaching Rathmor alive."

"A traitor . . ." she struggled to say.

"I found him."

"Good." For once she was not concerned about the punishment the man had received, even though she was certain that Alexander would have killed him, as would have any man.

When Ailis finally went to sleep, Alexander left Kate to watch over her while he sought out Jaime. He found the man in the great hall changing the baby's linen on a rug before the fire. Alexander crouched by his son and carefully studied the child's sturdy little body with utter fascination. Despite seeing the child with his own eyes, Alexander still found it difficult to believe that he was a father again.

"He has all he should have," Jaime said as he cleaned the child off. "Aye, and 'tis all in its proper place. He is healthy and strong. 'Tis hard to believe, but he seems to suffer no ills at all from the journey here."

When the baby clutched Alexander's finger in a surprisingly strong grip, Alexander felt himself swell with emotion. That amazement he had felt at first still lingered in his heart. He could not believe that he had had a part in creating such perfection. He found himself thanking God that the strength of his passion for Ailis had prevented him from exercising his usual caution and keeping him from fulfilling his heartbroken vow to remain forever childless.

"I am hardly a blameless man," he murmured, "but I canna understand, have never been able to understand, how any man or woman could harm a child." He thought of his poor Elizbet and wondered if he was being given another chance.

"Donald MacCordy could do it. Ailis wasna foolish for worrying. That man will kill anything when he has a sword in his hand. I have seen him. With this wee bairn he was striking close to ye. Aye, and he would have been hurting Ailis, who continued to refuse to have anything to do with him. He is badly eaten up with hate for ye, of any and all MacDubhs. Ye have made him look the fool. Twice MacDubhs have taken women promised to him. Aye and filled the bellies of each of those women with MacDubh bairns."

"I will take his accursed life yet. Tell me all that happened." Alexander picked up his son and led Jaime to the head table. Once seated, Jaime told Alexander the details of their imprisonment and escape. When Jaime was done, Alexander said nothing for a long while, then shook his head. "So, it appears I owe Sir Malcolm MacCordy two lives. I swear that he willna die by my sword."

Not yet, Jaime mused silently.

"And I shall do my best to see that he isna cut down by my people. Although I still consider the MacCordys my enemies, I can no longer count Sir Malcolm as a part of that feud. By his act of saving the lives of Ailis and my son, Malcolm has washed my father's blood from his hands." He scowled as jealousy briefly leapt to the fore of his emotions. "I am very glad that Ailis was heavily swollen with our child, then newly upon her childbed, or no doubt Malcolm would have demanded some payment from her for his efforts on her behalf."

Jaime was startled by his own capability for duplicity. Deceit had never been his way, nor had he thought he had the wit for it. He merely nodded as Alexander talked, giving no hint of any deals or promises made. He still hoped to put a stop to it, but if he could not, he would do nothing to mar what little time Ailis had left with Alexander.

When Angus arrived with a wet nurse, Alexander finally relinquished the care of his son. He made his way to his bedchamber to take Kate's place at Ailis's side. Instinct told him there would be a few rough days ahead, but he was not pleased when his instincts proved correct.

Ailis often cried out for him when delirium seized her, and he was needed to calm her. She was clearly tormented by visions of his death prompted by her last word of him as having an arrow in him. Due to her fever, she had little memory of returning to Rathmor, and Alexander was often hard-pressed to convince her that he was all right. He almost felt guilty when she revealed such signs of how she cared for him, and they touched him deeply despite his efforts to fight their allure.

The hardest thing he battled was her continued fears for

their son. In her fevered mind she would see Donald Mac-
Cordy carry out his vicious threats. Alexander found her
visions unsettling and worked unceasingly to put a halt to
them.

There really was little to be done. Ailis was kept warm
and clean, forcefully fed a hearty broth whenever possible,
and kept calm and resting as much as could be. Alexander had never felt so utterly helpless. He could do little
more than watch as she fought with an enemy that had no
fear of him or his sword.

The day after Ailis and Alexander's son arrived at Rathmor, he was christened Moragh Tamnais MacDubh. He was
loudly proclaimed heir to the Laird of Rathmor, but any celebration over that long-awaited event was delayed until Ailis
was well again. Alexander kept his promise to Ailis and held
the priest at Rathmor, all the while praying that it would be
to perform a wedding and not a funeral. The sympathy and
prayer he got from others revealed that Ailis had gained a
goodly amount of loyalty from his clan despite her MacFarlane blood. It surprised Alexander a little, but he was glad of
it. It would assuredly make her life a great deal easier as a
MacDubh.

Alexander was alone with Ailis when, after nearly a
week, her fever finally broke, and he was fervently glad of
it, for he discovered tears on his cheeks. For once he made
no excuses to himself for the show of emotion. When he
felt suitably under control, he dragged Kate from her bed
so that she could help him tend to Ailis. As soon as that
task was completed and Kate was gone, he shed his clothes
and joined Ailis in bed. For the first time in far too long he
fell asleep—quickly and deeply.


Ailis slowly opened her eyes. She looked around her in
confusion. When she caught sight of the golden-crowned

head next to hers and looked down at the elegant hand gently cupping her breast, she smiled as her memory came rushing back. Her dangerous trek had been successful.

"Ailis?"

She turned her head and smiled into Alexander's clearing eyes. "I made it."

"Aye—barely." He could not bring himself to be angry or to lecture about the risks she had taken, for he fully understood what had driven her to it.

"Well, aye, I did grow a bit ill."

"Oh, aye—a bit."

"Our bairn!" she cried and clutched him by the arm as some of her fears returned.

"Hale and hearty and properly christened."

"What did ye name him?"

"Moragh Tamnais MacDubh."

"A good strong name. What do ye think of your son?" she asked with a hint of shyness, for although she had no doubt about his wanting the child, she still felt a deep need to hear him actually say so.

He answered her with a kiss so full of tenderness it left Ailis speechless with some hope for the future. It seemed to her to be impossible for a man to kiss a woman so if he felt absolutely nothing for her. Although she scolded herself for succumbing to the allure of such speculation, she was unable to stop herself.

"There isna a fairer lad in all of Scotland," he said.

"He has your eyes," she said in a voice still husky from his kiss.

"Aye, and my temperament."

"The poor wet nurse," she murmured, her eyes bright with laughter. "The woman will never survive until he is weaned."

"Witch." He gave her a brief hard kiss. "How do ye feel?"

"Ravenous."

"Aye." He brushed his thumb over the tip of her breast until it grew taut. "I ken that feeling." He quickly left the bed, for he knew that he would try to make love to her if he did not, and he knew she was not ready for that.

"Where are ye going?" she asked as she watched him dress, keenly feeling his loss at her side.

"Away from temptation. I am also off to fetch a meal and the priest."

"Alexander, I am not dying. I am getting better." She watched as he strode to the door. "I need no priest."

"Ye do if ye are to be wed, lass."

"I am still abed," she squeaked in protest even as her heart skipped from a burst of eagerness. "Canna it wait?"

"I said we would be wed by the church as soon as I could set hands upon a priest. I have one, so we will be wed. There will be no chance left for anyone to try and deny our son his birthrights. I will send Kate to ye."

His high-handedness irritated her, but she did not argue. She wanted this union sanctioned by the church. Foolish or not, it would make her feel more secure. Alexander was a man who respected vows, and honored them, and those spoken before a priest were far more binding than the implied ones of handfast. She firmly pushed aside the memory of a promise and Malcolm MacCordy.

The priest was young and nervous, clearly perturbed by the irregularity of the wedding, but he performed it. Ailis suspected that he was more concerned about angering or offending Alexander. There was also the hint that the priest felt it was far past time to sanction the union.

When it was all over, Alexander firmly, and quickly, cleared the room. Ailis could no longer hide how weary she felt. The combination of her first meal in days plus being married had sapped what strength she had. She clasped her new husband's hand in hers when he sat down on the bed. It was frustrating to think that there would be no wedding night for a while.

"Ye are stuck with me now, Alexander MacDubh," she murmured as she closed her eyes.

"Aye." He pressed a kiss into her palm, still holding her hand even though she was asleep.

He studied her sleeping face. She was his now. The sense of calm that gave him surprised him only a little. He was growing accustomed to uncharacteristic emotions where she was concerned. Handfast had served its purpose, but now she was his in the eyes of God and the church. It would take both those powers to protect any man who tried to take her from him.

# 16

For two long weeks Ailis had been kept in bed. For two more even longer weeks she had been forced to play the semiinvalid. She was heartily sick of all the pampering that had been heaped upon her. All around her spun the rumors of the MacCordys and the MacFarlanes preparing an attack, but she was protected from all of that. She knew that she had to take it easy, but her well-intentioned multitude of nursemaids carried matters much too far. It seemed to her that she was more well rested, more well fed, and far more healthy than she had ever been in her entire life. In the last two weeks she had begun to wean them all of their protective roles. Now she planned to end Alexander's excessive gentleness with her and—specifically—his continued, self-imposed abstinence.

"Ye dinna need to build that fire up any more, Kate. 'Tis summer or did ye forget that? Sweet heavens, I will soon be seared on this side," Ailis grumbled as she got into her tub.

" 'Tis to keep away a chill." Kate stubbornly put another log on the already-roaring fire.

"The only reason I contracted a chill was that I had to push myself so hard so soon after bearing Moragh."

"Well, a body canna be too careful."

"That proverb has recently been proved a great fallacy,"

Ailis snapped. "This particular body has been 'carefuled' to death."

"Why must ye bathe? Ye had a bath but two nights past."

"How old is Moragh, Kate?" she asked.

Kate stared at Ailis in slight confusion. "Two months."

"Exactly." Ailis sent Kate a look she was sure a blind man could read and understand.

"Oh, I see." Kate blushed furiously, but then brightened. "I have just what ye need." She hurried out of the room.

After wrapping herself in a warm drying cloth, Ailis sat before the fire to let the heat dry her hair. She was busily plotting the best way to convince Alexander that she was not only able but quite willing to resume their lovemaking when Kate returned. Ailis took one look at the light, sultry linen and lace nightrail Kate held up and clapped her hands in delight. It was one of those pieces of soft flirtation every woman craved and most men found very alluring.

"Are ye sure ye are ready?" Kate asked as Ailis slipped on the thin nightrail.

"I willna embarrass ye by answering that," Ailis drawled, but grinned when Kate giggled. "This ought to change his lairdship's ways. Or, should I say, bring them back. I had never suspected that Alexander was hoping to be declared a saint. I hope he willna find the failure to obtain that lofty goal too painful to bear."

Alexander felt near to breaking under the strain of his self-imposed celibacy. The last few days had been the worst. He had barely seen Ailis at all. To be close to her yet to be unable to touch her was more than he could bear.

After his bath he sprawled on his bed with a tankard of wine in his hand and wearing only a drying cloth wrapped loosely around his hips. He had hoped that feeling chill would keep away the fever for Ailis which consistently burned inside of him, but he could sense that it was not really working. The rich wine helped a little if only because it finished what hard work had begun and eventually sent him to sleep despite his aching need for Ailis.

A sound at the door that connected his bedchamber to the room Ailis now used drew him from his sullen slumber. He stared with widening eyes and slowly sat up as Ailis entered his bedchamber. She wore a white nightrail of the finest sheer linen trimmed with delicate falls of lace and pale blue ribbons. The gown heightened the soft golden hue of her skin and the deep blue-black color of her hair. Desire gripped him so fiercely he was unable to move.

"Do ye want something, Ailis?" he asked in a weak, hoarse voice as he struggled to lift his gaze from her well-displayed breasts to her face.

Ailis smiled as she walked over to his bed and sat down. "I see ye so little during the day that I thought we could sit and talk now."

"Talk? What do ye wish to talk about?" He wondered frantically how a woman could look so seductive yet so innocent at the same time.

"I dinna ken. There must be matters of some sort that a husband speaks of with his wife."

"Aye. Must be."

No matter how hard he tried to think of some subject to discuss, Alexander found that he could only think of one thing—hurling Ailis down onto his bed. Her scent engulfed him. He was painfully aware of her slender thigh brushing up against his leg. A badly stifled groan escaped him as he lay down and closed his eyes.

"I would dearly like to talk with ye, lass, but I am far too weary this night," he mumbled. "Ye had best go back to your own bed. We can try this at some other time, loving."

Ailis slowly stood up, her hands set squarely on her hips. The little he wore was not enough to completely disguise his arousal, yet he was sending her away without even offering her a kiss. She wondered crossly just how long he felt she needed to heal from the birth and her fever. It also hurt that he did not seem to be as eager as she was to share some time together before the fighting began. She decided she would not wait for him to do something; she would act. Carefully she slipped out of her nightrail, laying it neatly over a stool near the bed. With far less care than speed she reached out and yanked off Alexander's brief covering.

Alexander cried out in surprise, his eyes opening wide as he sat up. "What are ye about, ye mad lass? Jesu!" His words choked to a halt as he greedily looked her over, her inviting nakedness barely shielded from him by her thick hair.

"I said I was wanting to have a wee talk," Ailis said.

"Talk?"

"Ye squeaked." Ailis could not stop herself from giggling over hearing such a sound escape such a strong, beautiful man.

"I didna squeak," he grumbled, then tried to speak with some air of command. "Put your clothes back on."

"Nay." With far more speed than grace she climbed into bed beside him.

"Ailis!" Alexander finally realized that Ailis was not really after some conversation, and he was a little surprised at how much passion had dulled his wits.

The sight of Alexander's long lean body taut and beautiful in arousal had Ailis aching for him. She grabbed him by the shoulders and pushed him back down onto the bed, then sprawled on top of him. Ailis knew his confusion was what made her aggressiveness such a success, but it was still exciting. She cupped his face in her hands and brushed her mouth over his.

"Ye have been very ill," he protested in a hoarse voice. "Ye have just borne a child."

"That child is two months old."

"The fever only left ye recently." He wondered why he was arguing so strongly for abstinence.

"Recently? 'Twas over a month ago. I am hale and hearty. Prepare yourself, Alexander MacDubh," she said in a voice that was rapidly growing thicker as she rubbed her body over his.

"Prepare? For what?" he asked in some confusion as, just as he finally reached for her, she pinned his wrists over his head with one small hand. He could easily break the hold, but he made no effort to do so, patiently awaiting her reply and very curious as to what she intended to do to him.

Ailis's voice held a seductive mixture of passion and laughter. "Because ye are about to become the first man in all of Scotland to be forcibly taken by a desperate woman."

The laughter that her playful remark stirred inside of him faded along with hers as Ailis eased their bodies together. Her aggressive game and his stubborn opinion that abstinence should be maintained a while longer shattered together. He was not sure who grasped the lead in the resultant fierce lovemaking, shifting as it did from one to the other until ecstasy's release gripped them both, and he did not care. He held on tight and let the pleasure they shared sweep over him. It was a long time after their shared release that he was able to move or to think very clearly.

"I do feel a bit ravished," he murmured when they finally stirred enough so that he could pull the sheet over their sated bodies.

"Only a bit?" Ailis snuggled closer to Alexander, rubbing her cheek against the hard warmth of his chest.

"Aye. Ye will have to try much harder next time," he drawled, laughter invading his voice.

"Well, I fear there is a price for such ravishment, and 'tis one ye may not be wishing to pay."

"Oh? And what is that price?" He slowly combed his fingers through her unbound hair, savoring its thick silkiness.

"Three or more months without me in your bed."

"It takes that long for ye to feel the hunger?"

"Nay. It takes that long for me to become so deranged with it that I grow this bold." She laughed with him.

"I was becoming a bit deranged myself," he murmured.

"To speak truly, I did think that ye were acting a wee bit strange . . ."

"Did ye, now."

"Aye, I did. I canna think that ye have often told a naked woman to put her clothes back on."

When Alexander finished chuckling, he turned so that he and Ailis were on their sides face to face. "Not that I can recall. I have certainly not thought on telling ye that since the very first time I set eyes on ye. Ebony and gold," he murmured. "Soft night and warm sunrise."

"Ye make the curse of my looks sound like a blessing." Ailis flushed slightly with pleasure over his soft flattery.

"Sweet wee Ailis, your looks arena a curse. Ye have paid far too much heed to the talk of fools. I wouldna put my name on a whore. Nay, nor an ugly woman if I could avoid it. " 'Tisna ugliness that continues to set my blood afire each time I look at ye." He gently kissed her. "Spanish women can be most alluring," he said, smiling faintly as he saw the breathlessness his kiss had left her with. "Aye, and Scottish lasses can be very fair. Ye have the best of both breeds. How ye do blush when ye are flattered, lass." He caressed the high color in her cheeks with his fingertips.

"I am unused to it, 'tis all."

"Aye, I canna see ye hearing many kind words from the MacFarlanes or the MacCordys. 'Tis to my shame that I havena given ye much of pretty words and compliments. I used to be very skilled at such things." He lightly brushed a few stray wisps of hair from her face.

"I dinna need pretty words," she mumbled.

"What do ye need, sweeting?"

She avoided meeting his gaze, afraid to meet his rich blue eyes directly because of what he might be able to read in her eyes. His question was a difficult one for her to answer. Although he had married her and set aside his vengeance, at least as it concerned her, he had given her no real clue as to his feelings. Pride demanded that she keep her love for him a secret until she could be certain that it would be returned. If she was not very careful in replying to his question, however, that secret would be revealed. Although there were hundreds of times when she ached to speak her heart to him, it was a weakness she knew she would not give in to. Aside from her pride, she feared the hurt she would suffer when Alexander offered no similar declarations.

Alexander sensed Ailis's reluctance to respond, and he frowned. He grasped her by the chin and gently forced her to face him. It was hard to read much more than wariness in her eyes, but that was enough to pinch at him. He knew he deserved it just as he knew that he was not fully sure of her yet. All thought of making her a part of his vengeance had left him, and although he knew he had done little to assure her of that, he knew that she knew it. Nevertheless, they remained wary of each other. He was suddenly weary of it all. Only when they were caught up in the full glory of their passion was there nothing between them, and that was simply not good enough any longer.

"Come, loving, from the first time she is born, a lass kens her destiny is to be wed, and she begins to make plans. Didna ye ever make any plans or nurture any hopes?" he asked.

"Well, there was one—I hoped that whoever took me as his wife would also take in Mairi's children and love them. Although what happened wasna at all as I had expected, I have gained what I have wished for."

"I canna believe that it is all ye thought on."

"Nay." Ailis tried to think of some way to phrase her hopes without declaring herself or appearing to demand some response in kind from him. "I did wish for a man who wouldna be too old nor too ugly. I also wished for a man who wouldna beat me nor shame me by bedding nearly everything in petticoats. 'Tis no more than most lasses wish for, I suspect. 'Twas as I grew older that I began to wish for something a wee bit different."

"Oh aye, and what was that?"

"That I would be wed to one who wouldna try to force me to be some meek and mindless wench who must bow to his every whim and willna argue, will agree with his every utterance. I had wished hard for a man who wouldna find what I am naught but a source of fury and shame. I wanted a man who might see me as more than someone to breed his heirs, and more than someone to keep his household in order." She gave him a crooked smile. "I was just never sure of quite what that more was."

Although he sensed that she held something back, Alexander decided not to press her on the matter. "Well, now I think I can, and have, filled every one of those wishes. I willna surround ye with squawling bastards. Whilst I would never swear that I would never succumb to a weakness of the flesh, I willna seek lovers and lemans. I willna treat the vows we took as if they are naught but words tossed to the wind." He touched a gentle kiss to her mouth. "Ah, lass, ye warm a bed well enough for any man."

"Even for one rumored to have bedded half the women in Scotland?"

"Aye, even for him, though I never met the greedy fool myself." He smiled when she giggled, but then grew serious again, lightly tracing the shape of her face with his fingertips as he spoke. "Nor do I want a meek wife, for all I may bellow and order ye to recall your place. 'Twould drive me to a fury to spend year after long year with a lass who did naught but smile and agree. Nay, a wife with some strength and wit can only be good for a man. What soured that in my stepmother, my wives, and Barra's wife, Agnes, was that they also held greed and guile. Ye dinna taint the good with the ill, lass. I hold no fear that ye will plot behind my back if ye disagree with what I say or do."

She heard that fleeting expression of trust and felt elated but said nothing. Instinct told her that, if she made a great ado about it, she would halt what was a revealing conversation because Alexander could suddenly realize how open he was being. He had said it, confessed his trust, and she decided that was good enough.

"Is that what Agnes and the others did, Alexander—plot and betray ye?" she asked, hoping that she would finally hear the whole story, would finally discover why he had soured toward women.

"Aye." Alexander sighed and his face hardened as he remembered the wrongs done to him and Barra. "They held no guilt about using treachery or betrayal to gain what they craved. Power and coin were their only goals, their only loves. Their games and plots brought naught but misery to Rathmor. Aye, and a death or two. The lies my stepmother told and the promises she made as she tried to grasp all the power she could gained us more enemies than allies. 'Twas

one of her twisted plots that led my father to your uncle and
his death."

Ailis wished she had not asked about the women. The
very last thing she wanted was to remind Alexander of the
anger and hatred he had for her uncle and the MacCordys.
She had already taken a chance by reminding him of the
grievance he had against women. Although he could see her
as being unlike those other women, there was no way for
him to see her as not akin to a MacFarlane. She cautiously
met his glance and breathed a silent, hearty sigh of relief
when she saw none of that fury directed toward her. It was
there, simmering behind his fine, desire-softened blue eyes,
but it was not directed at her. Finally he saw her simply as
Ailis, not simply as a MacFarlane.

"And they also started a war that is yet to be decided,"
she murmured.

"It will be done on the morrow."

It took Ailis a full moment to understand the implica-
tions of what Alexander had said. She stared at him with a
growing look of openmouthed surprise only faintly aware
of how closely he watched her. Then she grew angry and
sat up, the sheet clutched to her chest.

"On the morrow?" she repeated in a quiet, taut voice.
"There is to be a battle on the morrow?"

"Aye—on the morrow." Alexander was not surprised by
her anger, but he was fascinated by the way it turned her
lovely eyes black and stormy.

"And just when did ye plan to tell me about this?"

"On the morrow."

"In time to dodge the first arrow, I pray."

She knew that she had been purposely kept ignorant,
and it infuriated her. Some of her anger was directed at
herself. She had seen the signs of an approaching battle;
they had not been able to hide everything from her. Yet she
had never questioned, never asked for more information,

never pressed for the details. She had been too concerned about her own private troubles, about her child, her ills, and her husband.

What she did not really understand was why—why would they keep her ignorant? Then a chilling thought settled in her mind, one that struck her to the heart. Alexander had kept news of the impending battle from her for one reason—he feared she would betray him. She muttered a curse and leapt from the bed, too furious to be concerned about her nudity.

"Ye dinna trust me. Ye just said that ye kenned that I wouldna plot behind your back, but 'tis plain to see that ye didna mean in every way." She bit out the words as she gathered up her flimsy nightrail and started toward the door to her own sleeping quarters.

"Ailis, what are ye babbling about?"

She turned to glare at him, wondering how he had the audacity to look so confused, so handsomely irritated and befuddled. "I speak of my insult, and ye call it babbling?"

"What insult?" he bellowed. He was truly astounded that, for the first time in his life, a woman had him totally confounded.

"Cease this game, Alexander MacDubh." She jabbed her finger in his direction, giving it an occasional firm shake to stress her words. "Ye waited until now to tell me of this battle because ye feared I would turn spy for my kinsmen."

"Ye are mad! Get back here and listen to some sense."

He sounded so arrogant, so condescending and commanding that Ailis briefly considered marching back over to his bed—to punch him right in that perfectly shaped nose. "Nay. I believe I have played the fool enough for now. In truth, I am so glutted by it that I could be ill." She started back toward the door to her chambers.

Alexander cursed and leapt from the bed. He bounded after Ailis. She saw what he was doing, but too late to escape him. He grabbed her from behind and, ignoring her curses and flailing limbs, strode back to the bed. He tossed her down, wrestled her onto her back, and then pinned her down with his body. When he finally looked at her, face to face, he had to grin. Her hair was in such a tangle over her face that there was little more to see than two glaring eyes peering through. He pushed her arms up over her head so that he needed only one hand to grasp both of her wrists and then began to gently clear the hair from her face with his free hand.

"I have never had such difficulty with a female," he murmured, dropping a kiss on her nose when he uncovered it.

"Now I am a 'difficulty,' am I?" The way he felt pressing his body against hers and the way he was touching soft kisses to her face as he idly brushed aside her hair was making it difficult for her to keep a firm grip on her anger. "Get off of me, ye great blond oaf." The last thing she needed was to have her righteous anger quelled by his beauty and her own passion, yet she could see just how easily that could happen.

"Ye couldna possibly guess just how much of a 'difficulty' ye are, lass," he muttered. "I didna think that ye would betray me or the people of Rathmor to your kinsmen, loving. In truth, ye betraying me never entered my head in all of the battle planning I did, and that was when I realized how much I trust ye."

She fought against allowing his soft words to stir her hopes to life again. "Yet ye have done your best to keep me completely ignorant of the battle to come. I had heard some of the rumors, but I thought my oversolicitous nursemaids sought to protect me from it all and that was why I heard or was told so little."

"To protect ye was exactly what I was trying to do. Dearling, we are about to fight your uncle, the last of your kin. This battle we face on the morrow is between your blood kin and your wedded kin. 'Tis your uncle on the attack against the kinsmen of your child and Mairi's children. 'Twas a quandary I but wished to protect ye from."

"For ye feared which side I would choose to stand on."

"Nay, I kenned very well which ye would choose—me and mine. 'Tis another thing that told me that I was no longer seeing ye as a MacFarlane whom I happened to be cursed with a desire for, but as the lass I desired who just happened to be a MacFarlane. It has been a very long time since ye were all part of my vengeance, lass—a very long time. Didna ye ken that?" He felt that the tension, the resistance in her had ceased and loosed his grip upon her wrists. He had far better things in mind to do with his hands.

Ailis did not wish to be distracted, but the way Alexander ran his hand slowly down her side from shoulder to hip was accomplishing just that. She tried to fight the seductive allure of his skilled touch, to resist the way it pushed all thought from her mind. What he said, the way he explained his actions, made sense, yet she was not sure she ought to completely trust him. He idly smoothed kisses over her throat and breasts and she decided she had better decide on his truthfulness before she completely forgot her grievances against the man.

"Why should I believe ye?" she asked, her voice little more than a breathless gasp as he slowly lathed the tips of her breasts with his tongue. "Ye have made your mistrust of women clear."

"I have, but—answer me this—have I e'er lied to ye?" He gently rubbed his body against hers and watched her face, loving the way her cheeks grew flushed and her eyes became heavy-lidded.

"That doesna mean that ye wouldna. If we are to have a reasonable talk, then ye must halt your play. I canna think straight when ye are doing that." She trembled when he slowly drew her swollen nipple deep into his mouth.

"What else is there to be said; what else can be said? I have told ye why I tried so hard to keep ye ignorant of this battle. I canna prove that what I have said is true. I can only swear to it. On my oath, I but sought to save ye the ordeal of having to turn against your kinsmen. Do ye believe me or nay?"

"Oh, aye, I think I do." She twined her arms around his neck and held him as close as she could while he suckled her breasts.

"Ye *think* ye do?"

"In truth, I can think little at the moment." When his stroking reached the upper inside of her thighs, she opened herself to him and sighed with unrestrained pleasure over his intimate caresses. "I fear that the way ye touch me steals all of my wits."

"Good, I much prefer a witless lass."

Ailis laughed, knowing that he was jesting, then gave an audible sigh of delight as he teased her midriff with soft kisses and teasing licks. "For a man who was working so hard to be a monk, ye have become most greedy."

"Ye have recalled me to the pleasures I was so foolishly denying myself. I mean to drink my fill ere I face the battlefield on the morrow."

The reminder of the impending battle briefly checked Ailis's soaring passions. Although she wanted to wholeheartedly believe in a MacDubh victory, she could not ignore the chance that she could find herself back in the grasp of her kinsmen. Her child she might be able to protect—even if she had to proclaim him dead and allow some other woman to take him away—but there would be no sure way to save Alexander. This could be her last night with him. This particular night of pleasure could be the one that formed her last memories of him.

At that moment he touched his soft warm lips to the inside of each of her thighs. She fought her usual modesty when he then replaced his tenderly stroking fingers with his mouth. There was nothing she would deny him tonight. There was nothing she would deny herself. She gave herself over freely, with complete abandon, to his intimate kisses and savored his words of approval as much as she did the pleasure he gave her. It was a pleasure she intended to return to him tenfold. When he strode out to do battle in the morning, he might not have all the rest he should have, but she intended to have loved him so well that he would kill anyone who tried to prevent him from returning to her.

"Alexander?" she asked when she finally recovered from a fourth round of heated lovemaking.

Sprawled on his stomach at her side, Alexander found the strength to slip his arm about her waist and tug her closer. He knew he ought to get some rest, but he was starved for her. Each touch made him want more, each kiss made him crave another one. Each time they made love, he was eager to recover his full strength so that they could make love again. He discovered that he also liked just lying there with her or talking to her—depending on what she wished to discuss, he mused with a wry smile.

"What is it, sweeting?" He lazily nuzzled her ear.

"Just how is this battle to be fought?"

" 'Tis an acre fight."

"An acre fight."

It was to be as horrid as she had feared. She shivered a little, edging a bit closer to his warmth. "Why canna ye hold at Rathmor and let them try and take ye? Ye could win then. My uncle and Donald MacCordy wouldna be able to breach these walls."

"Mayhaps not, but we wouldna truly win, either. Aye,

'twould appear as if we were victorious, for we would still hold Rathmor and our enemy would retreat, probably with some large losses. And then what?"

"We could have some peace and respite from the turmoil?" she asked, but there was no hope or conviction in her voice, for she knew what he was going to say and she knew she would have to acknowledge the truth of it.

Alexander lifted his head enough to kiss her cheek. "I wish I could give ye that. And, mayhaps, I can, but it willna be by staying up on my walls. Nay, such a battle will only allow us to poke at the body of the adder that is coiled against us. We must cut off the adder's head. That can only be done by meeting our enemies on an even ground and sword to sword. Those who lead must be cut down. I am sorry, lass, for they are your kinsmen, but that is how I feel it must be if there is ever to be an end to all of this."

"No need to beg my forgiveness. I have the sense to see the truth of all ye say."

"Then come, kiss me, smother me in your sweet passion, so that I will march to meet my enemies with a sure step and victory as my fate."

Ailis kissed him and heartily prayed that she could do just as he had asked.

# 17

Flanked by the twins, Ailis stood on the battlements and watched Alexander lead the men of Rathmor to the chosen battlefield. She would be able to see the battle, but the distance would make seeing each man distinctly a little difficult. Alexander would not really be distinguishable from his men except that he would be in the lead, but in the fever of battle, who led would soon be difficult to determine. Even his banner might cease to be an exact marker. She ached to be closer, to be near enough to keep a close eye on Alexander, but there was no chance of that. He had left orders that she was to be very closely watched. The command revealed that he knew her far better than she had realized, but she did not appreciate that at the moment.

Alexander turned to wave a final farewell, as did Barra and Jaime, who would guard Barra's back. To Ailis's pleasant surprise, Angus also waved. She readily returned the gesture, then looked to Kate, who stood off to her right and held Sibeal in her arms. Both of them also waved to the men. Ailis found herself deeply relieved to see no sign of concern or fear on Sibeal's face. It had to mean that Sibeal had not seen any troubling visions, had had no dark dreams. Ailis told herself not to put too much faith in that, but it was hard not to have a little more hope.

"This must be hard for ye, mistress," Kate said as she set little Sibeal down. "The father of your son marching off to clash swords with your clan and your kin." Kate shook her head. " 'Tis sad."

" 'Tis sad that men canna find a better way to solve their differences," Ailis grumbled.

"What sets between the MacDubhs and the MacFarlanes is far more than mere differences. 'Tis far deeper than that."

"Oh, aye, I ken it." She rested her forearms on the cold stone. "I do but vent my anger, my helplessness."

" 'Twill be fine, Aunt Ailis." Sibeal patted Ailis on the arm, then let Rath take her by the hand and lead her away.

Ailis watched her niece carefully led off of the walls by her nephews. "Now, was that merely a courtesy, or was she trying to tell me something?"

" 'Tis probably as well not to ken exactly what it meant. What I should like to ken is—is Jaime a skilled fighter?"

As she met Kate's worried gaze, Ailis suddenly realized that she did not really have an answer for that. She felt briefly guilty, then shook the feeling away. It was not her fault. Jaime had not done much fighting, and it was not really a skill she was knowledgeable enough about to be a good judge. Then she saw how Jaime had been placed in the battle order and felt she had her answer.

"He has been set to guard Barra's back, Kate. Someone must think that he is skilled."

"Ye have never seen Jaime fight? I thought he was your protector?"

"Aye, but he never really needed to wield a sword to do that. Now, if ye asked me—if ten men charged Jaime, could he knock the fools aside?—I could say aye in all confidence. A sword fight? I simply canna be sure. But I point again to the fact that he has been placed at Sir Barra's back. Some man who can judge such things far better than I has judged Jaime fit enough to guard one of the heirs."

Kate grimaced, then nodded and smiled faintly. "I worry

too much. Jaime often tells me so. There is one other thing that I do worry on, and that is that he might be confronted with his own kinsmen, face to face, sword to sword."

"And will our softhearted Jaime have the stomach to protect himself against them?" Ailis finished and smiled at Kate. "The chances are very few that Jaime would meet any of them on this battlefield. His father and elder brother died long ago, and the rest arena soldiers, mere arrow fodder at best, but mostly left behind to plow or reap muck out the stables. Even if they are there and by some strange twist of fate Jaime should meet them, he willna hesitate to protect himself if they attack. His fear of them has eased, and he has learned not to meekly accept anything they say or do, but to fight back."

"That does ease my mind, but can ye say the same?"

"Can I protect myself against my own kin and the Mac-Cordys? Aye, without hesitation. What kin I had any affection for have all died. The lot who march against Rathmor and Alexander are naught to me. 'Twill be sad to accept that there can never be anything, but that isna my fault. They chose the path they walk down. Since it is me and mine they wish to hurt, I feel I can cut all ties to them. The few I still care for at Leargan willna be out on the field."

"And the ones ye care about shall survive this day."

"I pray we both shall have cause to smile when this is all over." She reached out to briefly clasp Kate's workworn hand. "Dinna forget what ye promised me."

"Nay, I willna. If the MacCordys and the MacFarlanes succeed, and please God they willna, your son will be safe. There isna a man or a woman here who would turn that child over to our enemies. I will claim him as mine, and if I fall, there are women aplenty ready to step forward and claim him."

Ailis relaxed, her fears soothed for the moment. "So, there is naught else to do but wait."

Alexander drew his mount to a halt. He could have easily walked the distance from Rathmor to the chosen field, but that would have lacked presence. His men found added strength in the appearance he presented, and, he hoped, it would make the enemy view him with some respect. Once dismounted, he met with the men he had sent out to watch the MacFarlanes and the MacCordys.

"Have they tried any of their sly tricks?" he asked his men.

Red Ian grimaced. "They did try. There were several archers placed so that ye wouldst be pelted from all sides. 'Twould whittle down your strength until MacCordy could win."

"But ye took care of the rogues?" Alexander was disgusted that his enemies could not even fight their last battle with honesty.

"Aye, that threat is no longer. There is only one other wee thing of interest. It concerns Sir Malcolm MacCordy."

"He has joined his kinsmen again, I presume."

"'Tis difficult to say." Red Ian dragged his fingers through his bright copper hair. "He no longer rides with them but has camped a few yards beyond the western line of trees. He claims he has had enough of his cousins' feuds and pointless battles. 'Twas a loud argument, so I believe I ken most of what was said."

"He had broken from his kinsmen, then," Alexander frowned and rubbed his chin. "Do ye think we can trust to that? 'Tis true that the man was never that close to his kinsmen, but he could also be very sly."

"Oh, aye, a rogue, but I think the break is a true one." Red Ian looked at his companion, who nodded, then he looked at Alexander. "He has camped and a few men have stayed with him, but 'tis difficult to ken if they are friends or guards. It did appear as if his kinsmen wanted him close at hand so that they could . . . curse it—what did they say?"

"So that they could make him see the error of his ways after they beat ye, sir," answered the other man.

"Ho, such boasters. If the ground is dry and cleared of treachery, then victory is ours. If the battle is an honest test of skill, then the MacCordys and the MacFarlanes have no chance of winning. They have relied upon murder and black-hearted betrayal for so long that their true fighting skills are no longer as honed as they once were. See to the safe securing of our mounts, Red Ian, and prepare yourself."

As soon as the two reconnaissance men left, Barra, Angus, and Jaime stepped over. Alexander could see the reflection of his own growing confidence in their faces. He felt his become even stronger. Most of the men of his clan had turned out for the battle, and he was moved by the sign of loyalty.

"A fine showing of brave men, eh, Angus?" He smiled at his man as he tugged on his mail gauntlets.

"Aye. They are eager to clash swords with this foe, eager to put an end to this long and bloody feud."

"Do ye truly believe that it will end here?" asked Barra as, with Jaime's aid, he laced on his mail shirt.

Alexander nodded. "It will. No matter which way the tide turns, the feud will end here—today. I pray 'twill end in a victory for us, but 'twill end nonetheless. I offered a truce to these fools, but 'twas refused. They have never wished peace, for in peace they would have to cease stealing all that is ours."

"Here they come," murmured Jaime. "Laird Colin comes ahead under a flag of truce."

"Mayhaps they have finally changed their minds," suggested Barra.

"Aye, or they have discovered that we found their hidden archers and ended that threat. So now they want to treat with us to gain time so that they can set yet another snare." Alexander shook his head. "We will hear what that black-hearted Colin wishes to say, but we willna trust in it. Always wary, my friends. We must be ever vigilant."

Colin halted and allowed himself and his two companions to be fleetingly searched by Angus and Jaime before stepping closer. For one brief moment he contemplated switching allegiances. The MacCordys had stolen everything from him, leaving him with no power within his own clan. One look into the MacDubh brothers' eyes cured him of that brief treacherous thought. There would be no mercy there. The MacDubhs wanted blood for blood. He had murdered their father, and they would not allow that crime to pass unpunished.

"What do ye want, MacFarlane?" demanded Alexander. "The terms of the battle are very clear and have already been agreed upon."

"I was but sent along to give ye one last chance to end this."

"Oh? Are ye to return to me all that is mine? Including my murdered father?" he snapped.

Ignoring that last furious demand, Colin answered, "We want ye to return what ye have stolen—my niece and the bairns who were abducted from MacFarlane lands."

"From MacDubh land. Leargan is MacDubh land. Your niece is also mine. She is the mother of my child." He smiled coldly at the stunned look upon Colin's face. "Did your fine allies neglect to tell ye about that? Well, there is something else that ye may be surprised to learn, then—ye canna have the bairns back, either, for they are my brother Barra's spawn."

"The bairns are MacDubhs? My niece's lover was a MacDubh?" Colin could hardly speak; he was red-faced and breathing hard. "And ye say that the MacCordys kenned all of this?'

"Aye."

A low, guttural sound escaped Colin MacFarlane. He turned and snatched his sword from a startled Angus. The two men with Colin stood confused as Colin started back toward the MacCordys with long, purposeful strides. When Colin gave out a bellow of rage and began to run straight for the three MacCordys, the two men finally moved and ran after him, but they were too late to catch him. Colin raced up to the MacCordys, who started to draw their swords and tried to get out of the way. The first swing of Colin's sword cut down William MacCordy. The second swing was successfully blocked by Duncan MacCordy, and Donald stepped over to impale Colin on his sword with a thrust from behind. Colin MacFarlane's death scream echoed over the suddenly quiet battlefield.

"Two enemy dead and we havena yet bloodied our swords," murmured Angus.

"Aye, but it looks as if the MacCordys feel that we are to blame for this as well." Alexander scowled toward the MacCordy forces, watching as Donald ranted and raved while Duncan briefly knelt by an obviously dead William.

"How could Colin not ken that Ailis was carrying your bairn?" Barra asked.

"Well, I suspicion that he kenned she was pregnant, but he didna have to ken that it was by me. The true parentage could be all that they kept hidden. He was shocked because he realized he had been lied to by men he had trusted. As much as a man like that trusts anyone. Mayhaps he suddenly just realized exactly how much of a fool and a pawn he had become."

Jaime nodded. "I saw that he had no power left when Ailis and I were prisoners at Craigandubh. Lady Una kenned more than Laird Colin by then. He grew more vague as she grew sharper."

"Well, mayhaps she will grow even sharper now that the source of her torment is gone." Alexander silently waved his men to take up their battle positions. "It appears that Donald's raging has either convinced many of the MacFarlane men to fight, or he has simply scared them all into staying. I dinna see many fleeing now that their laird is dead."

"I think their laird had been one of the MacCordys for many a month."

" 'Tis their curse. For 'tis a MacCordy who shall lead them to their deaths."

Alexander drew his sword and readied himself to match the assault he could see his enemy preparing. He felt a touch of regret that he had not been the one to end Colin MacFarlane's life, that neither he nor his brother had been able to avenge his father's murder personally. On the other hand he was very grateful. He had not wanted to be the one to kill Ailis's closest kinsmen. Those emotions surprised him, for his thirst for vengeance had been such a part of him for so long. He had sensed a change in himself, but he had not realized that it was a subtle easing of the bitterness he had nursed in his heart for so very long.

The MacCordys and the MacFarlanes bellowed their threats and insults, so Alexander fixed his attention on the front lines of the enemy warriors. Soon the charge would be starting, and he did not want to miss any of the signs that would proceed it. It was not a good time to be distracted or musing about any changes in himself. If he kept his mind on the battle to come, he would have plenty of time for such contemplations later.


Ailis heard the dull roar as the battle started in earnest. The MacCordys and the MacFarlanes screamed the last of their insults, bellowed their battle cry, and charged. The MacDubhs gave their full-throated reply and moved toward their attackers. Ailis could almost feel it when the two armies slammed into each other. Even Kate grunted softly.

Try as she would, Ailis could make no sense of what she watched. Although it was at a distance, Ailis did not think that made any difference. She doubted she would have understood it even if she was a lot closer. The men were too muddled up together, too thoroughly mixed. The number of men that became unmoving bodies upon the ground began to grow. From where she stood, it was impossible to tell which of the fallen were friend or foe. She ached to draw nearer but knew that would not be allowed.

"Can ye see how we fare, Kate?" she asked the woman who shared her tense vigil on the battlements.

"Nay. I can see nothing. It but appears to be some mad melee, as if no one has any battle plan."

"Aye, but they must have one. I thought it would help me to watch, but I believe it has made it worse. Mayhaps the best place to have spent this time was in the church or the like."

"That has never worked for me. At least, not when ye must sit for hours ere ye ken the fate of the men in your clan. Come and take heart," Kate advised Ailis. "At least from here ye will ken exactly when the battle has ended and which men flee the field. 'Tis better than naught."

"Aye, 'tis better than naught. And we can always pray for our men from up here."

Ailis smiled faintly when Kate began to do just that, taking her rosary from her pocket and beginning the calming chants. But Ailis had said so many prayers that she could no longer think of one. All she wanted was for Alexander and the others she cared about to survive and be victorious. If there had to be a choice, then she would accept mere survival. She simply did not want Alexander to be one of those unmoving shapes upon the battlefield.

Alexander fought his way toward Donald. He was eager to cross swords with the man. Vengeance for past wrongs was no longer the main reason he ached to fill Donald MacCordy's heart with cold steel. Every reason Alexander could think of at the moment had to do with Ailis. Donald was her betrothed; Donald had struck Ailis; Donald had threatened the life of their son, thus forcing Ailis to risk her own life in fleeing from those threats. Each of those memories were in the forefront of Alexander's mind as he battled his way to Donald. Once there, Alexander felt a cold, satisfying sense of victory as Donald whirled to face him. Donald was red-faced and grunting, sweat dripping from his face. Alexander felt cool, rested, and efficient.

"Now we meet as equals," Alexander called out to him, "although it causes a bitter taste in my mouth to call ye a knight or sir." Alexander looked the burly Donald over with contempt. "Ye bring shame to every honorable knight in Scotland."

"Then 'tis a good thing that I dinna face one now, isna it. Nay, I face an adulterer, a pretty-faced seducer—a carpet knight whose only spurs were earned riding maids in their boudoirs."

"I hope ye have made your confessions, MacCordy, for ye will die here on this field."

The first clash of their swords told Alexander that he was not fighting with a poorly skilled man. Donald's weakness was not in his arm or in his swing. Donald's weakness was that he could not control his emotions. He could spit out foul insults with ease, but he could not ignore them with calm. He too easily lost his temper, too quickly fell from skilled fighting into a brutal, fury-controlled slashing. It took but one or two clever, sharp insults to steal what skill Donald MacCordy had. Alexander did not stoop to such games, however, but he recognized that his reasons were far from noble. He wanted Donald to sweat, to know that even when he was fighting his best fight, he was not good enough. Alexander wanted Donald to see his own death approaching.

"Ye are willing to toss away your life and what few riches are left to ye for the sake of that brown-eyed slut?" Donald blocked Alexander's sword and tried to stab his stomach with his dagger, but Alexander easily eluded the clumsy slash. "Are ye even sure that the bairn is yours and not the offspring of that simpleminded fool she keeps so close at hand?"

Alexander was a little dismayed to discover that he had a weakness as well. It was difficult not to react with a blind fury to such insults against Ailis. He wanted to pin Donald to the ground and cut his tongue out with a dull knife. Such emotional responses had no place in a fight. Any emotion—from merciful to murderous—could be fatal. Alexander forced himself to remain untouched by Donald's ugly words.

"Cease sharpening your tongue on a lass and hone your blade on me instead," he ordered Donald. "There is no gain in going to your death with insults upon your breath."

"'Tisna me who shall be doing the dying here, my pretty knight."

A shock went through Alexander's arm as Donald's sword hit his. It was a powerful blow, but Alexander had faced enough opponents to know that Donald could not continue like that. Donald was one who fought a short fight well, but used up all of his strength far too quickly.

In a very short time Alexander saw that he had judged his opponent perfectly. Donald was soon awash in sweat and panting hard. The man's sword strikes, even the occasional lunge with the dagger, became awkward. For one brief moment Alexander contemplated toying with the man, prolonging the death blow they both knew was inevitable. Then he discovered that he really did not have the stomach for it. When the moment came, he ended Donald's life swiftly, with one clean direct sword thrust to the heart.

It was as he watched the man sprawl on the ground that Alexander realized the battle was as good as over. He turned his head to find Barra calmly watching him. His brother's whole attitude was one of calm and victory.

"So—we have finally won," Alexander said as he crouched by Donald's body to clean off his sword on the dead man's jupon.

"Aye, brother, we have finally won. Your insistence on an acre fight was clever. These fools were too arrogant to say nay."

"True, and they thought I wouldna guess the tricks they would use to ensure a victory." He glanced to the far end of the small battlefield to see a horseman approaching very cautiously and holding a white flag. "Malcolm."

"He wishes to treaty with us? The battle is over. His people lost it."

"He had no side in this. 'Tis probably what he wishes to remind us of now. Dinna scowl so, Barra. Instinct tells me that the man is no fool. He probably wishes to keep hold of what little he now holds. That will, of course, be a gain for him, for it would now belong to him alone. He willna be his cousin's slavey. I say let him keep what he holds. I have Leargan back. I can be generous. Dinna forget, he did much to help Ailis."

"Aye, and I still canna stop asking myself one question—why?"

It was a question Alexander had often asked himself, but he had consistently shied away from the answer. Malcolm had risked a lot to aid Ailis, and while Alexander did not want to insult the man, he could not feel that chivalry was the sole cause of such assistance. He was all that was polite to the man, however, when Malcolm halted before him. Alexander reassured Malcolm that all that had been his before the battle would remain his. As he was leaving, Malcolm extended his kind wishes to Mistress Ailis and the child, as well as an invitation for all of them to visit him whenever they were in Edinburgh. It seemed a curious thing to say, but the man left before Alexander could question it. With a shake of his head over the vagaries of some people, Alexander headed back to Rathmor, pausing only to make sure that Jaime and Angus had come through the battle unscathed as well. Once assured of their good health, his only thought was to get back to Ailis.

Even from a distance it was easy to see that the battle was over and that the MacDubhs had won the day. Ailis exchanged a brief exuberant hug with Kate, then joined the woman in hurrying off the walls. She was eager to get down to the gates so that she could see Alexander the moment he returned and see with her own eyes that he had escaped the battle unharmed. There was a good chance that she could reveal a lot of her feelings for him in that first moment of greeting, but she did not care this time.

Alexander had barely finished dismounting when Ailis flung herself into his arms. She briefly felt guilty that she could be so happy, for it had been at the cost of her kinsman's life. There was no doubt in her mind that her uncle was now dead, but she could muster no grief for him, and that did make her fleetingly sad.

"Your uncle is dead, lass," Alexander said as, with his arm around her shoulders, he started through the celebratory crowd of MacDubhs and into the keep.

"I was just thinking about that. He and the MacCordys

made it so that there was no other choice. Just death or victory. Of course, in their arrogance, they had not expected to lose." She paused just before they started up the stairs to their chambers to order a hot bath for Alexander. "So, 'tis all over now."

"Aye, 'tis all over."

Nothing more was said as they went up to their bedchamber. Ailis helped Alexander shed his armor and, as soon as the hot bath was delivered, the rest of his battle-stained clothing. Unlike many a time before, she was not stirred by the sight of his naked form. She was too concerned with assuring herself that there were no serious injuries. It was not until Alexander was dressed in his braies and sprawled comfortably on the bed, sipping a tankard of wine, that the silence between them began to grow a little awkward. When a maid delivered a tray with some bread, cheese, and apples, Ailis took it to the bed and sat down next to Alexander. The way he was watching her began to make her very nervous.

"It was a victory for ye?" she finally asked as she cut off a piece of cheese and put it on her bread.

"Aye, Leargan belongs to the MacDubhs again." He paused, then added, "I wasna the one who killed your uncle, lass."

"It wouldna have mattered if ye had been the one. I would have kenned that it wasna a murder but a fair fight. There is but one thing I need to ken—he didna suffer, did he? I truly dinna understand why that should matter to me, yet it does." She shrugged and gave Alexander a faint smile.

"He was the last of your close kin. 'Tis a bond that is hard to break." He told her how Colin had met his fate.

"Killed by his allies. Somehow there is a strange justice to that. When I was with them, I began to see that he had lost his power, that the MacCordys were the masters at

Leargan. And 'tisna so strange that word of who had fathered my child should be such a surprise to him. Even his poor befuddled wife felt that he had become more vague and dark-humored. He never came to see me, either, so a good look at my shape wasna able to rouse him to the facts. 'Tis a shame about William, I think."

"Wasna he the younger son? A somewhat witless fellow?"

"Aye, a wee bit slow, but I dinna think there was any real harm in him. He was but a pawn, pulled and pushed about by his father and brother. And what of Malcolm?" She tried to sound only politely interested but was not sure she had succeeded when Alexander gave her a sharp penetrating glance.

"Malcolm survived, but I believe he is good at surviving. He never joined the battle, but withdrew from it altogether ere his kinsmen took to the field. When the battle was done, we talked for a brief time. He asked to keep what little his kinsmen had given into his care, and I agreed. Then he said that we must come and see him in Edinburgh whenever we might chance to travel there." He watched her closely and realized, with a flicker of alarm that she was purposely not looking his way.

Ailis inwardly cursed Malcolm in every way she could think of even as she struggled to remain calm and only mildly interested. "Why should we chance to go to Edinburgh?" She wondered if the answer to her dilemma was just to ignore Malcolm completely. After all, she would find it very difficult to fulfill a promise to a person she never saw.

"I have a house there just as Malcolm does. It seems we both have some business there, and we like to go oversee it now and again. In a few days we shall travel to Leargan. After we put matters to right there, we shall travel on to Edinburgh. 'Tis a journey I make every year. Have ye ever been to Edinburgh?" he asked, and she shook her head.

"Ye will enjoy it, I believe." His curiosity grew as with each thing he said about Edinburgh, Ailis's mood grew more somber.

As Alexander talked, telling her of the sights and sounds of Edinburgh, Ailis wondered how she could possibly keep from going to the place. She briefly contemplated feigning some illness, but that would only give her a short respite. She would have to be ill whenever there was fine weather and talk of Edinburgh. That would certainly become suspicious after a while. An exerted effort to avoid any place was certain to arouse suspicions. In fact, any continued aversion to any spot would raise questions. Avoiding Malcolm or any place he was was clearly no answer. Neither was there any way to preserve her honor by keeping the promise, yet not betray Alexander by lying with Malcolm.

She put aside the empty goblets and food tray, then huddled closer to a quiet, relaxed Alexander. There was so much he and she could share now, but it would never be. Slowly Alexander had begun to soften toward her, she was sure of it, and now that those who had wronged him were all dead, his bitterness would ease, and things could only get better. Or they would do, she mused with a heavy sigh, if her promise to Malcolm was not poised like a dagger at her throat. That Malcolm would have the audacity to remind her of her promise by mentioning Edinburgh and inviting her and Alexander to come and see him was nearly more arrogance than she could tolerate. Malcolm had known that she would understand what he had meant, that the invitation to his home in Edinburgh was really him telling her where he expected her to rendezvous with him to pay her debt, and he had used her very own husband to deliver the message. She ached to slap the man—very hard and repeatedly.

"Come, Ailis," Alexander murmured, tilting her face up to his and brushing a light kiss over her mouth. "We were the victors today. 'Tis a time for smiles, not for such long, dark faces."

Although she gave him the smile he sought and a kiss or two, she ached to remind him that when some people had the pleasure of victory, it meant that someone else had lost. For every success there was a price. It was a lesson his wife was doomed to teach him.

# 18

Edinburgh. Ailis shivered despite the summer heat and cursed the word, the place, and the fact that she was there. Just as Alexander had said they would, they had gone to Leargan to be sure all was in order, then had gone on to Edinburgh. He reminded her that he had made the journey to Edinburgh at the same time every year. It was something that Malcolm had clearly known about when he had extracted the promise from her. Even then he had known when and where he would extract payment from her.

She cautiously looked at the man sprawled asleep at her side, his long, tautly muscled arm flung across her waist. Ever since the final battle with her kinsmen and the MacCordys, she and Alexander had been growing slowly, warily closer. His bitterness was nearly gone, the hateful remarks no more than a bad memory. She should have been filled with hope, her heart light as she worked to pull more than passion from her husband. For the first time since he had dragged her off to Rathmor, he was open to her, could be reached, perhaps even brought to love her, but she could do nothing about it. If nothing else, it would be inordinately cruel to grab for his love now that it was within her reach when she knew that she would have to betray him.

And I may as well hurry and do the deed, she thought as she eased herself out of bed and reached for her gown.

In the afternoon she and Alexander had wandered through the town, and there had been Malcolm. They had paused to be cordial, and Ailis passed a few awkward words with a quietly sad Giorsal. It had been made subtlely clear by Malcolm that he awaited the fulfillment of the promise she had made.

At first Ailis had given serious thought to postponing keeping her end of that infamous bargain. There had never been any particular time mentioned. Then she had seen that for the foolishness that it was. The bargain would not fade away. Malcolm would not disappear. Ailis knew she had to face the consequences of her promise and do so now. There was also the matter of the new, still changing relationship between her and Alexander. At last he was opening his heart to her, offering her chance after chance to stir far more than his lust, but she was now the one who held back. She would not be so cruel as to take whatever she craved from Alexander when she knew that she was doomed to betray him. If she did that, then she would be no better than the women who had left him such a scarred and bitter man.

"He will think I am no better than they were anyway," she mused to herself as she finished lacing up her gown.

Her heart beating fast and hard, Ailis slipped out of the room she shared with Alexander. She kept a very close eye on him, watching him for any sign of his waking up. To her relief he did not move at all. As softly as she could, she shut the door behind her.

In the outer hallway she found the candle and flint she had tucked into a niche just outside the door. The light it provided was very meager, but she felt more confident about getting out of the small manor house without incident. She briefly wished that Moragh had traveled to Edinburgh with them, for she would have dearly loved to see her child one last time. Ailis knew that once she fulfilled her bargain with

Malcolm Alexander would not want her any longer, and his rejection would assuredly mean the loss of her child as well.

"At least I had one last night with Alexander," she whispered as she slipped out of the house and hoped that the thought would be one to cheer her in later years.

Jaime cursed and slipped out of the house to follow Ailis. He knew exactly where she was going. Several times since she had made the bargain, he had tried to talk her out of keeping it. There was no honor in such a deal; therefore, there was none lost in refusing to fulfill the terms. Unfortunately, Ailis did not see it that way. She had agreed to a price for saving her child and herself, and she would pay the price.

He kept out of sight behind her as she made her way toward Malcolm MacCordy's residence. Although he could not stop Ailis, Jaime knew she might need protection going to and from the houses. He also knew that she would need help when it was all over. She would be heartbroken and would probably have to get away from the MacDubhs, either because Alexander told her to or because her own guilt would torment her into doing so. Either way she would need him. Jaime just hoped that, wherever his allegiance to Ailis led him, it was not too far away from the MacDubhs and Kate.

Alexander waited until the door shut behind Ailis, then swiftly got up and got dressed. He stepped over to the window as he buckled on his sword, carefully keeping just behind the drape, and watched the street below. When he saw Ailis creep along the road back into town, he cursed. He was just about to go after her when he saw a shadowy figure trailing her. At first he tensed, fear for Ailis's safety briefly swamping his jealousy and fury. Then he recognized the man. The large shape became a familiar one.

"Ah, the ever-diligent Jaime," he muttered, then hurried out of the house, rushing to fall into step behind the pair before they disappeared into the narrow streets of town.

It was difficult for Alexander to remain as no more than a man in pursuit, following and attempting to learn exactly what was going on. It had taken a while to understand that something existed between Ailis and Malcolm. He had not wanted to see it, had not wanted to know anything about it, but some things were too hard to ignore. The meeting with Malcolm in the market square had finally forced him to open his eyes.

No matter how many times he told himself not to let the pain of the past taint his judgments, he could not help but believe he was about to be betrayed again. Each step he took as he followed Ailis confirmed his opinion that she was slipping away to meet Malcolm. Nothing he could think of could excuse it, and nothing stilled the pain. Alexander was astonished at how much it hurt.


Ailis held her cloak snugly around herself even though she did not feel any cold. For a long time she stood in front of Malcolm's studded door unable to rap. A little wildly she thought of every possible solution to her dilemma and, as had always happened before, found that none really offered her an answer. As she knocked on the door, she felt as if her heart had suddenly been weighted with leads.

Ailis heard Malcolm at the door and shuddered. He opened the door, looked around, and gently took her by the hand and pulled her into the house.

\* \* \*

Alexander paused to watch her rap on Malcolm's door, then go inside. Jaime moved in the narrow alley to the right of the house, and Alexander decided to follow him. He wanted to storm into the place and put the fear of God into the both of them. As he stepped up behind Jaime, he mused that he would like to put more than fear into Malcolm MacCordy—he would like to insert a length of cold, well-honed steel into the man's gullet. He moved up behind Jaime and waited for the man to stop peering in the open window and notice that he was no longer alone. A cold smile curved Alexander's mouth when Jaime finally turned, his eyes widening.

"Ye ken it all," Jaime whispered.

"What I ken is that my wife is meeting her lover, and ye are aiding her."

"Nay! Nay, that isna true."

"Dinna lie for her. Be silent and let me see the truth for myself." He continued to stand just behind Jaime and watch as Malcolm and Ailis entered the room, sat down, and began to share a drink of wine. The slightly open window allowed him to hear every traitorous word. He swore that he would hold calm, would learn exactly what was happening before he broke it up.

Malcolm led Ailis into the small great hall and silently urged her into a high-backed chair at a heavy round table. When he poured them each some wine, then sat down near to her, she did not know whether to weep or throw the sweet liquid at him. He was being so hospitable even as he prepared for a night that would utterly destroy her.

"Where is Giorsal?" she asked, thinking that the girl was yet another person she would be forced to betray and hurt.

"I told the girl to stay to her own quarters. She has

plagued me about this since the day I saved ye and your child."

"Ye need not remind me of all ye have done for me, Malcolm. I am quite aware of it. 'Tis the only reason I am here."

He slumped in his chair and frowned at her. "Ye could look less like ye are about to set your neck upon the chopper's block. Ye arena going to an execution, merely repaying an honorable debt."

"There is nothing honorable about this! Nothing at all!"

"Mayhaps not." Malcolm leaned toward her, took her hand in his, and pressed a kiss to her palm. "Yet, that need not stop it from giving us each some pleasure."

"'Twill give ye death," Alexander muttered from his hiding place outside, and he started toward the window.

Jaime quickly grabbed him, holding him firmly. "Hold. Dinna intrude now, m'laird."

"Do ye think I should hold back until they are locked in an embrace?" he hissed but ceased to struggle.

"Just listen. I beg of ye. Just listen." Jaime kept a firm grip on Alexander even when the man calmed down.

"For a wee bit longer. No more. And if this is truly no more than some adulterous tangle—ye will pay dearly for this impertinence."

"Fair enough." Jaime prayed that the truth would be said aloud.

"Pleasure?" Ailis laughed bitterly and shook her head. "Ye find pleasure in betrayal?"

"Ye see betrayal," Malcolm grumbled. "I see naught but a bargain made and kept."

"What bargain?" demanded Alexander, careful to keep his voice low so as not to alert the ones he and Jaime spied upon.

"Hush and listen."

"I think ye grow mighty impertinent," Alexander said,

but he did hush. Something about the agitation in Jaime's demeanor told him to try and be calm, to listen and watch before acting.

"And ye have no intention of releasing me from it, do ye?" asked Ailis, already sure of his answer.

"Nay. Do ye think I would demand such a thing if I didna want it very badly, indeed? Aye, I ken what ye think about MacCordys, but we werena—arena—all so depraved. However, I found that I wanted ye badly enough to stoop low, indeed."

"Even to demanding that I break sacred vows, play the whore for ye, to save the life of my child?"

"Aye, even to that." Malcolm finished his wine in one deep gulp, then refilled his tankard. A somewhat sullen expression settled on his handsome face.

Jaime felt a distinct change in Alexander's stance and, even in the dark, could see the arrested look upon the man's face. With continued caution he eased his hold on the Laird of Rathmor. When all Alexander did was to turn and look at him, Jaime breathed an inner sigh of relief.

"This was some sort of bargain made for my son's life?" Alexander could not believe what he was hearing.

"Aye." Jaime nearly retreated from the look of fury upon Alexander's face and was concerned about whom that fury would be visited upon.

"Tell me *exactly* what the bargain was. Now!" he demanded when Jaime hesitated.

"That Malcolm would do all he could to save her and her child if she promised to spend one night with him."

"And Ailis agreed to that?" Alexander was not sure who he wanted to strike down most—Malcolm for being such a dishonorable rogue or Ailis for being so foolish as to think that she had to keep such a bargain.

"What choice did she have?" Jaime argued. "She was wet to the bone, tired, and about to give birth. Aye, and

Donald MacCordy himself was close at hand. There didna seem to be any other choice to be made."

Alexander felt a sharp stab of pain penetrate his anger. He could so easily see poor Ailis—wet, exhausted, and in the most vulnerable state any woman can be in. Jaime had been there to help her, but he had his limitations. Alexander had always deeply regretted that he had not been there to help her instead was stuck at Rathmor. Now that he realized what situations she had gotten into, he regretted it even more. He also ached to make Malcolm MacCordy pay dearly for forcing Ailis into such a deal. When he took a step toward the window intending to pacify his need for action, Ailis began to speak again, and he paused. While a great part of him felt that he had learned all he needed to know, a small part craved more.

"Why, Malcolm?" she asked. "Why even ask this of me? Why demand of me something I was not willing to give ye freely? Surely ye can get all the women ye need? Ye shouldna have to threaten or coerce a woman into pleasing your lusts."

"Nay, I dinna have to, but they canna give me what ye can."

"What? What do ye think I can give ye? I have all the same parts any woman does."

Malcolm cursed and raked his fingers through his hair. "'Tisna the parts. I can buy the cursed parts for a ha'penny. 'Tis what ye have in here." He lightly struck his broad chest with his fist. "''Tis what ye give that thrice-cursed MacDubh."

"I can never give *ye* that, Malcolm," she said in a solemn voice.

"Oh, I ken that he has a bonny face and a sweet tongue—"

"Aye, his face is bonny, so bonny it can make me feel dim-witted when I look at it, for it so completely scatters my thought. I dinna think there is a bonnier man in all of Scotland. However, 'tis just a face when all is said and quiet. It could be burned or scarred into real ugliness in but a blinking. It makes very little difference to how I do and dinna feel for the man. As for a sweet tongue"—she laughed—"the man lost that skill years ago, and it hasna returned in much strength. I hear few sweet words from him."

"Yet I can see, I can sense, that ye give him such fire. That fire is what I want from ye."

"I canna give it to ye. It comes from the heart of me, and although I think we might someday be friends, I have no room in my heart for another lover." She shook her head. "Ye mean to take everything from me, and yet willna even gain what ye seek."

"Everything? What do ye mean, I will take everything from ye? I ask for but one night."

"And what happens come the dawn?" Ailis wondered how the man could be so blind to her feelings.

"Ye go back to the man with the bonniest face in all of Scotland, and all is forgotten."

"Ye mean go back and lie."

"Ye wouldna tell him, would ye?" Malcolm asked with shock softening his voice.

"I wouldna have to say anything. He would be able to tell. There would be a change in me. I would ken what secret lay between us, and I fear I would hold it there. I would forever feel that he would find out that I had betrayed him. I would also feel soiled, and 'tisna because it was ye who touched me, but because some other man had touched me—any other man. That, too, would come between Alexander and me. I dinna think I can explain it. What ye ask for I can only give to Alexander MacDubh."

Malcolm leaned nearer to her, gently cupped the back of her head in his hand and pulled her face closer to his.

"Then pretend that I am your precious Alexander." He touched his mouth to hers.

Ailis was just thinking that, despite how it could destroy her life, she at least did not find Malcolm's touch completely repulsive. Then he tensed. She waited for him to continue the kiss, but he slowly pulled away instead. She opened her eyes and gasped at what she saw. Alexander stood beside them with his swordpoint hard up against Malcolm's throat. Ailis felt all the color leave her face as she leaned back and looked into his fury-bright eyes.

"So, my wife, this is why ye had such an interest in Edinburgh?" Alexander knew Ailis had done no real wrong, but seeing her being kissed by Malcolm had stirred his jealousy.

Before Ailis could reply, there was a soft cry of alarm and Giorsal raced into the room. The girl pushed aside a startled Alexander, then placed herself between him and Malcolm. Giorsal was deathly pale and trembling, but she stood firm, determined to protect the man she loved.

"Giorsal, are ye mad?" complained Malcolm, but when he grasped her by her tiny waist to push her away, he found that she was not so easy to move. "Lass, ye are not to concern yourself with this."

"Not concern myself?" Giorsal snapped, surprising Malcolm into speechlessness. "Who do ye think will be left to bury ye if ye get yourself killed trying to steal something ye can never have?"

"I regret to say that I willna be killing the man," Alexander said, sheathing his sword, then taking Ailis by the arm and tugging her to her feet. "I should very much like to, but I do owe him a life. So, now I give him his." He turned to Jaime, who stood quietly behind him, and gently nudged Ailis toward him. "Take my foolish wife home."

"Alexander—" Ailis began as Jaime took her by the arm and started to leave.

"We will talk at home."

Ailis felt her heart contract and just nodded, allowing Jaime to lead her away. If she were not so despondent, so close to weeping, she could almost laugh, although the humor that prompted it was a bitter one. She had not done what she had agreed to, but she was going to pay the penalty anyway. It was the cruelest of jests.

The moment Ailis left, Alexander looked at Malcolm, and despite his fury at the man, he had to smile. An extremely irritated Malcolm sat shielded by the tiny Giorsal, who refused to be moved. When it came to women, Malcolm was clearly as blind as Alex himself had been.

"Ye survive this insult, Malcolm, because of what I owe ye. There will be no second chance."

"Your wife wouldna give him one anyway," said Giorsal.

Alexander smiled. "Nay, I ken it." He grew serious as he looked at Malcolm again. "I canna deride ye as much as I would like, for I have played the fool a lot lately. But, heed me in this, Malcolm MacCordy, if ye would but consider it for a moment, I believe ye have been trying to steal what is already nearly sitting in your lap." He heard Giorsal gasp and gave the girl a brief wink before he walked away.

As he strode back to his own home, Alexander wondered how he was to deal with Ailis. He had stepped so wrong so often that he no longer felt confident about his own decisions. He could not believe that he had once dared to counsel his friends about how to deal with their wives. If they could see him now, they would have a hearty laugh. Alexander prayed that this confrontation would force him and Ailis both to speak with an honesty they desperately needed.

Ailis sat on the bed in the chambers she shared with Alexander, wondering if she should even be there. As she listened to him approach the room, she stiffened her spine, determined to speak up for herself. She did not really believe that she would be allowed to defend herself or that she would even be believed, but she had to try. When Alexander strode into the room and looked at her, she felt her courage falter badly.

"So, ye made a bargain with Malcolm MacCordy." Alexander stood right in front of her, his hands on his hips.

"Aye." Ailis looked up at his stern face and inwardly sighed. She knew that his outer beauty was not why she loved him, but she was going to sorely miss it when she could no longer look upon it. "I needed shelter. There was a price Malcolm demanded for it—one night with me. Since without that protection my child was doomed, I agreed to the demand."

"Did it ever occur to ye to ignore it, that ye didna have to fulfill such a promise?"

"It was what bought our son's life. I *had* to pay the price."

Alexander shook his head as he sat down beside her and yanked off his boots. "I think a part of ye is aware that it was a price ye didna have to pay. It was one of those demands ye could agree to to save your life, then scorn when ye are free. What was Malcolm to do if ye said nay? He could tell no one about the bargain without shaming himself, not ye. He certainly couldna come and complain to me that ye had refused to honor a debt."

"Are ye trying to say that I went there because I wanted to bed him?"

"Nay, not at all. I just think that ye thought too much on how he had saved Moragh's life."

"Well, mayhaps," she mumbled, suddenly unsure of herself. "I thought honor demanded it."

"There is no honor in meeting dishonorable demands."

"So, I have lost everything and for no good reason at all."

"Lost everything?" Alexander stared at her in confusion.

"Aye, ye and the baby."

"Might I ask where Moragh and I are going?" Alexander knelt by her feet and removed her shoes despite her look of confusion.

"I betrayed ye, Alexander. Ye have never made a secret about how ye feel about women who betray ye." She wanted to leave before she began to cry, but he was now undoing her hastily pinned-up hair, idly tossing the bone hairpins aside as he pulled them out. "I had so wanted to change your mind about women, to show ye that not all of us are bad and that there are still those ye can trust." She gave a startled cry when Alexander suddenly straightened up, caught her up under the arms, and lifted her up until they were face to face.

"Do ye ken how many women I have had in my life, Ailis?"

"Thousands?" she grumbled, wondering why he had to remind her of his profligate past now.

"Aye—thousands. And of all of those thousands I have never been left so utterly confused as I have so often been by ye."

"Confused? By me?"

"Aye. By ye. Utterly confounded and puzzled."

He gently tossed her down onto the bed and then pinned her there. Ailis wondered how he could call her confusing when he was acting so strangely. Alexander should be sending her away, throwing her out, yet he was taking her clothes off. He was, in fact, not acting as if he felt betrayed or even particularly angry.

"I have betrayed ye, yet ye are acting as if naught has happened," she muttered, her words faintly distorted by her chemise as Alexander tugged it off of her.

"Ye havena betrayed me." Once Ailis was naked, Alexander sat back on his haunches to savor the sight of her before taking off the rest of his own clothes.

"I went to Malcolm."

"Ye didna bed down with him."

"I was going to. That was the price asked." She shivered when he eased his naked body back into her arms.

"For Moragh's life. Do ye think me such a little man that I would fault ye for doing anything and everything ye needed to do to keep our son alive? I can find a few faults in your thinking, but none in your motive. I ken what fears drove ye to it. How can I condemn ye when I ken full well I could sell my soul to the devil himself if it would buy our child even one more day of life?"

He gave her such a fierce kiss Ailis could only cling to him and return it. She felt the first stirrings of hope since the day she had agreed to Malcolm's demand. Then she lost all ability to think as he made slow, passionate love to her. With his every kiss and touch, he cherished her, stirred her. There was not a place upon her body that did not tingle from the touch of his lips or fingers, that was not deeply warmed by his passion. She felt as if he paid her some high honor. When he finally joined their bodies, she was already crying out with need for him. Ailis clung to him with all the strength her ardor could produce as he eased into her. She continued to hold on tightly as he took her to a blinding release, which left her weak and trembling, a release enriched by Alexander's sharing it with her.

"Does this mean that I can stay with ye?" she finally asked, smiling when he chuckled.

"Aye," Alexander replied. "Ailis, what is it that ye canna give Malcolm that ye can give me?"

"Love," she answered, then gasped.

Ailis groaned and closed her eyes, embarrassed by her own stupidity. She had answered without thought, simply blurted out the truth. In one small word she had opened herself up completely, and yet she had no idea of what Alexander would do with such information or how he would even react to it. She was not sure that the way she could feel him grinning against her skin was a particularly good sign.

"Poor Ailis, ye really didna want to say that, did ye?" He propped himself up on his elbows to smile at her.

"'Tis none of your business." She was becoming irritated by his intense good humor, yet was curious as to the why of it.

"None of my business? Ye dinna believe I should ken how my wife feels about me?"

"Not when ye trick the declaration out of her."

"Ah." He brushed a kiss over her mouth. "Ye need not look so wary, dearling. No harm is done."

"Nay? I am now laid bare to ye—heart, soul, and body. Where is what ye offer me? When do ye shed your armor?"

"I have been a guarded man, havena I?" He idly brushed a few wisps of hair from her face and wondered if she had any idea of how beautiful she was—in face, form, and nature.

"Aye, and what few things ye have said havena exactly been revealing or, at times, endearing."

"Nay, and rebuke deserved. Ah, Ailis, I think I kenned from the beginning that ye werena like the others. Nay, none of the others, even before betrayal after betrayal had soured my nature and hardened my heart. In truth, I believe 'tis why I treated ye so harshly at times. Even after I ceased to be so bitter, I pushed ye away." He lightly traced the shape of her face with his fingertips. "I could see how dangerous ye would be. However, it wasna until I thought I had lost ye to the MacCordys and your kin that I accepted how much a part of my life ye had become."

"Ye missed me?" Ailis was surprised she still had the power to talk, she was so stunned by Alexander's words.

"Words canna say how much, which didna please me much, but I soon grew accustomed to that. 'Twas as I watched ye go to Malcolm that I finally saw the whole truth. The thought of ye going to another man cut me in such a way that I could no longer lie to myself. Sometime during all the months I fought ye, I had lost the battle."

"Are ye saying that ye do care for me?" she whispered.

"In ways 'twill be hard to say," he replied in as soft a voice.

"Well—try." She smiled fleetingly when he chuckled, then held his gaze, not daring to believe the soft look in his beautiful eyes.

"Ah, lass, I love ye." He laughed when she exuberantly hugged him.

Ailis tried to hug him with every part of her. She also tried not to cry. Emotion so choked her that she could only stare at him, touching his face with trembling fingers.

"I have never dared hope that ye would return my love, Alexander," she finally said. " 'Twill be a while ere I dare to really believe it."

He picked up each of her hands, then pressed a kiss into each of her palms. "Believe it." He touched a kiss to the tip of her nose. "We were fated, lass. I needed ye to save me from a complete darkness of spirit."

"And I needed ye in so many ways 'twill take years to tell ye of all of them."

"Well, we have years now, dearling. Aye, my bonny dark wife, we shall have many a glorious year." He smiled. "Until I am withered and balding and ready for the cold clay."

"I am sure your headstone will read 'Still the bonniest man in all of Scotland.' Even if ye are a hundred ere ye need it."

"And ye shall be kenned as, 'The one dearest to his heart.'"

"Can ye love a wee brown lass till death do us part?" She twined her arms about his neck and tugged his mouth down to hers.

"Dearling, the love I have for ye canna be dimmed even by death's cold touch."

"Then—for once, my fine golden knight—we shall tread the same path."

Please turn the page for an exciting sneak peek
of Hannah Howell's newest historical romance
HIGHLAND CONQUEROR
coming in March 2005!

*England, 1472*

"Stop staring at me."

Liam Cameron cocked one brow in response to his cousin Sigimor's growled command. "I was but awaiting your plan to get us out of this mess."

Sigimor grunted and rested his head against the damp stone wall he was chained to. He suspected Liam knew there was no plan. He, his younger brother Tait, his brother-in-law Nanty MacEnroy, and his cousins Liam, Marcus, and David were chained up in a dungeon set deep in the bowels of an English lord's keep. They needed more than a plan to get out of this bind. They needed a miracle. Sigimor did not think he had done much lately to deserve one of those.

This was the last time he would try to do a good deed, he decided, then grimaced. It had not been charity that had brought him to Drumwich, but a debt. He owed Lord Peter Geldard his life and when the man had requested his aid, there had been no choice but to give it. Unfortunately, the request had come too late and the trouble Peter had written of had taken his life only two days before Sigimor had led his men in through the thick gates of Drumwich. It was swiftly made clear that Peter's cousin Harold felt no compulsion to honor any pledges made by his now-dead kinsman. Sigimor wondered if it could be considered ironic that he would die in the house of the man who had once saved his life.

"Ye dinnae have a plan, do ye?"

"Nay, Liam, I dinnae," replied Sigimor. "If I had kenned that Peter might die ere we got here, I would have made some plan to deal with that complication, but I never once considered that possibility."

"Jesu" muttered Nanty. "If I must die in this cursed country, I would prefer it to be in battle instead of being hanged like some thieving Armstrong or Graham."

"Doesnae your Gilly claim a few Armstrongs as her kinsmen?" Sigimor asked.

"Oh. Aye. Forgot about them. The Armstrongs of Aigballa. Cormac, the laird, wed Gilly's cousin Elspeth."

"Are they rievers?"

"Nay. Weel, nay all of them. Why?"

"If some miracle befalls us and we escape this trap, we may have need of a few allies on the journey home."

"Sigimor, we are in cursed England, in a dungeon in a cursed English laird's weel fortified castle, chained to this thrice-cursed wall, and condemned to hang in two days. I dinnae think we need worry much on what we may or may not need on the journey home. There isnae going to be one. Not unless that bastard Harold decides to send our corpses back to our kinsmen for the burying."

"I can see that we best nay turn to ye to lift our spirits." He ignored Nanty's soft cursing. "I wonder why there isnae any guard set out to watch o'er us."

"Mayhap because we are chained to the wall?" drawled Liam.

"I could, mayhap, with my great monly strength, pull the chains from the wall," murmured Sigimor.

"Ha! These walls have to be ten feet thick."

"Eight feet six inches to be precise," said a crisp female voice.

Sigimor stared at the tiny woman standing outside the thick iron bars of his prison. He wondered why he had neither seen nor heard her approach. The word *mine* ripped through his mind startling him into almost gaping at her. The woman standing there was nothing like any woman he had ever desired in all of his two-and-thirty years. She was also English.

If that was not a big enough flaw, she was delicately made. She had to be a good foot or more shorter than his six-feet-four-inch height and slender. He liked his women tall and buxom, and considered it a necessity for a man of his size. Her hair was dark, probably black. He preferred light hair upon his women. His body, however, seemed suddenly oblivious to his habitual preferences. It had grown taut with interest. Being chained to a wall had obviously disordered his mind.

"And the spikes holding the chains to the wall were driven in to a depth of three feet, seven inches," she added.

"Ye obviously havenae come here to cheer us," drawled Sigimor.

"I am not sure there is anything one could say to bring cheer to six men chained to a wall awaiting a hanging. Certainly not to six Highlanders chained to the walls of an English dungeon."

"There is some truth in that. Who are ye?"

"I am Lady Jolene Geldard."

If she thought standing straighter as she introduced herself would make her look more imposing, she was sadly mistaken, Sigimor mused. "Peter's sister or his wife?"

"His sister. Peter was murdered by Harold. You came too late to help him."

Although there was no hint of accusation behind her words, Sigimor felt the sting of guilt. "I left Dubheidland the morning after I received Peter's message."

"I know. I fear Harold guessed that Peter had summoned help. Harold had kept all routes to our kinsmen tightly watched so Peter sent for you. I am still not certain how Harold discovered what Peter had done."

"Have ye proof that Harold murdered Peter?"

Jolene sighed and slowly shook her head. "I fear not. There is no doubt in my mind, however, Harold wanted Drumwich and now he holds it. Peter was hale and hearty and now he is dead. He died screaming from the pain in his belly. Harold claims the fish was spoiled. Two others died as well."

"Ah. 'Tis possible."

"True. Such tragedies are not so very rare. Yet, ere that spoiled fish was buried, two of Harold's dogs ate some. They did not die, did not even grow a little ill. Of course, Harold does not know that I saw that. The dogs snatched some of the fish from Peter's plate when his sudden illness drew Harold's attention. I saw it because I had to push the dogs aside to reach Peter."

"Who died beside Peter?"

"The two most loyal to Peter. The cook presented the fish as a special treat for the three men as it was their favorite dish. It was claimed that not enough fish was caught to prepare the dish for everyone. They were also served the last of the best wine. I believe that is where the poison was, or most of it, but I can find no trace of it. Not upon the ewer it was served from or the tankards it was poured into. I did not get hold of them fast enough and they were scrubbed clean."

"Did ye question the cook?" asked Liam.

"He has disappeared," she replied.

Sigimor cursed and shook his head. "Then I fear Harold will go unpunished. Ye have no proof of his guilt, and I am nay in a position to help ye find any. It might be wise if ye find somewhere else to live now that Harold is the laird here."

"But, he is *not* the lord of Drumwich. Not yet. There is one small impediment left."

"What small impediment?"

"Peter's son."

"Legitimate?"

"Of course. Reynard is nearly three years of age now. His mother died at his birthing, I fear."

"If ye are sure that Harold killed your brother, ye had best get that wee lad out of his reach," said Liam.

Sigimor noticed that Jolene only looked at Liam for a brief moment before fixing her gaze upon him again. Liam might not be at his best, being dirty and a little bruised, but Sigimor was surprised that the little English lady seemed to note Liam's highly praised beauty, accept it, and then dismiss it. That rarely happened and Sigimor found himself intrigued.

"I have hidden Reynard away," she said.

"And Harold hasnae tried to pull that truth from ye?" Sigimor asked.

"Nay. I am very certain he would like to try, but I have hidden myself away as well. Harold does not know all the secrets of Drumwich."

"Clever lass, but that can only work for a wee while, aye? Liam is right. Ye need to get yourself and the bairn away from here."

Jolene stared at the big man Peter had hoped could save them. That the Highlander would honor an old debt enough to ride into England itself was a strong indication that he was a man of honor, one who could be trusted to hold to his word. It was certainly promising that not one of the men had yet asked anything of her despite their own dire circumstances, but were quick to tell her to get herself and Peter's son and heir out of Harold's deadly reach. They were also big, strong men who, if set free, would certainly hie themselves right back to the Highlands. Harold would not find it easy to follow them there.

It did trouble her a little that she could not seem to stop looking at the big man named Sigimor. Most women would be breathlessly intrigued by the one called Liam. Despite the dirt and bruises, she had easily recognized Liam's beauty, a manly beauty actually enhanced by the flickering light of the torches set into the walls. Yet, she had looked, accepted the allure of the man, and immediately turned her gaze back to Sigimor. At three and twenty she felt she should be well past the age to suffer some foolish infatuation for a man, but she feared that might well be what ailed her now. The fact that she could not see the man all that clearly made her fascination with him all the stranger.

She inwardly shook herself. There was only one thing she should be thinking about and that was the need to get Reynard to safety. For three days and nights she had heard Harold ranting as he had Drumwich searched and its people questioned. Last night Harold's interrogations had turned brutal, filling the halls with the piercing cries of those he tortured. Soon one of the very few who knew the secrets of Drumwich would break and tell Harold how to find her and Reynard. Pain could loosen the tongue of even the most loyal. It was imperative that she take the boy far away and, since she had no way to reach any of the rest of her family, these men were her only hope.

"Aye, I must get myself and the boy away from here, far away, to a place where Harold will find it dangerously difficult to hunt us down, if not impossible," she said and could tell by the way Sigimor stared at her that he was beginning to understand why she was there.

Sigimor's whole body tensed, hope surging through him. She said she was in hiding, yet she stood there within plain sight apparently unconcerned about being discovered. There was also something in the way she spoke of taking the boy to a place far away, a place Harold would have great difficulty getting to, combined with the intent way she was staring at him, that made Sigimor almost certain she intended to enlist his aid. He noticed that his companions had all grown as tense as he was, their gazes fixed firmly upon Lady Jolene. He was not the only one whose hopes had suddenly been raised.

"There are nay many places in England where he could go that Harold couldnae follow," Sigimor said.

"Nay, there are very few indeed. None, in truth. Trying to reach my kinsmen has already cost one man his life. That route is closed to me, as it was to Peter, so I must needs find another."

"Lass, it isnae kind to tease a mon chained to a wall and awaiting hanging." He caught his breath when she grinned for it added a beauty to her faintly triangular face that was dangerously alluring.

"Mayhap I was but trying to get you to make an offer ere I was forced to make a request. If you offer what I seek, I can ponder it quickly, and accept, telling myself all manner of comforting reasons for doing so. If I must ask, then I am openly accepting defeat, bluntly admitting that I cannot do this alone. 'Tis a bitter draught to swallow."

"Swallow it."

"Sigimor!" Liam glared at his cousin, then smiled sweetly at Lady Jolene. "M'lady, if ye free us from this dark place, I give ye my solemn oath that we will aid ye in keeping the bairn alive and free in any and all ways we can."

"'Tis a most generous offer, sir," Jolene said, then looked back at Sigimor, "but does your lord give you the right to make such an oath? Does he plan to honor your oath and share in it?"

Sigimor grunted, ignored the glares of his men for a full minute, then nodded. "Aye, he does. We will take the lad."

"And me."

"Why should we take ye as weel? Ye are no threat to Harold's place as laird of this keep." Sigimor had fully expected her to insist upon coming with them, but he wanted to hear her reasons for doing so.

"Oh, but I am a threat to Harold," she said in a soft, cold voice, "and he knows it well. If not for Reynard, I would stay here and make him pay most dearly for Peter's death. Howbeit, I swore to Peter that I would guard Reynard with my very life. Since I have had the raising of the boy since his mother's death upon childbed, there was no need to ask such an oath, but I swore it anyway."

And there was the reason to take her with them, Sigimor mused. She may not have birthed the child, but she was Reynard's mother in her heart and mind, and, most probably, in the child's as well. It also told him the best way in which he could control her, although all his instincts whispered that that would not be easy to do. None of that mattered, however. He had been unable to save Peter, but he was now offered the chance to save Peter's sister and his son. Even better, in doing so, he could save the men he had dragged into this deadly mire.

"Then set us free, lass," Sigimor said, "and we will share in the burden of that oath."

Her hands trembling faintly from the strength of the relief which swept through her, Jolene began to try to find which of the many keys she held would fit the lock to the door of the cell. Hope was a heady thing, she mused. For a brief moment she had actually felt very close to swooning, and she silently thanked God she had not shamed herself by doing such a weak thing before these men.

"Ye dinnae ken which key to use?" Sigimor felt an even mixture of annoyance and amusement as he watched her struggle with the keys.

"Why should I?" she muttered. "I have ne'er locked anyone in these cells."

"Didnae ye ask the one ye got them from which key ye ought to use?"

"Nay. He was asleep."

"I see. Weel, best pray some other guard doesnae decide to wander down here whilst ye fumble about."

"There will be no guards wandering down here. They are asleep."

"All of them."

"I do hope so."

"The men at arms, too?" She nodded. "Is everyone at Drumwich asleep?"

"Near to. I did leave a few awake, ones who might be eager to flee Drumwich once the chance to do so was given to them." She cried out in triumph as she unlocked the door, opened it, then grinned at Sigimor.

Sigimor simply cocked one brow and softly rattled the chains still binding him to the wall. The cross look she gave him as she hurried over to his side, the large ring of keys she held clinking loudly, almost made him smile. He sighed long and loudly when she started to test each key all over again on the lock of his chains, and he heard her mutter something he strongly suspected was a curse.

His amusement faded quickly when she stood very close to him. Despite her delicate build, his body was stirred by the soft, clean scent of her. He fixed his gaze upon her small hands, her slim wrists, and her long, slender fingers, trying to impress upon his mind that she was frail. His body continued to ignore that truth. It also ignored the fact that her hair, hanging down her slim back in a thick braid reaching past her slender hips, was black or nearly so, a color he had never favored. Just as blithely it ignored the fact that the top of her head barely reached his breastbone. Everything about her was wrong for a man of his size and inclinations, but his body heartily disagreed with his mind. It was a riddle he was not sure he could ever solve.

"Are ye verra certain Harold's men are asleep?" he asked in an attempt to fix his mind upon the problems at hand and ignore the soft curve of her long, elegantly slender neck.

"Aye. I kicked a few just to be sure." She found it more difficult than it ought to be to concentrate upon finding the right key and ignore the big man she stood so close to.

"Just how did ye do it?"

"I put a potion into the ale and wine set out to drink with

the evening meal. I also had two of the maids carry a physicked water to the other men the moment the ones who sat down in the great hall to dine began to drink. Near all of them began to fall asleep at the same time."

"Near all? What happened to the ones who didnae begin to fall asleep?"

"A sound knock upon the head was swiftly delivered. There!" She smiled at him as she released him from his chains, only to scowl when he snatched the key from her hand. "I am capable of using a key."

"When ye can find it," he drawled as he quickly freed the others. "How long do ye think your potion will hold Harold and his men?"

"'Til dawn or a little later," she replied, thinking that six big men chained were a lot less intimidating than six big men unchained, standing and staring at her.

"How long do we have until dawn?"

"Two hours at the most."

Sigimor put his hands on his hips and frowned at her. "Why did ye wait so long to come and free us?"

"I had to lock a few doors, tend to a few wounds inflicted by Harold, and help those who kindly helped me to escape from Drumwich. Then I had to collect up some supplies to take with us and gather up the things Harold's men took away from you. And, considering that *I*, a small woman, put every fighting man at Drumwich to sleep with the aid of but two maids, I believe your implied criticism is uncalled for."

"It wasnae implied."

"Sigimor," snapped Liam, before smiling at Jolene. "Ye did weel, lass."

"Thank you, kind sir," Jolene responded, returning his smile.

Subtlety, but firmly, Sigimor nudged Liam away from Jolene. He might not understand what drew him to this tiny, thin Englishwoman, but, until he cured himself of the affliction, he did not want any other fool trading smiles with her. Especially not Liam who already had half the women in Scotland swooning at his feet.

"How do ye plan to get us all out of here?" he asked her.

"We could march right out the front gates, if you wish," Jolene replied. "I had thought we would leave as quietly and secretively as possible. If there are no obvious signs of our leavetaking, it may be a while ere your escape is discovered."

"Somehow I think Harold will find a castle full of men still asleep or just rousing immediately suspicious."

"Ah, of course. You are right."

It sounded as if she was gagging on those words, Sigimor thought with an inner grin. "Lead on then. I want to put as much distance as possible between us and Harold ere he awakens."

As she started out of the cell, the men falling into step behind her, Jolene said, "Aye. The sooner we reach Scotland, the sooner we will rid ourselves of Harold."

Sigimor doubted it would be that easy, but did not say so as he followed her along a dark, narrow passage heading away from the cells. Harold had already committed murder to steal Drumwich. Lady Jolene clearly feared for her life and her nephew's. If the screams in the night were anything to judge by, Harold was using brutal methods to try to find her and the boy. A man like that would not stop chasing her down simply because she had crossed the border into a country that was not particularly fond of Englishmen. Sigimor felt sure of that. Harold would mean trouble for them for quite a while yet. As he watched the gentle sway of her hips, Sigimor inwardly cursed. Harold would not be the only trouble he would find in the days ahead.

## ABOUT THE AUTHOR

Hannah Howell is an award-winning author who lives with her family in Massachusetts. She is the author of seventeen Zebra historical romances and is currently working on a new Highland historical romance, HIGHLAND CONQUEROR, which will be published in March 2005. Hannah loves hearing from readers, and you may write to her c/o Zebra Books. Please include a self-addressed stamped envelope if you wish a response.